Praise for the Novels
of Gail Fraser

Lumby's Bounty

"A visit to the charming, whimsical town of Lumby is a refreshing change from our fast-paced lives. Challenged to host a hot-air balloon festival, its residents rise to the occasion: lives change, love blossoms, a wild and irrepressible young man matures. A delightful read." —Joan Medlicott, author of the Ladies of Covington series

"Drop in on the sweetest small town since Mayberry, where the worst people are still nicer than the best people you know, and life's problems are solved by a backhoe, an industrial sewing machine, or monks wearing light-up tennis shoes. Your own troubles will melt away. When they return—if you're a smarty—you'll visit the next warmhearted book in Gail Fraser's series and get lumbified all over again." —Bob Tarte, author of *Fowl Weather* and *Enslaved by Ducks*

"Lumby will astound readers with its sense of humor, quirky charm, its aura of magic and possibilities, and happy (if unexpected) endings." —Cozy Library

"Author Gail Fraser has the ability to take everyday life and make it interesting reading. *Lumby's Bounty* is a feel-good story by a writer who knows her audience." — BookLoons

continued . . .

Stealing Lumby

"In the tradition of Jan Karon's Mitford series, this engaging inside look at small-town life will draw a bevy of fans to its old-fashioned story combining a bit of romance, a bit of mystery, and a multitude of quirky and endearing characters."   —*Booklist*

"There's a . . . quality to the writing that lends an unrushed, meandering feel to the narrative as evildoers are dispatched and equilibrium is restored. Fraser's story is pleasantly easy reading and as small-town cozy as they come."   —*Publishers Weekly*

"*Stealing Lumby* is a classic cozy read, with good-hearted characters that face life's problems head-on. Readers can be certain that, despite heartache and loss, good will prevail and evildoers will get what they deserve. Although that doesn't happen often in the real world, at least not in the time frame we'd prefer, Lumby is a wonderful place where it does. I'm certain readers of the first book in the series, *The Lumby Lines*, will love *Stealing Lumby*."   —Cozy Library

"*Stealing Lumby*, second in the Lumby series, is as delightful as the first. . . . Where else will you find a moose wandering around a village with a folding deck chair enmeshed in his rack? . . . I loved the blind horse being ridden by its elderly, almost blind owner. And how about the Moo Moo Iditarod? . . . It's fun to become a part of the village and listen in to their solutions—some of which make one laugh out loud, while others are wise and knowing, and some are just plain crazy. Which should make *Stealing Lumby* scamper to the top of your must-read list. After *The Lumby Lines*, of course."—BookLoons

The Lumby Lines

"At a time when we seem to be taking ourselves all too seriously, Gail Fraser pulls a rabbit out of the hat that charms while it helps us relax. *The Lumby Lines* strikes just the right balance of playfulness, satire, and drama. A thoroughly enjoyable read!"
—Brother Christopher, The Monks of New Skete

"Unique.... You will be amazed by the great imagination of the author.... The reader is in for a treat. This book is a delight to read and one that you will thoroughly enjoy."   —Bestsellersworld.com

"Gail Fraser has assembled a wonderful cast of characters and plunked them down in the middle of a beautiful town that rivals Jan Karon's Mitford for pure fun. Of course, there are obstacles to overcome, mysteries to solve, even some romance and reconciliation along the way to a very satisfying conclusion. Altogether a wonderful story, highly recommended."   —Cozy Library

"*The Lumby Lines* goes straight to the heart. The simplicity, humor, and downright friendliness of the book make reading it a pleasure.... Readers will close this book with a sigh of contentment and a desire to visit Lumby again. The author has faithfully carved out a slice of small-town living and topped it off with a large helping of humor. This reviewer can't wait for her next visit to Lumby!"
—Christian Book Previews

"A setting reminiscent of Jan Karon's fictional village.... *The Lumby Lines* is a feel-good novel with lots of heart and angst. I was sorry to leave my new friends but have brightened since I learned that a sequel, *Stealing Lumby*, is coming soon."   — BookLoons

Books in the Lumby Series
by Gail Fraser

The Lumby Lines
Stealing Lumby

LUMBY'S BOUNTY

GAIL FRASER

NEW AMERICAN LIBRARY

New American Library
Published by New American Library, a division of
Penguin Group (USA) Inc., 375 Hudson Street,
New York, New York 10014, USA
Penguin Group (Canada), 90 Eglinton Avenue East, Suite 700, Toronto,
Ontario M4P 2Y3, Canada (a division of Pearson Penguin Canada Inc.)
Penguin Books Ltd., 80 Strand, London WC2R 0RL, England
Penguin Ireland, 25 St. Stephen's Green, Dublin 2,
Ireland (a division of Penguin Books Ltd.)
Penguin Group (Australia), 250 Camberwell Road, Camberwell, Victoria 3124,
Australia (a division of Pearson Australia Group Pty. Ltd.)
Penguin Books India Pvt. Ltd., 11 Community Centre, Panchsheel Park,
New Delhi - 110 017, India
Penguin Group (NZ), 67 Apollo Drive, Rosedale, North Shore 0632,
New Zealand (a division of Pearson New Zealand Ltd.)
Penguin Books (South Africa) (Pty.) Ltd., 24 Sturdee Avenue,
Rosebank, Johannesburg 2196, South Africa

Penguin Books Ltd., Registered Offices:
80 Strand, London WC2R 0RL, England

First published by New American Library,
a division of Penguin Group (USA) Inc.

First Printing, January 2008
10 9 8 7 6 5 4 3

 REGISTERED TRADEMARK—MARCA REGISTRADA

LIBRARY OF CONGRESS CATALOGING-IN-PUBLICATION DATA:

Fraser, Gail R. (Gail Robin)
    Lumby's bounty / Gail Fraser.
        p. cm.
    ISBN: 978-0-451-22288-6
    1. City and town life—Fiction. 2. Northwest, Pacific—Fiction. I. Title.
PS3606.R4229L89 2008
813'.6—dc22   2007016280

Printed in the United States of America

To Emma and Yoda,
who are my quiet companions while I work, patiently waiting
by my side until the very last word is written

❧

ACKNOWLEDGMENTS

Appreciation is extended to those who helped with my research into hot air ballooning, including Jill Wing, who braved an early-morning rise for a rained-out ascent—just one of the many ways she has shown personal and professional support for all that is Lumby. And warm gratitude to Ellie Conover, a very good friend who always offers so much of herself. And to Dave Cohen for his collaborative efforts and amazing technical skill used in building and supporting my Web sites.

Once again, my full respect and special thanks go to the great team at Penguin NAL, especially Ellen Edwards, an editor extraordinaire whose unflappable belief in my novels keeps me moving forward. And, as always, a special acknowledgment and thanks to John Paine, who was the first to read this manuscript and offered invaluable feedback and edits.

ൟ

ONE

Tibbs

The spirit of Lumby is rooted in the small community of forty-eight hundred warmhearted and well-intentioned people who carve out the best lives they can for themselves and for their neighbors. The relationships among many of the townsfolk have carried on from one generation to the next. Few merchants actually post store hours since everyone knows each other's schedules as well as their own. And restaurants frequently enhance their menus with recipes specifically requested by their regular patrons.

Seated together at a table at S&T's Soda Shoppe were two men who embraced the town's tranquility: Simon Dixon, the sheriff, and Jimmy Daniels, the mayor for two years and proprietor of the town's most frequented tavern, Jimmy D's. They were meeting that morning to discuss preparations for one of Lumby's most deeply cherished traditions: Tibbs Tailgating.

Simon, a brick of a man with a strong body and square shoulders, had proved his worthiness as a lieutenant in the Seattle police force before marrying Anna and moving to her hometown, Lumby. For more than sixteen years, he had watched diligently over the town and its residents.

Jimmy, on the other hand, had lived his entire life in close proximity to Lumby, and three days after turning twenty, got married and established his home on the corner of Main Street and Mineral Street with his beautiful but bashful bride, Hannah. Now, in his mid-forties, Jimmy enjoyed his public role as town leader as much as he valued the apparent comfort of his personal life.

Jimmy rubbed his eyes, tired from looking at the fairgrounds map. "It will just have to be first come, first served. If there's not enough space this year, the overflow can park down on North Grant Avenue."

"I think that's the best alternative, but there won't be much foot traffic down there," Simon said. "People might complain."

"I know, but Tibbs Tailgating has grown so much, it's almost getting out of hand," Jimmy said under his breath.

In Lumby, most of the residents cared as much about the history of a tradition as the tradition itself. This story was frequently retold to whoever would listen:

Thirteen years before, on a glorious Sunday in April, Tibbs Taylor walked into the Presbyterian church on Farm to Market Road, holding Martha's hand. As they had done for two decades of their married life, they seated themselves in the third pew on the left and listened to the sermon given by Reverend Poole. The message that morning was one of following your heart to God, but Martha, being as tired of her husband as she was of his pig farm, only heard "follow your heart." She was so swept away by the reverend's preaching that upon arriving home she packed up her one bag, apologized to Tibbs at the front door, and ventured out into a new world, hoping to find a happier life in California.

Tibbs held out hope for her return for exactly one week, but Martha was never to be seen again. Angered by his wife's betrayal, Tibbs threw all of her possessions, from a torn brassiere to stained teacups, into the back of his rusted pickup and drove it to town, parking on Main Street. Then and there he auctioned off every one of Martha's belongings. Three hours later he headed home, his spirit cleansed and his pockets slightly fuller for the experience.

Thereafter, on the second Sunday of each April, the people of Lumby gathered to sell unwanted items at a town flea market called Tibbs Tailgating. Although some cynics saw it only as an opportunity to exchange one man's junk for another's, Tibbs Tailgating had remained a significant event in the community for well over a decade. It marked a time to clear out the cobwebs of winter and get ready for spring.

"So, you're fine with the plans?" Jimmy asked Simon as he packed up their papers.

"If no one else signs up, we should be good to go," Simon answered. "Additional posters will be put on Grant the night before."

"Good," Jimmy said, following Simon outside. "I'll drop these off with Dennis and have him print up a hundred more catalogues than last year."

Simon accompanied Jimmy as far as the police station at the corner of Main Street and Farm to Market Road, where Jimmy headed for the Chatham Press building. Simon stood on the front stoop and surveyed the town.

Lumby sits quietly on the northern brim of Mill Valley, a lush vale of rolling pastures, rich agricultural fields, and grasslands dotted with white farmhouses. To the west, protecting both the town and the valley, are densely forested hills and low mountains. Beyond those rise the vast and majestic Rockies.

The natural beauty of the surroundings can be appreciated throughout the year, with each season revealing a new wonder. Summer offers the sights and smells of verdant croplands, while autumn brings the colors of a painter's palette, splashing brilliant yellows and oranges across the landscape. When cold winds sweep down from Canada, the first winter snow settles on the jagged mountain ridges and then slowly descends onto the town.

In spring, though, the streams swell and the trees bud along Main Street, officially named State Road 541 but frequently referred to as Old 41. Charming storefronts and small cafés line sidewalks of raised flower beds, scattered fruit trees, and brightly painted benches. As the temperature warms, yellow-, blue-, and green-striped awnings are rolled out with their edges flapping in the breeze.

Simon watched Jimmy enter the Chatham Press building, which housed one of the oldest family-run businesses in Lumby. The enterprise consisted of the town's bookstore, a bookbinding concern, and a substantial printing operation that published the local newspaper, among other periodicals and flyers.

Woodrow Beezer, who built the three-story stone office at the turn of the twentieth century, began the family enterprise, which was, in time, passed on to his son, William Beezer. William was a hard man who kept a keen eye on the bottom line and grew the business tenfold. After William's unexpected death two years ago, his estranged son, Dennis, followed in his footsteps.

Jimmy looked at his watch and walked inside, jogging up the stairs two at a time.

At the top of the stairwell, he heard a loud voice. "What the hell have you done?"

And then silence.

Entering the publishing floor of *The Lumby Lines*, he first noticed Dennis's assistant, Kim, working at her desk, her head lowered. She looked up and quickly pointed to Dennis Beezer's office. As did everyone in town, she knew that Dennis was a good man with a long fuse, but today something—or someone—had obviously set him off.

Through the frosted glass of his office door, Jimmy saw Dennis pacing back and forth, occasionally frowning at the person seated in the chair in front of his desk.

Jimmy considered leaving—this was obviously very bad timing indeed.

Just then Dennis slammed open the door. "Kim," he said, forcing calm into his voice, "would you please get Jimmy on the phone?"

"He's standing right there," she said, pointing.

Dennis waved him over. "I was just calling you," Dennis said, shaking the hand of his close friend.

"So I heard," Jimmy said cautiously. "What's up?"

Dennis ran a hand through his hair in frustration. "I think you need to come in and sit down."

Walking into the private office, Jimmy saw Dennis's nineteen-year-old son, Brian Beezer, slumped in the chair. His head hung low, his dark brown hair mostly covering his handsome, angular face. His long legs were outstretched, with his feet knocking against each other.

Dennis handed a piece of paper to Jimmy. "Read this advertisement that was faxed over to us this morning. It's to be run in *The Lumby Lines* in a few weeks."

"Why are you giving it to me?" Jimmy asked.

"Please read it," Dennis said, turning with annoyance toward Brian.

Jimmy scanned the copy, taking note of the critical words: Balloon rides . . . Regional Balloon Festival . . . Lumby.

When Jimmy had digested its meaning, he started laughing. "Well, this is clearly a mistake, Dennis. We don't have any hot air balloons in Lumby, so it would make no sense that we would host a hot air balloon festival." He held out the fax. "I'm sure someone's just pulling your leg. That, or whoever submitted this just faxed it to the wrong local paper in the wrong town."

"No, they didn't," Dennis said, glaring at Brian.

Jimmy saw how angry his friend was. "What's going on?"

"Tell him," Dennis told his son.

Brian slid farther down in his chair. No one could do sullen better than the son of the newspaper's editor.

"Brian, tell him," he repeated.

"Well," Brian said at last, "Terry and I were looking at some magazines a few months ago, and saw this thing . . ."

"What thing?" Jimmy asked.

Brian hesitated. "An article. Anyway, it said they were—"

"Who?" Jimmy continued to press for clarity.

"The U.S. Hot Air Balloon Association. They were looking for a town to host this year's balloon festival." Brian continued to stare at his knees, which were nervously moving back and forth. "And we thought it would be cool if it was here, in Lumby. So we pooled some money at school."

Dennis was ready to explode once again. "How much?" he demanded.

"Two hundred and fifty dollars."

Both men looked at the teenager in disbelief. How could high school kids collect that amount without parental involvement or even awareness?

"Go on," his father said.

"We filled out the application and got a money order." His story abruptly ended, and after a few moments it was obvious that Brian had no intention of continuing.

Jimmy coaxed the boy. "And?"

Brian twisted in his chair. He went on very reluctantly. "Well, they wrote back several times asking for more information, and then about a month ago they sent us a contract."

Jimmy leaned forward, visibly confused. "Why would they possibly send a contract to you?"

Brian looked up at his father, hoping he would end the interrogation, but his father just glared back. When he saw no escape was possible, he lowered his head still farther down on his chest so he could barely be heard. "I told them I was the mayor."

Jimmy's jaw dropped. Part of him was impressed with how the boys had managed to win what must have been a competitive bid; the other part was disappointed in how they had done it. He quickly thought through the situation and found a seemingly obvious solution. "Well, no serious problem here. We'll just call them and courteously bow out—a thanks but no thanks reply."

"I've already tried," Dennis said wearily. "In fact, I've been on the phone all morning. I was told that the brochures and catalogues for the festival, along with countless advertisements, have already been printed and paid for. If Lumby reneges at this late date, it will cost us a significant amount of money in penalties." He paused as he looked for the contract on his desk. "As it was my son's doing, I would personally cover all penalties, but the amounts they quoted would financially ruin us. I even had Russell Harris over this morning to review the contract and he advised us not to break it."

Jimmy was still trying to find the silver lining. "Well, it can't be that big a deal. How many folks attend one of these festivals?"

"A thousand," Brian whispered.

"A hundred, you said?" Jimmy asked.

Dennis shook his head. "No, he said one *thousand*."

Jimmy let out a loud laugh. "But that's ridiculous! There are barely a hundred hotel rooms in a twenty-mile radius!"

"Seems Brian exaggerated those numbers as well," Dennis explained.

As the magnitude of the problem began to sink in, Jimmy's eyes widened. "What else did you write on the application that I should know about?"

"Here," Dennis said, picking up the papers that were on his desk. "You can read them for yourself."

Jimmy spent a few minutes perusing the documents. "Well, if our attorney says we can't break the contract, then we don't," he told Dennis. "I think we need to tell the town."

Dennis nodded in agreement. "Kim is already working on a short article. And Brian will be writing a personal apology to the town's residents."

"Brian, is there anything you haven't told us?" Dennis asked his son one final time.

The teenager glowered at his father. "Not that I can remember."

Dennis was tempted to reply sharply, but he restrained himself.

When the silence grew too heavy, the teenager jumped to his feet.

"All you can see are the problems!" he cried. "Don't you see the benefits? All these people will be coming to town with their awesome hot air balloons." He glanced at the faces of the two adults. "Come on. This will be the biggest thing that ever hit this town. It might turn into a great tradition, like Tibbs Tailgating."

But both men were so focused on the reality of the challenge that neither could envision what Brian saw: the skies over Lumby filled with vibrantly colored balloons of all patterns and shapes drifting silently toward Woodrow Lake. And Brian, still being young and adventurous, couldn't see the predicament he had brought upon the town.

T W O

Blinks

Although the warmer winds of spring had melted much of the snow throughout Mill Valley and the rolling hills to the west of Woodrow Lake, an unexpected storm the day before had left nine inches of fresh powder on the higher elevations, turning the road from Lumby to Franklin into a treacherous drive.

"Do you think we should turn around?" Pam Walker asked her husband.

Mark felt the Jeep fishtail and instantly clenched the steering wheel with both hands. "A mile farther and we'll be over the summit," he said, trying to comfort her.

Even their two Labrador retrievers were unusually quiet in the backseat. But when Clipper spotted a small herd of deer taking refuge in a pine grove close to the road, he pushed his nose hard against the window and growled. That, in turn, triggered Cutter's barking.

"Quiet!" Mark said tensely, taking his foot off the accelerator, which brought the car to a crawl. "This is worse than Priest's Pass."

Pam leaned forward and gazed up at the mountain peaks that flanked both sides of the road. She swallowed. "Did they ever find that couple lost under the avalanche last month?"

"Don't think about that," Mark said as he took another sharp curve. "Anyway, they were someplace called Claw's Path."

It was Pam's nature to worry when facing the unknown, to consider all possible outcomes either in or out of her control. On her husband's face, in contrast, she saw a slight smile that reflected his excitement in the adventure. Sometimes she deeply envied his carefree conviction that all would work out well. Other times, she wondered if he would be able to recognize real peril if it presented itself.

Just then they both saw the rusted plaque secured to a leaning metal post: BEARCLAW'S PASS.

"This is it," Pam groaned. "This is the same place."

"We'll be fine," Mark said.

He noticed Pam was nervously rolling up the papers that had lain on her lap since they'd left Montis Inn. "You're wrinkling his face," he said.

Pam looked down. "Oh no!"

She unrolled the magazines and gently curled the ends in the opposite direction and brushed her hand over the cover photograph, trying to smooth the pages.

"Do you think they know?" she asked, pointing at the most recent issue of *Northwest Living*.

Mark thought for a moment. "Probably not."

Pam opened the magazine, turning to the first page of the article Mark had dog-eared. She had read it several times since receiving the magazine that morning, and although she could have recited the first few lines from memory, she carefully read each word. "In a small and distant town—"

"Sounds like Lumby, doesn't it?" Mark interrupted.

During the last two years, he'd been happier than he'd ever thought possible. The time before that—their "corporate years," as both now referred to the prior decades of their life together—was spent swimming upstream, a constant struggle to prioritize their quality of life and relationships above quantity of possessions and job. Finally, in their late forties, they were fortunate enough to have found the answer in an old abbey that needed as much attention as did their marriage. Remaking Montis Abbey into a country inn had become a worthy focus of their considerable energy.

Mark loosened his grip on the steering wheel as they began their descent from the summit and the condition of the road improved with each passing mile. The dogs, too, settled back down and stared out the rear window.

Pam began to read again. "In a small and distant town that can only be reached by way of mountainous switchback roads that are often closed during the winter, the monks of Saint Cross Abbey are quietly administering one of the largest privately funded philanthropic efforts in recent times." She closed the magazine and studied the portrait of Brother Matthew on the cover. "It's a good photograph of him."

"He'll be embarrassed," Mark said.

"I think you're right, but I'm also sure they must have known that all of their good work would eventually attract some attention."

Once they were out of imminent danger on their slow trip to Franklin, Pam returned her attention to *Northwest Living*, skimming articles she hadn't read earlier. "That's interesting," she commented to herself.

"What's that?"

"Several local inns are advertising special room rates and packages for June fourteenth through the eighteenth," she replied.

Mark thought for a moment. "What's going on then?" he asked.

Pam riffled through more pages, hoping to find the answer. "I don't know," she said. "But I think we're fully booked for that weekend as well."

She laid the magazine on top of the other publication on her lap: *The Lumby Lines*. Pam had circled the article she wanted to show Brother Matthew.

The Lumby Lines

What's News Around Town

BY SCOTT STEVENS   March 21

A very slow week in our sleepy town of Lumby.

The owners of Lumby Sporting Goods are seeking interested volunteers to assist in the recovery of their Zamboni, which has been illegally parked at the bottom of Woodrow Lake since last January's unexpected thaw. Those bringing heavy machinery will be offered free fishing bait for the season. Please contact Billy.

The monks of Saint Cross Abbey, many of whom originally came from Lumby's own Montis Abbey, which is now Montis Inn, have been receiving national accolades for their global humanitarian projects. Preparations are being made for the town mayor to present the key to the city to the brothers, but inasmuch as Lumby doesn't actually have a key, a brass door knocker donated by Brad's Hardware will be used instead.

Consistent with the last dozen years, Tibbs Tailgating will be held at the fairgrounds on the second Sunday in April beginning at six thirty in the morning. A parking grid showing assigned spaces will be posted by the main entrance. Immediately following the close of this year's tailgating, the Rotary Club will be hosting a potato raffle by the east gate of the fairgrounds.

Brian Beezer and Terry McGuire, both 19, were voted Best Entrepreneurs by their fellow high school seniors for apparently maneuvering the Beezers' cat, Snapple, through the state's online university, from which she received a BA and an MBA, ranking second in her graduating class. Snapple then applied for and received a Small Business Association loan for $1,000 and a FEMA grant for $4,000.

Last night the town council voted 4–3 to deny issuing a permit to Steve Iron Enterprises for his proposed Main Street trolley initiative, claiming that the convenience of trolleying three blocks doesn't warrant the expense of repairing the streetlight at the intersection of Main and Farm to Market Road.

Arriving in the small town of Franklin, the Walkers were surprised to see so many cars parked along both sides of the road. Not only was the weather unpleasant, forcing many to stay home, but Franklin was a quiet two-block town with just a handful of shops that were only used by its few residents and the monks of Saint Cross Abbey. Tourism was one trade that would never threaten such a remote village.

"Do you think it's odd that there are so many cars here?" Pam asked.

Mark didn't give it much thought. "Maybe some folks stayed in town because of the bad weather."

Pam shook her head. "But the streets of Franklin are always so empty. We never see anyone here."

"Don't know, but I'm sure there's a logical explanation," Mark said, shrugging his shoulders.

By the time they drove the mile from downtown Franklin to the main gates of Saint Cross Abbey, the ice was accumulating so quickly that the Jeep's wipers couldn't clear the windshield. As they turned into the long driveway, the rear of the Jeep spun again, just missing a WELCOME sign.

"Let's not do that again," Pam said, referring to when Mark drove over the monastery's sign a couple years earlier.

"Yeah, but weren't the guys really nice about it?" he said.

She glanced over at her husband. "Let's not test their benevolence."

Normally Pam and Mark would be greeted by several monks working outside even during the winter months, but on that particular day the grounds were deserted. Ducks resting along the lakeside and smoke billowing out of the many chimneys across the monastic compound were the only signs of life.

As they approached the main building, both noticed that Saint Cross looked more somber than it had the many other times they had visited, but the beauty of the monastery couldn't be shadowed by the ice storm.

Saint Cross bore a likeness to an early-eighteenth-century stone church on the English landscape, with magnificent stained-glass windows and arched doorways. To the right of the main chapel was a common courtyard that, within months, would be awash with color from the several hundred roses planted by the brothers. The fragrance of the roses in full bloom carried throughout the abbey each summer.

At the west end of the garden, an open path of arched columns led to the monks' private courtyard, cloistered on all four sides by stone walkways. In the center, a carved wooden pergola stood over a small meditation pond. Ornamental trees offered shade to the many benches placed carefully throughout the court. Although this private cloister was always closed to the public, Brother Matthew frequently brought Pam and Mark there to visit.

Mark slowed the car as they neared the parking area. "I love coming to Saint Cross. I feel more spiritual here," he said.

Pam smiled. "Good thing, given it's an abbey."

"I even feel smarter here."

Pam started laughing. "What are you talking about?"

"It's true. Can't you feel it?" he asked, turning off the car.

As soon as the engine stopped, Cutter and Clipper went on alert. When Mark opened the driver's-side door, both dogs bolted over the seat, out the door, and darted across the open grounds.

"Get back here!" Mark called, keeping the decibels down in deference to the monks.

Pam jumped out of the car, put two fingers in her mouth and whistled, but the dogs were already halfway to the small lake. When the ducks finally noticed that the large canine masses were quickly descending upon them, they frantically flapped their wings, feathers flying, and loudly voiced their protest, shattering the calm.

Unfortunately, one duck was slower than the others and Cutter, who was well ahead of Clipper, caught it by its right wing and held the struggling bird in its mouth. Following his instinct, Cutter immediately returned to the car and sat in front of Mark, dropping the wounded animal at his feet.

"Do we have a blanket or towel in the car?" Mark asked as Pam bent down and gently placed the semiconscious duck onto Mark's jacket, which she had pulled from the backseat.

"But that's my new blazer," he protested mildly as she picked up the bird and handed it to her husband. Mark wrapped his arms loosely around the bundle.

After collaring their dogs and hustling them back into the Jeep, Mark and Pam knocked on the side door of the residents' building, a private entrance that few outsiders were invited to use.

Pam and Mark's unique relationship with the brothers had been defined two years before. When they first ran into local opposition while trying to restore the abandoned Montis Abbey, the monks befriended them and supported their efforts. Later, when the monks themselves were facing dire hardship, Pam worked relentlessly to ensure the monastery's financial solvency.

They knocked again and within seconds the heavy oak door opened.

A man in his early forties stood on the threshold. His dark brown hair and beard were trimmed short, and his lanky build and casual demeanor were those of someone comfortable in his own body. His large, dark brown eyes opened even wider when he saw the Walkers. "Well, hello, strangers!" Brother Michael said with a broad smile.

The Walkers had known Brother Michael for as long as they had known Brother Matthew. Both monks had returned to Montis shortly after Pam and Mark had bought the old abbey. Michael was many years Matthew's junior and had what the other brothers described as a free spirit and blunt honesty. If Matthew offered the voice of reason for the monastery, Brother Michael contributed the energy and enthusiasm. For that reason Mark and he had been good friends ever since the day they first crossed paths in the Montis orchard.

The heavy bundle in Mark's arms shook violently and Michael jumped back. A deafening squawk came from under the bunched coat. "My word! What is that?"

"One of your ducks, I'm afraid," Mark confessed.

Michael looked confused. "Well, come in, come in. What brings you out in such nasty weather—it wasn't to bring us a duck, I hope?"

The bird squawked again and Mark opened the jacket slightly, thinking the creature might need some air. To everyone's alarm, the duck sprang out of his embrace and flew down the corridor, crashing into Brother Matthew, who had just appeared from around the corner. Feathers scattered everywhere before the duck fell to the floor.

"What on earth?" Brother Matthew said, startled by the attack.

Brother Michael sprinted toward the duck, which was already limping in the direction of the kitchen.

Matthew brushed the feathers off his black robe. "Best not tell Brother John or it may be served with orange sauce for dinner," he called to Michael.

Brother Michael captured the renegade and quickly examined it before tucking it under his arm. "Its wing looks hurt. I'll take him to Brother Marc," he called back.

The duck bent his long neck, looked at Brother Michael, blinked once, and then opened his beak and tried to grab hold of the monk's beard.

"Ouch! He's attacking me!"

"One of God's creatures," Brother Matthew said with a smile, and turned to give Pam and Mark a warm embrace. "Our wayward friends—so good to see you again."

Pam stepped back and examined the monk. "You look well."

"I am, thank you," Matthew replied, leading them into the abbey's community room. He added several logs to the hot embers in the large fireplace. "It's chilly today," he commented, "but the room will warm up in a few minutes." He waited before adding one more log, and then sat down in his favorite chair next to the sofa. "So, what brings you to Saint Cross in such awful weather?"

Pam pulled the publications from her tote bag and handed Brother Matthew the copy of *Northwest Living*. "You're becoming famous."

He examined the cover and then turned to the article. "My word," he whispered.

Pam studied Brother Matthew as he read the feature story. She had always thought he was a handsome man. In his late sixties, he had thick gray hair and a closely trimmed beard that covered his square jaw. His eyes, behind bifocals, were steel gray surrounded by lines that deepened as he smiled. His black hooded robe appeared to add extra inches to his height of six feet four inches.

Pam also thought that he was finally looking well rested after the hardships he had faced the previous summer. Not only was he unanimously selected to lead the monks after their abbot had passed away, but he also shouldered much of the strain when Saint Cross suffered such financial austerity that they were weeks away from permanently closing their doors. But God had looked down on the monastery and smiled, and the tide had turned.

After a few minutes, Brother Matthew closed the magazine. "All of this is very unexpected."

"The article?" Mark asked.

"Yes. This one and others," he replied, standing to retrieve a stack of regional newspapers and magazines from the side table. "Let me return the favor in kind," he said, offering the pile to Pam. "In addition to Saint Cross, Montis Abbey is mentioned in several of them."

Mark leaned against Pam as she took the papers from Brother Matthew.

"Wow," was all she could say as she scanned the lead article on the front page of the living section from the *Seattle Times*' Sunday edition. Under the caption "Divine Interventions" was a large photograph of Saint Cross Abbey with Brother Matthew, surrounded by several other monks, standing in the cloistered courtyard.

She flipped to the next paper, the *Denver Post*, and then to a magazine, *Pacific Sunset*. Publication after publication featured Saint Cross Abbey on its cover.

When they were finished skimming through the stack, she looked up and congratulated her close friend. "You've done well."

Brother Matthew humbly nodded his head. "It started so simply. I remember the first day we convened to discuss how to best serve God with the windfall we were so fortunate to receive."

"Yes, fortunate, but all of you work tremendously hard," Pam corrected him.

"We try," he said, and then returned to the subject. "There was such dissension among us. Everyone had very good intentions, but each was directed differently. In our research, though, we stumbled on a field called microphilanthropy and microlending." Matthew's voice quickened with passion. "It's based on the concept that a large number of small grants or loans given directly to working people who are entrapped in poverty will be far more effective than one large donation."

"How small is a small gift?" Pam asked.

"Very, very small to you and me," he said. "Did you know that over one billion people live on one dollar a day—one billion? And three billion live on less than two dollars a day? I find that so shocking." Matthew bent his head. "Fifty dollars to someone trapped in that level of poverty can radically change the course of his or her life."

"Is the money for food?" Mark asked.

"No. That would only solve the problem for a month." Matthew turned to Pam and grinned. "The money is invested."

"In what?" she asked.

"Oh, the list is endless. In Asia, a water buffalo can allow a young woman to harvest four times the crop so she can sell most of what she reaps. In Africa, tools for working with leather will allow a craftsman to hire his brother to help make belts for the open market." Matthew pointed behind them at a blanket draped over the back of the sofa. "In Chile, a weave loom can employ four women in a small village. You are leaning against one of their products."

Pam and Mark turned and admired the colors and quality of the blanket.

Mark had another question. "How do you know where the money is spent?"

Brother Matthew spread his arms wide to convey the scope of their endeavor. "We have a growing international network in place, led by several of our brothers—two in South America, one in Asia, and so on. Each has a handful of volunteers to reach the villages and towns where our monies are most needed."

"I noticed you used the term 'microlending.' Is the money paid back to you?" Pam asked.

Matthew beamed. "Not exactly, and this is one of the greatest aspects of the program. When a gift is given, or loaned, to someone who has the capability of producing income, they agree to loan the same amount to another person in their village within a reasonable time after their own situation improves."

"Pay it forward," Pam said.

"Precisely," Matthew said, patting his knees.

Pam reached over and laid her hand on the monk's. "We're so proud of all that you've done."

"And you were there at the beginning, honey." Mark nudged his wife, referring to the great assistance Pam had given Saint Cross Abbey in defining a new business in which they made gourmet rum sauces.

Pam blushed. "And Charlotte Ross is looking down on us from heaven, smiling as well," she added.

"Charlotte's last act of generosity, leaving us a gourmet food company worth ten times our rum sauce business, was so unexpected but so deeply appreciated." Brother Matthew shook his head, still amazed by the kindness of their dear benefactor, who had passed away last summer.

Suddenly, sleet began to pelt the stained-glass windows.

"You will certainly be staying the night," Matthew said, rising from his chair.

"We really can't," Mark said. "Our dogs are in the car."

"Not a problem," Matthew insisted. "We can make accommodations for them. Brother Michael will show you to your room. Vespers is at five thirty."

After settling their dogs into vacant runs in the monks' small kennel, Pam and Mark rested a short time before venturing out in the ice storm. The private chapel was the smallest building on the monastery grounds, located well behind the main church and protected by a grove of old cypress trees. By the time the Walkers entered the monks' sanctuary, the sky had turned black and the wind was blistering—a final reminder that it had been a long winter.

Crossing the chapel's threshold transported the Walkers into another world of Gregorian chants, candlelight, deep prayer, and a rapt devotion to God. The one-room chapel was silent and still, even though the twenty-eight monks of Saint Cross Abbey were already seated. Each was in deep, contemplative meditation. The wooden pews glowed almost golden from the hundred candles.

The creak in the door hinge screamed through the silence, but none of the monks turned to see who had entered. Shutting the door quickly, Pam and Mark slipped into a back pew.

Several minutes later, without signal and in unison, the monks stood and the intense quiet was broken by the most extraordinary chanting. The voices were one but of three harmonic tones, and every corner of the chapel was filled with bass, baritone, and tenor adoration of God. Pam rubbed her arms, chilled by the wondrous moment. Mark was equally transfixed.

Halfway through vespers, a strong gust of wind penetrated the heavy door and blew out many of the candles in the back. That's when Mark noticed a glow coming from under many of the monks' robes. Oddly, the glows were of different colors: some pale green, some red, and others blue.

Mark squinted, straining to see the source of the lights. When he sank into the pew, lowering his head to try to peer under the robes, Pam hit his leg gently. But before straightening up, he finally realized what was making the various auras: the soles of the sneakers worn by the monks. As they walked or shifted their weight while standing, small lights in the heels of the sneakers blinked on and off. Mark stifled a laugh.

After vespers, Mark went up to Brother Michael, who was closer in age to Mark than was Brother Matthew.

"Nice sneakers," he told the brother.

Brother Michael grinned and brought his finger to his lips. "A Saint Cross secret. Nike sent a pair for each of the brothers," he explained. "It's just amazing; you really feel like you're walking on cushions."

As another monk walked toward the altar, Pam realized what they were talking about.

Blink . . . Blink . . . Blink . . . Blink.

Michael added, "The light shows aren't exactly what folks would expect from a bunch of monks, but my feet are in heaven."

After the front candles were blown out, many of the monks congregated at the back of the church, awaiting a break in the heavy sleet falling outside.

Moving slowly with his head slightly bowed, Brother Matthew walked down the center aisle and joined his visitors. "Although it wasn't planned, we are so glad you could join us for vespers."

"This is the first time we have ever been to a service in the chapel," Pam commented. "It really is breathtaking."

"Thank you. Most of us prefer its intimacy to the main church, but we can only seat a few visitors, as you can tell." Brother Matthew caught the eye of a young man standing close by. "Ah, good. I would like you to meet our retreatants." He waved to two men who had been sitting directly behind the brothers during vespers. Both had very dark complexions, but their hair was caramel colored, distinctly lighter than their skin. Their eyes, too, were uncommonly pale brown for such dark features. Pam guessed they were in their late twenties.

"Please join us," Matthew said, gesturing to the men. "Jamar and Kai, these are our close friends Pam and Mark Walker. Pam and Mark, this is Kai Talin," Matthew said, looking at the younger of the two men, "and his brother, Jamar. They are missionaries visiting us from Indonesia. We have contributed to their town's efforts in building a new school."

"Very nice to meet both of you," Mark said congenially, shaking their hands.

"And you," Jamar replied. "Your names have come up in several conversations."

Mark shot a mock concerned glance toward Matthew. "You didn't tell him everything, did you?"

Matthew laughed, shaking his head. "Not to worry. I don't think they would believe some of your stories anyway."

"You're from Lumby?" Jamar asked Pam.

"Just south of the town, yes," she answered. "We purchased the old Montis Abbey and converted it into an inn—with the help of many of the monks here, in fact."

"We would certainly like to visit before returning home. Franklin really doesn't give us much excitement," Jamar said, obviously hoping for an invitation.

"We didn't come for excitement," Kai said under his breath.

"Yes, but God would certainly want us to experience all that your country has to offer before returning home," Jamar maintained.

"How long are you here for?" Mark asked.

"A few more months," the younger brother said with a delightful smile.

"At which time Kai and Jamar will be returning home to their island of Coraba to pursue the priesthood," Matthew added.

"How commendable," Pam said.

Jamar grinned. "There are many ways one can be of service," he said, adding a cavalier wink at Pam. He stepped back, intending to lean on the end of a pew, but somehow he missed it and stumbled across the aisle. To his credit, he straightened himself in a flurry and then brushed back his hair. "Must be a different height than our pews," he said quickly.

Kai rolled his eyes before turning back to Mark and Pam. "So, you bought the brothers' old monastery."

"Quite old," Mark teased.

Kai blushed, thinking he had used the wrong word. "I meant previous."

"Perhaps Brother Matthew can bring you over one day."

Jamar's eyes widened. "Would tomorrow be too soon?"

THREE

Legacy

The following afternoon, Caroline Ross sat in a small conference room reviewing her notes. She had driven to Wheatley, a small city thirty minutes south of Lumby, to meet with two partners from the firm of Spencer Associates. One of them, Brooke Shelling Turner, had become a close friend during the previous year. Initially, they had been united by their mutual affection for Caroline's grandmother, Charlotte Ross.

Spencer Associates, one of the oldest architectural firms in the state, was steeped in tradition. The room featured furnishings of high quality: a large mahogany table surrounded by chairs richly upholstered in dark burgundy, and original oil paintings on the walls.

Caroline was stunningly attractive, as her grandmother had been. She had inherited Charlotte's straw-colored hair, hazel eyes, and a beautiful face with a determined chin. At twenty-eight, she exuded the same self-confidence and positive demeanor for which Charlotte would forever be remembered.

Caroline shared another attribute with Charlotte, the reason why she was at Spencer Associates that day: Caroline had a strong business mind. In Charlotte's last will and testament she had named Caroline to head the Ross Foundation, knowing that Caroline was most capable of carrying on her legacy.

Almost eighty years ago, with her first husband, Charlotte Ross had helped to mold Lumby into the town it was today. Although their small orchard was located in Rocky Mount, their home remained in Lumby. After her husband died, Charlotte single-handedly expanded Ross Orchards into one of the largest fruit-producing enterprises in the Northwest. The Ross Foundation had been established close to forty years ago and was funded by a small percentage of the company's profits. As Charlotte's apples grew, so did the foundation's net worth. And with success came personal windfalls that were substantial enough to allow her to make significant, usually anonymous gifts to the town of Lumby.

Her granddaughter meant to continue that tradition. Caroline slid the foundation's financial report into her briefcase, then scanned the newspapers that were laid out for visiting clients. She passed over the *Wall Street Journal* and picked up that morning's issue of *The Lumby Lines*.

The Lumby Lines

Sheriff's Complaints

BY SHERIFF SIMON DIXON   March 25

7:12 a.m. Betsy Miller involved in fender bender with parked car at the corner of Hunts Mill and Main Street. While driving son to school, pet turtle crawled under the brake pedal.

7:13 a.m. Cindy Watford on Cherry Street reportedly found live duckling in mailbox.

7:58 a.m. Moose vs. Volvo on State Road 541 one mile west of Priest's Pass. Guardrail damaged but no injuries.

8:47 a.m. Caller reported baby duck or goose found in mailbox on North Grant. Animal pooped on morning newspaper.

10:43 a.m. Assistance requested by Lumby Episcopal Church. Owl in belfry has six-pack plastic holder wrapped around its neck and wing. EMS dispatched.

3:53 p.m. Lumby Sporting Goods reported clothes missing from female display mannequin, again.

8:54 p.m. Concerned resident reported that an unusual amount of smoke was rising from one of the mounds at the landfill.

10:46 p.m. Resident reported that two teenagers are up to no good inside the public phone booth on the corner of Main and Mineral.

11:32 p.m. Jeep vs. buck on Farm to Market at MM 13. Both sustained serious damage. Buck being delivered to Dr. Campbell's place.

Caroline looked up when the conference room door opened.

"Hello, Brooke," she said with a wide smile. "It's been too long—perhaps a few days?"

"Your margarita party last Friday night, if I remember correctly,"

Brooke joked, sitting down beside her. "It took Joshua and me several days to recover."

Although Brooke and Caroline were opposites in physical appearance—Brooke having a mass of long brown hair and dark brown eyes—they shared a common approach to the world: one of caution, where trust was earned before it was given. Brooke also had the same determination about her, an energy that she had tapped when building a successful architectural firm in Virginia before moving to Lumby a few years before.

"But we did have fun, didn't we?" Caroline whispered as an older gentleman walked into the room.

"Caroline"—Brooke's voice became more formal—"have you met Donald Spencer?"

"No, but it's a pleasure," she said, shaking his hand. "I'm well aware of your quality work."

"Thank you," Donald said, staring at Caroline's vibrant beauty while taking a seat directly across the table from the two women. He caught himself and blushed slightly. "I'm sorry. You look remarkably like your grandmother," he explained.

"I know that you and she were good friends. I'm sure she would be pleased that we may be working together," Caroline said.

Brooke leaned forward. "So, what can we do for you?"

Caroline addressed both partners. "As you may be aware, I oversee the Ross Foundation, and I would like your thoughts on a project we are considering—a memorial for my grandmother." Caroline immediately noticed Brooke's reaction. "You look surprised. Is something wrong?" she asked.

"No, not really. I suppose—" Brooke began, then stopped to collect her thoughts. "I was given the rare opportunity to get to know Charlotte, and the woman I knew shied away from anything put in her name or in her memory."

Caroline smiled. "Oh, I certainly agree with that."

"But you're considering a monument?" Brooke asked in bewilderment.

"Oh, no," Caroline said and laughed, "not a monument, a memorial. Specifically, an arts center."

"An arts center?" Donald repeated.

"My grandmother loved three things: literature, art, and music. Her dream for expanding the town's library was realized last summer. She wanted to offer a similar opportunity for the arts. So, we believe a perfect tribute to my grandmother would be a center for artists and musicians."

"What a wonderful idea," Brooke said. "Charlotte dragged me to every concert within a hundred-mile radius." Her face lit up with a sudden memory. "One time she and I went to Rocky Mount and wandered into a pottery studio. We ended up staying for hours while she tried to make a bowl on the wheel." Brooke laughed, remembering that day clearly. "Clay was everywhere, on the ceiling, in her hair, but she loved it."

Donald returned to the matter at hand. "Where would this center be located?"

"Certainly in Lumby, but specifically, I don't know," Caroline said.

Donald opened his leather portfolio and began taking notes. "Have you given any thought as to how large a building would be needed?"

"I have a concept but no actual dimensions. The center should be able to provide separate studio spaces for at least twenty artists in addition to practice and composition rooms for half as many musicians." Caroline paused before voicing her next thought aloud. "And it would need an open area for concerts and exhibitions."

Donald looked at Brooke for confirmation. "There are several nice pieces of land available quite close to town that you might consider."

Instead of commenting, though, Brooke slowly stood up and began to pace around the table, rubbing her hands together.

"Brooke, what are you thinking?" Caroline asked.

Brooke stopped short, her figure silhouetted by bright sunlight shining through a large window. "I think I have the answer."

"What is it?" Caroline asked.

"Bricks."

Donald and Caroline stared at Brooke, waiting for her to go on. Citing a common building material didn't tell them anything.

Suddenly, Caroline's eyes opened wide and she gently slapped the table. "Of course! Bricks! I've heard rumors about it—if any of them are true, it sounds wonderful."

Donald was more confused than ever. "What is bricks?"

"That's what local residents call the old Round Station," Brooke explained.

"The deserted train station north of town?" he asked.

Caroline nodded. "That's the one, but I hear it's not a train station."

Brooke returned to her seat and began sketching rapidly. "It's a massive circular brick building that was used for repairing railroad cars and engines decades ago. There's only one set of tracks going into it, so once the boxcar was brought inside and reconditioned, it was literally swung around three hundred and sixty degrees and then sent on its way, thus the reason for the circular shape."

"But that track hasn't been used since the seventies," Donald said.

"Probably earlier than that," Caroline replied, trying to recall. "I believe the Rocky Mount line stopped running to Lumby in the early sixties."

Donald seemed reluctant to embrace the idea. "And the building is still standing?"

Caroline shook her head. "I've never actually seen it, but there's no reason to believe it's not just as it was left."

Donald continued to sound doubtful. "The elements have a way of demolishing deserted buildings."

"And the one road that goes to the Round Station has been closed for decades," Brooke added. "Joshua and I tried to find it last fall and it was impossible to get anywhere near it because of the undergrowth."

"Who owns it now?" Caroline asked.

"That's anyone's guess," Brooke answered.

Donald looked at his watch and stood up. "Well, it sounds as if we're in agreement," he continued. Seeing that neither Brooke nor Caroline followed his lead, he said, "I really need to get to another appointment. It was a delight meeting you, Caroline, and we look forward to working with you."

"If you don't mind," Caroline asserted, "I would like to work directly with Brooke on this effort."

Donald looked at her with surprise, since most clients generally preferred to work with the most senior partner possible, then he offered a cordial smile. "That would be fine. Brooke is one of our finest architects."

After Donald left the conference room, Caroline laughed. "Well, that was abrupt."

"Sorry about that," Brooke said. "The closer he is to retirement, the more impatient he becomes. But the firm would be delighted to see you through the project."

"Brooke, I'm in total agreement with what you said. Bricks may be the perfect solution and we should move forward as quickly as possible."

"But you haven't even seen it."

"That's something we need to remedy right away. If you're available on Thursday, I suggest we go for a hike."

Brooke was both surprised and impressed by Caroline's eagerness to get started. "Thursday is fine. That buys me a few days to make inquiries about the property. It wouldn't be one of my better moments if my client and I were arrested for trespassing."

"You worry too much," Caroline said. "I just know this is going to work."

"Charlotte always said you have some of the best business instincts she ever encountered. Still, let's take it one step at a time. It's an old deserted building—anything could be out there."

Surprises

"Our trusted law enforcement keeping watch," Brooke said as she walked into the police station the following day.

Simon looked up from reading the local paper. He had just finished the article Dennis and Jimmy had written about the balloon festival, which was immediately followed by a heartfelt, although painfully brief, apology from Brian Beezer. "Well, good morning."

"What's happening in the park today?" Brooke asked.

"Nothing that I'm aware of, but I've been buried in paperwork since sunrise. Why do you ask?"

"There are quite a few folks gathered across the street," Brooke said.

"I'll take a look. But first, what can I do for you?"

Brooke was running late and declined to take a seat. "One of my clients is interested in Bricks."

Simon's eyes widened. "Really?"

"The Ross Foundation is exploring the idea of building an arts center there."

Simon chuckled and shook his head in total admiration. "Charlotte Ross continues to give to this town even a year after her death. That woman was just amazing."

Brooke smiled. "She was indeed, and I think she would be delighted with Caroline's plans."

"Bricks certainly is a gem in the rough," Simon reflected. "It would be great if that building could be put to good use."

"So you're familiar with it?"

"I've been there more times that I can remember, but not recently . . . not within the last six months," Simon said.

"Caroline and I would like to look at it, but we don't want to trespass," Brooke explained. "Could you advise me on how best to proceed?"

Simon thought for a moment. "I'm sure we can arrange for the two of you to go out there. You do know it's quite a hike, don't you?"

Brooke nodded. "I'm embarrassed to admit it, but Joshua and I tried to find it last year," she said, blushing. "The woods were so dense we didn't get farther than a half mile."

Simon heard shouts outside and tried to look through the window. "When did you want to go?"

"Day after tomorrow. If you could help, that would be great," Brooke said. Through the increased noise from the street, she heard someone yell out Simon's name. "I think you're being paged."

"If you would excuse me," Simon said, almost running to the front door. "I'll call you tomorrow."

As he stepped outside, Simon saw a large crowd gathered in the park a half a block down Main Street. More onlookers stood on the Episcopal church property adjacent to the park, while others stood on the sidewalk across the road. Simon jogged down the road to join them.

All of a sudden, someone yelled, "Pull," and to Simon's astonishment a silo, which had been lying on its side, was raised above the crowd. It lifted higher into the air, and then, after oscillating for a few seconds, gently came to rest in the vertical position. The crowd broke out in an almost thunderous cheer.

Simon nudged his way through the crowd of spectators, finally breaking into the clearing. He first noticed the cows, some twenty black-and-white belted Galloway cows standing around the silo.

Then he saw rolls of spare agricultural fencing that were being used to erect a barricade along the west perimeter of the park.

"Morty, what on earth are you doing?" Simon asked, walking up to a small man who was at least thirty years his senior.

"Grazing my herd, Simon," the man answered, taking off his hat and wiping the sweat from his brow. "I didn't think she'd go up that easily—must not weigh anything when it's totally empty," he added, looking straight up at the silo.

"Morty, you're in the town park," Simon said, thinking that dementia may have warped the man's thinking.

"Well, I know that, Simon. That brush fire a few days ago got most of my grass."

Simon shook his head in disbelief. "But you just can't move your cows to the center of town."

"Actually, I can," the old man confirmed. "I'm exercising the town's grazing law of 1891."

Simon looked dumbfounded. "What on earth is that?"

"Read the books, Simon," he said almost defiantly, shaking his index finger at him. "It says that any civil servant can use town-owned property for grazing livestock three months out of the year. And since I was the postmaster for twenty years, I'm now claiming my rights."

"But, Morty, you know full well that that law was written a century ago when there were only a couple hundred people in Lumby."

"Still on the books," Morty replied, and then yelled over to his sons and grandsons, "Let's get these ropes off the silo and set up the water troughs."

Simon watched as Morty's grandsons rolled hoses from the back of Morty's tractor. He raised his hand to signal the boys to stop.

"All right, we'll find some grazing land for you, but it will take awhile," Simon conceded. "So why don't you stop what you're doing and just give me a little time."

"This will do just fine," Morty said. "Look at how my cows like that rich sod."

"Exactly!" Simon said. "Your cows will ruin the park!"

"Law of 1891, Simon, 1891," Morty reminded him.

Simon realized his only options were to either forcibly remove one of the founding fathers of the town (or so Morty always claimed to be) or to quickly find greener pastures for his cows.

"Morty, I'll be back shortly. Just hold off fencing. I'm sure we can resolve this to everyone's satisfaction."

Morty waved his hand in the air. "I'll be here, Simon. Not planning on going anywhere."

&

Dennis Beezer and his wife, Gabrielle, sat alone at the back table in the Green Chile, their small restaurant on Main Street. The eatery served not only the best margaritas in town but also savory Mexican cuisine from recipes that Gabrielle had brought with her from Veracruz. Her Central American upbringing was also reflected in the interior design of the restaurant, which was tastefully decorated with tablecloths that matched the green-and-yellow-striped curtains.

Although lunch would not be served for another two hours, Gabrielle had several Mexican stews cooking in large pots on the stove as well as tortillas baking in the oven. As usual, the small eatery was filled with exotic aromas.

Timmy, her eight-year-old son, came running in from the kitchen. "Mom, guess what? There's cows in the park! I was watching from the upstairs window."

"Is someone there with them?" Gabrielle asked.

"Mr. Dixon is talking to Mr. Alberts in the middle of the street and one of the cows is chewing a church shrub. Can I go watch?" he said. "Please?"

Gabrielle glanced at her husband and then back at her son—how very alike they were. Timmy had always been such an easy child to raise. "And when you cross Main Street?" she asked.

"I know," he said with the impatience of a boy on an important mission. "Stop and look both ways."

"Okay. But for only twenty minutes," she said.

Gabrielle watched her younger son bolt out the door.

Before Timmy had interrupted, Gabrielle and Dennis had been talking about Brian's latest transgression. Although she and Dennis agreed that Brian should be disciplined, she continued to feel the pain of disappointment in his lack of maturity and good sense.

Gabrielle wrung a napkin between her hands. "I feel I'm to blame for not teaching Brian better," she admitted.

"We both raised him," Dennis said.

"Obviously not well enough."

Her words stung because Dennis knew how true they were. "I know we were too lenient—at least I was," he said. "But—"

"No buts this time, Dennis," Gabrielle pleaded. "He could have cost us everything we have. Thank God Jimmy is such a good friend and agreed to go along with this prank."

Dennis took Gabrielle's hand and patted it gently. "It might actually turn out to be a good thing for Lumby."

"I hope so, because everyone's fingers are already pointing in our direction."

There was a tap on the window. Russell Harris, the town's attorney, was peering in over the CLOSED sign to see if anyone was inside. Behind him stood Jimmy D.

"I asked Russell and Jimmy to drop by after they had a chance to take a closer look at the contract," Dennis explained and waved them in.

The small bell chimed when the door opened.

"Come join our family meeting," Dennis said as Gabrielle stepped into the kitchen to fill two more cups of coffee.

"Well," Jimmy began after taking a seat, "I talked with folks from Wheatley and Rocky Mount, and both towns will be rolling out the red carpet for the balloon festival."

Dennis's spirits lifted. "That's great."

"And I'm being swamped with calls from townsfolk who are offering to rent out their available bedrooms."

Russell laughed. "For a premium, I suppose."

Jimmy rubbed his neck. "Well, that's what I was expecting, given that some folks haven't yet embraced the spirit of the festival, if you know what I mean."

Gabrielle rolled her eyes. "We absolutely do."

Jimmy continued. "But most of them said they are only looking for ten or twenty dollars a night, which is more than reasonable. Tomorrow afternoon, all those folks who are interested in converting their homes into small bed-and-breakfasts will be meeting at Jimmy D's to discuss it. You're all invited to attend."

Gabrielle looked at Dennis. "That's the least we can do. We'll be there."

"Will you also be talking about the balloon?" Russell asked as he stacked papers on the table.

Dennis and Jimmy looked at the attorney as if he were speaking a foreign language.

"What balloon?" Dennis asked.

Russell was equally surprised they didn't know. "Lumby's balloon, of course."

Jimmy laughed lightly. "No, no," he said, shaking his head. "We're just hosting the event. At best, some of the residents might pay for a ride during the festival, but that's just about it."

Russell pulled a file out of his briefcase. "Didn't you read the contract, Jimmy?"

"It's still in my in-box." The mayor winced at the admission.

"Well, let me find the appropriate clause." Russell quickly scanned the contract in front of him. "I quote, section III.2.A: 'In the spirit of aviation history and in the tradition of the regional balloon festival, the hosting town will construct and pilot the lead balloon in the festival. The balloon will be no less than one hundred thousand cubic feet, to be piloted as the lead balloon for the opening sunrise ceremony.' " Russell looked up from his reading. "You really didn't know about this?"

Jimmy and Dennis looked at each other in disbelief.

"Gabrielle!" Dennis called out. "Do you know where our son is?"

"Brian went over to the hardware store a little earlier. He said something about helium," she answered.

Dennis gritted his teeth in anger. "Well, obviously *he* knew."

"Speaking of the prodigal son," Jimmy said, pointing out the front window.

Dennis turned and saw Brian walk past the restaurant with Terry McGuire close behind. He jumped from his chair and ran to the front door, quickly collaring his son and dragging him inside.

"Did you know about the balloon?" Jimmy asked as Brian sank down in the chair next to him.

"What balloon?" Brian replied, feigning innocence.

Dennis glared at his son. "You know full well."

Brian shrugged off the adult stares. "There's the lead balloon that Lumby will need to build. But that can't be a surprise. Everyone knows that the hosting town always floats the biggest and best."

"And who do you think will pay for it?" Jimmy asked.

"The town will!" Brian asserted.

"The town is already tremendously unhappy with you," Dennis said. "There'll be a lynching party after you once they're told this festival is going to cost them thousands of dollars."

"But we'll reuse it, selling rides each year at the fair. It will pay for itself in no time," Brian tried to explain. "The guys in Rocky Mount think the balloon should be at least a hundred and twenty thousand cubic feet."

Dennis stared at his son in disbelief. "What guys in Rocky Mount? And when were you over there?"

"Terry and I have gone over there a few times. This guy I met there owns a hot air balloon and he gives flying lessons so you can get a balloon pilot's license."

Gabrielle's gasp was heard by everyone at the table. "You've been up in a balloon?"

"Oh, yeah," Brian said, his eyes shining. "It's great. The math formulas are pretty hard, but I think I get it now and the written test should be a breeze."

Dennis glanced first at Gabrielle and then at his son, as if the boy were a complete stranger. Not wanting to get into a family fight, he said, "We'll talk about this at home."

"Wait a minute," Jimmy said, then paused for a moment while he thought out his plan. "This might be all right. I mean, how hard can it actually be to fly a hot air balloon? It's not exactly physics or anything."

"That's exactly what it is," Russell said flatly.

"But it's really easy," Brian interjected.

"Well," Jimmy continued, "there must be someone in town who has experience with balloons, and I'm not talking about just a few flights, young Mr. Beezer. I say we should look at this as an opportunity for Lumby. We just need someone crazy enough to lead the troops."

Just then Jimmy looked out the window and saw Mark Walker taking a seat on one of the stone steps leading up to the library.

"And there's our man," Jimmy said.

"Mark Walker? Why would you think he knows anything about balloons?" Dennis asked.

Jimmy's smile widened. "Oh, I'm sure he doesn't, but if there's anyone with enthusiasm for a new project, it's our Montis man." He dropped his voice to a whisper. "Also, he's great friends with Chuck Bryson—"

"So?" Dennis interrupted, not making the connection.

"—who taught physics at Berkeley and must know a thing or two about aeronautics."

"But can Mark oversee such a large project?" Dennis asked skeptically.

"Oh, I think so. When he gets serious he's as focused as anyone. And he puts more heart into what he does than most men I know. Look at all he's accomplished down at the monastery."

"I thought that was mostly Pam's doing," Gabrielle commented.

"She managed a part of it, but Mark also jumped into something he knew nothing about and worked with the contractors. And he's as honest as the day is long."

"Good enough for me. Let me grab him," Dennis said as he headed for the door.

Through the window the others watched a pantomime of Dennis speaking to Mark, then escorting him into the Green Chile.

"Afternoon, gentlemen," Mark said with a smile, joining them at the table. "Don't tell me you're making secret plans to evict good old Morty and his dozen cows from the park?"

"If it was only that easy," Russell said with a groan.

"Oh." Mark drew the word out with a menacing sound. "Those aren't good words, coming from the town's attorney. You guys should know the gazebo is leaning quite a lot from all the cows rubbing their itchy ass—"

"Rumps," Gabrielle interjected from the kitchen.

"Boy," Mark said, looking around to see where Gabrielle's voice had come from, "she's as good as Pam."

All the men laughed.

"So, seriously, what can I do for you?" Mark asked.

Jimmy first glanced at Dennis and then leaned toward Mark. "We have an interesting proposition for you," he began.

For the next ten minutes, Jimmy explained the town's challenge and outlined what they wanted Mark to do. When he was done explaining, Mark's eyes were as big as saucers. "Wow!" he said.

"It would entail you rallying the troops and coordinating the town's resources to build the lead balloon," Dennis reiterated.

"Wow!" Mark repeated.

"We think you would be the perfect . . ." Dennis searched for the right word.

"Ambassador," Jimmy offered.

"Exactly," Dennis said. "An ambassador to lead this effort. But the details need to be kept between us for the next few days, until we have a chance to explain it in full to the residents of Lumby."

Mark straightened up in his chair. "Oh, I can't keep something this big from Pam. She always knows when I'm hiding something."

"Good for her!" Gabrielle shouted from the kitchen.

"She'll know in an instant," Mark warned his friends.

Jimmy shrugged. "Then just be vague for a while. Everyone will find out soon enough. And you're the guy they'll be turning to for leadership."

"Wow."

FIVE

Wading

Most folks in town were preparing for Tibbs Tailgating, in one way or another, well before the event. Hank, being the enterprising plastic pink flamingo that he was, chose to display his wares several days in advance. He placed himself squarely on the grass median in front of the Lumby Bookstore, where he could maximize sales from the traffic converging at Main Street and Farm to Market Road.

Toting a Radio Flyer wagon filled to the brim with valuables he had collected over the past year, Hank had hung one large sign from the handlebar that read CASH ONLY, NO BARTER. Although such inflexible terms annoyed some, most called him well principled for being so forthright about his business policy.

"Perhaps we shouldn't trade this year," Pam said, reading Hank's sign as she and Mark drove through town. "Last year we came home with more junk than we sold."

"But that's the fun of it," Mark replied. "It's not about the money but who ends up with the best stuff."

"So, mission not accomplished last year?" Pam asked facetiously.

"You'll be so surprised to see how many great things we have in the basement that we can recycle this year," her husband assured her.

An hour later, however, after scouring Montis Inn for "personal heirlooms and other collectables" they wanted to unload, the only items they had found were three bent tomato cages and a handful of torn paperback novels.

They moved on to the root cellar, a belowground storage room abutting the back of the main dining room.

"Can you see anything?" Pam called down to her husband from where she was standing by the entrance, struggling to keep the ponderous metal door open. Mark stood on the stairs several feet below her.

"Nothing—it's too dark. Could you move over so more light can come in?"

"Sorry," Pam said, trying to step aside. "It's really heavy. Can't I let go of the door?"

"No, please don't," he answered quickly. "The hinge is broken. This will only take a minute." Looking back down into the dark void, Mark asked, "So, how many steps are there?"

Before Pam could answer, she heard a large splash followed by a groan.

"Mark?"

"Six," he answered himself. "But the last one is a killer."

"Are you all right?"

"Wet."

"From what?" Pam asked.

"About six inches of muddy water," Mark answered, waiting for his eyes to adjust to the darkness.

"Is it really cold down there?"

"No, surprisingly not. This must be well below the frost line. But this is hopeless—I can't see a thing. Could you get me a flashlight?"

"There should be a large one on the ledge," Pam said.

Mark felt around. "This is disgusting," he grumbled. "I think there are mouse turds down here. Oh, wait, I found it."

Suddenly the root cellar was flooded with light, almost startling Mark.

"Wow, this is much bigger than I remembered," he called up to Pam. "And wetter."

She leaned over and tried to look down the stairs. "It was bone dry down there last summer. Where's the water coming from?"

Mark slowly panned the flashlight above his head and along each of the walls.

"I see some water flowing through the left wall."

"*Through* the wall?" Pam asked.

"Yeah, it seems to be seeping out of the dirt," Mark answered. "Wait—oh, God, something's got me . . . it's grabbed my sneaker!"

Pam was alarmed. "What's going on?"

"My sneaker's gone!" Mark shouted out. "There's quicksand down here—I felt it pulling me under."

"There's no quicksand around here," Pam said skeptically.

He sounded like an aggrieved child as he replied, "Tell that to my sneaker."

"Is the ground soft?"

"Just in that one place. I'll be glad to get out of here." Mark waded several steps through the water toward the rear of the storage room. "There are some crates down here. Are those what you want?"

Pam didn't know about any crates. "I don't think so. How many are there?"

"About six. They're all over in the far corner. I don't remember ever seeing them before. The bottom one is sitting in water, but the others look dry."

Pam was becoming curious. "Why don't you pass them to me."

"And there are a couple of boxes behind them, they look like wine crates. Should I bring those up as well?"

"Let's get them out of there before they rot," Pam suggested and propped the metal door open.

"Or before something sucks them into hell," Mark said under his breath as he began carrying the crates and boxes up the stairs, where he passed them to Pam.

"I'm glad we're finally doing this," she said, setting the crates on the ground outside. "Our guests will find the root cellar fascinating."

"A waterlogged room dug in dirt?" Mark challenged. His muddy, wet sock looked ludicrous without its shoe.

"Where the monks stored much of their food a hundred years ago, yes," Pam countered.

Mark picked up the last of the boxes. "Some of these are really heavy," he said, pushing them up the stairs.

After Mark crawled out, Pam closed the metal door. She looked at her husband, then at his dripping cotton sock. "Where's your sneaker?"

Had Mark not been so tired and wet, he might have become annoyed. "I told you, it's gone. It got sucked up."

Pam thought it best not to ask him to go back and retrieve it.

After carrying the boxes into their private residence at Montis Inn, Mark headed promptly for the shower to wash off the muck. Pam stoked the wood-burning stove, heating the damp air of the large room that served as both their kitchen and living room.

It had been two years since they had bought Montis Abbey, a fire-ravaged monastery that dated back to the late 1800s. With time and most of their savings, they had carefully restored the property and opened it as an historic inn. Their initial plan was to move into the main building once the renovation was complete, but they had become comfortable in the smallest house in the complex, the five-room rambler that they called Taproot Lodge. It offered what they had come to value most: privacy from the guests and workers at the inn.

While Mark was in the shower, Pam moved the four crates closer to the table and began unpacking them. She carefully removed papers and smaller boxes from the first.

Mark finally emerged from their bedroom, fully dressed. A towel hung around his neck.

"Feeling better?" she asked.

"Less turdy, thanks," he said, leaning over to kiss his wife. "So, did you find the missing treasure of Montis?"

Pam's eyes opened wide. "There's a treasure?" she asked.

Mark laughed. "Just teasing, honey. You're the only treasure here."

"You're sweet." She leaned her head against his hand for a few moments.

Mark noticed that Pam had set four places at the kitchen table for lunch. "Are we expecting company?"

"Chuck was going to work on the beehives today. He's probably already up in the apiary with Joshua. I thought they might like something to eat. Would you ring the bell for them?"

Mark put on his boots and walked outside to the main building. By the front porch, fifty yards from Farm to Market Road, stood a six-foot metal post with an old tower bell hanging from its horizontal arm. Mark pulled the heavy cord and a familiar sound rang out throughout the Montis property. He rang again: two tolls for a meal, three if the barn animals had escaped.

By the time Mark returned, a large pot of chili was already heating on the stove and Pam had resumed going through the boxes.

"Look at all of these photographs," she said, placing two more shoe boxes on the table.

But Mark was more interested in sampling Pam's cooking. He looked up only when he heard the dogs bark.

Pam opened the front door as Joshua rounded the corner of the inn. "Just the person I wanted to see," she said.

Joshua Turner was not a tall man, but he conveyed a self-confident strength. He had thick, sandy auburn hair and intense dark blue eyes that caught everyone's attention, especially that of Brooke, his wife. More often than not he wore an open, relaxed smile and had an easy laugh. Pam never found it hard to envision Joshua as a monk in his younger days, when he spent several years in contemplative prayer at Montis Abbey.

"Keep on saying that and your husband will get jealous," Joshua joked, taking off his jacket once he was inside.

"It's fine—you can have her," Mark said, winking at his closest friend. "Is Chuck with you?"

"He had one more hive to repair but said he would be down in a few minutes."

"So how are things up in the fields?" Mark asked, still sampling the chili from the pot.

"The good news is that the tupelo gum trees seem to have survived the winter," Joshua answered.

Mark looked up with a broad smile.

"Really?" Pam asked in amazement.

"I know," Joshua said. "I'm more surprised than anyone. When you had those shipped up from the South last year, I was sure they would be dead by Thanksgiving."

"Ye of little faith," Mark said, waving his spoon at the others.

"But, Mark, you have to admit the plan was flawed," Pam said.

"Not at all," Mark said. "I knew the burlap would protect them. That and the microclimate that Chuck insists we have over our orchard."

Joshua laughed. "That must be why you asked Brother Matthew for divine intervention when you planted them last year."

"A momentary lapse in confidence," Mark said with a grin.

Joshua's eye caught the boxes on the table. "What do you have here, family photos?"

"Yeah, yours, not ours," Pam answered, surprising Joshua. "We found them in the root cellar this morning. They seem to be mostly of Montis Abbey and the monks."

"May I?" Joshua asked, removing the lid from the box nearest him. It was crammed with old black-and-white photographs. Over the decades, the black had softened to a brown umber and the white had dulled to yellow beige.

Pam tapped the edge of one box. "We'll be returning them to Brother Matthew when we visit Saint Cross later this week, but I thought you would enjoy looking through them."

Joshua gently picked up one of the smaller photographs, no larger than two inches by three inches, which lay on top of the stack closest to him, and began to scrutinize the blurred image. He laughed softly.

"Look at this one," he said, handing it to Pam.

She studied it as Mark pulled himself away from the stove and looked over her shoulder.

"Do you recognize him?" Joshua asked.

She moved the picture closer and studied the face of the young monk, a man in his early twenties sitting on the front steps of Montis Abbey.

"Is that Brother Matthew?" she asked.

"That's amazing," Mark said, taking the photograph from his wife. "He looks so young, but he has the same thick hair and square jaw."

"The same light gray eyes," she added.

Mark turned over the photograph and saw the faded writing: 1956.

"That must have been taken close to when he joined Montis," Joshua said, looking through other photographs in the pile. The memories he cherished from his four years as a monk of Montis Abbey flooded over him like warm water.

"Who's this?" Pam asked.

Joshua studied the picture of a man in a long black robe standing by a beehive, and then looked at the next photograph of the same monk standing by the corner of the monastery's main building, smiling broadly with his arm around a man dressed in a suit. "This must have been taken in the 1950s as well. That's the monk Benjamin Beezer with his brother William Beezer."

"Dennis Beezer's father? Really?" Pam asked, looking carefully at the picture. "He caused us so much trouble when we first bought the abbey. Do you remember, honey?"

Mark was still standing behind her, staring at the image of the young men. "Yeah. I thought he hated Montis."

"He did," Joshua replied. "Benjamin died in the orchard during a horrendous storm and William never stopped blaming those at the monastery for letting his brother go out that evening to tend the beehives."

Pam studied the faces of the two brothers. "Young Brian Beezer is the spitting image of his granduncle. They both have the same eyes and mouth," she said, and then laughed gently. "It's funny, but the two couldn't be more different."

"One was a monk and the other is a hell-raiser," Mark quipped.

"Oh, he's not all that bad," Pam said, still studying the photograph. "But the resemblance is uncanny—almost eerie."

"How about this one?" Mark asked, handing Joshua another picture that was partly torn. "Your name is on the back."

Joshua looked at it but didn't say anything. It was a photograph of a very young man asleep on a cot with an older man sitting next to him. Joshua looked up with an odd expression on his face.

"I'm not sure when this was taken," he admitted. "But that's me in the bed."

"Was it taken at Montis?" Pam asked.

"Yes, over in the main building—the room upstairs at the end of the hall." He paused for a moment before continuing. "Anyway, I'm going over to Saint Cross tomorrow or the day after. Would you like me to give these to Matthew?"

Pam closed one of the boxes. "That would certainly save us a trip."

"Hello?" Chuck called, knocking on the door as he opened it slightly.

"Come in," Mark said, waving his arm. "We're just heating up the chili."

Entering the room, Chuck saw the old photographs on the table. "How delightful," he said. "Family photos?"

"No," Pam answered. "They seem to be mostly of the monks, all taken a long time ago. We were in the root cellar—"

"Speaking of which," Mark interrupted, "why don't you keep your jacket on? Could you spare a minute to look at a small water problem we may have behind the dining room?"

"Ah. That would make sense," Chuck said, surprising everyone. "Several underground streams converge close to the foundations of the dining room and kitchen."

"How in the world would you know that?" Mark asked.

"Many years ago the brothers asked me to witch the area," Chuck explained.

Pam raised her eyebrows. "Witch?"

"Dowse," Chuck clarified, but Pam still looked confused. "To find underground water with a hazel stick."

Mark glanced suspiciously at Chuck. "You're kidding."

"Oh, no, not at all," Chuck said. "An amazing thing, really. The limb bends toward the water. I'll be glad to show you anytime. In any case, I found a large spring about twenty feet from the cellar."

"I sometimes feel you know Montis better than we do," Pam admitted.

"That's understandable," Chuck said with a smile. "I helped the brothers around Montis Abbey for nearly thirty years."

"Would you mind coming to take a look?" Mark asked.

"Fine. Then we're off," Chuck said, and left with Mark.

For the next ten minutes, Pam and Joshua pored over the sepia-toned images of Montis.

"Oh, look at this. That might answer Mark's question," Joshua said.

Pam leaned over to see the picture Joshua was holding. It showed several old buildings in the back part of Montis Abbey—the scribing room, where for over half a century the monks came together to pen their calligraphy, and the original kitchen. What caught Pam's attention was the small shed, not larger than five feet square and six feet high, behind the kitchen, close to the entrance to the root cellar.

"What's that?" she asked.

"A spring house," Joshua answered. He looked at the back of the photo. "It seems there was enough water in 1936 that they had an active spring back there."

Mark burst into the kitchen, followed by Chuck.

"Guess what, honey?" Mark said. "We have a spring. It's about fifteen feet away from the cold cellar."

Pam looked at Chuck, who nodded his agreement.

"It could mess up your plan to use the root cellar as it was originally intended," Mark added.

Pam looked down at the photograph of the spring house and thought for a moment.

"You could have a trench dug to divert the water," Chuck offered.

Pam looked up at Chuck. "Why are we only seeing the water now?"

"The water level changes during the year depending upon rain and snowfall. I'm quite sure you had water in your root cellar before but just didn't see it at the right time."

"Or wrong time," Mark corrected him.

"When we go through a dry spell, how low do you think the water drops?" Pam asked.

"Oh, just below the surface," Chuck answered. "It would never dry up completely."

Mark looked at Pam and recognized her gaze. She was developing an idea. "What are you thinking?"

Pam grinned. "I'm thinking of a pond, a spring-fed koi pond. We could make the back of Montis spectacular. Our guests in the dining room could look out on a beautifully landscaped water garden."

"Charming," Chuck said.

To Pam's surprise, Mark didn't jump at the idea. "But, honey, we have so many other projects in progress," he said, thinking about the balloon festival. "And you're always saying we need to prioritize, and a fish pond, well . . ."

"Is an extravagance, I know. But we've always ignored the backyard, and since we have to spend money to fix the water in the root cellar anyway, we might as well get some benefit from it." She paused, thinking through the details. "If I do the work myself, it would cost very little."

Mark looked at Pam skeptically. "You're going to shovel tons of dirt?"

Chuck laughed. "Oh, no. Pam would need a good-size tractor and backhoe to do the job."

"And how hard can that be?" she asked. "It would take me an hour to learn and a day to dig."

"Excavate," Joshua corrected her.

"Exactly," she said. "Just imagine it, honey. Within a few days we can have a charming scene back there: a pond with a small waterfall or fountain, some benches, and perhaps a small willow tree at the far end."

Mark's eyes lit up as he began to share Pam's vision. "You're right, this could be great," he said. "Maybe we can put a hammock between those two elm trees."

"Absolutely." Pam jumped up and kissed her husband. "It will be perfect and I'll take care of everything."

"Are you sure you don't want to hire someone to do the job?" Mark asked.

"Definitely," Pam assured him.

"Well then, let me get you started by renting the tractor for you, and then the project is all yours," Mark offered.

"Agreed. It will be paradise back there in less than a week, I promise," Pam said, glowing with excitement.

Seeker

The Lumby Lines

Calling All Prototypes

BY CARRIE KERRY   April 1

As Lumby prepares to host the regional hot air balloon festival with opening ceremonies scheduled for June 14, the town is soliciting scale-model prototype designs for the hot air balloon that will be constructed and piloted by the residents of our great town.

The prototypes can be no larger than twenty feet high but must carry a minimum of one hundred pounds. (Sandbags will be provided by the Department of Transportation.)

All prototypes will first be evaluated on the ground and then flown immediately following Tibbs Tailgating, around 11:00 a.m. The winner will receive $100 and some kind of acknowledgment in the festival's catalogue.

Entry rules and balloon specifications are available at Lumby Sporting Goods. All questions should be directed to Mark Walker at Montis Inn. The potato raffle that was scheduled for that time has been indefinitely postponed.

The Lumby Police Department reminds everyone that ample parking will be available at the fairgrounds as well as along the north side of Fairground Road. They request that everyone stay off Wilbur's front yard—he just reseeded his lawn.

To Joshua's surprise, after reading about the trial balloon contest in the paper, he considered entering. As he drove to Saint Cross Abbey that morning, he began thinking about potential designs. Mark had already told him that he was involved with the festival, so Joshua was certain that Mark would want to put his best foot forward and build a prototype that would stupefy all. But the thought of his close friend playing around with propane burners sent shivers up Joshua's spine.

As Joshua entered Franklin, the traffic slowed, an anomaly for the small village. Equally unusual was the number of pedestrians filling the sidewalks, looking into the windows of the few stores in town. Perhaps a farmers' market was being held nearby, Joshua thought as he stopped the car again to allow more people to cross the street.

One stranger approached Joshua's vehicle and slapped his hand on the hood. "Hey," he yelled, "give me a ride to the abbey."

Before Joshua could respond, the driver behind him blasted his car horn, forcing Joshua to move on. Passing the stranger, Joshua shrugged his shoulders apologetically, to which the man yelled an obscenity. Taking a closer look, Joshua noticed how shabby the man looked. In fact, most of the pedestrians appeared seedy, dressed in soiled clothes. For the most part, the men were unshaven. What had brought such a rough lot to the area?

Although the trail of visitors thinned as Joshua drove out of town, there were still several walking along the street. One group strolled down the center of the road, taking up so much room that Joshua had to drive up on the soft shoulder to pass.

Arriving at Saint Cross, Joshua saw more people sitting on the lawns in front of the abbey. As he continued slowly toward the main building, many stared at him so intently that he was glad when he finally got inside the monastery.

The dining room at Saint Cross Abbey was large enough to accommodate two dozen visitors along with the twenty-eight monks in residence. Six walnut refectory tables formed two rows lined with straight-backed Alexander chairs, made of the same walnut. When the brothers ate alone, they sat along the outside of the tables facing each other, but with guests, both sides of the rowed tables were used.

Although the room was spartan, the construction reflected a scrupulous attention to detail. The hand-carved furniture represented the finest craftsmanship, as did the dry-stacked stone fireplace. Religious paintings and icons, either made at the abbey or given to the monks by generous benefactors, were carefully positioned on each wall.

Joshua always found tremendous solace in that room, sitting among the brothers, several of whom he had lived with when he, too, was a monk at Montis Abbey. During his visits and when time allowed, they often reminisced about the earlier days when the small brotherhood at Montis managed the orchard and apiary while producing nationally acclaimed religious calligraphy. "Penning" was the extraordinary gift the monks of Montis gave the world.

The photographs Joshua brought that day called up more memories.

"Look at this one," Brother Aaron said, holding up a picture of a very young Brother Matthew sitting in the Montis scribing room applying pen to parchment. He read the date on the back, "1959."

"A lifetime ago, my friend." Matthew sighed. "You had already been at Montis for some time when I joined."

"Indeed I was," the older monk said.

Joshua raised his index finger. "And they were good years."

Brother Matthew closed his eyes and smiled. "Many," he said before looking at Joshua. "These photographs are quite a treasure. Please tell Pam and Mark how delighted we are that they found them."

"I thought you would particularly like to see these two," Joshua said, handing him the photographs.

Matthew removed his glasses. "Ah, Brother Benjamin," he said sadly. "How I have missed him." Matthew continued to look at the photograph before turning to the one under it. When he did, his expression immediately changed. "This must have been one of the few times William Beezer came to our abbey. Now he and Benjamin lie side by side in the Montis cemetery." Matthew paused. "How sad that so much of William's life was spent in such anger."

"And Benjamin couldn't have been more opposite—such a forgiving soul," Aaron reflected.

"When Pam saw that picture, she said that Brian Beezer is the spitting image of his granduncle, Benjamin," Joshua said.

Matthew took a closer took at Benjamin's picture. "I suppose she's right, although I've only seen the young man a few times."

"No surprise," Joshua said. "Brian is a bit on the wild side and a church is about the last place I would expect to see him."

Suddenly the bell rang throughout the community house, and several of the men rolled their eyes.

"Another seeker, no doubt," Brother Michael said, getting up quickly. "I'll go this time. I haven't had my fill for the day."

"Seeker?" Joshua asked.

"These days Saint Cross Abbey appears to be the journey's end for many people searching for something they don't have," one of the older brothers explained.

Joshua leaned forward, interested in this new development. "Are those the people I saw in town? Who are they?"

Matthew began to explain. "Within the last few weeks—"

"Mostly since the article in the *Seattle Times* came out," another added.

Matthew nodded in agreement. "Yes, definitely since then. Our monastery has been—" He paused, searching for a word.

"Besieged," Brother John barked, walking into the dining room.

Several of the brothers laughed.

"I was going to say 'visited,' " Matthew corrected him. "Some are asking for money, while others would like to join the abbey."

Joshua's eyebrows lifted as he recalled the crowd he had seen in town. "Really?"

Michael continued. "Our guesthouse is full to the brim. We even have some folks sleeping on the floor, which actually might be more comfortable than some of the old mattresses we have in there. And every room in Franklin is filled."

"Was that the cause for the traffic in town this morning?" Joshua asked.

Another brother added, "There would be sleeping bags on the grounds if it wasn't for the spring rain."

Joshua leaned back in his chair, considering this unexpected consequence of the monastery's great success. "So, what are you going to do about it?"

All of the brothers looked at Matthew. "Pray for guidance while being as hospitable as we can," he answered, folding his hands over his chest. "We are all sure this will pass in a few days and our lives can return to normal."

"Why would you think that?" Joshua asked.

Brother John scoffed. "Because we don't dare contemplate the alternative."

There was a brief knock on the door and Jamar Talin stuck his head through the opening. "I've convinced my brother to test a kite I put together last night. Why do all the running if he will? Would anyone like to join us?"

The monks looked at each other and shook their heads.

"It's too crowded out there," one said.

"But that's what will make it interesting," Jamar replied. "We haven't had this kind of excitement in months."

"And why a kite?" Matthew asked before one of the brothers said something more derogatory about the crowds.

"Oh, it's a poor substitute for the hot air balloons we used to fly in Coraba."

Brother John raised his brow. "You own a hot air balloon?"

"Oh, no," Kai said, stepping into the room from behind his brother. "Our family could never afford one, but there are a few in town that we have flown since we were young."

"And you do that for sport?" John asked.

"They are wonderful for catching the interests of young women, if you know what I mean," Jamar said with a wink.

"No, probably I don't," John retorted.

Jamar continued, oblivious of John's comment. "But they're primarily used for the tourists who want an aerial view of the archipelago."

"But landing must be precarious at best if there are only a few islands to choose from," Joshua chimed in.

"Hundreds of islands, and the thermals offer almost unlimited flight."

"Well," Matthew said, "don't be too disappointed if you don't find the same flying conditions here for your kite."

"When I heard about the hot air festival next week," Jamar said, "I thought we would improvise and at least enjoy testing out the crosswinds caused by your mountain."

"Perhaps you will want to go to the back fields that have not yet been discovered by our unexpected guests," Aaron suggested.

"That's all right," Jamar said casually. "Spending some time with the seekers might be a good experience. You never know what something like that can lead to."

"No, you certainly don't," Matthew said, lowering his head to hide a grin, hoping Jamar's antics were more innocent than they sounded.

Jamar waved as he disappeared behind the swinging door, which closed quickly, smacking him in the back end.

ю<del></del>

SEVEN

Decisiveness

Anchoring the west side of town on the corner of Main and Mineral, directly across from the Lumby Feed Store and diagonal to Brad's Hardware, sits one of Lumby's most frequented joints: Jimmy D's. Although called a restaurant by its owner, the small, unpretentious establishment is, nonetheless, a simple local tavern that offers cold drinks and homemade cooking.

Much of the atmosphere at Jimmy D's is a carryover from the Rusty Brogue, the Irish pub that preceded Jimmy D's before closing down after a bizarre karaoke mishap.

The menu is limited: coffee and muffins in the morning, and Guinness beef pie, burgers, bangers, and the world's best fish and chips all other times. The only dessert is an Irish whisky cake whose recipe is a well-kept secret by the chefs, Danny and Shannon O'Brian, also from the Rusty Brogue days, whom Jimmy D retained.

The tavern has a regular clientele, which is keenly aware of Jimmy's unwavering adherence to state, county, and town drinking laws. In the morning, Jimmy D's caters to the women of Lumby who, after dropping their children off at school, need a coffee break before facing tedious chores at home. Businessmen and -women venture in during the four-hour window between eleven and three in the afternoon to meet with suppliers or have an out-of-office discussion with a troubled employee. Generally, the soft-spoken conversations are shared over burgers or beef pie and, at worst, a cold beer.

In the afternoon, after the high school lets out and before parents expect to see their teenage charges at home, Jimmy D's is a second home to some of the young men of Lumby who want to learn the finer lessons of pool and darts, and a temporary stop for some of the young women of Lumby who want to meet those same young men. They sit in dimly lit tall-backed pine booths sipping Cokes. The wood is rough from the names, dates, and pool scores that have been engraved into the tabletops over the years.

Shortly after the teenagers leave, several high chairs are brought out to accommodate the younger members of families that frequent the establishment for dinner. By nine, and slightly earlier on weekends, the restaurant takes on all the characteristics of a small-town bar, with Jimmy D keeping a tight rein on all that happens in his small corner of the world until closing at two in the morning.

Given the number of beers served there, it's no surprise that both the Feed Store and Brad's try to stay open as late as possible—not to suggest that they take advantage of semidrunk patrons who decide they need twenty guinea hens and twenty feet of galvanized piping at eleven o'clock on a Saturday night, but one never knows. Nonetheless, there is a regular late-night flow of traffic from Jimmy D's to the other stores in that part of town.

Adjacent to the back of Jimmy D's sits his home, a four-bedroom split level with the address of One Mineral Street. It is a well-maintained structure with extensive rock gardens and a beautifully manicured lawn. A brick patio in the back faces a pool that, because of the climate, is used only three months out of the year.

Jimmy D need walk only sixty feet from the back door of the tavern to the door of his kitchen to join his family for meals—a convenience that he especially appreciated in winter. A disadvantage of this arrangement, though not in his mind, was that there was no distance, no time or space, separating work and home. Perhaps it was for that reason alone that Hannah, his wife, seldom ventured into Jimmy D's. In fact, Hannah seldom ventured very far at all from One Mineral Street.

As robust and extroverted as Jimmy was, Hannah was the opposite: a painfully shy thirty-eight-year-old woman with a high-pitched voice that quivered when she spoke of something that mattered.

Jimmy was the first, and perhaps only, person to see Hannah's inner beauty. Throughout her high school years, she steadfastly supported Jimmy in all of his extracurricular activities and ensured she was the first to laugh at his jokes. She needed to admire and he found strength in having an admirer.

After marrying Jimmy when she was seventeen and having her son Johnnie eight months later, she began to withdraw from everything and everyone that didn't involve her husband and son. As Johnnie grew from adolescent to teenager, Hannah's social obligations with other parents decreased. She found private comfort in her own invisibility.

Over the years, Jimmy unconsciously assumed the lead for both of them, his dominance filling the void left by her retreat. The more she relinquished control, the more he took charge over Hannah for, as he sincerely saw it, her benefit and the well-being of their marriage.

Her appearance, too, was ordinary: a small woman with mousy brown hair and a common face that was never pampered or made up. To all indications, she was, in fact, bland.

But unseen by all, including her husband, a small fire burned in Hannah's belly. She cared passionately about her country, and had strong unvoiced opinions that ranged from the state of public education to farming rights. In fact, unknown to even her famiily, after Jimmy left for the tavern and Johnnie was off to school, she escaped to her sewing room above the garage, where she turned on National Public Radio and spent the entire day listening to national and international shows.

Fairground Road

North Deer Run Loop

North Grant Avenue

Trade Store

Bank

Dickensons

Main Street

SR 541

The Green
Chile

Chatham Press

Lumby Police

Lumby Episcopal

Cherry Street

The Bindery

Farm to Market Road

Funeral Home

South Deer Run Loop

To Deer Trail

To Wheatley

Lumby Presbyterian

Town of
Lumby

Est. 1862

While expanding her understanding of the world, Hannah was also improving upon the one great talent she had recognized in herself since childhood. She had a gift for embroidery, crochet, and especially tailoring. She was so good, in fact, that her husband's and son's wardrobes were filled with Hannah originals, which most people thought they bought in Wheatley's finer men's shops.

"I need your help making a trial balloon," Jimmy said to his wife over dinner. "Being the mayor, I think it's important that we have a prototype to fly on the fourteenth."

Hannah looked up from her plate. "I don't know anything about balloons."

"How difficult can it be?" Jimmy asked. "You're great with the sewing machine. All you need to do is stitch some nylon together."

Hannah put down her knife and fork. "I would prefer not to, Jimmy," she said in her reserved tone.

"Well, that's not a good reason," he pushed. "Everyone in town will be expecting me to have a balloon."

"And I'm not stopping you. I just don't want to be involved."

"But you need to be," Jimmy said more firmly.

That was one line Hannah had heard too often in their long marriage. She threw her napkin on the table. "That's the problem. If it's your project, why do I need to be involved?"

"But, Hannah, you're my wife," he said impatiently. "And occasionally you talk about getting out more often. Well, here's your big chance."

"Sewing a balloon that could easily embarrass the both of us is not a 'big chance' in my opinion," she said, trying to remain calm. "I'm willing to get out, but you telling me when and where to do it is only making matters worse."

"You'd stay in this house forever if I didn't say anything," Jimmy argued.

"No, I wouldn't!" she barked. "And I'm tired of everyone expecting me to be like you when I go out. I don't like our lives to be such an open book. Just because you own a tavern and you run the town of Lumby doesn't mean I can become the extrovert you want me to be."

Jimmy softened his voice, feeling a pang of guilt. "I want you to be yourself."

"You don't give me much of a chance when you tell me what to do and where to go, do you?"

⌒

A few blocks up from Mineral Street, Brooke sat on the bench at the corner of Main Street and Farm to Market Road. Across the way she noticed Hank, who was still displaying his wares in the red wagon. A car horn beeped, grabbing Brooke's attention, and she waved at some friends driving by.

"You look happy today," Caroline said, walking up to her friend.

"I am. The clouds are breaking and it's a great day for a stroll." She picked up the hiking boots on the bench beside her.

Caroline chuckled. "Aren't those a little commando for our hike?"

Brooke took off her sneakers and started pulling on the boots. "Prepare thyself, O client of mine." When Caroline didn't respond, Brooke looked up and saw that she was staring intently down the street. "See someone you know?"

"Ed Randolph. He just crossed Main and walked into the bar."

Brooke looked surprised. "You're not still dating him, are you?"

"No. But what a disaster that was. I really wasn't interested, but he was so charmingly insistent and the first few dates were wonderful. He was thoughtful and interested in my work, and from all accounts an honest guy." She fell silent.

"So what happened?"

"One night last month I ran into the Feed Store just before closing. Coming out, I saw Ed strolling into Jimmy D's with his arm around another woman. I asked him about it, and he lied, saying he was just helping a friend through a difficult time. You know," Caroline said and sat down next to Brooke, "I wasn't looking for a monogamous relationship and it would have been fine if he wanted to date someone else. But he denied it. He looked into my eyes and blatantly lied to me."

"Are you sure it was Ed you saw?"

"Unfortunately, yes. A few days later, I accidentally ran into the both of them having breakfast at S and T's. It was so awkward, I just ordered coffee and left."

Brooke sighed. "I wish I could help in some way."

A man walking down the sidewalk passed in front of them, turning his head for a second look at Caroline. Out of the corner of her eye she saw him gawking and cringed.

"You can start by telling me where I can find a nice guy who cares more about my feelings than my looks and who isn't interested in any of the foundation's money."

Brooke patted her friend's knee. "In time, you'll meet him. Just be patient."

Simon Dixon leaned out of the front door of the police station. "Are you ladies ready?"

Brooke called back, "In just a minute."

He fluttered a brief wave and went back inside.

"Is this really necessary? A sheriff's escort?" Caroline asked.

Brooke finished tying the other boot. "Consider Simon to be both scout and bear slayer," she said, winking at her friend. She looked up as Simon approached. "So, how goes your day, Sheriff Dixon?"

"On the hunt for grazing land. I suppose neither of you ladies has a five-acre parcel that the town could use temporarily?"

Caroline grinned. "Don't tell us you're trying to find a home for Morty's cows?"

"None other," he said. "And more calls come in each day about the growing ... bovine bouquet, as one of our elderly residents called it this morning." Simon pulled his car keys from his pocket. "But enough about Lumby's sewer smells. Are we off?"

Within a few minutes, the team of three was in Simon's patrol car heading out of town. From North Grant Avenue they turned onto Fiddlers Elbow, a town-maintained dirt road that meandered up to the base of the mountains. After several miles, seemingly in the middle of nowhere, Simon pulled over and turned off the engine.

"We're here," he said, pointing to a heavy chain that crossed what forty years earlier had been another dirt road, but was now so overgrown one would never notice it. It was the original entrance to the depot.

"If we are unsure who owns it, isn't this technically trespassing?" Caroline asked as she stepped out and eyed the dense woods that awaited them beyond the chain.

Simon dismissed the problem. "All taken care of. Russell Harris ensured the necessary paperwork has been filed in my office and at the town hall, giving us permission to walk the property in the absence of contacting the owner—he referred to it as a case of eminent domain due to abandonment. So, Brooke, were you able to get any more information on its ownership?"

Brooke rolled her eyes. "I spent the better part of yesterday driving between Wheatley, Lumby, and Rocky Mount, looking at old land deeds and abstracts," she explained. "The Pacific Railroad officially closed the station in September of 1961 and donated the hundred-plus acres of undeveloped land, without any mention of the building, to the National Parks Trust. There was an outstanding loan that the government didn't want to cover, however, so they immediately sold the property. Three changes of ownership and twenty years later, a judge ruled that back in 1961 the government never took rightful possession and had no legal grounds to sell the land."

"So it reverted back to the Pacific Railroad?" Caroline asked.

"Not exactly," Brooke explained. "It appears to have reverted back to the bank that held the loan, but by that time the bank no longer existed."

"So, how did it get resolved?" Caroline asked.

"To the best of my knowledge, it hasn't been."

Simon stepped over the chain. "Let's see what's out there. We have a good mile hike ahead of us."

The old dirt road leading to Bricks disappeared within twenty yards of the entrance, and the three found themselves surrounded by dense woods. Simon took out his compass and forged ahead, frequently using his machete to clear a path. Their pace varied from a fast walk as they crossed open pine groves to a crawl while they cut their way through the vast mesh of entangled berry bushes and wild vines.

Coming to a stream, Brooke leaned over and drank the clean water.

"Do you think we're close, Simon?" Caroline asked, using her shirt sleeve to wipe the sweat from her face.

"There was a stream that ran behind the station. If this is it, the station should be right over there," Simon said, pointing ahead of them.

They proceeded another hundred yards and the forest suddenly opened.

"Wow," Caroline whispered as she stepped into the clearing.

In front of them was an expanse of several acres filled with trees much younger than those in the surrounding woods and scattered around several buildings. Or was it just one building? Caroline asked herself.

Brooke's jaw dropped. "This is just amazing."

"I'm confused," Caroline said. "I thought it was a roundhouse."

"It is," Simon said. "We're looking at the back side of the depot. Those rectangular buildings are bays."

Caroline cocked her head. "I don't understand."

Simon pulled a pad from his shirt pocket and drew a simple sketch.

"This engine house is a polygon of sixteen equal sides with three rectangular bays in back. The center of the depot is a massive turntable with a maze of rail lines around it. The locomotive was brought in, put on the turntable, and rotated to align with an empty bay and then rolled into that stall. When the work was done, it was—"

Caroline was nodding her head. "Rolled out, spun, and sent on its way."

"Correct," Simon said.

Brooke laid her hand on Simon's arm. "You put me to shame. You know more about the architecture of this place than I do."

Simon laughed. "Boys love trains. It was the only thing I read about when I was a kid."

The three headed toward the building. Brooke guessed the round-house to be a hundred and eighty feet in diameter with a dome-shaped slate roof about forty feet high. Massive windows that had long been boarded up filled each wall of the polygon, with smaller rows of windows lighting the bays. The brick walls were the color of worn terra-cotta, and they seemed to be in good condition.

As they circled the building, they spied a thirty-foot-wide path leading away from the entrance and disappearing into the woods.

"That must be the original railroad track," Brooke commented.

Although dense undergrowth had covered the ties, the shrubs on the track were smaller and there were no trees, probably because the gravel underlying the track bed had stifled most vegetative growth.

The front of the roundhouse was as magnificent as Caroline had hoped. She immediately pointed at the padlocks on the massive metal doors used for the trains.

"How do we get in?" Caroline asked.

To the right was a standard-sized door that had been used by the workers. Simon put his elbow through a pane of glass.

"Simon!" Brooke said.

"We'll repair it within the week," he assured her as he reached in, slid the dead bolt, turned the lock, and smoothly opened the door. "Ladies first."

Taking a step over the high threshold, Caroline looked up and the sight cut her breath short. "Seems they left something behind," she said, stepping aside to allow the others to follow.

"This is unexpected," Simon said, staring at a huge locomotive parked right in the middle of the roundhouse.

"I've never seen anything like it," Brooke exclaimed.

"What? The building or the locomotive?" Caroline asked.

Brooke turned, her eye following the ceiling line. Then she glanced at the train again. "Both, I think."

Caroline spread out her arms. "This is amazing. Look at the placement of the tracks."

"Here's one of the toggle switches," Simon said, pulling on a four-foot-tall lever that was part of the control platform on the north side of the track's turntable. As he heaved the iron bar, a small portion of one track slid over five feet, aligning with another section leading to a repair bay.

"Amazing it's still greased enough to move," Simon said.

Caroline was walking along the inside wall, looking up at the windows. "This place will be perfect, Brooke," she said loudly. Her voice echoed through the cavernous space. "We can use the bays for individual studio space. And in the center, over here, we can build an amphitheater for music in the round. Directly above it, we can build a second floor for an open gallery to display the artists' works."

Brooke followed her client's thinking. "And the far bay can be soundproofed and used for practice rooms."

"Yes, that would be excellent," Caroline said, walking back to the center of the depot. She looked around once more and beamed. "This is it," she stated emphatically. "This will be Lumby's new arts and music center."

EIGHT

Practice

The Lumby Lines

Sheriff's Complaints

BY SHERIFF SIMON DIXON   April 8

6:26 a.m. Resident on Cherry Street reported mallard ducks have taken up residence in her new Sears hot tub.

6:42 a.m. Phillip called again. Young black bear discovered unconscious behind Wayside Tavern. Back door of stockroom smashed, numerous empty bottles on ground and keg clawed open.

7:04 a.m. Morning cleaning crew reported an unidentified man sitting in library wearing Speedo swim trunks and flippers.

7:09 a.m. Timmy Beezer's left hand is stuck in ice dispenser at the Green Chile. EMS dispatched.

8:44 a.m. Reverend Poole reported that two elk are running through Presbyterian cemetery, knocking over tombstones.

3:29 p.m. Baton thrown by majorette during twirling practice crashed through second-floor window of high school. LPD asked to respond.

3:33 p.m. Stalled farm equipment in front of Montis Inn blocking traffic in both directions on Farm to Market Road.

5:48 p.m. Patron from Jimmy D's reported that several of Morty's cows have left the park and are walking down Main Street heading for Goose Creek.

8:54 p.m. Allen Miller, age 8, called to say that he superglued a bone to his dog's tail and can't get it off.

9:01 p.m. Owner of Feed Store reported that ticket booth for second-floor theater has been wallpapered without his permission.

11:51 p.m. Van swerved to miss deer on Mineral Road. Van in ditch and requires towing but no humans injured.

After Wheatley Tractor Supply delivered the Kubota tractor, Pam spent several hours of several days sitting on it, combating her feelings of intimidation. She had been diligently reading the owner's manual every free minute she found, and when she was uncertain about the position or movement of a lever, she would walk out to the large machine to look at the controls. But again and again, Pam walked away from the tractor without even turning on the engine.

The only part of the project still on plan was Mark's promise to honor her request to stay away from the construction site behind the inn's dining room. She wanted to surprise him, Pam had explained with forced enthusiasm. Finally, on the fourth morning after Mark asked her how the pond was coming along, Pam put on her leather work gloves, picked up the keys, and went to confront her demons. Turning the corner of the building, she saw that the tractor was severely tilted. She ran toward it, thinking that soft ground had given way to the weight of the machine, but then stopped and groaned: the rear tire was flat. She took off her gloves and rubbed her face in frustration.

"It can't be as bad as that," a voice said from behind her.

She whirled around.

"Brother Matthew!" she said in surprise.

Wearing his long black robe, he took a step forward but then stopped where the grass turned to mud. "You look immersed in thought," he said.

"Buried is more like it. We've had the tractor for four days and all I've done is move a few levers without even turning it on," Pam said, blushing. "I'm so embarrassed—I don't even know how to start."

"As I feel about many of my projects." Brother Matthew smiled as he thought back to fifty years before, when he had planted six trees to begin the Montis Abbey orchard that ultimately expanded to six acres of various fruit trees. "So, might I ask what you are doing?"

Pam put her gloves back on and leaned against the deeply grooved tire. "It doesn't look like it, but I'm trying to excavate for a fish pond."

"Ah," Matthew said. "Very good." He bent over and picked up a rake. "May I?"

Pam nodded.

"Do you know the size—the shape and the depth?" he asked.

She pulled a torn and dirty piece of paper from her shirt pocket and handed it to him. "Here's my sketch. I was thinking forty feet long, twenty wide, and six feet deep. The center would be just about there," she said, pointing. "Chuck Bryson said there's a spring there."

"Very good," Matthew said, turning the rake over and using the handle to draw a line in the soft ground. "First, the perimeter of the pond."

"You're getting filthy," Pam said, watching him walk through the mud.

"Not to worry," he replied as he began to demarcate a large kidney shape that encompassed both Pam and the tractor. "If I may suggest, dig on your right and deposit on your left, and then use your front loader to remove the dirt. But don't push it too far—you may want to berm up around the pond."

Pam watched her friend intently. "How do you know so much about this?"

"You didn't think those ponds at Saint Cross are natural, did you?" he asked in surprise.

"I never really thought about it, but, yes, I assumed they were— they certainly look it," she said, encouraged for the first time that day.

Matthew stepped carefully out of the work zone. "And this one will as well. Be patient with yourself."

Pam nodded. "Can you stay for lunch?"

Matthew looked at his watch. "I really just dropped by to bring you our latest rum sauce flavor, but lunch would be very nice. Thank you."

"If you could give me about thirty minutes. I need to call down to Wheatley about the flat tire and clean up a little. Mark is at the stable if you'd like to visit him."

"More animals?"

"No, I don't think so. He's working on some secret project to do with the balloon festival," Pam replied, rolling her eyes.

Brother Matthew laughed. "That sounds dangerous."

"Perhaps you can wander down and be my spy?" she suggested with a grin. "Just to make sure his project is harmless."

"That's a word that doesn't instantly come to mind when I think of your husband's schemes."

"I know, but he's such a good man," she said with a broad smile.

"That he is," Matthew agreed. "Would you mind if I first walked through the orchard?"

"Not at all. They're as much your trees as ours."

As her friend strolled away, Pam turned and eyed the tractor. It certainly looked less intimidating, resting at such a severe angle. In fact, at that moment it almost seemed farcical that Pam felt outwitted by several tons of steel and hydraulic pumps. Glancing at the lines Brother Matthew had drawn in the dirt and then back at the Kubota, Pam felt a new confidence. *As soon as the tire is repaired, I'll be ready.*

৹৯

Each time Matthew returned to Montis, he relished the opportunity to once again walk through the fields and among the trees that he had cared for during his many years there. The trees had all grown older; some had already died and been replaced. It was still too early for them to bloom, but the orchard was greening out nicely. Spring cleanup was well under way, with the cut dead limbs piled at the end of each row waiting to be hauled off. Mark and Pam were indeed excellent caretakers of the property, he noted with satisfaction.

The stone bench the brothers had moved to the corner of the lower grove forty years earlier was still in place. As he sat and rested, Matthew looked down onto Woodrow Lake to the south and Montis Inn to the east. How he missed the calm and the quiet. He certainly didn't look forward to returning to the disruption caused by all the seekers at Saint Cross Abbey.

He was gazing down at the stable when suddenly Mark ran out of the barn, holding what looked like a long piece of rope that was clearly on fire. He threw the rope on the dirt and stomped out the flames. Then he picked up the rope and carried it back inside the barn. That didn't bode well, Matthew thought. Maybe it was time to go down and visit him.

"Is it safe to come in?" Matthew called out as he approached the barn.

Mark came to the opening of the large sliding door. "Well, if it isn't my favorite monk. What brings you to Montis?"

"I was down in Wheatley and thought I would drop off a sample of our newest rum sauce. Pam invited me to stay for lunch, so perhaps we can try it afterward."

"So that means you're here for a while? Great. Perhaps you can lend a hand," Mark said, leading Matthew into the barn. He returned to the task of tying ropes around a barrel that was attached to a pile of white sheets.

Matthew backed up slightly, not knowing what to make of what he was seeing. "Should I ask what you're doing?"

"Testing my first homemade hot air balloon," Mark said proudly. "Lumby will be hosting the balloon festival next month, and I've been asked to head up the project, and that includes building the town's entry."

Matthew eyed the whisky barrel. "And this is it?" he asked skeptically.

"Oh, no," Mark said. "We're all submitting model-size prototypes after Tibbs Tailgating. The winner will get one thousand dollars . . . or maybe one hundred, I can't remember which."

Matthew remained doubtful. "And you're familiar with hot air balloons?"

"Not really. Actually, I've never seen one in person, but how hard can it be? Look at all the books I got from the library," Mark said, pointing at the hardcovers stacked on the bench.

"Ah, I see. And this is—?" Matthew asked, putting his hand on the barrel.

"A makeshift basket, of course." Mark clapped his hands, sending dust into the air. "This will be so easy. I made the balloon out of sailcloth and bought that propane tank," he explained, pointing at the large torpedo-shaped cylinder, "but obviously it's a tad big."

"A tad, I would think," Matthew concurred. The tank had to weigh at least two hundred pounds.

"Right," Mark continued excitedly. "So, I bought these small propane burners."

He picked up an object the size of a toaster and passed it to Matthew.

"If you could hold it over the barrel while I attach it, that would be great."

After spending several minutes roping the components together, Mark tilted the barrel and rolled it out on its rim, with Matthew close behind carrying the burner and makeshift balloon.

"Is Joshua around?" Matthew asked warily.

"No, he's off this morning. Down at the university. Why do you ask?"

"Just in case you need help."

Mark waved off the idea. "We won't need any help. It's really quite simple. They were doing this back in the 1700s using ducks and sheep."

Matthew, still holding the burner, looked up. "Did the animals survive?"

Mark cocked his head. "I actually don't know. But I was reading that the first person went up a few months later, and he survived. Well, he only flew for twenty-two minutes, but I thought that was pretty impressive."

"Mark," Matthew said hesitantly, "I don't think you want the rope that close to the burner. It will catch on fire."

Mark looked at his last knot. "Good point," he said, untying the cord.

Seeing Mark retie the knot over the burner on the other side, Matthew thought it best to make another suggestion, but chose his words carefully. "Do you remember the two missionaries you met at Saint Cross—the ones from Indonesia?"

"Yeah. They seemed like nice fellows," Mark replied.

"It's my understanding they know how to fly balloons and also produce some of the finest hot air balloon wicker baskets in the world. Perhaps they could help."

"No need," Mark said. "I think we're good to go. Matthew, if you could spread the balloon out, I'll turn on the fan to start blowing hot air into it."

Matthew did as directed and then stood back as Mark lit the burner, rotated the fan, and began blowing hot air into the small sailcloth envelope. Matthew had originally guessed the balloon was only ten feet long, but as it inflated, it expanded exponentially in volume. Within a few minutes, the irregularly shaped balloon had lifted off the ground and was hovering over the small whisky barrel, which was tethered to the ground by two ropes wedged under Mark's foot.

"Is this great or what?" Mark called over to Matthew, who had prudently stepped back into the barn.

The balloon appeared to have large white blotches along the seams.

"How did you make the balloon?" Matthew asked.

Mark gestured up to the envelope, pleased with his design. "I glued pieces of nylon sailcloth together."

"Glued?" Matthew asked.

Mark pointed over toward where Matthew was standing. "Yeah, with that stuff on the bench."

Matthew picked up the can. The front was marked "Highly Flammable."

"Mark, did you notice that—"

"Hold on—liftoff!" Mark called. He opened up the propane burner slightly and the balloon lifted gently off the ground. "And here we go," he said as he opened the valve all the way.

The flame shooting from the burner tripled in size and almost singed the sailcloth. The balloon rose fifteen feet off the ground before catastrophe struck. There was a muffled explosion, and then the balloon burst into flames and crashed to the ground, landing scant feet from where Mark was standing.

As Matthew would later relate to Pam, Mark's reflexes were impressive. Within seconds he grabbed the barn hose and doused the burning sailcloth. He then put out the flames in the barrel, which had caught fire after smashing to the ground.

The animals responded as one would expect. The chickens, which had been pecking the ground close to the launch site, sent feathers everywhere, trying to fly away. The three sheep stampeded for higher ground. The draft horse, snoozing peacefully in the field, was awakened by the commotion and trotted through the flimsy gate Mark had constructed. Its mane flapped in the wind as it headed north on Farm to Market Road.

Amid the mayhem, Mark beamed. "Wow, did you see that?" he asked. "It actually floated!"

Matthew stared at him in disbelief. "You were almost killed!"

"Ye of little faith, Brother Matthew," he said, turning his back on the smoldering remains. He headed into the barn. "Here, let me show you my second design."

Once in the dim interior, Matthew looked at the sketch of a lawn chair attached to a much larger balloon. "You have got to be kidding."

ɔ

NINE

Junk

Several hours before dawn on the morning of Tibbs Tailgating, the wind began to blow from the west, pushing out the clouds that had hung over Lumby the preceding day. The spectacular sunrise promised a fine morning as cars began to arrive.

Years before, when the large crowd outgrew the space in Main Street, Tibbs was moved to the fairgrounds, allowing ample sales room for all. Originally, the town tried to restrict each resident's "sales space" to one vehicle, but creative individuals tried to skirt the rule by using huge buses, flatbeds, and in one case a UPS truck, to display their wares.

After a bizarre accident involving a farm combine ended those practices, it was decided that all Lumby residents would be allocated as much space as they needed on a first-come, first-served basis. Further, a "parking map" was drawn up accordingly. Latecomers or last-minute additions were put on the east side of the fairgrounds away from the general traffic and close to the Porta Potties, which was enough incentive to most to get their reservations in early.

By six a.m. as many as fifty vehicles of all styles and dimensions were parked in long rows, with another fifty on their way. Cattle cars filled with furniture and flatbeds hauling used water troughs were flagged in and directed to their respective slots. Even children pulling Radio Flyer wagons piled with old toys were allocated individual spaces. The only noticeable absence was that of Hank, who had, in past years, announced the commencement of the sale using his preferred foghorn.

Pam and Brooke sat shoulder to shoulder on the open tailgate of the Jeep and drank coffee from a large thermos. Their cars, parked next to each other, were well positioned in the middle of a center row.

"Good placement this year," Brooke said drowsily.

"This is missing a price tag. How much do you want for it?" Joshua asked Brooke as he and Mark hoisted a large rocker onto the top of their station wagon so it would be in good view.

"Ten dollars," Brooke replied.

Pam peered up. "That looks like an awfully nice chair for ten dollars."

Brooke watched Mark and Joshua tape a sale sign on it. "You can't see it from here, but there's no seat, and most of the wood is cracked."

"Ah," Pam said, and returned to her coffee. "I hate getting up early."

"Remember last year? It was a downpour. And we only made eighteen bucks—just enough to pay for lunch afterward."

Pam laughed. "Well, we made about fifty dollars, but in turn Mark spent around two hundred."

Brooke looked surprised. "Buying what? It's all—"

"Junk? Yeah, well, whatever it was, we're reselling most of it this year." Pam shrugged her shoulders and leaned back against a rolled-up sleeping bag.

"You should keep the sleeping bag—it might come in handy," Brooke said. "I heard Jimmy is asking town residents to rent out their empty bedrooms for the balloon festival."

"That's a good thing. We're fully booked and have a wait list a mile long," Pam said. "Are you thinking of renting out rooms?"

Brooke looked over at her husband. "Yeah, we are. We have those three bedrooms upstairs and more space in the finished basement."

"Do you know what you will charge?"

"No, but it will be nominal. We're doing it just to help out."

At 6:30 exactly, the horn blew over the fairgrounds' loudspeaker, and Tibbs Tailgating officially began.

Brooke jumped to her feet and pulled on Pam's pant leg. "Okay, let's go check out everybody's stuff."

"You're kidding," Pam said, refusing to budge.

"Let's go before the good things are gone. The guys can handle our sales."

After more coercing, the women refilled their coffee mugs, instructed their husbands to sell as much as they could without giving away the barn, and ventured out. They started on the west end of the field and strolled down the rows systematically.

The tailgaters used an astonishing variety of selling techniques. Some had mounted large signs on their roofs listing sale items and prices. Others had taped flags to their antennas. A few had even wrapped colored Christmas lights around their vehicles, powered by the cars' cigarette lighters.

In front of one van squatted a huge green plastic frog with an obscene hole in its mouth. One eye was missing and his face was covered with small dents.

"A rare find," the frog owner said. "He was the fourth hole at Rocky Mount's miniature golf course for two years running."

"That explains that, doesn't it?" Brooke said, trying to lift the frog to show Pam. "Would you like this for your pond?" she joked.

When Pam glared at her and walked away, Brooke knew she had touched a nerve. "Are you all right?" Brooke asked, catching up to her friend.

"I don't want to talk about it," Pam said, uncharacteristically obstinate.

Brooke put her arm around Pam's shoulder. "Why not subcontract the excavation? They could be done in less than a week."

Pam stopped short. "Because I don't like failing," she said almost bitterly.

"But this is out of your—"

"League? Is that what you were going to say?"

"No," Brooke replied carefully. "It's out of your realm of expertise."

"So you don't think I can do it either?" Pam questioned.

Brooke was backpedaling furiously. "That's not what I said. In fact, I'm sure you can do it—you can do anything."

That didn't help either. Pam ran her hands through her hair. "God, I'm so tired of hearing that."

"All right, end of discussion, but remember I'm on your side. You can call me if you need help," Brooke said.

Pam finally cast off her black mood. "I'm sorry," she said. "You're right, let's change the subject. How was the Round House?"

"That old rail station is one of the more amazing buildings I've ever seen. It would be perfect for Caroline, but there are some hurdles."

"Such as?"

"A forty-ton locomotive parked inside." Brooke laughed. "But, more seriously, I can't seem to get to the bottom of who actually owns the property."

Pam looked puzzled. "What does Joan say?"

"Which Joan?"

"Joan Stokes of Main Street Realty. She knows the history of every acre of property in Lumby. I guarantee she'll give you the right answer."

"That's a good idea."

"Look, over there, it's the bird lady," Pam said, pointing to a dilapidated van stuffed floor to ceiling with cages. Yellow canaries sung from every perch.

Brooke whispered to Pam, "I heard she has over a hundred birds flying free inside her house."

"Look at the hat she's wearing—it has a bird feeder on top!" Pam said in amazement.

"And you see those two turkey vultures in the tree up there?" Brooke asked, subtly pointing to the woods. "If they get hungry, she's a goner."

Brooke pulled on her friend's arm when they passed in front of an old memorabilia table. "Look at this," Brooke said, picking up a copy of *The Lumby Lines* dated 1955.

The Lumby Lines

The News of the World to the News of Lumby

BY WILLIAM BEEZER   November 14

Without jeopardizing this newspaper's indisputable journalistic integrity, and contrary to our long-standing practice of giving no endorsements, a product was patented within the last few months that is no less than revolutionary, one for which the residents of our fine town need to take note.

Velcro, a new two-sided fastener, was invented by George de Mestral in 1948, and will replace the zipper in a matter of years.

An amateur mountain climber, de Mestral came upon the concept of a two-sided resealable attachment when he returned home from hiking one day to find his pants and his dog covered with burrs. Upon microscopic examination, he discovered the secret of the seed-bearing burrs: minuscule hooks on the burr grabbed the fine fibers of his woolen trousers. From that, he ultimately replicated the fastening by using nylon sewn under infrared light.

Velcro will soon be available at Woolworth's on Main Street—certainly something we will all want to try.

As Pam and Brooke explored the fairgrounds, Mark was focused on the balloon contest, letting Joshua handle any sales that came their way.

Mark held the diagram as he explained his design. "It's really simple. Even Brother Matthew was impressed by the design."

"Why do I doubt that?" Joshua said with good humor.

"All right, not exactly impressed, but he did help me with an earlier version. And this one is so much better," Mark guaranteed. "Okay, so you're in on this?"

There was a long pause. "Mostly," Joshua said reluctantly. "But I am not getting anywhere near the flames."

"No need to. This thing will fly itself," Mark assured his friend. "Here's my digital camera. The propane test flights will begin as soon as the tailgating is over, so I'm sure there will be some balloons lying around. Why don't you go scout out the other designs so I can study them before the competition?"

Joshua was taken aback by the suggestion. "You want me to *spy*?"

"Exactly!"

Joshua squinted at him. "Have you forgotten that I'm a former monk? I never dropped that integrity thing, you know."

Mark thought for a moment, trying to reconcile morality with astute planning. "Then just ask them if you can take a photo, like for the newspaper or something."

"You're impossible," Joshua said, and shuffled off with camera in hand.

To Joshua's surprise, he did see some balloon entries, and their owners eagerly encouraged him to photograph them. When he reached the last row at the far end of the fairgrounds, he came upon his wife and Pam haggling with a tailgater.

Brooke examined a wok she was holding. "Four dollars," she offered.

The heavyset woman shook her head. "Six is the lowest I'll go."

"She'll take it," Joshua said, walking up to the women.

Brooke turned and smiled. "Thank you, dear."

As the three continued to stroll past the open trucks and rear van doors, they saw everything imaginable and even some things that weren't.

Pam asked, "So, how goes the sale of our stuff?"

"Mostly gone," Joshua replied. "I took pity on some old man who very much wanted our rocker, so I gave it to him for a dollar."

Pam laughed. "You have such a soft heart. I'm surprised you took the dollar."

"Mark said it was a matter of principle. Oh, wait, I need to take a photo of that balloon basket over there."

Pam frowned. "Let me guess. Mark sent you out on a reconnaissance mission?"

"He's getting nervous about the competition," Joshua explained.

Pam turned to Brooke. "He's pretty serious about his new responsibilities to lead the town's hot air balloon efforts. He feels that if he doesn't win the trial balloon contest today, his leadership will be called into question, if you know what I mean." Pam winked.

"Well, if anyone can do it, I'm sure it's Mark," Brooke said.

They rounded the bend and saw Mark sitting on top of the Jeep with papers in hand. He was so engrossed in the owner's manual for the booster that he didn't hear them approach.

"Hey, honey," Pam said.

He looked up in surprise, then quickly recovered. "These instructions are missing pages five through seven," he complained.

"Here are some of the other designs," Joshua said, handing Mark the digital camera. He started avidly screening the photographs.

"Some of them look amazingly . . ." Joshua searched for the right word, "real."

For the first time that morning, Mark showed serious concern. "Real?"

"Perfect replicas of full-scale hot air balloons in miniature," Joshua explained. "Very impressive."

Mark considered that notion but then waved away Joshua's assessment of the competition. "They don't have what I have."

"And what, pray tell, is that?" Joshua asked.

Mark jumped down from the roof, reached into the backseat of the Jeep, and withdrew a torn-up microwave oven box.

"You're going to cook your balloon?" Pam joked.

With great dignity Mark lifted the top flaps. "No, that's just what it was mailed in." Leaning over to let Joshua look inside, Mark quietly disclosed his secret. "It's a turbo booster for a propane burner."

Joshua's eyes opened wide in sudden panic. "Where did you get that?"

Mark looked around to make sure no one was listening. "Off the Internet—some company in New Mexico."

"And they sent it to you in an appliance box?"

"Yeah, I asked them about that. They said these things aren't supposed to be shipped without a lot of paperwork, so they just use microwave boxes for convenience," Mark explained. "It makes sense to me."

"It sounds illegal to me," Joshua replied.

Suddenly, the horn blew again, marking the end of Lumby's annual Tibbs Tailgating.

The fairgrounds loudspeaker crackled. "Is this thing turned on?" everyone heard Jimmy D say. He continued in a more official voice. "This is to remind everyone that registration for the balloon contest will begin at twelve thirty. A helium balloon to determine wind direction and speed will be sent up at twelve fifty-five over by the Porta Potties, and the first prototype flight will be at one, followed by launches every five minutes. Be sure your envelopes are inflated and ready to go when it's your turn. Thanks."

More crackle was followed by a short, ear-splitting screech before someone turned off the microphone.

Mark carefully returned the booster to the backseat. "We need to strategize," he said. "I think we want to be about in the middle of the line, so we should go over there now and wait by the desk."

"Mark," Pam said, checking her watch, "we still have a few hours."

He was all seriousness. "You can never be too ready. We want the largest crowd to see our balloon. Too soon in the competition, a lot of folks haven't arrived yet. Too late and people are already going home. So timing is everything," he explained. "I guarantee my entry is going to astonish everyone."

"My concern exactly," Pam said, patting her husband's arm. "I just want you to come out of it alive."

∽

Although Dennis and Gabrielle Beezer were not as well positioned at the fairgrounds as they would have liked, they still sold most of what they brought, primarily due to the charming sales antics of their young son, Timmy. That was one of the few similarities between the two Beezer brothers—they both had a natural gift for free commerce.

"Timmy, would you run this over to Mrs. Walker," Gabrielle said, handing him a small ceramic dish. "Do you remember where they're parked?"

"Sure, Mom," he said and dashed off, holding the bowl with both arms.

"I haven't seen Brian this morning," Gabrielle said to her husband.

Dennis stood tall and scanned the fairgrounds. "I'm hoping our talk with him really got through."

Gabrielle began organizing the back of their car. "You don't think we were too harsh?"

"I don't think that's possible with Brian."

"And do you believe that he's stopped taking those balloon flying lessons?" she asked.

Dennis shook his head. "I just don't know. We have him on a pretty tight rein right now, but I also know that when Brian's determined to do something, he usually finds a way."

"Let's hope that will become a positive character trait in his adult life," Gabrielle said. "So, we did pretty well today, I would say."

"Except for that," Dennis said, pointing.

Unfortunately, the one item that the Beezers wanted to dispose of this year, and every other year they had attended Tibbs, couldn't even be given away. So Dennis once again returned the three-foot-tall ceramic palm tree to the back of their station wagon.

"Can't we take it to the landfill and be done with it?" Dennis pleaded with his wife.

"No," she said. "It was a wedding gift."

"From a bunch of drunken college friends we haven't seen in twenty years," he protested.

Suddenly, a blast came from the direction of the Porta Potties and fireworks began to shoot into the sky. Over the loudspeakers screeched Tchaikovsky's 1812 Overture.

"What in the world is going on?" Gabrielle asked, stepping up on the car's bumper to get a better look. "Oh, my word," she groaned.

Just then, a small hot air balloon rose in the air.

"Who is it?" Dennis asked.

They both stared as the balloon rose higher until the ropes tethering it to its payload snapped taut. There it floated for a moment, stalled by the heavy anchor. The burner, being operated by remote control, opened suddenly, and the balloon rose higher, lifting one of the Porta Potties several feet off the ground. When the balloon listed, the Porta Potti swung sharply, releasing chemicals and other more displeasing fluids from the holding tank in its base.

A woman screamed as fluids splashed to the ground not far from where she was standing. Everyone else kept their eyes on the sky. It was indeed an amazing sight—a hot air balloon lifting a portable john as aqua chemicals seeped through the floor.

"Whose balloon is that?" Dennis said.

"Brian!" Gabrielle yelled to her son. "Stop that balloon this instant!"

When Dennis heard his son's name, he darted around the parked cars and headed toward where the balloon had launched. Terry McGuire and Brian Beezer, holding a remote control, stood with their backs to Dennis as he rapidly descended on them.

Grabbing his son by the collar, Dennis spun Brian on his heels. The jolt caused him to jar the control lever, sending the balloon and haltered lavatory upward another ten feet. Catching a slight breeze, the balloon began to drift slowly over the cars, with the Porta Potti spilling its contents onto every roof and inside each convertible it passed.

"What the hell are you doing?" Dennis shouted.

Brian, who had been thinking his balloon was a great opening for the prototype contest, was startled by his father's anger. "Nothing," he blurted, trying to pull away from his father's grip.

"Get it down now!" Dennis demanded.

"Let go of my arm," Brian said, shaking loose. "It will come down on its own in a minute."

Dennis watched as the Porta Potti slowly dropped. Then his eye caught what was in the toilet's direct path of descent: the Episcopal church van. Had the winds kept it afloat a few seconds longer, the latrine would have cleared the vehicle by several inches. Unfortunately, the raised sun roof caught the floor of the outhouse and caused the structure to flip on its side, crashing into the windshield and excreting its final wastewater onto the dashboard.

"Not a spectacular landing," Brian mumbled to Terry.

"I've had it!" Dennis yelled. "This is the last straw."

"But Dad," Brian griped, "this was going to be an amazing inaugural flight. I was even paid by the Feed Store to put their banner on the balloon, but it took off too fast."

"I don't want to hear about it, Brian. You've been totally irresponsible," his father barked. "And forget about sitting around, doing nothing all summer. You'll take that job Mrs. McGuire offered you and you'll pay for every penny of damage you've done here today."

"But, Dad."

"No buts. Your mother and I have had it with your irresponsible behavior." Dennis was so angry he was shaking. "Like it or not, your life is going to change as of today. You're taking that job with Mrs. McGuire and, right this minute, you're going to see every owner of those cars that were splashed with the wastewater and arrange a time for *you* to hand-wash their cars, inside and out."

"But, Dad, that's like thirty cars. It'll take days."

"At least that long," Dennis said, glaring at this son. "Because I'll be inspecting each and every one of them myself."

TEN

Adrift

Within thirty minutes, most of the Tibbs Tailgating cars had left the fairgrounds, leaving only a dozen scattered across the field. The food stands were also packed up and rolled out. Gradually, the cars that remained were repositioned over by the west end of the fairgrounds, closer to the registration desk, and the balloon prototypes were removed from various trailers and vans. One exceedingly large preassembled entry needed to be hoisted from a flatbed.

Most participants set up their entries in the open area behind the launch pad. Since the rules were less than well defined, there was a wide range of sizes and designs, but all had three common components: the envelope, which was to be made out of nylon donated by Brad's Hardware; a vessel or basket that was attached to the balloon and could carry a minimum of five pounds for each vertical foot of the envelope; and some remote-controlled burner mechanism.

An aerial view of the fairgrounds that afternoon would surely have been an impressive sight. A dozen balloons ranging from three feet to twenty feet tall, all brightly colored with dyed cloth or paint, bobbed on their tethers while others spread over the grass were slowly inflating.

As with most Lumby events, Sal Gentile and his wife, Melanie, were asked to judge the proceedings. Sal, who owned the only liquor store in town, was a well-respected merchant and a good friend to many. Likewise, Melanie, who had worked at S&T's for many years, was thought to have a good heart and a quick mind. Over time, they had become the town's custodians of whatever quirky event someone mustered up. And it was a role that both took quite seriously.

Sal and Jimmy D reviewed the entry rules as people began lining up at the registration desk, where Melanie efficiently logged in each balloon, its builder, and its pilot. During the flights, she would also record the results as jointly determined by Jimmy and Sal.

"How's registration coming?" Sal called to Melanie.

She looked down at her clipboard. "We have most everyone. There are fourteen entries."

At 12:56, Sal released a blue helium balloon from the launch area and everyone fell silent as they watched it float upward. One participant clapped, appreciating the lack of wind. Suddenly, though, the test balloon hit a crosswind and was quickly carried toward town, gaining more distance than altitude by the second.

Sal blew the horn, giving the first pilot a five-minute warning. Jonathan Tucker, Lumby's most respected woodsmith, came forward carrying an oak box attached to a well-inflated balloon no more than five feet tall. Setting it on the cement pad, Jonathan relit the burner while his wife held down the balloon.

"Are you ready, Jonathan?" Sal asked.

"As I ever will be," Jonathan said with a chuckle.

Sal held up his stopwatch; he and Jimmy had arbitrarily decided that "time adrift" was one of the criteria that would be used to determine the winner.

"Let it go," Sal said, and started the clock.

Jonathan's wife jumped back, and Jonathan increased the fuel, using a remote control. Nothing happened.

"It takes a minute," he said, and opened the burner to medium.

Slowly the balloon lifted, but then it stalled when the basket cleared ten feet off the ground. It was later said that some participants thought they heard a metal thump from inside the box, but Jonathan, confident that his balloon could go higher, opened the throttle on the remote control for a maximum flame. Although the balloon went no higher, within thirty seconds the wood began to smolder. Another thirty seconds and flames erupted from the boards on the right side, which then ignited the ropes. In the next thirty seconds Jonathan's well-carved box was ablaze, as was the balloon, which crashed to the ground a hundred yards away from where everyone had gathered.

The fire department responded immediately, and at Dennis's request the EMS truck pulled closer to the launch pad.

"Next!" Sal called out.

The flights of the next two prototypes were surprisingly uneventful. Both followed true to course: up fifty feet followed by a quick descent, landing on fairgrounds property. Several people applauded afterward.

Joshua and Mark looked on as another balloon went up.

"Boy, that floats nicely," Joshua said.

"Traitor," Mark joked.

They returned their attention to their own balloon, and Joshua continued to tie knots in the rope as Mark had instructed.

"Have you ever tested yours?" Joshua finally asked.

Mark shook his head. "This one? No, I didn't have time."

"Have you seen Chuck Bryson?" Joshua asked, sounding more nervous. "With his physics background, I would have thought he'd be at the front of the line."

"He would have, but he had a seminar in Berkeley and won't be back until Friday."

"How unfortunate. I would welcome his advice right now."

"Next!" Sal yelled.

A well-constructed albeit boring twelve-foot envelope carrying a wicker flower basket was placed on the pad. Because of the nominal weight of the basket, Sal attached several sandbags on each side and added a solid cement block in the center.

"Let it go," Sal instructed and started the timer.

When nothing happened, Sal repeated with some impatience, "Let it go."

"I am," the owner said, and walked up to the basket to check the burner. Peering in, he saw the small flame flickering.

He turned around, looking for Sal. "I'm out of gas."

Several of the onlookers broke out laughing.

"Next!" Sal called.

What the following entry lacked in technical ingenuity it made up for in creativity: a brilliantly colored balloon with eight bands of color spiraling from the bottom to the top, knotted by dyed rope. Acting as a basket and securely holding the burner was an empty three-foot-long wooden *Kon-Tiki* replica that the owner normally used for serving sushi.

The pilot nodded to Sal.

"Let her rip," Sal directed.

It began as the most ethereal of flights—a wonderful-looking balloon above a bamboo boat floating gently on the wind. Then, seemingly out of nowhere, another model-size hot air balloon floated above the tree line at the edge of the fairgrounds, heading straight toward the *Kon-Tiki* balloon.

Sal jumped up on the table and looked toward the forest to see who had launched the challenger, but he caught only a glimpse of a red shirt running through the dense brush. Rejoining Jimmy, Sal watched as the second balloon approached.

It was only then that the townsfolk witnessed an implausible sight: Hank was strapped into a small wicker basket, his skinny flamingo legs dangling from the bottom. From all appearances, he was piloting the balloon and on a collision course with the *Kon-Tiki*.

"Everyone, look! Hank's flying!" a woman hollered over the noise of the crowd.

Jimmy was flabbergasted. "In all my years . . ."

Someone yelled, "They're going to crash!"

Within seconds the two envelopes collided, then bounced off each other, leaving Hank's legs swinging in the wind.

"Watch out, Hank!" a resident yelled, but it was too late. Hank's balloon had gained altitude and, caught by the crosswinds, was quickly carrying him away. Within a few minutes he was a pink speck in the sky, heading toward Woodrow Lake.

"So, what do you think of that?" Jimmy asked Sal under his breath.

"I truly don't know," Sal said, still watching Hank. "I'll head down Farm to Market Road after we're done here to make sure he's all right." Then, in his deep voice, he called out, "Next!"

"That's us!" Mark said, pulling his sights off Hank. "Come on, Josh!"

Mark scrambled to collect the basket and firing mechanisms with Joshua right on his heels holding the folded balloon. Running up to the launch pad, he rolled out the envelope and attached the tethers.

"They're supposed to be inflated already," Sal said in frustration. "You'll disqualify on the time limit."

"No, I won't," Mark yelled back.

"Four minutes," Sal said, and began his timer.

Within fifteen seconds, Mark had the burner attached to the envelope and the booster connection clamped to the burner. He turned on the fan, angling the flow into the mouth of the balloon, and started the burner. Nothing noticeable happened. But when Mark turned the key for the booster, a muffled boom was heard, and the balloon abruptly inflated. Within thirty seconds, the envelope was beginning to lift off the ground. Within a minute it was filled. Mark lowered the booster and placed it in the basket.

Taking the remote control from Joshua, he turned to Sal. "Ready."

"Then let it go."

Mark turned the knob that controlled the booster, opening it up fully. He then increased the booster to maximum. Nothing.

"The ignition may have blown out," he said, walking up to the balloon and leaning over to look into the basket.

Just then the basket shot up at such a speed that Mark was almost decapitated. He fell backward, dropping the remote control, which split open on the ground.

"Wow, look at that thing go!" Jimmy said.

"It's a damn rocket!" someone yelled.

Gasps were heard throughout the crowd. The balloon went up so high and so fast it soared over Lumby, heading toward the mountains, caught in an unexpected crosswind that carried it westward instead of down the valley.

"What a flash in the pants," a woman said loudly.

The balloon was careening out of sight.

Mark, still flat on his derriere, looked over at Joshua with wide eyes. "Did you see that? That was just amazing! We have to get another one of those."

Extending a hand to his friend, Joshua said, "I think our piloting days are numbered."

Mark gave a wily smile. "Oh, they're just beginning."

An hour later, after the last balloon, christened the *Condor*, crashed into the back of the town library, most participants packed up their belongings and headed home, having been told that the winner would be announced at some later date.

Mark joined Jimmy, who was seated behind the registration desk organizing papers. "This was just fantastic," Mark said. "Fine job."

Jimmy didn't respond.

Mark leaned over the table. "Really, it was great."

Jimmy gazed scornfully up at him.

"What's wrong?"

Jimmy was irritated. "What do you think?"

Mark shrugged his shoulders. "Haven't the foggiest."

"We will look like idiots, Mark," Jimmy said, leaning back in his chair. "Our town has to host a hot air balloon festival and none of us knows a darn thing about hot air balloons."

"But they were great today," Mark argued.

Jimmy pointed a finger at him. "And you and I will look like the biggest idiots of all. Think of it: a hundred experienced balloonists and a thousand spectators spend a lot of money to come here, expecting a real event. Maybe not Albuquerque, but they don't want to see a hokey pie-eating contest. Some of their balloons cost fifty thousand dollars—it's not a game to them."

Seeing the intensity of Jimmy's reaction, Mark began to sense the enormity of the challenge. The more he thought, the more dire the prospects became.

"You know, maybe I'm not the right person to head up this thing," Mark finally admitted.

Folding the papers, Jimmy commiserated with him. "I agree, but none of us is—that's the problem."

"Then we just bow out, take our losses and walk away."

"That is *not* an option," Jimmy said. He had no intention of explaining how Mark's suggestion would put Dennis's family into near bankruptcy.

Mark was surprised by Jimmy's unusual show of temper and knew best not to press the issue. "So," he countered, "we bring in help."

"And who would that be?" Jimmy asked.

"I'm not sure, but a good place to start might be up at Saint Cross Abbey."

Jimmy raised his brows. "To pray for help?"

Mark slapped his hand on his knee. "That's a good one." He laughed. "But, no, I think we're way past that. Brother Matthew said they have two Indonesian retreatants who make some of the best hot air balloon baskets in the world. And they know something about flying in them too."

For the first time Mark saw a flicker of hope in Jimmy's eyes. "Really?"

"That's what Matthew said, and monks normally don't lie, if you know what I mean," Mark said, jabbing Jimmy in the side. "Don't worry, we'll do this together, and we'll do it right."

Just then, a muted explosion behind them made both men jump. Jimmy didn't even bother to turn around.

"I don't want to know about it," he said, laying his head on the table.

ELEVEN

Burned

Mackenzie McGuire idled at the end of a short line of cars awaiting admittance into Saint Cross Abbey. Next to her, her son, Terry, fiddled impatiently with the radio, trying to find a rock station with no static—an impossible challenge in the small town of Franklin, which was surrounded by mountains. In the backseat, Brian Beezer sulked, still angry that his father insisted he work for Mrs. McGuire as part of his punishment for the trial balloon mishap.

Mac looked in the rearview mirror at Brian, then at her son. She smiled. At nineteen, Terry was looking more like his father every day, although he had inherited her own vibrant red hair. It had been several years since his father had left for younger and greener pastures, leaving Mac to raise the boy alone. They had not only survived those turbulent times but had developed a healthy respect and appreciation for each other. Although Terry had stumbled into mischief a few times during those years, he was clearly coming into his own now. In recent months, the more responsibility and independence his mother offered, the more he rose to the occasion.

"You know," Mac said, "I'm really proud of you."

Brian jabbed his knee into the back of Terry's seat. Terry glanced over at his mother and blushed. He would have normally shrugged off such a compliment, especially one made in front of his closest friend, but having just finished a hard carpentry job the day before, he appreciated her comment.

Someone behind them tapped the car horn, catching Mac's attention. The gap had widened in front of her. As she moved the car forward, she leaned out of her window and saw a makeshift wooden gate at the beginning of the driveway. A man in a long black robe was leaning over, talking to the occupants in the car four or five spots ahead of hers.

Brian took note as well. "Boy, who'd have thought that God would be so popular on a Tuesday afternoon."

"They must be having a convention or something," Mac commented as two more cars pulled up at the end of the line.

"With so many construction jobs in Lumby, why did you want to drive all the way up here to Franklin?" Terry asked.

Mac released the brake and the car crept forward. "As a special favor for Pam and Mark. Also, the change of scenery might do all of us some good."

"Mom," Terry said, rolling his eyes, "we're nineteen. Being surrounded by a bunch of monks isn't our idea of a good time."

"Keep your mind open, and you, too, Mr. Beezer," Mac said. "You may be surprised by what comes your way."

Finally, they reached the gate. A young-looking brother holding a notebook smiled. Mackenzie's unruly hair blew across her eyes as she opened the window.

"Welcome to Saint Cross Abbey. How may we help you?"

"We're here to see Brother Matthew," Mackenzie answered, pulling her hair back.

The brother appraised her and the two boys. "Is he expecting you?"

"Yes," she said. "Mackenzie McGuire. We had an appointment scheduled with him ten minutes ago, but the traffic has been unbelievable."

"We apologize for that," the monk said, looking down at this pad. "Please drive to the chapel and then bear left," he instructed, pointing toward an ancillary road off the main driveway, "and take the service road around to the back of the community house. I'll let Brother Matthew know you're here."

"Thank you," she said, and drove on as the monk waved to the next car.

Brian scoffed at the monk as they passed. "Was that supposed to be a security checkpoint?"

"I don't know. But look at all those people on the lawn over there," she commented. "I've only been here once before, but it was really dead."

"Appropriate word," Terry said, pointing to the cemetery they were passing.

When they circled behind the main building, Mac saw a tall man in his sixties wearing faded blue jeans and a short-sleeve shirt standing by the open door.

Mackenzie lowered her window. "Excuse me," she said, "Brother Matthew?"

"Ah, Mackenzie McGuire," Brother Matthew said in his deep bass voice.

"May we park here?"

"That would be fine." He extended his hand as she got out. "Thank you for coming. I believe we met at the barn building last year, or perhaps at Charlotte's funeral?"

"Yes, both," Mac answered.

"The Walkers have always been so complimentary of your work. They say you are the finest carpenter in the state," Matthew said.

"Thank you," she replied with a slight smile. "This is my son, Terry."

Matthew smiled back. "Very good to have you here as well, Terry," he said, and shook his hand.

Terry was surprised not only to see a monk wearing jeans, but also to be treated as an equal. He straightened his back and stood taller.

"And this is another of my fine workers, Brian," Mac said.

Matthew looked at the young man's face for several moments. The eyes looked familiar but he didn't know why. Even the forced smile the teenager wore when he shook his hand snagged a distant memory.

"What can we do for you?" Mac asked.

"You can see the damage best from over here," Matthew said, leading them through the back entrance of the courtyard. He pointed up to the wide expanse of the roof.

Mackenzie and Terry saw a blackened patch surrounding a small chimney. "Oh, no, what happened?" Mackenzie asked.

"We had a small fire," Matthew said gravely.

Mac squinted harder, seeing what she thought was a piece of fabric flapping out of the chimney. "What's that?"

Brian looked up, shading the sun from his eyes. "It looks like part of a hot air balloon," he said.

"Yes," Matthew answered. "As improbable as it sounds, we think a balloon crashed into our roof a few days ago."

Terry took several steps back and stood next to Brian. "Good thing you're keeping up with those balloon flying lessons," he said under his breath.

Brian glared at him. "Shhh. No one knows but you."

Matthew continued to explain. "This is a double chimney. The right stack vents the first-floor fireplace in the kitchen and the left draws from the meat smoker, also in the kitchen. We were using the smoker at the time, so we're not sure if the burner on the balloon started the blaze or if the nylon caught fire from the heat of the rising smoke."

Mackenzie finally made the connection. "The balloon was from the trials in Lumby?"

"No doubt," Matthew answered.

"It looks like an old roof," Terry surmised.

"It is. Wooden shakes that have been patched over the years."

"And how would you like it repaired? With the same shakes?" Mac asked.

"I'm afraid so. We know that it's not the most cost-efficient and certainly not the safest when it comes to fire, but we are trying to retain the authenticity of the monastery as it was in the 1800s."

Terry squinted as he studied the roof. "Is there access to the roof through a window, or perhaps we can borrow a ladder to take a closer look?" he asked.

"You can crawl out through the north window in the library on the top floor. Be careful, though, the pitch is alarmingly steep."

Mackenzie said, "If you could show us the way."

But Matthew stood still for a moment. He placed his finger over his lips in thought.

"Is something wrong, Brother Matthew?" Mac asked.

His eyes narrowed behind his bifocals. "Not at all. In fact, since you are here, perhaps you could look at one more project after we return from the library. We have a need for additional rooms and have discussed the idea of partitioning our larger bedrooms in the guesthouse. With bunk beds we could almost triple the sleeping capacity."

Mackenzie looked around at the other buildings, not knowing which was the guesthouse. "We can certainly give you a bid on that."

Before going inside, Mackenzie reached into the backseat of her car. She produced *The Lumby Lines* and handed Matthew the copy. "Pam asked me to give this to you. She said you enjoy reading our little paper."

He smiled. "Indeed, I do."

The Lumby Lines

Lumby Forum

April 15

An open bulletin board for our town residents

Don't let depression destroy your life—the church will help. Join us Saturday nights at the Lumby Presbyterian Church for pot-luck dinners—prayer will follow.

Allergies. Cheap to a good home: 6-month-old golden retriever or 28-year-old boyfriend. One has to go. Will take best offer on either. Call Sara 925-3771.

2001 riding lawn mower parked in front of Jimmy D's two nights ago is missing, I think. If you know where it is, come see me at the bar and I'll buy you a beer. Harry.

SWM seeks companion—flexible. Call Phil: 925-3928.

Lost. Snapple, a 4-year-old calico cat with advanced college degree. Reward. Neutered. Like one of the family. See Dennis Beezer at Chatham Press.

In search of short brunette seen in bookstore on April 14—I think we were meant for each other. Call Phil: 925-3928.

Icelandic socks just arrived. Stock up for the winter. Limit one per person at Wools Clothing Store on Main Street.

Woman's Auxiliary Rummage Sale. Get rid of those things not worth keeping around the house. Husbands welcome.

A dozen chickens of unknown ownership were left on the back porch of the Feed Store last Thursday night and are now creating havoc with the goats. Please claim immediately or they'll be roasted.

Brother Matthew cherished the few minutes of retreat he found sitting in the corner of the library while Mackenzie and her workers were on the roof inspecting the shingles. Life at the monastery had changed so abruptly when the seekers arrived, first in small groups and then in large masses. Matthew felt, as did all the monks, deep conflict between shutting the gates to the invading world and openly embracing those who sought sanctuary. He laid the newspaper on his lap and closed his eyes, relishing the silence.

"Brother Matthew, you are wanted on line two," a voice came over the intercom.

Matthew reached over the desk and picked up the phone without hesitation.

"This is Brother Matthew."

"Hi." The man spoke tentatively. "This is Jimmy Daniels from Lumby."

Matthew took a moment to recall the name. "Ah, yes, the town mayor. I believe we've met before."

"On a few occasions, yes," Jimmy replied politely. He was never comfortable when he thought formal etiquette was in order. Contrary to his feelings, this was one time when it wasn't.

Matthew leaned back in the chair. "What can we do for you, Jimmy?"

There was a slight pause. "We find ourselves in a fix," Jimmy began. "Our town will be hosting a hot air balloon festival this summer."

"Yes, we've heard."

"Oh, very good," Jimmy said, brightening. "Unfortunately, we are a little short on experience and know-how. If the truth be told—" Jimmy said, immediately smacking himself in the forehead for using that expression with a monk. "Well, of course, the truth is always told," he stuttered. "Our balloon trial was a disaster."

Matthew laughed. "So we assumed."

Jimmy was mystified by the remark. He hadn't seen the brothers of Saint Cross Abbey at the fairgrounds. "You were there?"

"No, but one of the balloons found its way to the roof of our monastery," Matthew explained.

"Gives a whole new meaning to Ascension Sunday, huh?" Jimmy blurted out before he could pull back his words.

Matthew laughed deeply. "A new meaning indeed."

"Anyway," Jimmy said, coughing, "Mark Walker mentioned that two of your visitors might know something about hot air balloons, and if so, we would really appreciate talking with them. Perhaps they could give us some pointers."

"Ah, I see," Matthew said, pushing his glasses higher on his nose. "Yes, both Jamar and Kai Talin, who are visiting us from Indonesia, know quite a bit about hot air flying. Supposedly their village weaves some of the finest balloon baskets in the world."

"Wow, that sounds great," Jimmy said.

"But you understand," Matthew added gently, "that their participation is not under my control. I will certainly discuss your request with them today."

Just as the conversation was concluding, Brian climbed through the window and stepped onto the short ladder below the sill. Mackenzie followed.

"So, how does it look?" Matthew asked after hanging up the phone.

Mackenzie tied back a handful of loose hair that had sprung free. "Probably not as bad as you're thinking. About forty shingles need to be replaced. The fire damage was only on the surface—everything underneath looks fine."

"Well, that's very good news."

Terry climbed through the window with the ease of an athlete and stood next to Matthew.

"We should also replace the flashing," Terry said, tucking in his shirttails. "It wasn't damaged by the fire, but it has warped and cracked with age. I'm surprised it's not causing leaks below."

Brian dropped his head, slightly embarrassed that he had nothing to contribute.

Mackenzie, though, only noticed how carefully Matthew listened to her son. And seeing the two males side by side, she was startled to notice that Terry was only a few inches shorter than the monk, who was no less than six feet four inches. Terry had grown in so many ways during the last year.

"The roof may be leaking, but we are never in that part of the attic," Matthew confessed. "Very good, then. Perhaps that's something you can begin as soon as possible?"

"We can." Mac nodded.

"Now, if you would like to look at our guesthouse?"

"From the crowds that I saw gathered on the lawn," Mac commented, "I'm assuming you will need those extra beds sooner rather than later?"

"Sooner may not be soon enough," Matthew said with a weary sigh.

Brian looked out the window. "Don't you want them here?"

Matthew had to think a moment before answering. "Well, they have arrived . . . unexpectedly," he finally said, selecting his words carefully.

"In other words, they're uninvited," Brian said.

Brian's bluntness almost made Matthew laugh. "This monastery is for the worship of God, so our doors are open to whoever wants to join us in prayer."

Brian looked squarely at Matthew. "So, they come to your services?"

Again, Matthew was caught off balance. "No," he admitted. "I can't say that they do."

"Hey, Beezer, come on," Terry said.

Matthew raised his eyebrows. "You're Brian Beezer?"

"The one and only," Brian answered.

Ah, of course. Matthew smiled, thinking back on Brother Benjamin. *He is indeed the spitting image of his granduncle. And from all appearances, he's just as brutally candid.*

⤎⤏

TWELVE

Expectations

Heeding a request from Brother Matthew for a brief meeting at three that same afternoon, Kai and Jamar Talin arrived separately in the community room. Several minutes early, Kai sat on the couch and opened the book he had been reading, *In the Spirit of Happiness* by the Monks of New Skete.

The younger of the two brothers at twenty-seven, Kai had impressed all the brothers at Saint Cross with his sincerity. He was devoutly committed to his Christian calling and strove to embody all that his beliefs encompassed. Not as tall or physically commanding as Jamar, Kai was soft-spoken and more selective of his words than his brother. As a result, frequently it was Jamar who spoke for them when they were together.

"Good afternoon, brother," Jamar said with only a trace of an accent as he entered the room. He picked up a copy of *Condé Nast Traveler* lying on the table along with several other magazines the monks had been given. He looked at a photograph of Vancouver Island on the cover. "We really need to do some traveling before time runs out," he remarked.

Kai looked up from his book. "I don't think the villagers would want us to spend their money that way."

"Oh, there are other ways of paying one's way," Jamar said with a crafty smile.

He collapsed on the sofa next to Kai and flipped through the magazine. The facial similarities between the brothers were dramatic. They did indeed carry the genetic imprint of islanders from Coraba and a handful of surrounding islands in their remote region of the world.

The largest island close to Coraba is Sulawesi, formerly known as Celebes until Indonesia established its independence in 1945. With a coastline of over three thousand miles, primarily due to its many long, thin peninsulas that extend out into the balmy waters, Sulawesi is the northern anchor of a string of islands off its southeastern coast. Some of the islands of the archipelago are so small that they vanish entirely when the waves are high. In the middle of this chain lies Coraba.

One of eighteen thousand islands that make up Indonesia, Coraba is oblong in shape, seventy-two miles long and forty-four miles wide. There are only two townships on Coraba, each staking claim to roughly one-half of the ever-eroding land. The northernmost township is Timbora, which Kai and Jamar called home. Ranaki, a village of comparable size, sits on the southern shores.

Neither town reflects the country's predominantly Muslim religious alignment due to a band of young Dutch missionaries who permanently settled on Coraba in the early twenties. The ministry passed down the religious stewardship to their offspring, but then suffered when many laypeople decided to return to their homeland. The one surviving pastor who cared for all the souls on Coraba had died in a fishing accident the prior fall, leaving the islanders to look within their own community to select and educate a canon. Kai Talin, who was all but the associate pastor in the church, was immediately identified, as was his brother, who might have lacked a deep religious commitment but was so well liked that he was able to entice the young ladies to come to the pews each Sunday morning.

Following island culture, both brothers were sent to the United

States to be mentored by the brothers of Saint Cross Abbey, who had recently donated funds for their new school.

"Do you know what Matthew wants to talk about?" Jamar asked.

Kai, trying to read, just shook his head.

Bored, Jamar dropped the magazine on the end table and looked around. "You're not very talkative today," he said. At twenty-nine, he believed that his younger brother should be more attentive, so he jabbed him in the side.

"Stop," Kai said.

Jamar jabbed him again, but got no response. He looked at his watch just as Brother Matthew joined them.

"I'm sorry for my delay," Matthew said. "I hope this meeting doesn't interrupt your schedule of study."

"Not at all," Jamar said. "I was out talking to several of the seekers. I'm excited by all of the activity they've brought to Saint Cross."

"Ah," Matthew said, wishing he could share such enthusiasm. "And, Kai, how are you doing?"

"Very well, thank you," he said, closing the book.

Matthew sat and crossed his hands over his chest. Looking at both brothers, he approached his subject slowly. "We have so enjoyed your company and community involvement during the past several months. I hope this retreat has met some of your spiritual needs and has helped identify the paths each of you will take when you return home." He paused. "As we said when you first arrived, we can't provide any of the answers, but hopefully Saint Cross can offer you some of the foundation you will use when you decide how to best serve God."

Jamar nodded his head, for reasons quite different from what Brother Matthew was talking about.

Kai looked at Matthew in concern. "It sounds as if we're being asked to leave."

"Ah, no, not at all," Matthew assured him. "We hope to enjoy your company for another few months, as you had originally planned. We are keenly aware that you, Kai, are giving serious thought to making

the Church your life commitment. We want to provide an environ-
ment, albeit one that's a little noisy right now, that would offer both
self-reflection and growth."

"You have done that with your generosity," Jamar added with too
much charm.

"If you need anything," Matthew continued, "especially when we
are so busy looking outward at the crowds that seem to grow by the
day, you must be sure to ask."

Jamar, not one for letting an opportunity slip by, said, "My brother
and I thought it would be beneficial to see the surrounding area, the
local towns, before we leave, if that would be possible."

Kai glared at his brother. They had never discussed that idea, and
he had no interest in leaving Saint Cross Abbey.

"Actually, that's really why I asked to see you this afternoon. The
small town of Lumby, located one hour east of us, has called and
asked if either or both of you would be interested in meeting with
some of their townsfolk," Matthew said. "Perhaps I misspoke, but I
told them that you were knowledgeable about hot air balloons and
were proficient basket makers."

Kai leaned forward. "Why would they want to talk to us?"

"Lumby will be hosting a balloon festival in several weeks. The
balloon that struck our roof"—Matthew pointed upward—"was one
of their trials."

Jamar almost jumped from his seat. "This would be very good,"
he said. "We could explore the area while helping those in need. Kai,
you know everything about balloons. What do you think?" Jamar
glared at his brother enough to intimidate him. He was not going to
let Kai's religious habits interfere with an opportunity to venture as
far away from Franklin as possible.

Kai bowed his head to Matthew. "I don't have any desire to leave the
monastery, but if this is something you would like us to do, I will."

"It would need to be your decision, Kai, but they are friends
and we would very much appreciate any assistance you could give
them," Matthew said.

When Kai hesitated, Jamar filled the void. "We'll do it," he said. "When can we leave?"

◡৩

In a charming Victorian house on a quiet street in Lumby, Brooke looked over her husband's shoulder and read the same article.

The Lumby Lines

What's News Around Town

BY SCOTT STEVENS   April 15

A canister of Woodmen's Bear Repellent, purchased on sale at Lumby Sporting Goods, was accidentally discharged at the Wayside Tavern two nights ago. The bar is expected to remain closed for several more days, and the owner has offered to testify as to its effectiveness against patrons.

At the town council meeting last night, Morty Alberts submitted a petition to rename Lumby, returning to the original name used prior to incorporation in 1862. When challenged as to the historical authenticity of the proposed amendment, Morty showed town books dated 1859 referring to Albertsville. However, when the councilmen further investigated, they found Mudsend to have been the town's name in 1856. Petition was unanimously denied.

All individuals who would like to help with the hot air balloon festival are encouraged to attend

the committee meetings held each Tuesday morn-
ing at 10 o'clock in the community room at Montis
Inn. All questions should be directed to Mark
Walker.

"Are you planning to go?" Brooke asked.

Joshua laid the paper down on the dining table. "Hopefully not.
I'm just too busy. But Mark keeps trying to lasso me into helping
him."

Brooke removed salad plates from the refrigerator. "You don't
sound happy about that."

"I am, but—"

"But?"

He strummed his fingers on the table. "I know nothing about hot
air balloons. And I'm not like Mark. I can't just jump into a project
with wild abandon and have absolute belief that everything will turn
out fine." Joshua paused, thinking about his close friend. "In some
ways I wish I could be more like him."

Brooke walked up to Joshua and kissed him. "I love who you are,
and I wouldn't want you to be any other way."

The doorbell chimed just before seven thirty. They had a standing dinner with Caroline Ross for every other Monday evening, and
Caroline had never been a minute late in all of the times they had
gotten together.

"Come on in," Brooke called out.

"Your guest has arrived," a woman called from the foyer.

Joshua stood up from his chair as Caroline entered the kitchen.
She was wearing crisp navy pants and a blue-and-white-striped shirt
with a high collar. Her hair was pulled back with a navy ribbon.

Taking the large wicker basket she was carrying, he kissed her
cheek. "So, what have we here?"

"Only the essentials." Caroline smiled. "Wine and dessert."

Brooke held out a frosted glass. "A frozen margarita to start the evening?"

"Perfect," Caroline said. She gazed around the kitchen and then strolled to the window, placing her hand on the curtains. "Even after all this time, it's still a little bittersweet coming here."

"We understand," Brooke said, putting an arm around her. "Your grandmother lived in this house for over fifty years. We're so pleased we were able to buy it after she passed away last year."

"I'm the one who's pleased," Caroline said. "After she died, I actually thought about selling my place on Cherry Street and moving in. I so love my home but dreaded the thought of someone horrendous moving into my grandmother's house."

Joshua laughed as he set the wine bottle and brownies on the counter. "If that happened, I'm sure Charlotte would rise from the grave to haunt them personally."

They all laughed, recalling fond memories of the woman who had touched each of their lives in very different ways.

"So," Caroline said, wanting to change the subject, "how goes your investigation into Bricks?" She glanced at Joshua. "I'm sorry. Do you mind if we talk business for a minute?"

"Be my guest," he said. "I find your project intriguing."

"How kind," Caroline said, raising her glass. "Let's hope the town council feels the same way."

"Not if we don't clearly determine who owns the property," Brooke said. "I met with Joan Stokes and she was kind enough to go back into her personal records. Unfortunately, they showed nothing new, but she did confirm the same real estate transactions I had pieced together."

"So, we are no closer," Caroline said in frustration.

"Not necessarily," Brooke replied after taking a sip of her margarita. "Yesterday I met with Russell Harris. After reviewing the documents I gave him, he said that Bricks would meet the definition of 'legally abandoned property.' "

"How can that be?" Joshua asked. "Someone must have been paying taxes on it for all these years."

"Actually, no," Brooke answered. "The tax bill hasn't been paid since 1977."

"So?" Caroline asked.

"Per Russell, the town can take possession of the property and auction it off for back taxes and outstanding liens."

Caroline stood up and walked over to the kitchen island to refill her glass. "But if the liens are with bankrupt companies, how could they be repaid?"

"They can't be—it's simply dead debt. But some legal steps need to be taken to tie up those loose ends so there's a clean title."

"So, has Lumby taken ownership of Bricks?" Joshua asked.

Brooke shook her head. "That's what puzzled Russell. It's something that fell through the cracks, or perhaps the town discussed it and decided they didn't want to spend the money to legally erase the deeds and clear the title."

"So Russell is now going to advise Lumby to do just that?"

"He can't," Brooke answered.

Caroline raised her eyebrows in consternation. "Why not?"

"Because I hired him yesterday to represent you, and he would have a conflict of interest if he now advised the town council to take action. I suggest you meet with him as soon as possible, and bring your checkbook. The town might want a quick resolution, in which case it might be as simple as paying back taxes for twenty-odd years. A substantial sum, but that would certainly be far less than buying it outright at today's market value."

Caroline beamed. "Wow, you're good. Let's celebrate."

As the two women settled at the table to chat, Joshua went out to his car to fetch some college papers that he needed to grade that evening.

"You're so fortunate," Caroline said as she watched him leave. "You two seem very much in love."

Brooke looked out the window above the sink and saw her husband pass by. "I think we love each other more than we are *in* love," she said.

"But that's what lasts, isn't it?"

"I certainly believe so," Brooke answered.

Caroline stared wistfully off into the distance. "He's a very good man, isn't he?"

"He has a heart of gold," she replied. "And I've never met a more honest man."

Caroline smiled weakly. "That's hard to find, isn't it?" she said, almost talking to herself. "There's such promise when a new relationship begins and you get swept away by the charm and the excitement. But then the smooth exterior wears off and you wonder what happened and how you could have such lousy judgment."

Brooke saw the sadness in Caroline's eyes. "Unfortunately it's hard to see what a person is made of on a first date."

"Exactly. Then, months later, when you do find out that honesty and integrity aren't words in his vocabulary, you're crushed." Caroline sighed deeply. "I know I'm happy without someone by my side, but it would be so nice to share my life with someone I respect, someone with a higher moral purpose than deciding what beer to drink on a Friday night."

Brooke laughed. "That's exactly what I thought before I met Joshua, and look what happened. Give it time. Someone will come along when you least expect it."

THIRTEEN

Needling

Jamar Talin, frustrated that he was unable to get his own ride to Lumby, nudged his brother over as they squeezed into the front seat of the abbey's only pickup truck. Brother Michael was already in the driver's seat. The town meeting was to begin in a few hours and no one wanted to be late. In fact, if they were there several hours early, it would only please Jamar more—ample time to meet some of the charming women of Lumby, no doubt.

"Do you want to refer to a map to see where we're going?" Michael offered the brothers.

"Not necessary. But we are ready for the experience," Jamar said with forced politeness, trying to suppress his impatience.

Jamar had left the monastic grounds only twice since their arrival, and both ventures took him to the small town of Franklin. He had thought about asking a stranger for a ride just to get farther away, to see the great America he had heard so much about, but he knew there would be serious consequences if he followed his impulsive nature.

Although the brothers and the Church were all Kai needed to further his religious study, on that specific day he, along with Jamar, would see a breathtaking part of the country.

Lumby is not a town one would easily stumble upon while traveling. The privacy it affords has always been deeply embraced by its residents. Anyone venturing north from Wheatley would find only one thoroughfare to Lumby—Farm to Market Road, which passes Woodrow Lake, an irregularly shaped reservoir three times longer than it is wide. The Army Corp of Engineers takes credit for the lake's overall design, although the residents of Lumby maintain that Mother Nature and three million years of glaciers left a far more impressive imprint than man ever could. Regardless of its origin, it provides spectacular views from every vantage point.

As Farm to Market Road veers away from the last cove at the northernmost point of Woodrow Lake, it follows Beaver Creek into Mill Valley. The first homestead one encounters is Montis Inn, just off the road at Mile Marker Five. At that point the road gently winds through rolling green fields protected by densely forested foothills to the west.

Kai and Jamar stared out the window with their mouths open. Although they came from an island paradise, the sheer beauty of Chatham County, dotted by large farms with white barns and livestock grazing in the higher pastures, left them speechless.

A few miles south of Lumby, Beaver Creek bends toward the northwest and Farm to Market Road continues straight to intersect with State Road 541 in downtown Lumby.

"How charming," Kai said to Brother Michael as they turned onto Main Street.

"Are your traffic lights normally blue?" Jamar asked, looking up at the blinking light.

Michael laughed. "No, usually they're red and green. But this is Lumby, and the residents seem to march to their own drummer. The town is eight blocks long and three wide—much larger than Franklin."

He began to tell Kai and Jamar what he knew about the town. One of Lumby's oddities, he explained, was that much of the town's commerce took place one level above the street, on the second floors of the stores that lined Main Street. The entrances leading to many of the upstairs merchants were almost impossible to find by those who didn't have the unique pleasure of living in the vicinity. The post office, for example, occupied the second floor of the police station and had a private entrance on Farm to Market. Prior to its expansion the previous year, the library was located above the town hall. On the south side of Main Street, Jodi's Antiques rose above the Green Chile, and Notes, the town's only music store, occupied the second floor over Lumby Bookstore.

"Very interesting," Jamar said as he spotted three young ladies window-shopping at Wools.

Michael parked the car in front of Jimmy D's.

Kai looked at the BAR sign and heard music coming from inside. "Is this where they're having our meeting?" he asked apprehensively.

"No, we'll be gathering in the theater above the Feed Store," Michael answered as he pointed across the street. "It's one of the town's oldest buildings."

A large red store with a steeply pitched roof over the front porch looked well weathered from the hundred years it had been standing. An impressive cupola, almost the size of a tiny barn, adorned the roof's peak.

"They sell most everything here," Michael said as they crossed the street. "Animal feed and the animals to eat it, hay, and wood shavings. We've bought all of our gardening clogs here."

Walking inside, the Talin brothers were given a glimpse into history that few Americans experience, although much of what the brothers saw held little meaning for them. The walls of the Feed Store were covered with decades-old posters and public notices that had all curled and yellowed with time. Coolidge and Harding billboards asked for the people's votes, and Health Department letters reminded all to get the new polio vaccine. Advertisements for cars, going back to a Model T priced modestly at $465, lined the east wall. On a large corkboard behind the cash register, recent articles from *The Lumby Lines* were thumbtacked on top of old ones, three and four issues deep.

The back half of the Feed Store was an open barn that held the store's grain inventory—primarily horse, goat, and chicken feed stacked in forty-pound bags, six feet high. Behind that were pens of small fowl—three- and four-day-old guinea hens, Cornish Supers, Barred Rocks, and Rhode Island Reds. A few lambs were tied to a cross post, and one mare occupied the only available stall. Jamar was unsure what was worse, the offensive noise or the unpleasant smell.

Sam Hopper, the store owner, darted through the store waving a broom. "I chased them around back!" he yelled to one of his sons.

"I think one's stuck in the pipe, Dad," the son shouted from the back porch.

"Shut the door so they don't come in again!"

"What's going on?" Kai asked.

After returning the broom to the wall, Sam finally noticed the men. "Well, Brother Michael, we haven't seen you in several months," he said, shaking his hand. "How is everything at the monastery?"

Michael raised an eyebrow. "Interesting, to say the least. Should I guess you're still trying to evict your porcupines?"

"The very same ones for a year," he said. "But instead of four, they're now a family of nine."

Michael laughed. "Another few years and they'll be running *you* out with a broom."

"One made of quills, no doubt," Sam said.

"Matthew wanted me to thank you for allowing us to use your theater for the town meeting. Can we go upstairs?"

"Please help yourself," Sam said, watching the islanders follow Michael. "There are some critters in the attic that might stir, but just ignore them."

"Will do. We're going up one level," Michael told the brothers, pointing at the staircase adjacent to the horse stall.

Walking up into the theater offered the visitors a rustic, aromatic perspective of Lumby. First built as a vaudeville theater, the space had gone through many legal and illegal incarnations before being rebuilt almost twenty years earlier. At that time it became the town theater, which could seat almost fifty comfortably and another thirty, who bought half-price tickets, uncomfortably.

Two chalkboards brought over from the high school were positioned in front of the seats. Next to them were two metal chairs and a small podium.

Jamar walked around with some bravado, nodding his head in approval. "This will do," he said.

Downstairs, the mare whinnied and kicked her front hoof against the door. That, in turn, stirred the fowl, which screeched in unison.

Kai looked apprehensively at Michael.

"You'll just need to speak louder to be heard," the monk advised.

⁂

Jimmy stood in his living room and looked at the wall clock. "The meeting is in thirty minutes, Hannah," he called upstairs.

Hannah, wearing a clean pair of slacks and a pressed shirt, walked halfway down the staircase and then abruptly sat down on a step. Her hair was tied up in a knot. "I really would prefer not to go," she said softly.

"You need to at least make an appearance," he said, looking up at her. "Everyone in town will be there."

"Except me," she corrected him.

Jimmy was already nervous about the gathering, and another uneasy encounter with his wife was the last thing he wanted. "It's my meeting. It would look pretty bad if my own wife didn't bother showing up."

"But, Jimmy, that's my point. It's *your* meeting. You don't need me to be some ornament hung on your arm."

"I never think of you like that," he snapped.

"I do, every time we go out together, every time someone comes up and talks to you without even noticing I'm there." Tears burned in Hannah's eyes. "I'm invisible when I'm with you, and I hate it."

"Well then, make yourself visible," Jimmy said loudly.

Hannah grabbed a spindle of the railing, clenching it so tightly that her knuckles turned white. "It's so easy for you to say. Everything is so easy for you," she yelled. "You have no idea what it's like to be someone other than the outgoing, ever-popular Jimmy D."

"Hannah, it's not that hard. Just be yourself."

Hannah stared at Jimmy. "I don't know who that is anymore."

Jimmy waited for a few moments, hoping that Hannah would change her mind. "I really thought you would enjoy getting involved with the balloon festival, Hannah. You can't fault me for that."

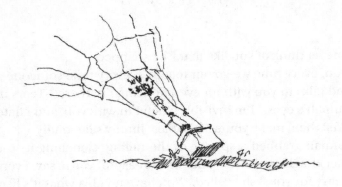

F O U R T E E N

Enlightened

After nudging several chickens away with his foot, Jimmy Daniels walked through the front door of the Feed Store.

"Your animals are out of control, Sam," Jimmy said to the owner, who was standing behind the counter.

"Those damn porcupines are driving me nuts," Sam replied.

"Porcupines? I'm talking about all the chickens out front."

"Oh, yeah, those," Sam said, waving off the problem. "Someone seems to think I'm running a boardinghouse for stray poultry. Every week another half dozen join the flock."

Jimmy laughed and headed upstairs. As he entered the theater, Jimmy sighed in relief when he saw Brother Michael and his two guests standing by the chalkboard. Mark Walker was also there, looking at a picture of a hot air balloon drawn on the blackboard.

One of the brothers was leaning over the table, reading a newspaper article out loud and laughing.

The Lumby Lines

No Forwarding Address

BY CARRIE KERRY   April 19

Reverend Poole of Lumby Presbyterian Church
has ventured as far as our state capital in defense
of his parishioners. His most recent grievance has
been with the state's electric company, which sent
Ken Abbott a March bill for $4.32, although Mr.
Abbott has been resting peacefully, buried seven
feet under, at the Presbyterian cemetery for well
over a year.

"After I assured company officials that Mr. Abbott
was in no condition to write a check, they insisted
on obtaining a forwarding address for the customer,"
Reverend Poole explained.

"It was similar to when we needed to obtain county
and church permission to have a horse buried next
to his lifelong owner. The papers provided by the
Ecumenical Council required that the deceased animal sign its name on the application."

"You must be the Talin brothers. Welcome!" Jimmy said.

Jamar put down the paper. "I'm Jamar, and this is my younger
brother, Kai," he said, shaking Jimmy's hand.

"I'm Jimmy Daniels and this is Mark Walker. I suppose we're the
official welcoming committee," he said, smiling broadly.

Brother Michael stepped forward and said to the Talins, "These are the two men who really need your help."

"You are both responsible for making the hot air balloon?" Kai asked.

Jimmy and Mark grimaced at each other.

"What a sobering thought," Mark said. "But, yes, I suppose we are."

A group of six townsfolk arrived and sat in the front row.

"How many people are you expecting?" Jamar asked.

Jimmy looked at his watch; it was 3:35.

Dennis Beezer walked in alone and stood at the back of the theater. Although his son wanted to attend, Brian was grounded until further notice because of his prank at the fairgrounds.

"This may be it," Jimmy said with obvious disappointment. "Why don't we begin? I'll introduce you—Brother Matthew gave me some of your background—and then the floor is all yours."

Kai did not understand what he meant by the floor being anyone's, but Michael, who normally explained idioms, had already walked away and taken a seat toward the back of the theater.

Jimmy stepped up to the podium and addressed the few people in the audience. "Welcome," he said awkwardly. "Thanks for—"

"Wait a minute!" someone called from the staircase. "Don't start yet!"

Brooke and Joshua hurried through the door, followed by Pam Walker. The three quickly took seats in the second row.

"Sorry we're late," Brooke apologized, "but a truck dumped a ton of organic fertilizer one block over and we were stuck in traffic."

A crowd of people immediately followed and rushed into the room. Within a few minutes every available seat was taken and another twenty people were standing in back.

A frowsy woman with dyed auburn hair stood next to Dennis. "I'm glad you're here," she whispered.

Dennis recognized her but didn't know her first name. "Can I help you?"

"I wanted to tell you how much we appreciated your son's help in completing Jerry's college loan application. We just heard back the other day, and the university is giving him full tuition. We never thought that was possible, but Brian must have said the right thing."

She patted Dennis on the arm and went and sat down, leaving him speechless.

Jimmy D coughed and everyone quieted down. "Thanks for coming," he said loudly, as there was no microphone on the podium. "I'm so pleased to introduce Jamar and Kai Talin from the island of Coraba, Indonesia. They are visitors at Saint Cross Abbey and have offered to share their knowledge of hot air balloons. I've been told that both brothers have been around balloons their entire lives. Not only is it one of their village's means of traveling between islands—"

"How can that be?" Pam whispered to Brooke. "Wouldn't they just float into the Pacific Ocean?"

"That would be the Indian Ocean, I think," Brooke corrected her.

"—but Corabans weave some of the highest-quality baskets in the world," Jimmy continued.

"Out of palm leaves?" Pam whispered again.

"Shhh," Brooke hushed her friend.

Jimmy coughed. "We have invited them to Lumby to share with us what they know and perhaps bring us one step closer to hosting our festival in just six weeks' time."

Some people had brought pads of paper and were already taking notes. Others just nodded in agreement.

"So, let me turn the stage over to Jamar, in the bright yellow shirt, and Kai." Jimmy abruptly left the stage and joined Simon Dixon and Dennis Beezer at the back of the room.

"What do you think?" Jimmy asked.

"I have no idea," Dennis said. "The drawing on the chalkboard looks real accurate, but who would actually know?"

As Jamar walked to the podium, his toe caught the edge of the riser and he stumbled forward. Within a second, though, he straightened up and ran his hand through his hair, immediately regaining his composure. He looked out at the audience, smiling broadly.

Brooke leaned over to Pam. "What a great smile. He's really good-looking, isn't he?"

Pam shrugged one shoulder. "A little too suave for my taste."

"Thank you for inviting us," Jamar said with a mild accent that sounded European. "It is a privilege to come to your fine town. I can see that *everything* they said about its residents is very true." He was eyeing two young ladies in the third row, all but winking at them. "You are as smart as you are hospitable, and we offer ourselves in any and all ways. My brother and I have been involved with hot air balloons since we were children, when we were first taught to weave two-man baskets, and by our late teens we were both licensed pilots. So, with that experience, hopefully we will be able to answer most of your questions. Now, I'll let my brother, Kai, begin by explaining the basics."

One of the young women raised her hand.

"Yes?" he said.

"Are you a monk?"

Jamar laughed. "No, absolutely not. Perhaps we can meet afterward and I can explain," he said with a wink.

Many in the audience laughed, but Kai shot his brother a glance, which he ignored. "We simply came to Saint Cross for a four-month retreat," Jamar said. He turned to his brother as he left the podium. "Kai?"

Kai walked to the front of the small stage.

"If no one objects, perhaps I should begin with the fundamentals," he said. "The first manned hot air balloon was initially tested in 1783. One hundred and seventy years later, gas balloons were used to drop leaflets over Eastern Europe during the Cold War."

The scampering of a small animal was heard directly above the stage.

"That's probably just another chicken," Jimmy called out.

When Kai looked up, some straw floated down from the loose attic boards and landed on his shoulder.

"The local residents don't seem interested," Kai joked tensely. "Anyway, from there, a few people began experimenting with very simple polythene balloons using a blowtorch to heat the air."

"What a great idea," Mark whispered to his friends standing in the back.

"With U.S. Navy backing, research showed that nylon and propane-powered burners were most effective. In 1960, the first modern hot air balloon heated by a propane burner was flown in Nebraska. So, your country is really steeped in the evolution of what you are exploring now," Kai said, nodding.

Pam nudged Brooke. "I like him a lot."

Kai turned to the blackboard on which he had sketched a balloon, his drawing large enough to be seen easily from the back of the theater.

"Very simply, there are three components," he explained, pointing to each section as he spoke. "The envelope is what many might think of as the balloon. Usually made of nylon and filled with hot air, envelopes can range in size from forty to over two hundred thousand cubic feet."

"How big is that?" asked a man standing by the door.

"It all depends upon the shape of the balloon, but a medium-size envelope, which would be about one hundred thousand cubic feet, might be well over sixty-four feet high with a sixty-foot diameter."

The collective oohs and ahs from the audience were loud enough so that no one heard the door open and close. Caroline Ross sneaked into the theater, scanned the audience, and quickly took the empty seat next to Brooke, which had been saved for her.

"How's it going?" Caroline whispered.

"It's just getting started," Brooke said.

Kai returned to the blackboard and continued lecturing. "The deflation port is a flap at the top of the envelope that is used to cool the balloon." He paused, half expecting a question. "All right. The second component is the heater system, which is made up of the propane storage tank, the burner or burners, and fuel lines carrying the propane from one to the other. The more heat, the more lift. The third part is the rattan wicker basket, which holds the fuel tanks, the pilot and his instruments, and of course the passengers."

On the blackboard, Kai quickly drew a few lines that were taken to be three human figures standing in the basket.

"Some support equipment we should discuss before launching," Kai went on. "An inflation fan is used to direct and blow hot air into a deflated envelope that is lying on the ground. At least three crew members will be needed—the pilot at the burner and two others at the mouth."

A woman who was taking copious notes asked, "Where is that? The mouth?"

"I'm sorry," Kai said, turning back to the blackboard. "At the bottom of the envelope is the skirt—here." He pointed with a long, graceful finger. "The mouth is where the skirt and the envelope meet—here."

"Thank you," the woman said with a small wave of her hand.

"You will also need a chase vehicle large enough to carry the basket and balloon to the launch site. The chase vehicle follows the balloon during the flight so that the ground crew is in place at the point of descent. And then, finally, there are smaller items, such as a drop line, igniter, and so on, all of which we can talk about as we discuss the lift."

Brooke looked at Caroline, who was studying Kai intensely. She seemed captivated by the slim young man with the chiseled bones and exotic features.

"So what's on your mind?" Brooke asked in a sly tone.

"How a man of God with such a gentle voice can be so . . ."

"So what?" Brooke asked.

"Enlightened," Caroline answered.

"Ah," Brooke said, noticing that Caroline's stare hadn't wavered. Kai continued to talk for the next hour, frequently stopping to answer questions. Since he didn't know any of the U.S. laws that governed pilot certification, he wrote several questions on the second blackboard, to be investigated and answered by others.

After he took the group through each step of a flight—inflating, launching, and landing—Kai spent the rest of the afternoon talking about flight maneuvering: ascent, level flight, and descent. He discussed various types of wind at length, always prefacing his comments by saying that his experience was limited to the flying conditions over Coraba and the surrounding islands.

Kai also strongly recommended the use of pibals—dark-colored nine-inch-high helium pilot balloons that are sent up to different altitudes to give the pilots a better understanding of the local wind currents.

When he felt he had covered all that could be digested in one session, he simply said, "Thank you," and stopped talking.

An awkward silence fell over the room. One person began to clap, and then another, and quickly the entire theater was filled with applause.

In the back of the room, Mark leaned over to Jimmy and Simon. "I think that went quite well," he said, clapping along with the others.

"But are we any closer to achieving what we need?" Jimmy asked.

Mark considered the question. "We know a lot more than we did, but I see what you mean."

As the ovation subsided, Mark walked down the side aisle. "Kai," he said, speaking so that all could hear, "you know that as part of the festival we need to build our own balloon—the reason why we asked you here today. If you were presented with this challenge, what steps would you take to accomplish it?"

Jamar stood up, but Kai started speaking before his brother could respond. "If broken into steps, the task is not as overwhelming as you might think. Take each of the components—the envelope, the heater, and the basket—and find people in your community who have the skill and talent to create that one element. For example, there are many plans available for laying out the gores and panels of nylon, but you need someone who can operate a heavy-duty sewing machine and is familiar with handling large pieces of fabric. Possibly the hardest part of the envelope is the sewn-in webbing. As for the heating system, that is technical, so anyone knowledgeable about burners could assist. Finally, the basket—the materials can be bought inexpensively, and if no one in town has the experience, I can teach a few how to weave." Kai looked out over the crowd and saw worried faces. "It's very doable if you break it into small tasks, one step at a time."

Jamar stepped up to the podium. "I agree with everything my brother says and offer my expertise as well. In fact, if it would be a benefit for me to stay in town, that can easily be arranged."

Jimmy joined them at the front of the theater. "We would all like to thank you for such an informative lecture," he said, to a round of weaker applause. Turning to the audience, Jimmy added, "If anyone here would like to work on any part of the Lumby balloon, please come up and talk with Mark Walker. Also, all of you who have offered to open your homes to the visitors and rent out a room or two will need to gather for a few minutes to walk through some of the specifics. Thank you all for coming."

As people began to rise and mill about, Jamar noticed a stunningly attractive woman with long legs in the front row. She was turned slightly, watching the men in back, so her black hair fell over her shoulder. She had a slightly darker complexion than most who had come that day. Perhaps she was of Latin descent, Jamar thought.

He approached while she was still alone. "Lumby certainly has beautiful ladies," Jamar said, flashing a quick smile.

Gabrielle was slightly startled by both the man's sudden appearance at her side and his suggestive comment. Seeing it was one of the two brothers, though, she excused his unusual introduction as that of a foreigner with different social customs.

"Thank you," she said, holding out her hand. "I'm Gabrielle

Beezer. You and your brother are doing a wonderful favor for our town."

Jamar held her hand for several seconds too long, enough to confirm she was not wearing a wedding ring. Had he known that Gabrielle had left it by the kitchen sink in her rush to attend the lecture, Jamar would have approached the situation differently.

"It was all my pleasure," he said.

Gabrielle gently pulled back her hand. "To show you our appreciation, please come by my restaurant for lunch the next time you're in town. It's the Green Chile, just down a few blocks on Main Street."

"A lovely woman like yourself owns her own restaurant?"

"I do," she said proudly.

"You must be the perfect example of elegance in the kitchen," he said, winking at her.

"I don't think that when I'm up to my elbows in dishwater. But please come by," she said, wanting to end the conversation.

"I most certainly will," Jamar said before rejoining his brother, who had begun erasing the blackboard.

"I love this town." Jamar beamed.

Kai laughed. "I think you would love just about any town other than Franklin these days."

"Perhaps, Kai," he responded. "And best yet, I have been asked out by a beautiful woman."

"The one you were just talking with?" Kai asked, wary.

"At her own restaurant, she said," Jamar added.

Kai told his brother sternly, "Our village sent us to Saint Cross Abbey in good faith, and we are here for that reason."

Jamar gave a sly smile. "Well, God works in mysterious ways, doesn't He?"

A good-sized crowd had gathered in front of the theater. In fact, to Jimmy's surprise, most of the townsfolk who had attended the presentation were awaiting directions on how the small town of Lumby could host the more than one thousand participants who were expected to attend the festival.

Once you subtracted the hotel rooms within close proximity and the accommodations available in Rocky Mount and Wheatley, Lumby was still short several hundred beds. Although a handful of residents saw this as a fortunate turn of events that would benefit their wallets, almost all had an earnest desire to do whatever was necessary to ensure the festival's success. Several had even told Jimmy they would offer rooms free of charge if need be.

Jimmy stood on a small riser and raised his arm. "Could I have everyone's attention, please." He waited a moment. "This is a great turnout. From the preregistration forms we have received, it looks like there are about three hundred folks who are looking for local lodging."

"How do we get their names?" someone asked.

"Are bunk beds all right to use?" another man asked from the back of the group.

Jimmy held out his hand. "Okay, hold on. Let me explain what I have so far and then answer your questions." He opened a folder and scanned the first page. "It's really going to be easy. We'll provide the information but we're not going to set down any rules. Each of you will need to write up descriptions of your accommodations—you can offer any rooms you would like, with one or many beds, with or without a private bathroom. If you want to include meals, that's your prerogative as well. And you need to determine how much you want to charge per day, or perhaps you want one price for the entire weekend. You need to get all that information to Dennis Beezer in the next few days, and he will consolidate the listings, run off copies, and mail them out to those who have requested lodging information. And then the tourists will contact you directly if they are interested in renting a room from you."

"What about requesting advance deposits?" the same man asked.

"That's up to you," Jimmy answered.

"Should we include photographs in our description?" a woman asked.

Jimmy nodded. "If you like," he said. "The only thing we really require is accurate descriptions—please don't embellish them to the point where expectations won't be met when the guests finally arrive."

From the group's silence, Jimmy worried that his short speech had fallen on deaf ears.

"So, it's all up to us?" asked an older woman standing in front.

Jimmy shrugged his shoulders apologetically. "Pretty much," he said. "With everything else we have going on, about all we can do is get the word out and make sure everyone knows of your accommodations. This is one time when each of you will need to step forward and take the reins."

"Well, I can do that," the woman said.

"Yeah, me too," someone else added.

"Gabrielle, how much are you going to charge?" a man asked, which began a loud exchange of ideas and comments that lasted for thirty minutes.

Given the notes that everyone was carrying out of the Feed Store, it appeared that there had been a valuable sharing of ideas and plans among the new hosts and hostesses of Lumby.

FIFTEEN

Sinking

The following morning, Mark was showered, dressed, and halfway to town before Pam even began giving serious thought to beginning her day. It was a day she didn't want to face, and three times she pulled the pillow over her head to avoid the inevitable. Only after bribing herself with a promise of blueberry pancakes did she find enough motivation to get up, pull on a torn T-shirt and an old pair of dungaree overalls, and face what lay ahead. Not wanting her wedding ring to get marred or lost during her excavation adventures, she removed the gold band and placed it on her nightstand.

After breakfast, she procrastinated yet another hour by having three cups of coffee, which only raised her anxiety.

"All right," she said to herself, "the time has come."

She grabbed the leather gloves off the side table and a single key from the row of hooks by the door and walked outside. It was a glorious day—seventy-four degrees without a cloud in sight. A mild breeze rustled the tops of the trees in the orchard across the street.

Pam called out to the dogs, but neither Clipper nor Cutter could be seen. No doubt they were exploring distant corners of the Montis property and, knowing it wasn't mealtime, had far more interesting things to do than to obediently respond. Pam shut the screen door and marched onward.

Turning the corner by the dining room, she almost ran into Hank, who was perched a safe distance from the tractor. Evidently he had ventured down to the inn to offer a hand, or wing, as the case may be; he had donned a construction hard hat and fly-fishing waders that covered most of his formidable physique. Realizing how muddy the job was going to be, Hank had opted for a rain parka that came down to his knobby knees. Although he eyed the bright orange Kubota with suspicion, he knew that the fish pond could ultimately offer him easy pickings for several meals.

"Don't know if you really want to be here, Hank," Pam advised. "It could turn ugly."

Hank opted not to reply and instead offered Pam a supportive glance.

Pam had had several nightmares about driving the tractor. Even worse, she had continued to lie to Mark by saying that steady progress was being made on the pond. So Mark, having kept his promise to stay away from the construction site, would never have guessed that Pam had not once been out there since the flat tire had been repaired.

She stood next to the rear wheel, the top of which came to her shoulder. She warily eyed the step up to the seat, a good twenty inches off the ground. Then she looked up at the dining room window and reminded herself how wonderful it would be sitting there, having dinner overlooking a beautifully landscaped water garden. Pam groaned, took a deep breath, and pulled herself up into the seat.

She mentally rehearsed the checklist she had studied so carefully, and then began. Slowly, she went through the process step by step: depress the brake, depress the clutch, disengage the PTO, turn the ignition key, shift into low gear, engage the PTO, release the clutch, lift the backhoe, lift the front bucket. So far, so good.

Pam finally pressed her heel down on the back part of the hydrostatic pedal, and the Kubota crept backward. Applying slightly more pressure, she increased her reverse speed to four miles per hour.

Suddenly, a dog screamed out in pain and she slammed on the brakes, lurching backward and then forward. Shaking, she turned around, expecting to see one of their dogs under the tire. Instead, both Cutter and Clipper were twenty yards away tugging on a tree branch. No doubt the yelp was Clipper's response to Cutter taking the bigger end of the stick.

Pam's nerves were shot, her hands shaking. She concentrated on reversing the process to turn the tractor off, and then there was silence. Hearing the racket had stopped, the dogs ran over to her and started to explore. Cutter jumped into the front loader and Clipper peed on the tire.

"I agree." Pam laughed as she stepped down. "But you two need to go inside before something bad happens."

After putting the dogs in the kitchen, Pam skimmed the owner's manual once more before her second attempt of the day. This time, getting back onto the tractor felt different. For the first time, it wasn't totally foreign and daunting. Pam didn't struggle to remember each step, and for a few fleeting seconds her movements with the pedals and levers became second nature. Also, the noise, which was once deafening, was now an encouraging indicator that all was well with the engine.

With the front loader and backhoe well off the ground, Pam pressed the accelerator with the ball of her foot and the tractor rolled slowly forward. She was executing the plan she had developed the night before: begin at the beginning. Simply drive around the backyard and perhaps, at best, circle the inn a few times to get the feel of the tractor. Forward and reverse, slowly and cautiously.

She found that when she hit a bump, the impact would travel through her right leg and affect the pressure she had on the pedal—jerking the tractor forward or too quickly slowing it down—so she deliberately tried to "ride" through the bumps with her foot remaining still, as she would when holding a cup of coffee in a car. She also discovered that although the tractor was at least twenty feet long with the front and back attachments, it had a surprisingly tight turning radius and good maneuverability through the power steering.

After her third trip around the inn, Pam practiced figure eights between the lodge and the guesthouse. On the north side, she stopped and reversed between two trees, correctly gauging distances to within a few inches on each side. Her confidence was growing as she looked around for another challenge. She saw Joshua up in the orchard and headed his way, crossing Farm to Market Road like a true farmer.

Joshua waved as Pam drove past, carefully maneuvering between the apple and pear branches. She was beginning to "feel" the tractor, to listen to the engine and know when to throttle up or down.

One step at a time, she thought with a grin. After traversing most of the upper fields, she followed a path back down to the barn. Approaching it slowly, she steered the tractor so that when she came to rest, she was squarely in front of her target: a six-foot-tall mound of mixed manure and hay.

With her foot still on the brake, she put her right hand on the joystick and slowly moved it forward and backward, right and left, watching how the front bucket responded. Again and again she lowered the bucket, raised it, and tilted it in and out.

Finally, she put the loader parallel to the ground, stepped on the gas, and, as the bucket moved into the manure, she maneuvered the joystick so it lifted and cradled inward, scooping up a large quantity of manure.

"Wow," she said softly.

She then reversed and drove the tractor toward the raised garden beds on the lake side of the barn and dumped the manure into their large compost bin. She repeated the exercise until there was nothing left to move. Only once did she mistakenly raise the front loader so high that the manure poured out over the back of the bucket, onto her and the tractor hood. But better manure than rocks raining down on her. All in all, it was a successful learning experience.

Driving down the barn's access road, she turned left onto Farm to Market and returned to Montis Inn, waving at passersby. For the first time since taking ownership of "the guppy project," as Mark referred to it, she actually felt good about her accomplishments.

Maneuvering the tractor behind the dining room, she slowed to a crawl and, backing up, positioned herself several feet away from the natural spring. She then raised the throttle, stood up, moved to the rear of the Kubota and sat behind the backhoe, which was facing the standing puddle of water.

She remembered Matthew's words: dig on the left, drop on the right. Or was that begin on the right? In her anxiousness she grasped the two levers too quickly and the backhoe jolted forward, sending vibrations through the tractor. She immediately realized she had not dropped the outriggers, the stabilizing legs, and lowered them so that they dug into the ground. She gently began to experiment. One lever controlled the boom retraction and extension, as well as left and right movements, while the other controlled the bucket retraction, extension, and curl. What delighted her was that the more tender the touch, the more control she maintained.

Very ingenious.

She then extended the arm and dropped the bucket and made a first dig into the earth. Pulling the bucket toward her, she scooped out a full load of dirt and deposited it to her left, where she could push it away with the front loader. Repeatedly she scooped until there was a worthy hole in front of her, six feet in diameter and four feet deep in the center.

But she hadn't calculated the correct reach of the arm, and she needed to increase the width of the hole. Several trees blocked her access from the other side, so she took the only option she saw: she inched the tractor forward down the slope and partially into the hole, far enough so she could continue to dig out on the far side. The tractor was at a precarious angle, but Pam felt comfortable knowing that, at worst, it would slide a few feet to the bottom of the pond. Its huge tire treads would surely get her out of any predicament.

Stepping from the tractor to the backhoe seat, she noticed how soggy the mud was, but she was confident there would be enough traction to back the tractor out when the time came.

After another few minutes of digging, Pam turned off the engine and looked around in triumph. She had excavated the first part of the pond.

Needing a break, she jumped down and pulled herself out of the hole and headed back to the lodge.

Only after having a light snack did Pam feel exhaustion stream through her arms and back. She stretched out on the sofa, and soon she and the dogs were sound asleep. It was well past dark when Mark finally returned home and woke her. Without saying more than a few words, she kissed him and went to bed, too tired even to take a shower. She was in such a deep sleep that she never heard the thunderstorm that moved through Mill Valley in the middle of the night.

Ꮮ

By morning, the rains had passed, although it was still cloudy. After soaking her sore muscles in a long bath, Pam was ready to begin phase two, the excavation of the north end of the pond.

Circling around the building, she saw the Kubota and knew instantly that something was radically wrong: the top of the tractor was several feet lower than when she had left it the day before.

"My God! What happened?" she yelled out.

When she ran up to the excavated hole, she saw water everywhere. Rain the night before and seepage from the natural spring had raised the water level to halfway up the rear tire, almost to the seat. The engine looked like it was barely dry.

"No, this can't be happening!" she said as she frantically waded through the water and climbed into the seat.

She held her breath when she turned the ignition, but nothing. She tried again and this time the engine turned over. She shifted to four-wheel low and gently pushed on the pedal. No movement, not one inch. The rain started again, which was incentive enough for Pam to push the pedal as hard as she could. The wheels spun, throwing an arc of mud and water through the air, but instead of moving out of the hole, she was slipping farther down. She continued spinning the wheels, making deeper tracks into which the tractor slid.

Suddenly, the engine sputtered and died. Water had flooded any hope of salvaging the machine. A clap of lightning brought on a downpour.

Soaked through and through, Pam yelled out in frustration. Water rose higher than the seat, drowning everything below her hips. She couldn't remember a time that she had felt as frustrated and beaten as she did at that moment. She dropped her head and began to cry.

"Are you all right?" a man yelled.

Pam jumped in her seat.

"Are you all right?" he repeated.

She wiped her eyes with her muddy gloves, smearing dirt on her face, and tried to see who was speaking. There was a man in a dark raincoat with a hood pulled over his head.

"Yes, I think so," she said, shaken.

"You really should get off the tractor. Not a place to be in a lightning storm."

Pam looked up at the sky and quickly stepped down into water, which came up to her chest. She tried to claw her way up the bank, but it was muddy and slippery. Seeing her struggle, the stranger extended his hand.

Once she was pulled out of the hole, Pam took off her gloves. "Thanks," she said.

The man, no taller than she, pushed the hood off his head, and Pam saw that it was Jamar Talin.

"Jamar! What are you doing out on such a nasty day?"

"I'm looking for Mark. I'm supposed to talk to him about the design of the balloon. I knocked on your front door, but no one answered."

Pam ran a hand through her wet hair and Jamar noticed that she wasn't wearing a wedding ring. Perhaps there was more of an opportunity here than he had thought.

Pam looked up and saw the storm passing. "Mark was in the orchard, but he probably went down to the barn when it began raining."

"So," Jamar said, thinking how best to use this rare opportunity of being alone with Pam, "this is your pond project?"

She looked askance at the muddy hole. "If one could call it that. Yes, I'm afraid it is."

"It's quite an admirable effort for a woman to undertake," he said, winking at her.

Pam shrugged her shoulders. "Had I known what I know now, I might not have been so willing to take it on."

"Well, in our country, beautiful women such as yourself are revered and never asked to do manual labor."

Pam laughed. "That's how it was here among a certain class of women a few hundred years ago."

"Well, perhaps I can offer some assistance. There would be nothing more satisfying than working close to you," Jamar said.

Pam wanted to assume he was just being polite. "Thank you for the offer, but this really is a one-person project."

Jamar applied more pressure. "But you are all alone back here, obviously wanting companionship. It could be our private matter." Jamar gave her another wink and brushed back his hair.

This is unreal, Pam thought. *He's hitting on me!* "Actually Mark gives me about all the companionship I can handle right now. But I appreciate your concern." She extended her hand to offer a polite, formal closure to their conversation, but one of her gloves dropped into the pond.

Jamar immediately seized the opportunity to be chivalrous. "Let me get that for you." But the glove had floated away from the bank and was several feet out of his reach.

"Here," Pam said, handing him a stick.

He stretched as far as he could. "Just a few inches more," he said, extending the branch with his fingertips.

Suddenly, Jamar's right foot slipped in the mud and he sailed forward, landing facedown in the water.

He grabbed the glove and stumbled to find his footing in the pond. "Anything for the lovely lady," he said, and winced.

As Jamar climbed out, covered with muddy water, Pam laughed. "You're quite a sight."

He looked down at himself. Then, with a grin, he squeezed his arms together, posing as if he were in the Mr. Universe pageant. He changed to a side pose, bringing one arm above his head and flexing his muscles, which obviously couldn't be seen under his drenched clothing. He then turned around and offered Pam a back view, flanking one leg out toward her.

She slapped her hands together and started laughing.

"Impressive, wouldn't you say?" Jamar asked.

"I was going to use the word 'daunting,'" Pam said. "You need to get back and take a shower."

Jamar raised one eyebrow. "All alone?"

Pam looked at him from the corner of her eye. "I certainly hope so."

SIXTEEN

Sewn Up

Hannah sat by the window of her sewing room, holding back the curtains so she could watch pedestrians cross the intersection of Main Street and Mineral Street. Some, no doubt, were leaving Jimmy D's, while others were venturing into the Feed Store or Brad's Hardware.

From her safe vantage point, she enjoyed watching everyone and often laughed when she saw what they brought to, or from, the merchants. Hannah also observed with envy the casual interactions of the townsfolk, chatting on the steps of the stores or even stopping in the middle of the street to catch up with friends.

For as long as she could remember, she had never felt comfortable with people, except of course with Jimmy, who patiently became her protector when they were in their mid-teens. When they first met, her shyness only seemed to strengthen Jimmy's determination to become a comfortable focal point in her life. Once that occurred, they fell into a loving relationship, with Hannah well sheltered from the world and Jimmy the center of her attention. Even the birth and raising of their son had little effect on that fine balance between husband and wife.

Although the years had passed complacently for Hannah, recently she had begun to feel uneasy with her own invisibility. It was a gradual awareness that started as a mild annoyance and then grew into a piercing agony. But she didn't know how to crack the shell that she and Jimmy had built around her. And over the months, her emotions had turned toward anger; first at herself for being who she was and not knowing how to change; and then at Jimmy for . . . being Jimmy.

She could have attended the meeting in the theater, she reasoned with herself. After living in Lumby for so many decades, she knew most everyone in town by name and had a polite if distant relationship with the other wives. She might have gone if it hadn't been Jimmy's affair, or if Jimmy hadn't pushed. Self-contempt welled up within her when she realized she was, once again, letting Jimmy indirectly control her life.

She let the curtain drop when she saw her husband turn the corner and head toward home.

"Hannah?" he called up to her from the foyer.

He was several hours early. Hannah turned off the radio and went downstairs to the living room.

"Is everything all right?" she asked, since she seldom saw him during the day.

Jimmy opened the curtains as far as they could be drawn, and then looked around the room. "Just great," he said. "Come sit down."

She watched him straighten the stack of newspapers on the coffee table.

"What's going on?" she asked apprehensively, sitting as requested.

"I had a wonderful idea this morning," he began. "You know that a few fellows from the monastery came and talked to us about building the lead balloon for the festival."

"The meeting in the theater," she said.

"Well," Jimmy added, "I think it would be great if you sewed the envelope."

"What's an envelope?"

"The main body of the balloon," Jimmy said, making a large circle with his arms above his head.

Hannah thought he must be teasing her. If she didn't want to sew a small test balloon, why on earth would she agree to be responsible for the real thing? "That's not very funny," she said, and hurried into the kitchen.

He was right on her heels. "No, seriously, Hannah. You are the finest seamstress in town. I have seen you sew everything from dolls' clothes to my suits. You even made Chuck Bryson's sails for the *Calypso* last year."

"But a full-size balloon, Jimmy? That's crazy."

He pulled a piece of paper from his pants and flattened it out on the countertop. "But it's all just panels sewn into long strips, and then the strips are sewn together," he explained.

Hannah looked at the diagram. At first glance, it seemed easy enough, but she knew the difficulty would be the special seams that held the panels together against the internal force of the hot air and the external force of the winds.

"No, thank you anyway," she said, and opened the refrigerator to begin dinner preparations.

Jimmy came up behind her and put his hand on her shoulder. "Honey, we really need you to do this."

"We, as in the town?"

"Yeah, all of us."

"Definitely not," Hannah said more firmly. "You know I'm not comfortable around people. I hated when you ran for mayor, but you said it was important. But this time I'm saying no." Her voice was beginning to shake. "I'm not going to put myself in a position of being the focus of everyone's attention."

The front doorbell rang.

"Will you just keep an open mind and come meet someone?" Jimmy asked more forcefully.

Hannah stared at him in anger. This was typically how Jimmy

got his way—he bullied her with an arsenal of friends who wouldn't let her back out, who embarrassed her into going along with their plan.

Jimmy rushed to the front door and ushered in a handsome younger man whose eyes were lighter than his skin color. Hannah was certain she had never met him.

"Hannah, this is Kai Talin. Kai, my wife, Hannah."

"Thank you for inviting me to your home," Kai said in a soft voice with a unique European inflection.

Hannah was too flabbergasted and self-conscious to respond. Her gaze moved from Kai to Jimmy and back to Kai.

"Honey, Kai is from Indonesia and knows a tremendous amount about hot air balloons. I thought he could answer any questions you may have."

Hannah struggled to find the right words. She refused to be coerced into anything. "I'm sorry to have wasted your time, sir," she said formally. "My husband misunderstood. I won't be working on the project. So, if you would excuse me." Her face was beet red as she hurried from the room.

As soon as she was gone, Jimmy said in a low voice, "Don't worry about it. She'll come around in the next day or two."

"But she sounded sure of her position," Kai replied.

Jimmy grinned. "Yeah, but I can change that. Perhaps you can come by day after tomorrow. Hannah will have lots to ask you by then."

Kai wasn't so certain. "Honestly," he said, "I think this project will be hard enough even with people who are truly enthusiastic. Perhaps there are others who can sew the envelope."

"Not a problem. Hannah will do it," Jimmy said jovially. "See you day after tomorrow."

After Jimmy closed the door, Hannah appeared at the top of the stairs.

"You have done it again," she said, and now it was not only her voice that was shaking. "How dare you speak for me?"

"Hannah, you keep telling me you want to get out more. I guarantee that tomorrow you'll think it's a great idea."

She wanted to yell at him, but held back. "And if I don't, what then?"

"Well, of course you will," Jimmy said. "You have to. The whole town is counting on you."

She slammed the bedroom door behind her.

The Lumby Lines

Sheriff's Complaints

BY SHERIFF SIMON DIXON   April 22

4:43 a.m. Domestic dispute on Mineral Street.

6:53 a.m. Resident on Cherry reported that his backyard swimming pool had been filled with warm water and apparently used—two pairs of men's boxers were hanging on the clothesline.

7:02 a.m. Cindy Watford reported that someone put a "Silence Hank" bumper sticker on her car while she was grocery shopping in Dickenson's.

7:27 a.m. Dispute at Jimmy D's.

7:53 a.m. Clerk at bookstore called in complaint that sidewalk bench had been moved down to Wools.

9:04 a.m. Lumby Sporting Goods reported "Silence Hank" stickers covering private parts of display mannequin.

9:40 a.m. Pickup vs. loose steer on Loggers. Steer's horn still embedded in front grille.

9:42 a.m. Man on Hunts Mill reported car being driven by dog hit side of his house. Seems dog, left in parked car with engine running, jumped on gear shift and reversed down driveway.

1:20 p.m. Parks Department says an old man is sitting in an Adirondack chair sunbathing naked in middle of fairgrounds.

9:17 p.m. Jeremy Kidd reported that his still was tampered with and requested police to investigate.

10:36 p.m. Jeep vs. draft horse on Farm to Market in front of Montis Inn. No damage.

In the main building at Montis Inn, Mark had converted a second-floor guest bedroom into his temporary office, hanging a large poster of a hot air balloon on the door. Each morning he disappeared upstairs to call volunteers, place orders for needed materials, and refine timelines.

"Wow," Pam said, walking into the room for the first time. She picked up a rough copy of the festival catalogue. "I thought you were only responsible for making the balloon."

"I am," Mark said, his head still deep in paperwork, "but I'm lending a hand in all the festival activities."

Pam circled the room and examined a corkboard that held several different strands of rope, each one correctly named and priced. "I have to admit, I don't think I've ever seen you so organized. This is so unlike you."

"You've only skimmed the surface with me, honey," Mark said with a big wink.

"That's what I'm scared of," she teased. "Hey, we need to get going to Saint Cross if we're to join Brother Matthew for lunch."

"Sorry, honey, I don't have time," Mark said, pulling out a file from a makeshift cabinet.

"But they have a new recipe from their brandy sauce line they want us to try."

Mark shrugged. "I just can't. I've got to follow up on a hundred different items." He picked up a sheet of paper and began reading. "Almost everyone in town has offered to help board some of the visitors, and I need to finalize and post the list. And the draft of the festival program needs to be approved. The restaurants need to be told what to prepare for the town barbecue. Letters need to go out to all of the balloon pilots. Even the churches are waiting for a final count of tables and chairs to bring to the fairground for the opening banquet." He shook his head. "It just goes on and on."

"Well, I'm proud of you," Pam said, kissing him good-bye. "I'll see if Joshua wants to join me. Anyway, there are plenty of leftovers if I'm not back before dinner."

"Drive safe," he said and then picked up the phone to make another call.

Before beginning the trip to Franklin, Pam stopped off at the Montis stable just south of the inn. Joshua, who had been working there all morning, jumped at the opportunity to join her and visit his old friends.

"I really appreciate this," he said as they drove through the mountains. "The last time I was at Saint Cross, the town was busier than usual. Some unexpected visitors wanted to see the monastery, so we didn't have a lot of time together."

"Brother Matthew certainly sounded anxious when I spoke with him yesterday," Pam agreed.

Joshua kept an eye out for wildlife, specifically bighorn sheep. "He is always uneasy when the unexpected happens."

Pam grimaced. "I know the feeling."

Joshua was in the process of rolling down the window. "Oh, that's right. Now that you've brought it up, how goes your pond?" he asked.

Pam responded by biting her lips.

Joshua continued in a relaxed tone, "I noticed the guys from Wheatley Farm Equipment were back with some heavy equipment."

Still no response from Pam. She tightened her grip on the wheel.

Joshua wasn't giving up, though. "I heard they're taking the tractor away in a few days."

Pam hit the steering wheel with her palms, startling Joshua.

"It's a failure," she said in anger and frustration. "I'm a failure. For the life of me, I can't manage to dig a damn hole in the ground without causing a catastrophe."

"You looked like you were making progress when I saw you in the orchard."

Pam shook her head. "Driving is not the problem. Even operating the backhoe isn't too hard. But there's so much I don't know about excavating. I thought it was simple, but it's a chess game—you need to think four or five steps ahead or you'll be stranded with a machine that can't get out of the hole you've dug yourself into."

Joshua tried to offer reassurance. "But that happens to the best of them."

"Please don't tell Mark," she said.

"If you want, but," Joshua said and paused, "it might not be that bad to have Mark see you . . ."

"Fail?" Pam asked angrily.

Joshua held up his hands. "Well, how about not succeed on your first attempt?"

Pam beeped her horn at a deer by the side of the road. "Well, I've made my last attempt. The damn tractor is going to sit in the backyard and rust until the rental period runs out. I'm giving up."

Joshua couldn't believe his ears. "Just because it doesn't come easily to you?"

His words stung because she had been arguing with herself using the same logic. "My project has been a total waste of money and it's getting embarrassing," she informed him. "They must be laughing at me all over Wheatley."

"The best excavators need to be pulled out every now and then," Joshua consoled her. "And you're a beginner. They know that."

"I just can't do it." Pam's voice cracked and she waited several moments before continuing. "I have nightmares about the tractor driving off on its own," she finally admitted.

"Oh, that's nothing," Joshua said, trying to lighten her pain. "When I decided not to take my vows, I dreamt God came after me with a rolling pin."

Pam glanced at Joshua. "A rolling pin as in what's used for pie crusts?"

"Yeah. I figured it must be tied to 'Give us this day our daily bread.'"

Pam finally laughed. "So what did you do?"

"Persevered, as you will. It was hard at first, but I took it one step at a time and began to walk the path I was meant to live."

Pam smiled, beginning to feel much better. "Perhaps finishing the pond will be my own saving grace."

SEVENTEEN

Hiding

A mile outside of Franklin, the traffic slowed to a crawl.

"Someone must have hit a deer," Pam speculated, but then thought otherwise when she saw a man walking alongside the slow-moving cars wearing a Rotary Club vest and holding a large bucket for donations.

"I don't think this is about a deer," Joshua said dryly.

Pam moved the car closer to the center lane, trying to peer beyond the long procession. "It goes all the way into town."

A quarter mile farther, high school students offered a "waterless" car wash for two dollars. Shortly beyond that, a local farmer had set up a makeshift roadside stand of questionable sturdiness to sell radishes and greenhouse tomatoes. For three to the dollar, he was also selling peeping chicks that scrambled about in a small plastic trough.

Finally coming into Franklin, both Pam and Joshua were amazed by the town's transformation. The quiet two-block village of empty sidewalks, a few stores, and one infrequently visited diner was now an overrun municipality that was unsuccessfully accommodating the multitudes that swarmed its streets.

Pam's jaw dropped. "I've never seen anything like this."

The sidewalks had become a vendors' paradise. The front of the small pharmacy was taken over by a large metallic stand with T-shirts covering every inch of open space. One read, "Support the theory of evolution . . . 400 billion amphibians can't be wrong," and another, "Atheists are beyond belief."

"Must be agnostics," Joshua joked.

Below that T-shirt, a bright yellow polo was imprinted with "We fix problems with duct tape, God fixed problems with nails."

"Maybe not," he corrected himself.

Then Pam saw a poster hung from the next vendor's tent. It was a photograph of Brother Matthew's monastery, and below that, in bold letters, "Come bunk with a monk at Saint Cross Abbey."

"Oh, my God," she muttered.

"Appropriately said," Joshua teased.

Pam laughed at her gaffe. "The brothers couldn't have approved that."

"Absolutely not," Joshua agreed.

Pam gaped at the crowd of pedestrians. "Do you think they are all here because of Saint Cross?"

"Perhaps," he said, leaning out his window to listen to an evangelical preacher standing in front of the town's only bar, sharing his steadfast opinion on the sins of the flesh. Joshua raised his brows.

The mile from Franklin to the abbey on the west side of town was no less congested.

Finally, they approached the gate at the monastery.

"Look over there," Pam said, pointing at the expansive front lawn. Several tents had been erected, and cots and sleeping bags covered the ground. Small barbecue grills and coolers sat among cars and motorcycles parked randomly on the grass.

On the lower hill just past the rock wall, someone had built a makeshift stage on which a cardboard spaceship had been placed. On front of the fuselage hung a sign: TICKETS TO HEAVEN $10.

Pam pulled up at the entrance gate and Brother Michael looked into the car. "Oh, familiar faces!" he said, showing his first smile of the day.

"What has happened?" Pam asked in disbelief.

"The articles about our philanthropic efforts and our donations were reason enough for all these people to come," Michael explained.

"What do they want?"

He sighed wearily. "Many want money, some say they want to join the abbey. Others are just lost, looking for an answer."

"In your rum sauce?" Pam asked glibly.

"This is just unbelievable," Joshua commented, looking at the crowd gathered around the pond. There were so many more people than the last time he had visited.

"So, is there a secret code to get in?" Pam teased Michael.

He leaned closer so he wouldn't be overheard. "There needs to be, if you ask me. But it's a little quieter inside. Why don't you guys park by the small chapel and go in through the private entrance?" He opened the gate. "You'll probably find everyone hiding in the kitchen."

Pam drove through the gates but had to brake every few yards for pedestrians crossing in front of them. The same level of commotion continued in the back of the abbey, forcing Pam and Joshua to sneak in through a well-hidden side door immediately off the courtyard that was only used by the monks.

Walking through the building, they first noticed that the community room was empty. At the kitchen, the small window on the swing door was covered with a new sign that read in bold red letters: PRIVATE! DO NOT ENTER! THIS APPLIES TO YOU!

"Do you think that means us?" Pam said.

"I don't think so," Joshua said uncertainly.

Pam knocked lightly but there was no answer. She pushed the door open a few inches and looked in. On the far side of the room, several monks were gathered around a small table, eating.

"Excuse me?" Pam said softly, but no one heard.

Standing behind Pam, Joshua tried to peer in and accidentally pushed her into the room. Everyone looked up.

"Get in, quick!" one of the monks said.

Brother John stood and waved them over. "Come in."

A dozen monks were uncomfortably squeezed around the narrow table. Bowls and platters of food were pushed together in the center along with an open bottle of wine. The monks were speaking in hushed voices.

"Is it a religious day or something?" Pam asked Joshua as they approached the table.

He shrugged. "Not that I know of."

"Pam, Joshua," the familiar voice of Brother Matthew called out. "Come and sit."

"What's going on?" Pam asked. "Why isn't everyone in the dining room?"

"We're hiding," Brother John answered.

Joshua looked around. Other than the monks, the room was empty. "From whom?"

The front bell rang out through the abbey and several of the monks groaned.

"Them," Brother John said. "I'll get it."

Just as he left, the phone rang. "The answering machine will pick it up," said another brother.

"Assuming the tape's not full," someone commented.

"We're averaging one call every two or three minutes," Matthew explained. "Please sit and join us. Would you like some lunch? Unfortunately, our cook quit a few days ago because of all the commotion, but we have a buffet of leftovers. Help yourselves."

Pam quickly noticed how exhausted Matthew looked. In fact, all of the monks looked tired. The front bell rang again and the brothers blanched at the sound.

The door cracked open and three others slid into the kitchen: Mackenzie and Terry McGuire followed by Brian Beezer. Pam smiled when she saw Mac. They had become good friends when Mac spent the entire summer restoring Montis shortly after Pam and Mark purchased it. Pam was equally surprised to see Brian, having heard that the young man was seriously grounded because of his prank at the fairgrounds.

"Is the coast clear?" Mac whispered.

"It is now," Matthew said, "though we just escorted out several uninvited visitors in search of coffee and mayonnaise. Lunch is the same as yesterday, but please help yourselves." Turning to Joshua and Pam, he added, "I need to return a few urgent calls. Could we get together in about thirty minutes?"

"That would be fine," Pam said, helping herself to chicken salad.

One by one the monks cleaned their plates and left the kitchen.

Terry and Brian stood next to each other making sandwiches. "I've got to get to your mom's car," Brian whispered. "I hid my balloon pilot's manual under my jacket in the backseat and I need to study it over lunch."

Terry leaned closer to his friend. "I thought you were giving that up."

"No way," Brian mumbled. "It's great, but you get tested every week, so I've got to study."

Terry called to his mom, "We'll be outside."

The boys hurried out, leaving the three adults alone in the kitchen. While Mackenzie filled her plate, Pam picked up the paper and read the editorials.

The Lumby Lines

Letters to the Editor

April 25

CASTRATING IDEAS

At our most recent town meeting, our unenlightened councilmen voted 4–3 to adopt an ordinance prohibiting the feeding of stray animals on public property, specifically the park and the fairgrounds. Our residents haven't seen the likes of such a rubbish idea in years.

The cruel starvation of abandoned animals will not solve the problem of feral feline and canine overpopulation—castration will. The same should be done to our civic leaders who don't care about the welfare of these poor animals.

—Melanie Gentile and Cindy Watford

FOULMOUTHED FLAMINGO

Many in our good town have proven to be loyal supporters of our honorary avian resident, Hank. Some believe he should run for mayor during next year's election. However, before we raise him higher up the palm tree, a voice of reason needs to be heard.

The sad reality is that Hank coveted several of my farm's geese on at least three different occasions during the last month. When I was trying to evict him from my land, Hank shouted obscenities unbecoming of his species. I and others in the community think it best that he be relegated to the county zoo if he does not migrate to Wheatley for the summer months.

—A concerned Lumby resident

Pam pulled out a chair for Mackenzie. "I heard that you were working here. How's it going?"

Mac checked the door to make sure everyone else had left. "Almost impossible," she said, shaking her head of red hair.

Pam wasn't sure what she meant. "You're having problems with the brothers?"

"Oh, no," Mac quickly corrected her. "The monks have been wonderful. In fact, they are constantly apologizing. But some of the seekers have total disregard for the brothers' property and services."

Joshua poured some iced tea for himself. "What are you working on?"

"We were originally brought in to repair the roof. One of the Lumby balloons started a fire on the wooden shingles." Pam looked at Joshua out of the corner of her eye. "But now we're subdividing some of the rooms in the guesthouse and the boys are kept busy building quad bunk beds."

"How are they doing with all of the commotion?"

"Terry is less affected by it than Brian, I think," Mac said.

"You and Terry seem to have a good relationship," Joshua commented.

Mac smiled proudly. "It's getting there. He's coming into his own."

Pam put down her fork. "In truth, I suppose I'm surprised to see Brian Beezer here."

Mackenzie shook her head. "He had no choice. After Brian's disastrous balloon flight, his father laid down the law and insisted he go to work."

"And?" Pam asked.

Mackenzie looked down at her plate. "It's frustrating. He doesn't have a natural ability for carpentry the way Terry does, so he's constantly one step behind, which frustrates him. However—" She paused, thinking more about Brian. "I have to admit, the boy has more ideas in his head at any one moment than I've had in a lifetime."

"Ideas about what?" Joshua and Pam asked in unison.

Mac laughed. "You name it—everything from how the monks could better organize the visitors to how the pharmacy in town should rearrange their floor layout in order to"—she lifted her fingers and made quote marks in the air—"maximize sales."

"And Terry would prefer that Brian just swing the hammer?" Joshua asked.

"Yeah, he would. It's certainly a strain on their friendship."

Moving on to other subjects, Pam shared with Mackenzie news from Farm to Market Road. About forty-five minutes later, Matthew returned to the kitchen.

Mac put her plate in the sink. "Let me round up my crew and get back to work. I'll see you later."

"And if I'm not needed here, I would like to walk around your grounds," Joshua said just as the front doorbell rang again. He gave a brief wave as he left.

Matthew covered his ears in exasperation. "I would take you into the community room, but so many people look into the windows that we would have no privacy. Anyway, several people have asked to meet us to discuss forming business partnerships. We would very much appreciate it if you participated in the discussions."

Pam was pleasantly surprised. "I would be delighted to."

Matthew brought his index finger to his lips. "Good. I promise it will be interesting. So, if you would like to join me, there are several propositions awaiting our consideration."

As Matthew led his guest through the back corridors of the main building, Pam asked, "Have you ever talked to Brian Beezer?"

"Not at any length. I've met him—he bears a startling resemblance to Benjamin. But if Brian is at all like his grandfather, William, I suspect he would keep his distance from any monastery."

"I think Brian follows his own inclinations and doesn't walk in anyone else's shoes."

"Why do you ask about him? Do you think he might be interested in monastic life?"

Pam laughed under her breath. "Oh, I don't think so. But there might be more to him than meets the eye. Along with all the complaints about his undisciplined behavior, he also has been doing quite a lot of good lately. Gabrielle told me that he arranged for one boy to receive a full college scholarship. You might ask him what other ideas he has rolling around in his head right now."

"I'll certainly talk to the boy if he's willing," Matthew said.

EIGHTEEN
Pitches

Pam first noticed the woodwork of the vaulted ceiling.

"This is gorgeous," she breathed out as Matthew led her into a room that she had never seen before.

"This is Chapter Hall. The monastic community gathers here each morning to discuss the day's schedule, as well as for weekly spiritual readings. It is the third most important room in the monastery after, of course, our small chapel and larger church."

Pam noticed four tables arranged diagonally in the room with four seats in front. There were well over thirty chairs, enough for all of the monks.

"Pam Walker," her name came over the intercom. "Mark is on line three."

Pam blushed uncontrollably. "I'm so sorry," she said to Matthew. "Our cell phones don't work up here."

He raised his hand. "Not a problem. There's a phone in the corner that you can use."

Pam picked up the receiver. "Mark?"

"Hi, honey. How's it going at Saint Cross?"

Pam frowned and covered her mouth. "Fine, but you didn't call me for that, did you?"

"No, but I just had a nice talk with Brother Aaron. He's such a nice guy."

"Mark, what do you want?" Pam asked impatiently as she watched three brothers enter the room and take seats at the front table.

"You sound rushed. Am I calling at a bad time?"

"I'm surprised you're calling at all," Pam replied in a strained voice.

"Well, they don't mind—they like us." Mark laughed.

Another group of brothers walked in. "Actually, I've got to go. What do you want?"

"Okay. I picked up two large burners, about three feet each, at the post office yesterday. They were in the back of the Jeep. Did you notice if they're still there?"

"They're not. When I picked Joshua up at the barn, I asked him to take them out and set them inside the door."

"Great, honey. Thanks," he said happily. "Have a safe trip back. Love you."

Pam couldn't help but smile. "You, too."

Rejoining the others, Pam sat at the back table next to Brother Michael. Within a few minutes, another dozen monks arrived.

At two o'clock, Matthew stood up and cleared his voice. "Thank you all for pulling yourselves away from your work and joining us this afternoon. We have already met with those people who have a genuine interest in considering our way of life for themselves. We now need to offer time to some who have repeatedly requested a business arrangement with us and have shown an interest in helping us to further our philanthropic goals. As we discussed last week, Pam Walker is with us today to offer a different perspective as we begin to interview those who are interested in working with Saint Cross in some way. As these are preliminary discussions, what I think we want is a unanimous thumbs-up or -down so we can carry only the good ideas forward."

Matthew sat down just as a very short man, who appeared to have a perpetual tan, was escorted in and introduced as Finley Dryden. He remained standing in front of the group as he began his pitch in a Scottish accent.

For the next ten minutes, Pam listened to Finley's presentation in partial disbelief. She took no notes, a sure indicator that she saw no value in the idea. In fact, she had a hard time keeping a straight face while Finley spoke.

"So," he recapped, "the complex would be architecturally similar to that of your abbey and would carry its same name: Saint Cross Condominiums, One Step From Heaven. A nine-hole golf course would surround the living quarters on all sides, except on the southeast corner, where we intend to build an Olympic-size pool in the shape of a cross. In the shallow end, there will be a swim-up bar, and in the deep end a small altar. With your endorsement, we are certain to sell ninety percent of the units before construction begins. And, of course, two of the finest units would be reserved for your community. I'm sure that a few weeks in Lakeland, Florida, during the long winter would be a welcome break from . . . well, you know. It would be a nice break." He paused, trying to regain some composure. "Are there any questions before I get into the financial aspects?"

Matthew quickly stood up and spoke for the group. "I don't think so. As much as we appreciate your proposal, I don't think we are in a position to consider any more details quite yet. If you would like to leave that information with us . . ." Mathew let his voice trail off, not wanting to offer any false promises.

As Finley left, Matthew looked back at Pam, who quickly and subtly gave a thumbs-down.

Just as two other men were being brought in, the intercom buzzed. "Pam Walker, line two."

Pam dropped her head in embarrassment, avoiding the looks of many who turned her way.

"I'm so sorry," she said, running over to the phone. "What is it?" she almost hissed.

"Hi, hon."

Pam turned her back to the tables and pressed the phone to her mouth, speaking as softly as possible. "Not now, we're in a meeting."

"But this is important," Mark said.

Pam was exasperated. "What?"

"Wheatley Farm Equipment is here," Mark explained.

Pam turned toward the brothers and raised one index finger as if to say "one minute," mouthing the word "sorry."

"And?" Pam asked, her face beet red.

"They say your rental is up today. They'll take it back unless you want to make other arrangements."

"Oh, for heaven's sake," she said. "I don't know what I want to do. Tell them we'll buy the damn thing just to push them off until tomorrow."

"Will do," Mark said, and hung up.

"I'm so sorry," Pam said as she retuned to her seat. "He won't call again."

A few brothers chuckled.

The second presentation lasted no longer than the first and was met with an equally enthusiastic thumbs-down.

After a brief discussion, the men fell silent when a tall woman in an austere tailored suit walked forcefully into the room. The woman's facial features appeared more pronounced because of the makeup she wore, and her seemingly wet hair was pulled back into a tight bun. She carried a briefcase of richly tanned leather.

"Gentlemen," she began without preamble, "I will be brief. As you know, Amazon Coffee is the largest purveyor of gourmet coffee in the world. We are a four-billion-dollar conglomerate and were listed in *Fortune*'s top ten best-run companies for the last three years."

"Excuse me," Matthew interrupted.

"Yes?" the woman asked.

"What is your name?"

From the woman's expression, no one could tell if she was more annoyed by the interruption of her presentation or, as she saw it, the irrelevance of the question.

"Ashley Myers, Senior Vice President of Joint Ventures," she answered abruptly. "If I could continue, Amazon Coffee offers espressos and cappuccinos in congenial atmospheres for social interactions of upper-socioeconomic customers."

"What?" one of the monks asked.

Her rhythm broken, Ashley finally looked at her audience—and met blank expressions all around.

"Well, all of you have certainly had Amazon Coffee?" she asked almost accusingly.

Brother John laughed. "I doubt that."

"But you know who we are, correct?"

"Many of us don't, actually," Brother Aaron answered.

Ashley froze. She had never been in a meeting in which her company's formidable size and reputation didn't control the content of the conversation, let alone the outcome. She saw Pam in the last row and tried to make eye contact, but Pam looked away. Within seconds, the aggressive, in-control corporate executive visibly wilted.

To her credit, though, she recomposed herself and began again. Speaking in a lower voice, at half the speed of her initial pitch, she introduced the men to a company called Amazon Coffee, and quickly promised samples of their coffees to be delivered to them each month for the coming year.

"Given your position in the gourmet food business," she explained, "we thought it may be mutually beneficial for us to work together."

"How?" Brother John asked skeptically.

"We would offer a Saint Cross monastic brew from a custom blend of the most select beans we purchase in South America. Our Marketing Department suggested carrying an image of your abbey on cups that we would use during the promotion. In addition to a license fee for the use of your name and monastery, you would receive a royalty—a percentage of net income from those sales. Also, we would offer a bilateral agreement whereby you could purchase our coffee at wholesale and use our company's name."

"But we have no intention of opening a coffee shop here," one monk said.

"No, but you can add bags of beans to the many gift baskets sold by your subsidiary."

Ashley continued explaining the details of her proposal until all the monks' questions were answered. It was obvious that they were more interested in the espresso than in the condominiums, but that wasn't saying much.

Brother Aaron stood up and spoke before escorting Ashley out. "As Brother Matthew said, many of us need time to consider the idea, but if you could leave us your number we will certainly call within the next few weeks."

After they left, everyone in the room once again fell silent. Matthew stood to address the brothers. "That was the last meeting of the day and perhaps it's a blessing. It appears we all have a lot to think about. I would suggest we meet after dinner tonight to begin to share our initial thoughts."

After the monks left the room, Matthew walked up to Pam, who was still seated at the back table. He rearranged a chair to sit across from her.

"I had no idea what to expect," he confessed.

Pam laughed. "Nor did I, but I wouldn't have missed it for anything."

"You agree that the first two presenters offered nothing that we should consider."

"I agree wholeheartedly," Pam said. She looked at her pad of paper—not one word, because the first two ideas lacked substance and the third was so unexpected. "But Amazon Coffee—they might have something worth studying," she said.

"Indeed," Matthew said.

"And you're responsible for gaining consensus one way or another?" she asked.

"Not necessarily responsible, but I will try to lead that process."

Pam looked at her close friend. "So, what do you think?"

Matthew rubbed his eyes. "I don't know. If we could impose upon you once more and ask if you could review a copy of the proposal she left us, I would appreciate it."

"I certainly will," she promised. "And now, I think I should round up Joshua." She started to stand.

"Actually there's one other matter I would like to talk to you about if you have a minute," he said.

Pam returned to her seat. "What's that?"

"A favor, if at all possible. You have met Kai and Jamar Talin, the brothers from Coraba who are here on retreat."

"I have," Pam replied. "And I hear they've given invaluable assistance to Lumby as the town prepares for the festival."

"That's good to hear. I know Kai would much prefer to stay at the monastery, but their efforts in Lumby really call for them to be there most every day. Unfortunately, we are stretched so thin that the time required to drive them to and fro is more than we have right now."

"I can well imagine," Pam said.

"We thought it might be more practical for them to stay in Lumby for the next several weeks, but I worry that Jamar may want to experience too much of a good thing. So, we thought Montis, being slightly out of town, may ease his temptations."

Pam laughed softly.

"Is something wrong?"

"Not really. I had a misunderstanding with Jamar. He showed . . . interest." Pam blushed and then quickly said, "But we seem to have straightened that out. Do Jamar and Kai room together?"

"They do here, but that is your choice," Matthew answered. "And we will certainly pay your regular rates."

"Let's not worry about that right now. Have you talked to them about it?" Pam asked.

"We have. In fact, they could be packed in just a few minutes if you wouldn't mind bringing them back with you today."

"No, not at all," Pam assured him.

⸎

The return drive to Montis was a quiet one: Pam thought about Amazon Coffee as she drove. Joshua, who had had an unpleasant encounter with some of the seekers, was napping. Kai was praying for a speedy return to Saint Cross, and Jamar watched Pam while fantasizing about his approaching date with a beautiful woman named Gabrielle.

𝕿𝖍𝖊 𝕷𝖚𝖒𝖇𝖞 𝕷𝖎𝖓𝖊𝖘

Freezing Ermines
BY CARRIE KERRY   April 29

Admittedly, strange things have been found in back-
room commercial freezers of many restaurants. The
main chef of S&T's Soda Shoppe was startled to discover four live arctic ermines enjoying the balmy
zero-degree air while setting up home in a large box
that had been stashed in the corner.

So, how exactly did these weasels find their way to
our small town?

"I was trading up," explains Brian Beezer, who
quickly admitted ownership of the carnivorous var-
mints. "There's this new site on the Internet, eBay,
where you can buy and sell most anything. It's very
cool. So, I thought I'd try trading up. I started with

one bicycle tire—and three weeks later, I have four ermines. The possibilities are endless."

"Next time, I'm sure Mr. Beezer will first ask permission to use my freezer," the restaurant owner added.

"Is that Woodrow Lake?" Kai asked as he looked out the window of the second-floor bedroom he had been given at Montis Inn.

"Yes, it's only a mile away—a very enjoyable walk in the evening," Pam answered.

"And how far is Lumby?" Jamar asked.

"Several miles up Farm to Market Road. We'll be glad to give you a ride in, or if you just stand by the side of the road, most folks will stop to give you a lift," Pam said.

But when she considered the brothers' exotic appearance, she wondered if she had spoken too quickly about the congeniality of the residents. Although she had come to love Lumby, she knew that the townsfolk could be leery of strangers.

And she wondered about the Talin brothers—how they viewed their surroundings at Saint Cross and what they thought of this temporary request to help out the town. Did they view Lumby's townsfolk with the same caution as the residents did them?

"Would you like to join us for dinner tonight? There are no guests at the inn this week, so the meal will be something simple in our home."

"Do you live here?" Kai asked.

"In Taproot Lodge, the small building on the other side of the courtyard."

"Dinner would be very nice," Jamar politely accepted.

"Then we'll see you at seven o'clock. If there's anything you need, let us know."

Jamar unpacked immediately and returned to Kai's room, adjacent to his.

"Quite a fortunate turn of events, little brother," Jamar said, stretching out on the bed.

Kai was still gazing at the lake and surrounding mountains. "If it's only for a few days. There's still so much to learn at Saint Cross."

"We have our freedom now, so let's not waste it," Jamar said. "I've got to get into town tomorrow for a lunch date."

Kai frowned at his brother. "I still think that's a bad idea."

"Not if you saw her—she's gorgeous and very exotic," Jamar enthused.

"Is she single and of age?" Kai asked, knowing Jamar all too well.

"Yes, on both counts."

Kai raised his brow. "I like this town and the people in it, so promise me you won't wreak havoc like you normally do."

"Cross my heart," Jamar said. But his wink promised otherwise.

In the kitchen, Pam found Mark seated on the sofa, working his way through the first chapter of an aeronautics manual that Chuck Bryson had lent him. He had been studying the first chapter for several hours and was still lost in the terminology.

"Hi, honey," she said, leaning over and kissing him on the lips. "Did you have a good day?"

"Uh-huh," he said, not really having heard the question.

"Did you find your burners?" she asked.

"Uh-huh."

"Kai and Jamar Talin will be staying with us for a while. I put them in rooms 202 and 204, and they'll be joining us for dinner tonight."

"Ah," he said, and kept on reading.

As she began to clear the kitchen table, Pam picked up a large receipt placed under two sets of keys. It was a Wheatley Farm Equipment invoice for the Kubota sitting in the backyard with eighty-six running hours logged on the engine: $24,500. At the bottom it read "Paid in Full."

Immediate panic made Pam turn to her husband. "Mark? What is this?"

He looked up for one second and then returned to the book. "The papers for your tractor."

"*My* tractor?" she asked, straining to control herself.

"Yeah. You told me to buy it this afternoon," he said, not even raising his head.

Pam glared at him in disbelief. "And how exactly did you pay for it?"

"I wrote them a check, honey. You know I don't have that kind of cash in my wallet."

"Mark, look at me!" Pam snapped. "I didn't want you to buy the tractor. I wanted you to push them off a day or two so I could extend the rent when I found a few minutes."

"Well, I guess you don't have to do that now," Mark said, not understanding his wife's problem. "We need a tractor for the barn, and from what I saw, you seemed pretty good at operating it."

"But the check you wrote is going to bounce! We don't have twenty-five thousand dollars in that account."

"That's all right. Just transfer some from our savings."

Pam dropped into the chair. "Which we all but spent restoring Montis. It's been a thin couple of years."

"Well, you never talk to me about our finances," Mark complained.

"Because you never ask!" she retorted. "The few times I bring it up, you say it will all work out."

"And it does, doesn't it?"

Pam ran her hands through her hair in frustration. "Will you help me get ready for our dinner guests?"

"Oh, who's coming?"

She shot Mark a scorching look. "I've had it. I'm going to take a shower to cool down. Jamar and Kai will be here in thirty minutes."

"They're here? That's great. We can talk balloons all through the night. I have a hundred questions to ask them."

෴

The following morning, Jamar and Kai accepted a ride to Lumby. While Kai went directly to the theater to continue work on the hot air balloon basket, which no one else had volunteered to help make,

Jamar used his free hours to explore, wandering through various stores along Main Street and introducing himself to female patrons and cashiers.

At eleven o'clock, Jamar bought a small bouquet of flowers from the florist above Wools and proceeded next door to the Green Chile. Although the CLOSED sign hung on the window, he leisurely walked in, and was delighted to see that the restaurant was empty except for Gabrielle, who was in the kitchen softly singing a Spanish serenade as she cooked.

Jamar stood by the doorway. "You have a beautiful voice."

Gabrielle jumped, startled by the intruder. She turned and saw Jamar smiling suavely.

"What a surprise!" she said, forcing calm into her voice.

He moved forward and swung his arm from behind his back, scaring her further. But when he held out the bouquet, she exhaled.

"For you." He bowed slightly.

"Thank you, Jamar. How kind," she said, placing the flowers in an empty pot. She didn't know how forward Indonesian men were, but she didn't want to stay in the kitchen alone with him. "Why don't you sit and I will pour us some iced tea?" she suggested, leading him back into the dining area.

Gabrielle looked at the clock. The restaurant would open in twenty-five minutes.

"So, what brings you to town today?" she asked, putting the drinks on the table.

Jamar threw his arms wide. "To see you, of course," he said. "I've thought of nothing but your kind invitation since we first met in the theater."

Gabrielle groaned to herself. That was not the answer she wanted. "It's the least we can do," she said. "You and your brother have helped the town so much."

He looked deeply into her eyes. "You alone have made the long journey from my island to Lumby an unforgettable one."

Gabrielle was at a loss for words, but she attributed his brazen admiration to being a foreigner. Perhaps all natives of Coraba behaved so warmly. "And a long journey it was," she said with a polite smile. "So, how is your stay at Saint Cross Abbey?"

"We are now at Montis Inn—closer to town and those whom we want to see," Jamar answered.

"Oh, that's a wonderful inn—very romantic," she said, and then immediately recoiled for using such a suggestive word.

"If you were there," he said softly, and placed his hand on hers.

She jumped away at the same moment the door swung open. Dennis walked in and saw Jamar at the table.

"Did you open early today?" he asked, walking up to his wife and lightly kissing her cheek.

Jamar stared incredulously at the man.

Gabrielle stood and put her arm through her husband's. "Jamar, this is my husband, Dennis Beezer. Dennis, this is Jamar Talin."

Dennis shook his hand warmly. "Yes, I was at the back of the theater when you and your brother introduced all of us to hot air balloons."

Jamar looked at Gabrielle and was crushed. "I'm so sorry," he said. "I believe I misunderstood."

At his sorrowful tone, Dennis looked between the two. "Did something happen?" he asked rather sharply.

Gabrielle patted her husband's arm. "I may have accidentally misled Jamar by not wearing my wedding ring," she admitted.

"But you never do when you're in the kitchen," Dennis said.

"Jamar didn't know that."

Suddenly Dennis understood what was being implied and put his arm tightly around Gabrielle. "Why don't the *three* of us have lunch?" he suggested heartily.

When the resturant help arrived, Gabrielle was able to leave the kitchen and join Jamar and Dennis, who were already deep in discussion about Indonesia.

"It truly is paradise," Jamar said. "Beautiful beaches and more beautiful women, although you appear to have your fair share here," he added as Gabrielle sat down.

"I miss the tropics," Gabrielle said wistfully. "The warm air and fresh fruit year-round. If only we could escape to the beaches in South America a few weeks each winter."

"That would be good for both of us," Dennis agreed.

"Have you ever been to my corner of the world?" Jamar asked.

"No," Gabrielle answered. "Perhaps one day."

"You must visit," he exclaimed. "It's the country of forested islands, brilliant beaches with swaying palm trees. And, of course, there's Bali Hai. We have two hundred million people and several hundred languages and ethnic groups—a result of eighteen thousand islands spread across the Southeast Asian archipelago."

"*Eighteen thousand* islands?" Gabrielle asked.

"The smaller ones are bought and sold regularly," Jamar pointed out. "Actually, they are easy to acquire. Indonesia is very poor, so few natives could ever afford a private island."

Gabrielle's eyes widened.

"Some are beyond description," Jamar continued, sensing their interest, "with waterfalls cascading over mountainous cliffs, crashing into basins of azure blue water."

Even Dennis was following each word. "It sounds splendid."

"It is beyond anyone's wildest dreams," Jamar said. This lunch may not have been a total waste after all, he thought. "And it is just a plane flight away."

"For one vacation in a lifetime," Gabrielle said sensibly.

Jamar shook his head. "Oh, not necessarily. Several Americans have bought small islands and visit us once or twice a year."

"Really?" Gabrielle asked.

"Many of the islands have rattan tiki huts that are built on stilts just offshore. That way you can hear the waves lapping against the beach and you can go swimming out your front door."

"Oh, Dennis, doesn't that sound perfect?" Gabrielle said.

Jamar pushed the topic one step further. "I have some photographs in my room at Montis Inn. They were taken of an island that is now for sale—very small but breathtakingly beautiful. I'm sure it will be bought by a shrewd American who wants to visit heaven before he dies."

Jamar watched Gabrielle as she looked at Dennis. "It has a five-bedroom villa that overlooks the ocean."

"And how much would an island like that cost?" Gabrielle asked.

"Oh, I don't quite remember," he said, leaning back in his chair. "I really had no plans of conducting business on this trip."

"Business?" Dennis asked.

Jamar whipped out his wallet and gave them a card. "I'm a licensed island broker."

"Oh, I see," Dennis said skeptically.

Jamar put his finger to his temple. "But if I recall correctly," he said, looking up at the ceiling, "the island may be on the market for three hundred and eighty-seven thousand U.S. dollars."

Dennis whistled. "Heaven certainly has a high price these days."

"A bargain price if I've ever seen one," Jamar assured him. "And only eight thousand miles away—that's just a good night's sleep on the flight over."

"Can we go look at the photographs?" Gabrielle asked Dennis.

"Sure, honey. Just be sure you bring the rest of Lumby with you. If everyone throws in a hundred dollars each, you can buy your island tomorrow," he said facetiously.

Gabrielle's eyes lit up. "What an incredible idea!"

TWENTY

Friends

Shortly after Kai's first presentation to the town, the theater above the Feed Store was dubbed "Command Central" (or "Chicken Command Central" by those who noticed the growing number of free-range poultry pecking in the area). Within days, it was filled to capacity with supplies and materials for both Lumby's balloon entry and the organization of the festival. Cartons of tickets, printed brochure covers, and posters announcing the festival littered the floor. More boxes, arriving daily, were stacked on the rear benches. Over the movie screen, Jimmy had hung a four-foot-square sign reading ENDEAVOR, the name that Chuck and Mark had proposed for the balloon. Although real progress on the balloon was still being made at a crawl, the activity in Command Central suggested otherwise.

Working diligently in the middle of the disorder was Kai. Although he preferred to be back at Saint Cross, he felt committed to helping the town with its festival. The basket that he had single-handedly woven was close to completion. As he threaded the rattan back and forth over a frame made of vertical rods and aluminum tubes, creating an upper lip of the basket, Kai thought about the two things that were normally on his mind: God and how God wanted him to spend his life.

He was deep in reflection when Hannah Daniels walked up the stairs. Stopping in the doorway, she watched Kai interlace the fiber, knot it, and continue with another thick strip of rattan. As she shifted her feet, the old floorboards creaked.

Kai looked up and smiled. "Mrs. Daniels, come in," he offered, but didn't stop weaving.

"Please call me Hannah," she said as she slipped into a seat in the front row, watching intently. Several questions came to mind as she studied Kai's work. Why did he change the color of rattan, as he had when she first came in? What gave the basket a firm enough structure to lift five hundred pounds? But she remained a silent observer.

Kai continued to work in silence, not wanting to initiate meaningless chat.

Finally, in a soft voice, Hannah said, "Life is easy for Jimmy, and he thinks it's that way for everyone else."

Kai nodded, encouraging her to continue.

"But he may be right. I believe I could sew the envelope, as you call it."

Kai smiled at her. "I'm sure you could."

After having listened to Jimmy's gruffness for the better part of thirty years, she found comfort in Kai's gentle voice.

He continued, "I hear that you are one of the finest in the area with a needle."

Hannah looked down at her hands. "It's my escape," she confessed.

"We all have those in one form or another," Kai said. "Why don't I give you a little more information and show you some of the material?"

He searched about for some paper to draw on, but finding none, he tore off the cardboard cover of the box that the rattan had come in. He took a pencil out of his shirt pocket and drew a hot air balloon.

"A gore is a vertical section of fabric that is normally made of many horizontal panels," he said, pointing to the different sections of the envelope. "Most smaller balloons are sixteen gore, the larger ones are twenty-four gore. The gores are joined together with double locked stitches, French feld seam."

"Yes, I'm familiar with that," Hannah said, a little less timidly. "Why are there so many panels within one gore?"

"Two big reasons: the extra stitching provides ripstop protection and it allows unlimited options for colors and designs."

Hannah raised her brow. "Ripstop?"

"A way to end a tear in the nylon, if one should ever occur," he explained. "Also, this more modular construction allows for easy replacement if one of the panels gets damaged."

Hannah nodded.

Kai looked around for a sample of cloth. "The fabric is a tough one-point-nine-ounce ripstop nylon that has either a silicone or polyurethane coating. What we will be using is polyurethaned. Two challenges you'll have are the sheer volume of the fabric and its weight. When you are done, your envelope will weigh more than two hundred pounds."

Hannah was startled by the words "your envelope" but showed no reaction. "Ah," she said, "but that's surmountable if one or two men are around to assist."

"Exactly," Kai said, pleased that Hannah was not frightened by the size of the project. "At the mouth"—he returned to the diagram, pointing to the bottom of the balloon—"for the first panel, they use flame-resistant material. At the top is a standard flap or 'parachute' opening."

"Made of?"

"A heavier nylon because of its constant use," Kai explained.

"Is that it?" Hannah asked, looking closely at Kai's diagram.

"In concept, yes. The nylon and threads arrived yesterday," he said, pointing to a half dozen large boxes in the corner of the room, "and a commercial sewing machine will be delivered from Wheatley today or tomorrow."

Hannah jerked back, as if someone had pushed her. "Because

Jimmy told you I would cave in and do it?" she asked in a harsh, cold voice.

Kai was surprised by Hannah's fierce reaction. "No, I already talked to someone in Wheatley who agreed to sew it."

Hannah eyed him suspiciously. "But I heard Jimmy tell you that he'd talk me into it."

"He did say that. But I heard your voice even more clearly saying that you weren't going to." Kai had no problem seeing what was right. "This should be a fun experience for every person involved. If not, it's not worth doing."

Hannah's shoulders dropped as she began to relax. She looked around and saw no space free. "Would I sew here?"

"I don't see why not. In fact, I discovered a small room in back that might be perfect. It even has a small cot if you get tired. And the bathroom is through that hall," he said, pointing to the far end of the theater. "It's going to be a lot of work."

Hannah extended her hand to Kai. "I'll begin tomorrow morning," she said, shaking on the deal.

"Only if you want to do it," Kai said.

Hannah raised her head high. "I do."

"Then that would be wonderful," he said. "And several of us will be here to help in any way we can."

"All I need is the sewing machine," she replied, and walked out a happier woman, closing the door behind her.

After she left, Kai continued to weave the basket. Just a few more inches, he thought. In his peripheral vision he saw the door swing open again. Thinking it was Hannah, he didn't look up. "Well, that was fast. Did you think of another question?"

"Not that I know of."

The voice was different: succinct and self-confident. Kai raised his head and saw a tall attractive woman with fine blond hair. She looked as surprised as he felt.

"I'm sorry for interrupting," she said. "I didn't know anyone was up here. I just came to get some tickets for the library auction."

Kai raised his brows in confusion. "They're auctioning off the library?"

She laughed, thinking how nice he was to offer to help build the hot air balloon. "Not exactly, but with this town, one can never be too certain. I'm Caroline Ross."

"Hi," he said, smiling. "Lumby does appear to be unique."

"That's an understatement," she concurred. "You know, everyone really appreciated the presentation you gave."

"It was a pleasure," he said, and returned to his work.

Caroline was intrigued by the quiet Indonesian. Unlike most men, he didn't gape at her good looks. In fact, he didn't seem to have noticed them. She took a few steps closer to watch him skillfully intertwine raw materials with metal.

"I thought someone in town was going to make the basket," she commented.

Kai sighed. "I did too, but there were no volunteers."

"I'm sorry for that," she said with feeling. "You would probably prefer to be with the brothers at Saint Cross than alone in the attic of a feed store."

His face lit up with a beatific smile. "Being alone doesn't bother me at all. In fact, the silence is a nice change from the commotion at the monastery. However, yes," Kai said seriously, "I would prefer to be at the abbey continuing my studies."

Caroline carefully examined his face as he concentrated on his work. His high cheekbones were as chiseled as she had remembered. "Are you going to be a monk?"

His eyes, a honey brown that appeared lighter against his dark skin, sparkled. "Something like that, yes. Actually, a priest."

"Ah," was all Caroline could find to say.

"And what do you do, Caroline Ross?"

She sat in one of the chairs in the front row. "I oversee my grandmother's foundation."

Kai wrestled with one corner of the basket, tugging it into a tighter curve, even as he listened intently. "I don't fully understand."

"Shortly before my grandmother passed away last summer," Caroline explained, "she moved a large part of her estate into a philanthropic foundation—an organization that is now responsible for identifying and distributing charitable gifts and grants."

"To the people of Lumby?"

Caroline nodded. "To the town, certainly. But we do work all across the Northwest."

Kai was intrigued by the idea. "That sounds honorable."

Caroline gave him a funny look. "I never thought about it in those terms, but I suppose it is. I feel I am continuing Charlotte's legacy as well as being involved with many good causes." She paused. "It's very rewarding."

"Are any religious?"

"Hmm," she said. "I never analyzed the foundation gifts with that kind of secular-nonsecular separation," she answered, and then mentally ran through last year's projects. "Yes, we have made several donations to various churches, but to no one denomination. I would say that our projects are more community-based than—" She searched for the right word and then quickly gave up, "God-based."

Kai smiled. "I'm sure He won't hold that against you."

"Oh, believe me, He has so many better reasons to strike me with a bolt of lightning," Caroline admitted, blushing.

"And you? Are you religious?" Kai asked in the same lighthearted tone.

Caroline tapped her hands on her knees. "Brother Matthew endearingly calls me an enlightened agnostic."

"Enlightened?"

"Yes," Caroline said, realizing the term might have several meanings to an Indonesian. "I've wondered about that myself. Next time I see him, I'll be sure to ask him exactly what he means."

Kai went back to work and Caroline watched him in companionable silence. She was relieved he didn't feel the need to impress her. Everything he required was within. Just as she was going to ask him about the island of Coraba, a new voice broke the quiet.

"Isn't this cozy?" Jamar said, appearing at the doorway.

Caroline jumped but Kai was used to his brother's voice.

"You should knock, Jamar. You scared the daylights out of Caroline."

She rose to her feet. "I need to find those tickets," she said, and went into the back room.

Jamar swaggered over to Kai. "Seems I can't leave you alone for a moment," he teased.

Kai made a face. "You know me better than that."

"So, she's free game?"

"Leave her alone. She's too nice for you," Kai said.

Yet as Caroline came back into the theater, Jamar moved toward her. "I'm sure we haven't met," he said, extending his hand. "I would have remembered such a beautiful woman."

Caroline tried not to roll her eyes. The sense of peacefulness was lost.

"I'm Jamar, Kai's brother."

"I assumed," she said politely. "I'm Caroline Ross. It's very nice to meet you, but I really do need to run."

Jamar held her hand for one second too long, forcing Caroline to deliberately pull away.

"Kai," she said, "would you come downstairs and show me which rope you were talking about?"

At a loss as to what Caroline was talking about, he nevertheless followed her into the stairway.

Once out of earshot, she told Kai, "I want to hear about Coraba. Would you like to have dinner so we can talk?" She didn't want to give him the opportunity to say no, so she quickly continued, "I think you would love the Green Chile. Perhaps tomorrow evening at six?"

Kai smiled, the corners of his eyes wrinkling. "I look forward to it. I'll see you there."

She headed downstairs but Kai didn't move until she reached the bottom. Before she left, she turned to look back up at him. Their eyes made contact, and they both smiled.

Returning inside, Kai ignored Jamar and began putting away his materials and cleaning up his work area. He began humming a tune from his homeland. All of a sudden he felt very lighthearted.

"Apparently, I should leave you alone more often," Jamar remarked dryly.

Kai just turned his back to finish his work.

When Kai and Jamar left the Feed Store soon after, they both noticed Jimmy D standing outside his tavern directly across the street. He had been talking to patrons for the better part of an hour and had watched the comings and goings in the theater. He waved the brothers over.

"Can I buy you two a cold beer?" Jimmy offered, putting his arm around Jamar's shoulder.

"No. Unfortunately, we need to get back to Montis Inn," Kai answered before Jamar could accept the invitation.

"How is it going in there?" Jimmy asked, looking up at the theater.

"The basket will be done tomorrow, and hopefully it will only take a few days to sew the envelope."

"Oh, that's just great," Jimmy said, and then lowered his voice. "I couldn't help but notice that Caroline Ross was up there."

Kai wasn't sure how to respond, so he said nothing.

Jimmy raised his eyebrows. "I trust everything is all right. You know, she's one of our town's founding granddaughters and carries a lot of influence with most folks."

"She was telling me about the philanthropic work done by her foundation," Kai explained, although it sounded more like a justification for her visit. "It's admirable."

"She's great," Jimmy said. "Beautiful and intelligent. Will make a wonderful wife for some lucky man someday."

"I'm sure she will," Kai said. "We really need to be off, so have a good evening."

As they began to walk away, Jimmy grabbed Kai's arm and pulled him aside. "Also," he said in a softer voice, "it seems you'll have to hire someone to make the envelope. I don't think Hannah will do it."

Kai hid his surprise. "Have you talked to her today?"

"No, I'm in the proverbial doghouse," Jimmy said sheepishly. "She hasn't spoken to me for a few days and the situation is going from bad to worse, if you know what I mean."

"I'll be sure the envelope is ready on time," Kai promised, without offering any details.

TWENTY-ONE

Interests

As Mark leaned over the bed and placed a breakfast tray in front of his wife, he kissed her tenderly on the lips. "Good morning. I made pancakes just because I love you."

Pam rubbed her eyes and sat up, stacking pillows behind her. "I love you too, but it's six in the morning. What are you doing up so early?"

"I have a meeting over in Rocky Mount in an hour," Mark said. "And then I'll be with Chuck most of the day talking about the heater system."

"For Montis?" Pam asked, still in a sleepy daze.

"No, for the *Endeavor*," he replied as he buttoned his shirt.

"Oh, is that the name everyone chose for the balloon?" Pam asked. She saw Mark had included the day's paper on the tray and she put on her reading glasses. "I like it."

Mark sat at the end of the bed and slipped on his shoes. "So, what are you doing today?" he asked.

She slinked down between the sheets. "The fish pond," she mumbled.

"How is that going?" he queried brightly. "You asked me to stay away, and I have, but I'm getting really eager for the great unveiling."

"I am too," Pam said with forced enthusiasm. "Should be any day now."

"I'm really proud of you, honey. That's no small feat. It's one hell of a machine to maneuver."

"It is indeed," she said with a forced smile. "Will you be home for dinner tonight?" she asked, wanting to change the subject.

"It all depends on how much Chuck wants to get accomplished, but I'll call you," he answered and leaned over to kiss her again. "Be careful out there."

"You too. They haven't repaired the guardrail at Priest's Pass yet," she reminded him, "so drive slowly. You don't want to end up like William Beezer, dead from a fatal crash on that awful hairpin turn."

After Pam heard the front door close, she set the breakfast tray aside to lie down again. She removed her glasses and closed her eyes. Very few times in her life had Pam come up against an obstacle that she couldn't readily understand and easily overcome. She had a pragmatic, almost impersonal objectivity to many of life's tasks and believed that mind over matter accounted for most successful outcomes.

But this pond had been, to date, a miserable, expensive failure. To make matters worse, she had been unable to share her self-made fiasco with Mark. *Why?* she asked herself for the hundredth time. Mark always offered unconditional support and was the last to speak a critical word. He was never judgmental. So, why couldn't she tell him that she'd given it her all and it wasn't good enough? For that reason exactly, she thought; it wasn't good enough.

Not wanting to think about it anymore, she picked up *The Lumby Lines.*

The Lumby Lines

What's News Around Town

BY SCOTT STEVENS   May 6

A busy week in our small town of Lumby.

The average number of calls to Lumby Funeral Home has skyrocketed from three a week to over five hundred a day. No, the black plague has not descended on our village. Instead, a misprinted area code in *Northwest Living* has anyone interested in singles ballroom dancing calling the number for eternal rest. The response has been so tremendous that the funeral home is now entertaining the idea of renting out their parlor to Fred Astaire types. "It's a perfect place," the owner says. "No one here will complain about the noise."

Howard, the town's wayward moose, has roamed from his usual stomping grounds at Priest's Pass to the playgrounds at Lumby Elementary School. The six-foot-at-the-withers moose has repeatedly attacked the swing set with his antlers and become entangled in the chains. On two occasions within the last week, Doc Campbell was called in for intervention. The town council will be voting on Howard's future this week. All interested residents should attend. Also, donations are being requested to replace damaged playground equipment.

To pay fines for various infractions and indiscretions issued to Jeremiah Abrams and his mare Isabella by a certain unnamed councilman, last Thursday Isabella pulled Jeremiah and their financial restitution to city hall in her old wagon. With the assistance of several residents, including this reporter, Jeremiah deposited close to ten thousand pennies on the counter. Unfortunately, the very same councilman was present to deny the payment, due to its "small denomination." Since Jeremiah had no intention of asking poor Isabella to pull the payload home, the pennies remain piled in the lobby.

Mike McNear quickly eliminated the well-established vole population on his farm when he traded his favorite swine and one feeding trough for four arctic ermines previously owned by Brian Beezer. Thinking the ermines would substitute for ferrets, Mike released the wild animals in his back field. After three days, all rodents were eradicated. Unfortunately, two days later, most of his chickens were as well. The ermines are still loose somewhere on his property.

Having fought the urge to procrastinate all morning, an hour later Pam was dressed and out the door. Walking behind the kitchen, she saw her tractor parked on dry land close to the hole that she had begun to excavate, thanks to it being towed out by Wheatley Farm Equipment. The small pond, now absent one tractor and filled to the grass line with crystal-clear water, looked very inviting.

"But too small," she said, and headed over to the tractor. Standing next to the front loader, she began talking to the Kubota. "You know, I never liked orange, but you're now mine and your name is Bertha." Pam climbed up to the driver's seat and seamlessly ran through the steps to start the engine. "And we *will* work together, like it or not," she shouted over the engine noise.

Before moving forward, though, Pam carefully studied the ground, noting the wet spots, the small runoff from the pond, the trees and the slop. She considered her options and then decided where she was going to dig—three feet from the existing pond. That would be fairly dry clay. Only after she finished excavating the final footprint of the pond would she remove the land barricade between the two holes, thus allowing water to fill in the entire cavity. That was a sensible plan.

With the tractor well positioned, Pam took hold of the control levers of the backhoe, extended the arm, and dropped the mouth of the bucket until it cut into the soft ground. Manipulating both handles, she dug a long, wide swath across the grass, and swung the bucket around to pile the dirt to one side. The next cut was the same distance away but deeper by another two feet, forcing the bucket to claw out the ground. As she pulled the bucket inward, the whole tractor jerked and the arm of the backhoe shuddered—it had hit an immovable object. Thinking it could be a large rock, Pam extracted the bucket, dropped it again, and began the scoop with greater speed and force.

Clank. The teeth hit something and the tractor rocked.

"Now what?" she asked in frustration.

Pam took a deep breath. *Obstacles are surmountable,* she repeated to herself several times. With the backhoe, she began to scrape the dirt off the top of the object. The sound of the metal scraping against stone was as unnerving as nails on a blackboard. She then dug to the right and left, and front and back. To Pam's best guess, the object was about two feet square and heavy enough not to be nudged, even by the power of Bertha.

Once Pam cleared away as much of the dirt as she could, she jumped off and stepped down into the hole. With gloved hands she rubbed away the remaining soil.

How odd, she thought, staring down at a perfectly chiseled stone block. Her eyes widened. Maybe this was an old spiritual stone used by the brothers a century ago. Perhaps the monks of Montis Abbey found it in the woods and dragged it to this very spot. Perhaps this was the stone seat on which they meditated for hours on end. All of those possibilities appealed to Pam so much that the drudgery of excavating quickly became a sacred mission.

꧁

It was slightly after eight in the morning when Hannah left her home on Mineral Street—too early for Jimmy to be awake, which was what she wanted. Main Street was just stirring with merchants cranking out the colorful awnings and placing sales signs on the sidewalks. Hannah loved the small town, but she didn't like her life in it.

Walking through the Feed Store, she murmured hello to people she had known since childhood. For Hannah, each step leading up to the theater became a small declaration of independence. Each promised more distance between her and her mundane existence at home.

As she opened the door, she expected to see Kai working on the final details of the basket. But the room was dark and the theater quiet. More boxes had arrived, taking up the little free floor space that was left.

Hannah paused, not knowing exactly what to do. Would Kai be coming that day? If not, could she begin on her own? Battling her insecurities, Hannah switched on the lights and began looking through the boxes for the nylon that she would be using for the envelope. She was kneeling on all fours when someone pounded on the door. She leapt to her feet, her heart caught in her throat.

"You Kai?" asked a huge man in a filthy T-shirt.

Her eyes wide, Hannah was unsure what to say.

"Your name Kai Talin?" the man repeated.

Hannah shook her head. "No," she said softly.

"Well, we have a machine for him. You know where he wants it?"

Hannah took a small step forward. "A sewing machine?"

"Guess so," the man said, looking at the paper. "It says here a double needle lockstitch machine. Where you want it?"

Hannah dug her nails into her palms. "This way," she said, and led him to the back room. "Here, please."

"No problem, ma'am." Tucking the papers under his armpit, he yelled down to one of his coworkers, "We need more straps, Leo."

As the men struggled up the narrow staircase, jockeying the oversized sewing machine base through the door frame, Hannah turned her attention to the large boxes marked "Nylon." She systematically opened each, and after confirming the contents against the invoice, she arranged neat piles by size and material. By the time the men had positioned the sewing equipment against the wall, Hannah had stacked the various threads needed for stitching the envelope and was breaking down the empty boxes to free up floor space.

"Wow," Kai said when he entered the room an hour later. Order had replaced the utter chaos of the day before. "I'm amazed by what you've done."

Hannah surveyed the room, feeling proud of her small accomplishment. "I think I'm ready to begin now."

"And the machine?"

"It's in the back room," she said. "It's threaded and I've run some stitches on some scrap pieces of nylon the manufacturer included in the boxes."

"Good for you," Kai said, pleased by her initiative.

"It looks like there is only one color, red?" she asked.

Kai began drawing an outline of an envelope with twelve vertical gores. He shaded in every other one. "I think Jimmy and Mark Walker selected the simplest pattern and one solid color. So your only concern will be the order of the panels you sew for each gore."

Hannah studied Kai's diagram. "Sounds easy enough," she said. "But . . ." She hesitated.

Kai waited, encouraging her to say what was on her mind. "What is it?"

"Doesn't some value lie in the esthetic beauty of the more intricate patterns—the spirals and checkboxes?" she asked.

Kai smiled. "Yes, some of the multicolor balloons are breathtaking, but we thought it best to keep it simple this first time."

"All right," she said. "Let me get to work."

"Hannah," he called to her before she disappeared into the back room, "it's none of my business, but does Jimmy know you're here?"

"He will soon enough," she retorted, then marched into her small sewing sanctuary.

⊷

On the second floor of the Lumby Library, seated at a richly stained and heavily varnished oak table, Chuck Bryson scanned the half dozen open books that were in front of him, and scribbled additional numbers on his yellow notepad. He looked up at a group of people walking up the stairs, making their way to the conference room one floor up, but then returned his focus to the task at hand.

"Hmm," Chuck uttered as he chewed on the pencil eraser.

He pulled one of the books toward him and eagerly flipped through the index, running his finger along the entries. Finding his page, he compared the authors' notes with his own calculations.

"I'm sorry I'm late," Mark said, walking up and shaking Chuck's hand.

"Not to worry," Chuck said, pulling up a chair for his friend.

"You sound just like Brother Matthew when you say that," Mark commented.

Chuck laughed. "No surprise. He and I go back further than I remember. Anyway, I have pulled a few notes together for you." He handed Mark the pad of paper.

Mark looked at the scribbles and his eyes instantly blurred. Squinting made it no better—he still saw a page full of nothing but lines and numbers.

"They're fairly self-explanatory," Chuck added.

Mark continued to stare at Chuck's work. One formula was so long that it filled the width of the entire page, including the margins.

"Do you have any questions?" Chuck asked.

That question was one of the funniest things Mark had heard in a long time. He started to laugh uproariously.

"Chuck, you could be showing me your next formula for insect repellent. I have no idea what this means."

"Nothing but first-year physics," Chuck said, defending the simplicity of his formulas.

"If I took physics, I guarantee you it was so long ago I don't even remember how to spell the word."

"My mistake," Chuck said with a smile, taking back the pad. "These are just rough figures, probably all wrong. So, let's get down to it, shall we?"

Chuck tore off the top page and started fresh by drawing a balloon. His voice took on the timbre of the professor he had once been. "Flight is possible in one of two ways: aerodynamically, which uses thrust and forward speed to create lift, like an airplane. The other is aerostatically, which uses heated air or gases to produce lift. The overriding physics of ballooning is that hot air has less mass—or weight—than cool air."

"I didn't know air weighed anything," Mark said.

"In fact, it does. A cubic foot of cold air weighs about twenty-eight grams. Increasing that to one hundred degrees, the same amount of air weighs twenty-one grams, or seven grams less. So, each cubic foot of air in a balloon can lift seven grams of weight," Chuck explained while writing the numbers and drawing arrows on the page.

"Got it," Mark said, studying the diagram.

"So," Chuck continued, "to lift a thousand pounds, or about a half million grams, you would need about seventy thousand cubic feet of hot air, which is the size of a small two- or three-man balloon."

"So that's why the balloon sizes are in cubic feet," Mark surmised.

"Correct!" Chuck said. "The question then becomes, how does one heat such a large volume of confined air. That's where your burners come in. A single-blast valve burner can produce about ten million BTUs at one hundred pounds per square inch, which is about sixty degrees, and those numbers go up to thirteen million BTUs at one hundred and twenty-five PSI, at seventy degrees. Finally, a little under sixteen million BTUs at one hundred forty PSI, eighty degrees. With double-blast valves, you can increase the burner output by approximately fifty percent."

"What about triple valves?" Mark asked.

Chuck shook his head. "You don't want to go there."

An attractive older woman walked up to their table. "Will you two be joining us?" It was Joan Stokes of Main Street Realty.

"I'm not quite sure what you're talking about, Joan," Mark said.

"The meeting upstairs with Jamar about the island near Coraba," Joan answered.

Chuck scratched his head. "I've been away for a few weeks. Where's Coraba?"

"Indonesia, where Kai and Jamar are from," she explained in her sweet voice. "Jamar is an island broker and it's come to our attention that a small island just came on the market."

"The quintessential example of 'location, location'?" Mark grinned.

When Joan Stokes smiled, her eyes sparkled. "I would say so."

"And someone from Lumby is buying an island?" Chuck asked.

"Well, not yet, but there are about twenty folks in town who are considering pooling their money and going into the venture together."

"Wow," Mark said, "what a great idea."

"The investment would be quite small. I'm surprised Pam hasn't mentioned it. She looked at various financing alternatives for us. In fact, I have her recommendation right here," she said, patting her leather portfolio. "Jamar is already upstairs answering questions."

"And the island is nice?" Chuck asked.

"Paradise," Joan said with a Realtor's gusto. "White beaches, palm trees, even a small mountain on the north side. I'm going to Bali for vacation next week and have offered to take a boat over to see it." She added shrewdly, "I can also talk with their attorneys to ensure everything is on the up-and-up."

Chuck looked at Mark. "I believe an opportunity awaits us. Could we continue this after the Coraba meeting?"

"Absolutely, but I'm going to stay here and look at some of these books," Mark said, pulling the encyclopedia closer. "I'm curious about a quad booster."

Chuck rolled his eyes. "Think smaller," he warned.

ᴗ෨

It was seven in the evening before the group in the library disbanded. Joan Stokes, Russell Harris, and Jamar Talin were the last to leave. Had Jamar looked across the street once he walked down the library stairs, he would have seen Kai and Caroline sitting at one of the outside tables at the Green Chile, engrossed in conversation. But he didn't, because he was trying to read a contract that Russell had unexpectedly passed to him at the close of the meeting.

"I think most of my earlier decisions were influenced by Charlotte," Caroline said, responding to Kai's question about her grandmother. She looked down and twirled her wineglass. "My mother died of cancer when I was twelve, and my father spent most of his time at the office or in the orchards. So Charlotte stepped in and became role model, friend, and disciplinarian. I lived with her during the summer months when Dad was busiest."

"I hear so many compliments about her," Kai said.

"Some thought she was a wealthy eccentric, but she really was the salt of the earth—totally genuine, very much like you," she said softly. "I still miss her every day."

"Did you go away to college?" Kai asked.

"I did, again with Charlotte's persuasion. I went to an all-women's college in Massachusetts called Mount Holyoke."

"But you came back to Lumby?"

"After graduate school. Charlotte had done so much for me, I wanted to help her as much as possible. Between the two husbands that she had, I lived with her for about a year after she had a bad fall, but as soon as she was fully recovered, she lovingly kicked me out."

"It's nice to hear you laugh," Kai said, smiling at her.

"You've brought out a lot of fond memories," she said, touching his hand. "So, do you miss your family?"

Kai took a sip of water and thought for a moment. "My upbringing was so different from yours. Instead of one close family, I was part of the island village. Like all children on Coraba, I was really raised by the town elders, who took care of us as much as my own mother did. My father would go out on fishing trips for several months at a time and then be at home for four weeks before leaving again."

"Does he still fish?"

"Yes, but he stays in the harbor now and lets the younger generation battle the hooks and lines." Kai's eyes danced when he laughed. "On his last trip out, he hooked a large tuna that dragged him into the sea."

"Really?"

"He had to swim for hours to get back to the boat."

Caroline tilted her head and gave Kai an assessing look. "Your parents must be very proud of you, and the townspeople very appreciative."

Kai grimaced at the compliment as guilt washed over him. The town wouldn't appreciate him thinking how attractive Caroline looked that night. She was wearing a simple blue cotton dress with her hair pulled back. And their conversation was so relaxed and honest. "I think it's always hard to live up to a parent's expectation, let alone a town's."

Caroline looked into his eyes. "But aren't you doing just that at Saint Cross?"

He smiled weakly. "Yes, but I'm not at the abbey. I'm having a wonderful dinner with you."

"That's just one night. They would understand," she said, trying to ease his concern. "Are you looking forward to returning home?"

Kai stared at Caroline until her heart began to race. "There's no simple answer. But I do want to return to Saint Cross."

"What is it about monastic life that attracts you so?"

"I'm not as confused there." He laughed. "But really, I love the peace of the abbey and I deeply respect the monks. The monastery gives me a time and place to go look beyond my personal desires to something greater." He paused to give the question more thought. "To put God first, I suppose."

"And that is what is most important to you?" Caroline asked

before she could stop herself. She needed to hear the words, to end all hope that he had personal feelings for her, as she did for him.

He tilted his head. "I thought it was, but now I'm not sure."

"I know this sounds strange, but I've never felt like this before, as if we have known each other forever. I feel you can look into my eyes and know exactly what I'm thinking," Caroline whispered.

Kai leaned toward her. "I wish I could explain how I feel. But I'm not as fluent with words as my brother, and perhaps I see everything with far more complexity, which makes it more difficult to sort through." Kai paused, taking hold of Caroline's hand.

Sensing people staring at them, Caroline asked, "Do you want to go for a walk?"

"I would love to," he said.

After Caroline paid the bill, Kai stood and held Caroline's seat out for her. "Thank you for dinner. I'm sorry I was unable to take you out, but our village provided a very little stipend, thinking that we would be given all we needed at Saint Cross."

"And it sounds like you have been," Caroline said as they stepped away from the table.

The evening sky was clear and the air fresh. The streetlights gave a warm glow to downtown Lumby.

"Is there anything else you wanted to do with your life?" Kai asked as they strolled in front of Wools.

Caroline slipped her hand under Kai's arm. "Not really. My grandmother prepared me to lead her foundation and I always assumed she knew best. I still think she was right. And you?"

"When I was much younger, I thought I would enjoy teaching."

"Really?" Caroline said in surprise.

"Is it so strange an idea?" Kai asked. "I loved geography when I was a boy, perhaps because we lived on an island, and I wanted to explore the rest of world, which seemed so different and so far away."

Caroline chuckled. "I felt the exact same way right here in Lumby."

By the time they reached Hunts Mill Road and turned toward the fairgrounds, they were lost in discussion. The more they conversed, the stronger they felt a bond grow between them, an intimate connection that revealed how truly similar they were even though they came from very different cultures. Losing all sense of time, Caroline and Kai sauntered through the fairgrounds and along the roads on the north side of town. When they finally made their way back to Main Street, the lights were out in the Green Chile and all of the stores had long since closed. It was an evening neither of them would ever forget.

TWENTY-TWO

Trash

The second floor of Saint Cross Abbey housed many of the private sleeping quarters for the monks, small, modestly furnished cells with attached bathrooms. At the end of the long corridor, behind a heavy oak door that remained closed throughout the day, was the brothers' informal sitting room, with several sofas and large upholstered chairs. Many of the monks retreated to its comfort at the end of the day when chores and vespers were done. It held one of the few luxuries at the monastery: a color television set.

Most evenings the monks watched a news channel until nine and then turned to a drama or comedy chosen by majority preference. Frequently, a family member or friend would mail a movie to them, which they watched on their DVD player. After an hour of entertainment, they turned the TV off and retired to their rooms for prayer and sleep. Only on rare occasions, such as when recovering from injury or illness, would a monk relax in the common room during the day, and even then it would be only for a short time.

So, on that Tuesday, it was unusual that the door was cracked open and voices could be heard coming from that end of the corridor.

Brother John replaced the three books he had brought to the second-floor library and stopped by the door, trying to recognize the voices.

"Well, that sucks," a man said in a loud tone.

Brother John bolted down the hall and threw open the door, stunned by what he saw. A man was sitting on the sofa with his dirty bare feet up on the table, a beer can in one hand and the television's remote control in the other. Another man was standing by the TV turning the knobs, and a woman was curled in the chair closest to the fireplace.

Brother John was furious. "What the hell are you doing in here?"

"Cool," the woman said with a California Valley accent. "The monk swears."

John was so disarmed by the invasion of their personal space and property that he could only repeat the same question. "What are you doing here?"

"Trying to get MTV, but your channels suck," the man on the sofa said.

"Who gave you permission?" John said, unable to control his anger.

"We don't need permission," the man replied arrogantly. "This is a house of worship."

John was repulsed. This was the last straw of so many that had been thrown their way. "This is the monks' private sitting room and you are not invited in here."

"We'll leave when our show is over," the woman said.

"No," Brother John barked. "You will leave now!" He grabbed the arm of the man on the sofa and pulled him to his feet.

"Hey, get your hands off me."

"Get out now!" John yelled in his face.

"Fine, we're out of here," the woman said, joining her friends at the door. "This place is a dump anyway."

John stared at them until they disappeared down the stairs leading to the first floor. Shaken, he sat down and rested his head in his hands.

Matthew ran into the room. "I heard yelling. Are you all right?" he asked.

MTV was still blaring from the television. Matthew quickly clicked it off.

"Thank you," John said weakly.

Matthew looked around the room and saw magazines thrown on the floor and beer cans on the table. "What happened?"

"Some of the seekers got together, but apparently we weren't invited to the party," John said, trying to make light of the encounter. But his voice still cracked.

"They were in here?"

"Three of them, yes. I forced them to go in a very inhospitable way."

Matthew had seen how the stress of the seekers' intrusions had strained the community, but now he realized how deeply it had disturbed his close friend. "I'm sorry."

"I am too. I should have handled it much more benevolently."

"Seeing how they are, I doubt that very seriously," Matthew replied.

⁖

Mackenzie and Terry McGuire, with Brian Beezer in tow, returned to Franklin in hopes of completing several small jobs at Saint Cross Abbey that had been delayed because the crowds had made their work impossible. Arriving well after breakfast, they realized the situation had only worsened in their absence. The makeshift gate had been extended several feet higher and ran along the entire front of the monastery's grounds. The lawn resembled a large parking lot with tents, recreational vehicles, and mobs of people assembled in large clusters. Litter floated on the pond. As they drove past, the seekers stared at them.

After unpacking their tools, the three began where they had left off the prior week, replacing the snow-rotted horizontal trim along the bottom of the church walls. Brian was responsible for removing the rotted wood, Mac for measuring and cutting, and Terry for hammering the new trim in place.

Mac was standing by the table saw when Brother Matthew crossed the drive to join them.

"Good morning," she said, noticing how tired Matthew looked.

He rubbed his neck. "Truthfully, I don't know how long we can put up with this mob scene. But I appreciate you coming back."

"We'll give it another try," Mac said.

Matthew put on a pair of heavy gardening gloves. "Do you mind if I join you and do some long-overdue weeding in the beds?" he asked. "I promise to stay well out of your way."

"If you can stand the sound of the saw," she said.

"From what we have had to listen to day and night, the saw would be a delight."

Brian watched as Matthew, who wore faded jeans and a denim shirt, walked gently into the flower beds along the foundation and began pulling weeds. Brian looked where he himself had been working and noticed for the first time that he had stepped on some of the smaller plants.

"Sorry," he said.

Matthew waved the clump of weeds in his hand. "Small things tend to be overlooked."

Brian tried to straighten several flowers that had been crushed.

"Not to worry," Matthew said, appreciating the gesture. "They'll grow back."

As Matthew weeded, he kept Brian in the corner of his eye. It was obvious that although Brian was impatient with the tools he used, he was trying his best.

After an hour, Matthew sat on a large rock to take a break. Brian was several yards away, still removing trim boards.

"Do you enjoy the work?" Matthew asked casually.

For a moment, Brian was unsure the monk was talking to him. "Me?"

"Yes, you," Matthew said.

"Sure," he answered automatically, as he would with any adult in order to avoid conversation. Then he looked at Matthew again and thought twice. He shouldn't lie to a monk. "Not really," he said. "I'm not good at carpentry, so it takes longer than it should, which frustrates all of us."

"No one can excel in everything," Matthew pointed out.

"No, we can't."

"It would be an ideal world if we all could always do what we were best at," Matthew thought out load.

That struck Brian as a very good idea. "You must be an awfully good monk if you head up this place."

Matthew laughed deeply. "Just between us, I doubt that seriously, but I try, which I hope counts for something. And what are you good at?"

Brian stood up from kneeling and his eyes widened. "Deals," he said, smiling.

Brother Matthew tilted his head. "Deals? I don't understand."

Brian wasn't sure he should be talking to a monk about it, but he decided to plunge ahead. "Figuring out the deal or how to make something better. Or looking at a problem and knowing how to fix it or improve upon it to make a profit. I've been working on this barter project, leveraging items to be sold."

"In Lumby?"

"Yeah, but mostly on the Internet. I started with a bicycle tire a month ago, and after nine trades, a couple days ago, I ended up with a wooden kayak. Now someone's offered a purebred golden retriever puppy for the kayak, and they're worth four hundred dollars. Is that cool or what?"

"Very," Matthew said. "But where does it end?"

Brian's energy stalled for a second. He just stared at Matthew as if he were being spoken to in a different language.

"To what purpose is all of your trading?" Matthew added.

Brian struggled for an answer; he had never thought about the question. "I don't know. I guess the deal is the purpose."

"Journeys are always good, but it can offer more when one has a destination in mind, a purpose greater than oneself," Matthew offered. "So, it's the business you like?"

"The deal and solving business problems. One of my teachers called it process engineering—breaking something down into parts so that it can be improved upon."

Several seekers were yelling at each other, their voices echoing across the monastery grounds.

Matthew rolled his eyes. "And how would you improve upon our predicament?"

Brian stood up. "You want them gone?"

"Well, preferably not shot," Matthew joked. "But most of them are uninvited and are causing havoc in our community. We don't have the people or the money to support so many."

"Do you let in anyone who comes?"

Matthew looked over at the guesthouse. "Yes. Right now there are about thirty in the guesthouse, half on bunk beds and half sleeping on cots. We estimate another one hundred are camping on our property, and possibly the same number are staying elsewhere in town. Most of the townsfolk are renting out rooms and making an attractive profit."

"And how much do you charge?" Brian asked.

Matthew looked at him in surprise. "We don't. We ask for a donation of twenty dollars a day for lodging and meals or ten dollars a day just for meals."

Brian's eyes widened. "You're feeding and housing all of these people for twenty dollars a day?"

"Yes," Matthew answered. "It's certainly not fancy. We bring out tureens of food and drink three times a day. Some have their own dishware, but mostly we have reverted to paper plates and plastic utensils."

"And all are making donations?" Brian pressed.

Matthew grimaced. "Not very many, actually. In fact, we only collect about two hundred dollars a day."

"From the hundreds that you serve?" the teenager confirmed.

"Yes."

Brian shook his head. "What a rip," he said, but then noticed the monk's expression. "Sorry, but it's a simple problem to solve. Beginning tomorrow, tell them that effective immediately there will be a charge, not an optional donation, of thirty dollars for three meals and an additional thirty dollars per night for lodging."

Matthew leaned back as if he had been pushed. "But, Brian, one of our tenets is generosity," he said.

"Yeah," he said, "and your generosity should go to those who truly need it, not to a bunch of slackers. Believe me, I know something about this. But I can guarantee you that this will separate the—" He searched for the expression.

"Wheat from the chaff?" Matthew offered.

"Right. The freeloaders who just want cheap meals will leave and the religious guys who are meant to be here will stay. If they can't afford it, they'll let you know. Also, I think you guys should make church services mandatory," Brian said, then quickly refined his suggestion. "But not for us, of course."

Matthew chuckled. "Of course."

"And have them do the morning and evening things."

"Matins and vespers," Matthew clarified. "Matins are at six in the morning. It appears most stay up carousing until quite late."

Brian got excited, thinking through the solution. "But that's just it. If they really have a religious calling, they won't object. Basically, you're shutting down their party," he said, brushing his hands together.

Matthew considered the implications of the boy's radical recommendations. "I don't know if we can fit everyone into our church."

"You can always hold the services outside—that would be pretty cool. But if I'm right, I think you'll be amazed how few visitors there will be after tomorrow evening."

Matthew crossed his hands over his chest and was silent for a long moment. He clearly saw how the seekers were draining the energy of the abbey and felt a heavy burden to offer the correct solution to the other brothers. He thought through his next steps. "Will you be here later today?"

"I think so, but it's Mac's call."

"I would like you to join us for a community meeting so you can make your recommendations to the other brothers."

Brian backed up, raising his arms. "Oh, I don't think that's a good idea."

"Why not?" Matthew asked. "They're your suggestions."

"Yeah, and I could be totally wrong."

"At some point in your life, Brian, you need to stand tall and back up your ideas with conviction. For what it's worth, I think the monks will listen to your every word."

TWENTY-THREE

Missing

Caroline Ross sat impatiently in her attorney's office, located in the basement of the Chatham Press building. She looked out the high, narrow window and saw only the shoes and legs of pedestrians. Occasionally, a small dog would walk by and look down at her.

"I think we're all set, Caroline," Russell said as he reentered his office after making several copies of the contract. "The town agrees to sell the property to you for the cumulative back taxes and penalties on both the building and the land, which I think they have assessed fairly."

"As undeveloped land?" Caroline asked.

"For ninety-six acres, yes. The remaining acreage, main building, and the outbuilding were collectively assessed on a sliding scale starting at four hundred and fifty thousand in the early 1960s and ending with one hundred and twenty thousand as an abandoned property today."

"So the path is now clear to move forward with the Ross Art Center?" Caroline asked.

Russell, ever the realist, replied, "The first hurdle is behind you. The next will be to clear the title and deed."

Caroline frowned at this latest obstacle. "Isn't Lumby going to convey a clean title?"

"As far as they are concerned, yes. But the disputed real estate transactions that took place forty years ago left a trail of claims—"

"But those companies no longer exist," Caroline interrupted.

"I understand. But the title still needs to go through the legal steps to remove all liens."

Caroline shook her head with impatience. "And how long will that take, Russell?"

He was noncommittal. "We will move forward as quickly as possible,"

Caroline groaned.

"I know that's not what you wanted to hear. In the meantime, we can get started on the town council's application process. Although the art center will be a nonprofit organization, it still needs to be approved, as any other business does."

Accepting that she couldn't change Russell's time frame, Caroline stood up and collected her papers. "That's fine. Please begin the process and let me know if the foundation needs to supply any further information beyond what's in our proposal and business case, which I believe you have."

"I do," he answered. "We'll call you next week when a draft of the application is ready for your review."

Walking up the steps to Main Street, Caroline saw Kai standing by *The Lumby Lines* newspaper stand, smiling as he read that week's issue. She looked around and saw Jamar, half a block away, talking to two young ladies, his arms moving in an animated fashion that had the females giggling.

"Anything new?" Caroline asked Kai.

He looked up and grinned. "Your breaking news is about as interesting as what we have on Coraba. The only difference is that we have a weekly fish tally on our front page."

She vividly remembered all he had told her about that faraway place. "You miss Coraba, don't you?" she asked.

Kai tilted his head, slightly confused by the question. "I suppose so. It's the only home I've ever known." He closed the paper and folded it along its center crease. "I wanted to thank you for a wonderful evening. It was one of the most memorable nights I've had since arriving in your country."

"The pleasure was all mine," she said. "It certainly took me away from the challenges I'm facing."

"Troubles with your business?" he asked.

"Yes and no," she said. An idea came to her, and she impulsively asked him, "I'd like to show you something. Would you by any chance be free for an early-evening picnic today?"

Kai's face brightened. "I would."

"Where can I meet you?"

"I'll be at the theater finishing the basket."

Jamar, sauntering up to Caroline, overheard Kai's last comment. "You work too hard, brother."

"And you, perhaps, not enough," he retorted.

"Caroline Ross," Jamar began, placing his arm lightly around her shoulders, "there is so much we need to talk about. I understand you're at the helm of a large foundation. A beautiful woman controlling vast sums of money." Clearly Jamar was not seriously interested in Caroline, but he enjoyed getting the better of his brother and somehow he knew Kai had a soft heart for the beautiful blonde.

"Don't do that, Jamar," Kai warned.

"Oh, Kai. You're too sensitive. Caroline knows my intentions are honest."

"Honest or honorable?" Caroline asked, grinning at Kai in such a way that Jamar didn't see.

Jamar ran his hand through his thick hair. "Both, I assure you," he said, winking at her. "But you've never given me the opportunity to show it. So, perhaps you will give me that chance tonight at dinner?" He raised his brow and gave Caroline a come-hither look.

"No, thank you. I have plans," she said, smiling at Kai.

Jamar glanced first at his brother and then back at Caroline, and immediately sensed their connection. "With Kai?" he asked in surprise. "Oh, I can be so much more interesting."

Caroline blushed, feeling uncomfortable.

"Leave her alone," Kai said.

"Younger brother," he said in a humorously condescending tone, "this is when you step aside and watch your older brother's talents in international diplomacy." Jamar slid closer to Caroline.

Angered by his brother's brazen behavior toward Caroline, Kai lunged forward to push Jamar away. But Jamar saw his brother's advance, and he jumped aside, placing Caroline in Kai's path. Kai couldn't stop his forward momentum and bumped Caroline on the shoulder, pushing her into the street. She stumbled just as a car approached. The car's horn blasted and Kai's eyes widened as he yelled her name. Luckily, she found her balance and stepped aside just before a serious accident occurred.

"Are you all right?" Kai asked. "I'm so, so sorry."

Caroline was shaken and placed her hand on Kai's arm as they stepped over the curb and onto the sidewalk. "Yes, I think so," she said.

Several people had seen the commotion and gathered around them.

"That Indonesian fellow pushed her. I saw it," someone said.

Caroline, noticing the growing crowd, tried to collect herself. "I'm really fine," she repeated loudly.

"Why did Kai push you?" an onlooker asked, ignoring the foreigner.

Dennis Beezer, who was just leaving his building when the incident occurred, stepped forward from the crowd. "Are you sure you're all right? What happened?"

Caroline tried to smile. "It was just an accident. We were all joking around, and Kai and Jamar were roughhousing. I accidentally stepped into the middle of it."

Dennis turned to Jamar and Kai. "I suggest you two leave."

"Yes, everyone please just leave," Caroline urged the crowd.

Kai, though, thought she was also talking to him, so he shuffled away as quickly as possible, his brother not far behind. After crossing the intersection of Main and Farm to Market, Kai looked back and saw Dennis still talking with Caroline, whose head was down. Jamar had already crossed the street, heading for the library.

Why did that urge to push his brother come upon him? Kai asked himself. He would never hurt anyone. But Jamar had upset him when he invited Caroline out. Kai had only made matters worse by embarrassing and hurting her with his rashness. No doubt she wouldn't be interested in their picnic now.

∽

The following hours passed more slowly than Kai could ever remember. He tried to keep busy but finally gave up and paced the floor, twisting rattan string in his hands. Although he had given up all hope of seeing Caroline that afternoon, as she had suggested earlier in the day, he had to wait until Jamar returned so they could jointly find a ride back to Montis.

He looked at the clock. Only a few minutes had passed since the last time he had checked.

A car horn blew outside, probably someone waiting in front of Jimmy D's. It blew again, and then seconds later, again. Kai looked out the front window and saw Caroline's white Jeep parked in front of the Feed Store.

Kai couldn't run down the stairs fast enough.

When he reached her car, he leaned in through the open window. Caroline looked wonderful—she had changed into a bright yellow blouse and black slacks. Her blond hair hung loosely under a small hat. "You still want to go on a picnic?" Kai asked.

She smiled. "Absolutely. How about you?"

"Only if the posse doesn't find us," he said, smiling as the American term rolled off his tongue.

"Come on, get in," she said. "I want to show you something."

As Caroline and Kai drove out of town, Jimmy watched from his tavern's front window. He was going to make a comment to one of his patrons, but thought it best to keep his opinions to himself for the time being.

Not until they turned off of North Grant onto Fiddlers Elbow did Kai finally speak again.

"Are you all right?" he asked.

Caroline glanced over at him while trying to dodge the potholes on the dirt road. "I'm fine. And I'm so sorry for how people reacted," she said. "The folks in town are very protective of me."

"With good reason," he said, smiling. "So, where are you taking me?"

"Bricks," she said proudly.

"Your art center?"

Caroline laughed. "Well, it's more like a circular train depot right now, but it's all ours. We had just signed the papers when I saw you today. The Ross Foundation is now the official owner and I would like you to be our first visitor," she said as she pulled the car over and parked on the grass.

He was delighted by the prospect. "Congratulations! We should celebrate."

"We will," Caroline said, taking a large wicker picnic basket from the backseat. "There's a bottle of champagne in here. Do you mind a bit of a walk?"

"Not at all," he said, taking the basket from her. It weighed quite a bit, and he wondered what she had packed inside. "Lead the way."

After Caroline took a quilt from the trunk, they walked the path single file. Although Simon Dixon had cut back some of the brush and overhanging limbs, it was still rough terrain and slow going.

When they came to the clearing, Caroline paused.

"That's amazing," Kai said, viewing the circular brick building.

"Isn't it?" she asked with childlike excitement. "Come on," she said, taking his hand.

They walked through the field and up to the front of the building. Caroline began to laugh, pointing at Hank, who was perched by the main door, appropriately attired in a train conductor's blue-and-white-striped overalls with a matching hat. A whistle hung from his neck.

"How did you get here?" she asked the flamingo, who remained quite shy in front of the stranger.

"What is that?" Kai asked.

"It's more of a who," Caroline said. "This is Hank, one of our most esteemed town residents. Hank, meet Kai Talin."

Hank blinked so quickly that neither saw.

"What is he doing here?"

Caroline laughed. "I'm not sure, but given his clothes, I would say he's far more interested in the train depot than an arts center. Most times, we don't know what he's thinking."

"Most times?" Kai asked, bewildered. "Caroline, he's a plastic flamingo!"

"And one who doesn't share his opinion often," she noted. "He'll occasionally carry a sign protesting a change made in town, but frequently he goes about his business in silence."

Leaving Kai standing dumbfounded, she opened the door, leaned in, and tried the switch on the wall. To her joy, the lights came on.

"Wow! We have electricity," she said with a broad grin. "We talked to the power company only yesterday and they said it would take a few days to get this old building online again."

As Kai stepped inside, he stopped in the doorway, his eyes as wide as saucers. "There's a—"

"Train?"

"Yes, exactly," Kai said.

"Isn't it great?" Caroline asked. "Our table is waiting for us," she said, walking over and climbing up into the train. Caroline had converted the back half of the locomotive cabin into a small dining room with a café table and a checked tablecloth. Kai placed the basket on the table, and as he looked around in wonder, Caroline laid out assorted cheeses and meats and a freshly baked baguette. She poured champagne into glass flutes and brought one to Kai.

"Cheers," she said.

"That's not much of a toast, considering all that you have done," Kai said kindly. He raised his glass. "To the intelligence, perseverance, and generosity of Caroline Ross, whom I shall always hold close to my heart."

At his unexpected gesture, Caroline blushed. "Thank you, sir," she said, bowing slightly. "Now, come eat."

Their conversation over dinner was as engaging and relaxed as on their first afternoon together, and as the hours passed, time seemed to stand still for both of them.

⁊

Brooke had long since pulled the roast out of the oven. When she looked at the clock, she saw it was eight thirty. "Caroline should have been here an hour ago," she said. "I'm calling her house again."

After getting Caroline's answering machine, Brooke joined Joshua in the living room, where he was watching television.

"She's not there. I think something's wrong," she said.

"She may just be running late," Joshua suggested.

"I don't think so. We've been having dinner every other Monday for close to a year and she's never been late. Would you mind driving over to her home to see if she's all right?"

"Sure," he said, getting up and grabbing the keys. "I'll call you from her house if she's there."

But Caroline's house was empty. It was now dark outside and no lights shone through the windows. Her car was nowhere to be seen. Driving back through town, Joshua checked the parked cars along Main Street.

Coming to the intersection of Farm to Market, Joshua saw Simon cross the street, and he honked his horn.

"Have you seen Caroline?" Joshua asked. "She was due over at our place for dinner a while ago and Brooke is worried."

"She was with the Talin boys earlier today," Simon answered. "There was a small ruckus in front of Chatham Press."

"A ruckus?" Joshua asked.

"The younger brother pushed Caroline into the street. She said it was an accident, but her explanation seemed too contrived."

For Joshua, that didn't jibe with the Kai who had given the talk about balloons. "Have you seen her since?" he asked.

"No. I'm sure it's not a problem, but I'll keep my eye out for her car as I make the rounds about town tonight."

"Thanks, Simon. Will you have her call us if you see her?"

"Will do," he said.

⁓

Several hours later, Kai and Caroline turned off the lights and walked out of Bricks into the night. Bright moonlight broke through the trees.

Looking up into the sky, Caroline sighed. "I didn't realize how late it was."

"Nor did I," Kai said. "Do you think you can find the trail back?"

Caroline looked nervously at their surroundings. "I think so, but I've only been on the path two or three times."

Kai put his arm around her. "I have a good sense of direction. If you're up for it, let's give it a try," he said and led her around the back of the roundhouse to where he remembered the path began.

Out of necessity Caroline held Kai's hand to steady herself over the rough ground. When she stumbled, he grabbed her waist. For the remainder of the slow walk back to Caroline's car, Kai kept his arm tightly around her.

By the time they reached the road and walked the short distance to the car, it was close to midnight. Caroline and Kai were exhausted, and they rested for several minutes before heading into town. They spoke very little as Caroline drove, both thinking about the evening they had shared.

"Thank you for taking me there," Kai finally said.

Caroline saw him leaning against the car door, almost facing her. "I'm glad you like Bricks as much as I do. Your opinion means a lot to me."

The headlight of a passing car shone on Caroline's face and Kai couldn't resist looking at her. "You are captivating in so many ways," he said softly.

She waited a moment. "I hear a but coming."

"There is no but. You are one of the most extraordinary women I have ever met. The kindness in your heart, the passion of your convictions are so attractive," he said. "I can't help but be drawn to—"

Suddenly police lights flashed directly behind Caroline's car. Startled, she slowed down, and when the car didn't pass, she pulled over to the side of North Grant Avenue. Looking in the rearview mirror, she saw Simon Dixon approach.

Simon shined a flashlight into the car through the open window. "Is everything all right, Caroline?" he asked, glancing at Kai.

"Yes, fine," she said, tensing up. "We're just getting back from Bricks."

"Isn't it a little late to be out in the woods?"

Kai leaned closer to Caroline so he could clearly see Simon. "My fault entirely," Kai said. "I asked far too many questions about her arts center."

"We lost track of time," she added. "Is something wrong, Simon?"

"Joshua asked me to keep an eye out for you. He was worried when you didn't show up for dinner."

Caroline pushed her palm to her forehead. "Oh, no! I totally forgot our dinner tonight. I'll call Brooke first thing in the morning."

"I'm heading south of town. I can give Kai a ride down to Montis," Simon suggested.

"Thanks anyway. I need to drop something off for Pam."

"At midnight?" he asked.

"For tomorrow morning," she said. "So, if that's it, have a good night."

"Drive safely," Simon said, shining the light on Kai one final time.

As Simon walked away, Caroline rolled up the window. She placed her hand on Kai's arm. "I'm so sorry," she said. "They're well intentioned and very much care for me."

Kai put his hand on hers. "As they should."

When they arrived at Montis, instead of dropping Kai off in front, Caroline drove slowly into the parking lot, turned off the lights, and removed the keys from the ignition.

"Would you like to go for a walk? The orchard is almost ethereal at night with such a bright moon."

Kai wasn't the least bit tired and jumped at the chance to delay saying good night to Caroline. "I would love to."

As they crossed the street, they both reached out and took each other's hand. Kai glanced back and saw that all the lights were out on the second floor of the inn.

After they climbed the hill, Caroline found an open space that faced Woodrow Lake and sat down on the sweet grass. Kai remained standing, which allowed Caroline to lean back against his leg. When she moved her head, Kai felt her hair touch his fingertips. His heart raced.

Caroline lifted her hand and touched his. "Come, sit down," she whispered.

When Kai moved close to her, they each felt the charge between them, the pull that neither could ignore. Caroline looked at Kai, moonlight dancing in her eyes. He longed to take her in his arms, to feel her body against his and to taste the sweetness of her lips. He lifted his hand toward her, but then abruptly pulled away.

He forced himself to look down at the lake. He laughed softly.

"What is it?" Caroline asked.

He leaned back and looked up at the sky. "When I was a child, I felt God always watched me more carefully at night because most everyone was asleep so He had fewer distractions." He smiled at the memory. "During the full moon in particular, I felt I had to be on my best behavior because God could see everything more clearly in the moonlight."

"Like tonight?"

"In my younger days, I would be most assured that He was watching us right now."

"And would He approve?" Caroline asked.

Kai was caught off guard by the question, but then considered it carefully for several moments. "If only I knew, but I think He would be cautiously concerned," he finally said, standing up. He offered his hand to Caroline. "Why don't we walk through the fields?"

"He can't see us in the apple grove?"

Kai laughed. "Oh, I'm sure He can, but walking seems safer than lying next to you."

The two friends disappeared among the trees, arm in arm, talking quietly of anything and everything. It wasn't until dawn lightened the sky that they realized how much time had passed.

TWENTY-FOUR

Barricade

Later that morning, Jamar sauntered into Kai's room at Montis Inn.

"So, little brother, where were you last night?"

Kai didn't answer, knowing that Jamar would never believe the innocence of the situation.

"And here I thought you were holier than thou," Jamar taunted him.

"It was nothing," Kai said, walking into his bathroom and shutting the door, which Jamar immediately opened.

"To spend a night with a beautiful woman is never nothing," Jamar said enviously.

Kai fought being pulled into the lurid discussion Jamar wanted.

His brother was not put off, though. "My, my, our village was so sure they were sending the good and the pure. They'll be in for a shock when they find out you've taken up with a blonde you barely know," he teased.

"That's enough!" Kai said and pushed Jamar out of the room, locking the door.

By the time Kai had showered and dressed, Jamar was no longer in sight. After eating a light breakfast, Kai went out to Farm to

Market Road in search of a ride to Lumby. He had frequently been given lifts into town by residents returning from Wheatley, but that morning the owner of Wools drove by without a nod. A short while later, the librarian with whom he had chatted on several occasions drove past, glancing at Kai but as quickly looking away again.

After an hour of waiting, Kai was relieved when an SUV finally pulled over.

Joshua rolled down the passenger window. "Do you need a ride, Kai?"

"I would appreciate that," he said, getting into the car.

Driving off, Joshua asked, "Have you been waiting a while?"

He looked at his watch. "Over an hour. And usually someone picks me up within five minutes."

Joshua scratched his ear, unsure how forthcoming he should be. "I think it may be a show of resentment," he said cautiously.

Kai jumped in surprise and turned in his seat to look at Joshua. "Toward me? Why?" he asked.

"Because of last night," Joshua tried to explain as gently as possible. "When Caroline didn't show up at our place, folks became concerned."

"I know she feels badly about forgetting your dinner and not calling Brooke beforehand, but she's far from being an irresponsible teenager missing early-evening curfew," Kai said.

"This is a small town and everyone looks out for everyone else. Word spread quickly that you were with her until early morning."

"So? I'm not a bad guy. Why would people think otherwise?"

Joshua glanced over at Kai. "Well, for one thing, several people saw you push Caroline into the street."

Kai's face flushed with anger. "It was an accident. I was trying to push Jamar away from her."

"Unfortunately, stories become twisted."

Kai's shoulders dropped. "So what can I do?"

"Give it time," Joshua advised. "The people of Lumby don't accept strangers quickly."

"Because of prejudice?"

Joshua thought for a moment. "No, not against race or religion. They just don't immediately warm up to folks who aren't from around here."

"Perhaps it would be best for everyone if I returned to Saint Cross as soon as possible. That would take care of a lot of problems."

Joshua continued looking straight ahead. "Are other things not going well?" he asked, sensing Kai's unhappiness.

Kai was silent for the longest time. "Having left the monastery, perhaps you're the only person who could understand." He paused, and then slowly continued. "I have given my life to God and I am going to be a priest, but now I'm starting to wonder. I never thought I would question that."

Joshua heard the remorse and torment in Kai's voice. "Thinking we know our own destiny is a dangerous proposition."

Kai considered his words carefully. "But don't we? I was selected by the town's elders to become the spiritual leader of our community. When that happened, I knew how my life would play out."

"You might have thought you did, but don't the last few weeks prove otherwise? We don't know what's waiting for us around the next bend. It could be the death of a loved one, an unexpected opportunity, or . . . finally finding a soul mate."

Kai shook his head. "I find it disconcerting if we don't know where our lives are headed."

"But it can also be liberating. I think our lives can follow many different avenues. I could have taken my vows to become a monk, but in my heart I knew that wasn't the path I should take at that time in my life. And then I expected to be single, but meeting Brooke turned that upside down."

"So you didn't leave the abbey for Brooke?" Kai asked.

"No, I met her several years afterward." Joshua smiled, thinking about his wife. "Believe me, it would have been so much easier to leave the monastery if Brooke was there waiting for me."

"And you didn't feel you were turning your back on God?"

"Oh, no. Just the opposite. I became a better person, more authentic to who I really am. And I'm quite sure that's what God wants for each of us."

Kai rubbed his palms together. "It's not easy to see what's authentic within ourselves, is it?"

"No," Joshua said, glancing over at Kai. "It's even harder when so many people are telling you who you are supposed to be."

As Joshua turned onto Main Street, Kai looked in both directions, hoping to see Caroline, hoping for that sense of assurance she gave him with just one glance. But she was nowhere to be seen.

Pulling up to the Feed Store, Joshua stopped to let Kai out.

"If there's anything I can do, don't hesitate to call," Joshua offered.

"I wish there was, but unfortunately I think I need to work this out on my own."

❧

Just outside town, Caroline was sitting on the sofa in Brooke's house, nervously twisting her hair.

"When I finally got home, there were a dozen messages on my answering machine," she complained.

Brooke, seated in a chair next to her, said, "But it's understandable that we, and others, were worried about you."

"To be worried about me is fine," Caroline said. "To be worried about me because I was with Kai, whom no one seems to trust, is ridiculous. I just wish everyone would stay out of my personal life."

Brooke shrugged her shoulders. "But that's a consequence of small-town living."

"Two callers actually said that they were extremely disappointed in my lack of judgment. Can you believe that?" Tears welled up in her eyes.

"Those you just ignore," Brooke advised.

Caroline's face turned red. "But how dare they!" she yelled.

Brooke was startled by her friend's outburst. "Caroline, what's going on?" she asked gently.

Caroline stood up. "It's everyone and everything," she blurted out.

"No, it's not. I know you too well and you've never cared what other people thought of you," Brooke said. "What's really wrong?"

Caroline fell slowly back onto the sofa, tears beginning to roll down her checks. She tried to take a deep breath. "I don't know what to do," she finally said.

"About what?"

She pushed a pillow into the corner of the sofa. "Kai is such a good man, but I'm just making things worse for him. And I deeply resent how everyone is treating him. Why can't they see in him what I see?"

"We just don't want you to be hurt," Brooke said.

"When he leaves, that's going to happen anyway."

✧

After Simon finally secured leased grazing land several miles south of town, the relocation of Morty's cows from Lumby Park started in orderly fashion, then went terribly amiss. Due to the damage the cows might have done if they were herded down Main Street, Simon insisted Morty provide transport to the Galloways' new home. When the first of the cows were funneled through a rope path to the trailer, an old jalopy backfired ten feet away, startling the cows from their procession. The third in line broke through the ropes and galloped onto Main Street, where she had an unfortunate collision with two motorcycles. The cow, seemingly unhurt, then ran back toward the park, which riled the rest of the herd. Half the herd stampeded north up Farm to Market while the others ran west toward Jimmy D's and the Feed Store.

The latter was possibly the worst route to take on that specific morning. The townsfolk were moving the separate parts of the *Endeavor* from the Feed Store to the fairgrounds for a trial flight, so the west end of Main Street was blocked with trailers and vans, surrounded by balloon sections. Much of the envelope's sixty feet of nylon had been rolled out on the street for folding before it was boxed and driven up Fairground Road. The basket, too, was sitting unprotected in the middle of the street.

As the cows passed in front of Wools, someone ran out and tried to slow them by waving a red coat, but that merely increased their agitation.

Those town patrons who were standing outside Jimmy D's watching events across the street were riveted by the sight of fifteen belted Galloways running at full speed down the road toward the town balloon.

"My God!" someone yelled out. "Pick up the balloon!"

Instead, all of the patrons froze and watched the stampede approach.

Hearing the shouts, Kai ran out of the Feed Store. The cows were less than half a block away and gaining speed. He looked at the balloon, weighing several hundred pounds, and knew that there wasn't enough time to pull it to safety.

Instead, Kai ran into the street and positioned himself between the lead cow and the balloon. Hannah, who had followed him out of the Feed Store, also ran into the street and stretched out her arms, trying to create a human barricade.

"Get back," Kai cried when she grabbed his hand.

The Galloways were fifty feet away and approaching at a dead run.

Jimmy D flew through the tavern's front door and ran to Kai, standing to his left side with arms spread. Within seconds, another six people joined the blockade, and then another ten behind them, so that the barricade was two people deep.

But the cows weren't slowing. They were only forty feet away.

"Mooo," someone voiced as loudly as possible.

Another joined in. "Mooo."

Immediately, all twenty were mooing as if their lives depended on it.

The cows, stunned by the oddly familiar noise, locked their legs, skidded a short distance on the concrete, and finally came to a stop six feet away from the human wall. They looked blankly at the people in front of them, and then, smelling the oats that were stored in wooden bins behind the Feed Store, slowly turned and headed in that direction.

One person began to clap and then everyone burst into laughter and applause.

No one, though, came up to Kai and expressed gratitude to him for initiating the action that saved their balloon. No one except Hannah.

"You started it all," she said. "Thank you for saving my envelope."

"It was worth saving," Kai said.

Jimmy walked over to his wife and put his arm around her. "Are you all right?" he asked.

She had slept only a few hours in their house the night before, preferring the privacy and independence of her sewing room at the Feed Store. "I'm fine," she said softly.

Knowing this was not the time or the place to talk about personal matters, but realizing that his opportunities were limited, Jimmy blurted out, "Good that Johnnie is away for the summer. He might not understand why you're spending more time up in that theater than you are at home. In fact, even I don't get it."

Hannah didn't know how to explain either. Being out of the house made her feel liberated, and she was so busy sewing that she hardly noticed the hours passing. When she had finally gone home last night, it was past two in the morning. She had undressed and for three hours she lay next to Jimmy in silence. Then she rose, showered, and put on clean clothes before returning to her sanctuary across the street.

"Are you coming home at a reasonable hour tonight?" Jimmy asked.

She thought for a moment. "No, I don't think so," she said. "It's not that I don't love you. I just don't like myself when we're together."

Jimmy looked into his wife's eyes and, for the first time in their marriage, saw her pain. "Where will you stay?" he asked her.

"I don't know, Jimmy. But you'll be the first person I tell when I figure it out," she said, watching Morty Albert and his sons corral the cows behind the Feed Store.

Within minutes, the cows were funneled through makeshift fencing into the repositioned trailer that was to deliver them to their greener pastures. The envelope was rolled up and once again people on Main Street returned to their orderly pursuits.

Uplifting

The Lumby Lines

Sheriff's Complaints

BY SHERIFF SIMON DIXON   May 13

2:38 a.m. Man swerving down Main Street on riding lawn mower crashed into flower bed. LPD called.

6:41 a.m. Elk vs. dump truck on Mineral by town landfill. Elk shaken but walking.

7:29 a.m. Cindy Watford called to report that there are four pygmy goats in her pen—she only owns two. She wanted to know if it was all right to release the two that aren't hers.

8:54 a.m. Model plane hit transformer behind Dickenson's and burst into flames. No electricity at store or Episcopal church. LFD notified.

8:57 a.m. Power outage reported at Mobil gas station.

3:33 p.m. Resident called requesting assistance. Back went out carrying sofa into tree house. EMS dispatched.

3:36 p.m. Owner of S&T's called. Pallet carrying forty-pound bags of flour broke on the sidewalk in front of restaurant. Quite a mess.

3:47 p.m. Lumby Elementary called. Two pygmy goats are grazing in playground.

4:28 p.m. Red tricycle with red canopy top and yellow streamers missing from in front of candy store. Little Sara crying. Can't be that hard to find.

8:11 p.m. Unidentified caller reported seeing town cannon listed on eBay with last bid at $23.00.

It took five men to fold and lift the envelope into Jimmy's white van and another three to maneuver the basket and burner system onto its roof. With Jimmy in front, a long procession of cars led from Main Street up Hunts Mill Road and then onto Fairground Road. Driving through the fairground gates, which Hank was holding open, Jimmy crossed the open field and parked the van next to the cement pad that was used during the trials. Mark had arrived an hour earlier to set up the tables and chairs.

Within no time, most of the townsfolk had arrived and were tailgating or sitting on large tarps, waiting for the activities to begin. Brian Beezer, who never missed an entrepreneurial opportunity, walked the grounds selling refreshments, silk-screened *Endeavor* T-shirts, and beginner manuals on hot air ballooning.

The envelope was finally hoisted from the back of the van and carried into position about fifteen feet downwind of the launch site, where the basket would ultimately be placed. Jimmy, Mark, and Jamar began to unfold the balloon.

What people expected would be a simple balloon was, in fact, a balloon of solid red. As the full length and breadth of the nylon was revealed, weak applause broke out sporadically from the crowd.

Seated in her car, Hannah frowned. Every stitch wouldn't have been the same if some imagination had been put into the color, she thought.

After the basket was removed from the roof, Chuck Bryson installed the propane tank and began connecting it to the burner.

"Do you need any help?" Kai asked, walking up to him.

"There you are!" Chuck said, tapping him on the back. "Wonderful you're here. I was worried you were going to miss the big event."

"Sorry I'm late," Kai said glumly. "I had to walk up from Main Street."

Chuck was surprised. "With all the traffic headed this way?"

Kai leaned closer to Chuck so as not to be overheard. "It appears I've ruffled some town feathers because of my friendship with Caroline Ross."

"Not to worry. Everything will straighten itself out in time," Chuck said. "Now come help me with this contraption."

Once the basket was readied, Chuck, Jimmy, and Mark attached the rigging from the basket to the balloon while Kai slowly circled the envelope and scrutinized as many panels as he could see. He was impressed by Hannah's outstanding craftsmanship.

He then lifted the collar, confirming that each fitting and fastener was secure.

Placing the inflation fan next to the propane burners facing toward the inside of the envelope, Kai asked Chuck and Mark to lift the mouth of the balloon, forming a large opening into which the air would blow. He turned on the fan to test the direction of "the blow" and adjusted it so no air was being directed above, below, or to either side of the mouth.

The balloon slowly began to inflate.

"I thought you used hot air," Mark yelled over the sound of the fan.

"We do," Kai answered. "After it's inflated about sixty percent with cold air. Otherwise the partially filled envelope would begin to rise too quickly."

The crowd gathered closer to the balloon as it gained volume, although it was still lying on its side. At last Kai turned off the fan and felt each of the control lines, inspecting the connections and correcting the position of the vent cord. He circled the balloon again for a second thorough inspection.

"I'm turning on the burner," he announced to Chuck and Mark. "Hold the mouth as high and as wide as you can so the fabric is kept away from the flame. Also, don't look into the burner."

Kai adjusted the angle of the fan and quickly blasted one burner to ensure the blow was angled correctly. He then turned on the fuel burners and began to add hot air with short blasts of flame that lasted no longer than two or three seconds. He alternated between blasting and cooling until the balloon was just lifting from the ground. The mouth gradually pulled away from Mark's and Chuck's hands.

"Chuck, please stand next to the basket, and Mark, ensure the tether lines are secure," Kai called out as he turned off the fan.

Within seconds, both Mark and Chuck were standing by the basket and several others were managing the ropes. Kai continued blasting the flame in three-second intervals until the envelope was inflated and hovering directly overhead.

The crowd broke out in more convincing applause, and someone lit some firecrackers in celebration.

Kai swung around to Jimmy. "Tell them no fireworks!" he shouted. Turning to Chuck and Mark, he instructed them, "Put your hands on the basket. We need to reach equilibrium. Tell me when."

Chuck nodded at the good sense of the suggestion.

"What's equilibrium?" Mark asked Chuck.

"When the force of lift equals the force of gravity . . . when it floats perfectly level," Chuck answered and placed his hands on the basket rim. "When that's reached, two people should be able to keep the basket in place with the slightest hand pressure."

Kai continued to fill the balloon and suddenly the basket lifted a few inches off the ground.

"Ho!" called Chuck.

Kai immediately shut off the burner.

Hannah, who was now standing by her car watching the envelope inflate, grabbed a piece of red nylon from the backseat. Walking up to the basket, she leaned over to Kai. "Would you help me?"

Kai was unsure what Hannah wanted until she handed him one corner of the fabric. Lifting it up and unrolling it, he saw it was a framed banner with *Endeavor* skillfully stitched in white. Kai and Hannah attached the four corners to one side of the basket, and loud cheers resounded from the crowd.

"Perfect," Kai said, winking at Hannah, who smiled broadly.

Jimmy then filled the second blue helium balloon of the day and released it as everyone watched. There was no wind until two hundred feet, and then it appeared to be blowing toward the southeast. Kai watched intently, not taking his eyes off the weather balloon.

When he was satisfied the wind conditions were good, he stepped inside the basket and blasted to adjust for his added weight.

"Chuck, you're next," he said, and lent Chuck a hand as he climbed in. "Mark, your turn," he said. "Where's Jimmy?"

"He's talking with the chase crew over there," someone called back. "He's coming now."

Jimmy came running up and stepped carefully into the basket.

"Do all of you remember everything we discussed a few days ago? Stay inside the basket and hands off the lines," Kai said, and everyone nodded.

Then, quite unexpectedly, Jamar walked up to the balloon. "Kai, some folks are saying that I should pilot the balloon." He glanced back and several young women in the crowd waved to him.

"You don't have your pilot's license," Kai protested.

Jamar shrugged. "You actually think that matters in the United States? You know I've soloed before."

Kai shook his head. "I don't think it's a good idea. You weren't involved in building the basket and you're not familiar with this heating system."

"Well, we should let Jimmy decide." Jamar turned to Jimmy, who was watching the two brothers argue. "Who do you want as your pilot?"

For one of the few times in his life Jimmy didn't know what to say. "Whatever you guys think."

Hannah saw a way to end the dissension. "Why don't both of you go?" she proposed.

"Great idea," Jamar said, jumping into the basket, his foot brushing against the propane tank. "But I really don't think you're needed, little brother."

"Yes, brother, I am," Kai corrected him. Kai leaned out of the basket, looking upward. "I want to check the cord a final time," he said, stepping out of the basket.

Jamar quickly seized the opportunity. "Everyone stand back," he said with great bravado, and then blasted the burner for several seconds. The basket lifted a few inches off the ground.

"Jamar!" Kai yelled, grabbing on to the rim of the basket. "You were already at equilibrium—don't blast again!"

Then an unfortunate string of events took place over thirty seconds that would be forever remembered by the onlookers in Lumby.

Mark, wanting to take Kai's side in the argument, stepped out of the basket but smartly kept much of his weight leaning on the basket rim.

"Mark, what are you doing?" Jimmy asked nervously.

"I don't feel safe flying with Jamar," Mark admitted.

"Kai, come back in," Jimmy demanded.

Kai started to swing his leg into the basket, but Jamar caught his foot and pushed it out, throwing Kai off balance and knocking him to the ground. Mark spun around as he watched Kai's head smack against the earth. Jamar jumped out of the basket and ran over to Kai, determined to keep his brother pinned down.

With Mark's and Kai's weight removed, the basket began to rise.

"Wait a minute!" Jimmy yelled as the basket lifted another three feet. "I'm not going by myself," he cried, and jumped out.

Without Jimmy's weight, the balloon shot upward. Chuck Bryson, the only remaining passenger, called for help as the basket rose steadily.

The ground crew, thinking the balloon was lifting off, released the lines. The *Endeavor* made a fast ascent above the fairground, with Chuck looking down helplessly.

Kai pushed Jamar off him and jumped to his feet. "The vent cord," Kai yelled, and raised his hand, trying to mimic pulling the cord attached to the top flap that needed to be opened to release the hot air. But from such a height, Chuck assumed Kai was simply waving to him.

Not very appropriate, Chuck thought, unsettled. He took several deep breaths to calm himself, then finally lifted his head and looked around. In his fear, he hadn't seen the scenery below, but now, looking out over Lumby and all the way down to Woodrow Lake, he thought it was one of the most beautiful sights he had ever witnessed.

The silence was overwhelming. He was flying on the wind as quietly and smoothly as he could ever imagine. Now on to business, he thought, looking around the inside of the basket. He found the altimeter and saw that he had leveled off at two hundred feet.

He appeared to be heading south, following Farm to Market Road. The familiarity of his surroundings calmed any remaining nervousness he felt. He picked out the orchard and Montis Inn and even spotted the beehives that he had maintained for so many decades. The area's topography surprised him, though. How many times had he walked the path through the upper fields at Montis, never really knowing how those hills were set against the larger landscape?

He flew almost directly over the Walkers' new barn, low enough to catch the attention of their goats but high enough not to spook the draft horse.

He looked at the altimeter. He was descending and Woodrow Lake was directly ahead of him.

Instead of panicking, Chuck looked up at the top of the balloon and saw the flap that Kai had once mentioned. His eye followed the cord to the collar and then down to the basket. If he released air, there was a chance that he could land before hitting the water. Holding his breath, he pulled and watched the flap open wide.

He descended with alarming speed, but Chuck, focused on looking upward, kept on holding the flap cord. When he dropped to a hundred feet, the balloon caught a strong crosswind. It jerked due east toward the woods south of Montis and the Fork River. Flying over the rapids, he saw a hay field just beyond the forest edge.

The balloon continued to descend. A quarter mile before reaching the clearing, the basket became snagged in the treetops. The envelope swung into a branch, which tore a large gash in the nylon. The basket hurtled downward, breaking branches along the way, a support line snagged on a higher limb and stretched taut. The basket flipped, sending Chuck crashing to the ground.

His body was jarred so badly, Chuck dimmed into unconsciousness. He never saw how the fire above him started. It was later proposed that when the basket flipped, a wire or limb hit the release lever that blasted the burner. The blast probably lasted only a few seconds, but a second was all it took to set the nylon ablaze.

Chuck also never remembered being pulled from the woods by the many people who were following the balloon on the ground, and were within screaming distance when he was so abruptly hurled from the sky.

TWENTY-SIX

Blame

Pam Walker was unaware of the chase crew and caravan of cars that passed in front of Montis Inn after rescuing Chuck Bryson. The only sound she heard was the incessant splashing of Clipper and Cutter in the smaller of the two ponds. Since the pond had filled with spring water, the dogs had been swimming every waking hour.

"They're Labrador retrievers, honey. What did you expect?" Mark had commented the night before when, in their excitement, the dogs had broken through the screen door to deliver a large frog they'd recovered from the pond. "Be glad it's not a rare koi," he had added, which gave Pam considerable worry all night long.

"Get out of the water!" Pam yelled at Cutter, the one that would be more apt to obey. The dogs had brought a new volleyball to the pond and were testing its buoyancy.

Pam picked up a large stick. "Cutter, look what I have," she said, which got the dog to at least look up. But it was hot, and the ball in the water offered much more entertainment than a stick on dry land.

As a final resort, Pam walked in front of the lodge and opened the back of the Jeep and honked the horn. Both dogs flew around the corner and leapt into the air, crashing into the backseat. Then they did what dogs do after swimming—they shook their entire bodies, sending water everywhere.

With little patience left, Pam grabbed two leashes, harnessed the beasts, and led them to the lodge with whimpering complaints voiced along the way. Their expectations for a promised car ride were being rudely crushed.

"You look wetter than they do," Joshua said from his car as Pam stepped back outside.

Her response was a low rumble. "I can't keep them out of the pond."

"Because they're—"

"Labs, I know. Mark reminded me of that last night." Recovering from her bout of curmudgeonliness, she asked him, "So, what are you doing here? I thought everyone was in town for the launch."

Joshua laughed. "We were. It flew and then it landed."

"Is Mark happy?"

"At this moment," Joshua said in a long, low voice, "I would think not. But I'm sure he'll tell you all about it."

"Oh, I'm sure he will," she said with a raised brow. "Since you're here, would you look at something?"

She put her arm through Joshua's and led him to the excavation site.

"What's wrong?" he asked.

"Surprisingly, nothing. I just need you to solve a mystery," Pam answered as they circled around the back of the building.

"Wow," Joshua said when he saw two nicely sculpted and cleanly excavated holes dammed by a two-foot-wide stretch of land. One pond was filled with water, while the other was bone dry. "I'm really impressed, but I don't understand why you have two holes next to each other."

"Inexperience." Pam pointed to the smaller of the holes. "I began digging directly over the spring, and within a day the water filled in. I wanted a larger pond, but working in the mud trying to extend an already filled hole was disastrous. So . . . ."

"You dug the dry hole to the left?" Joshua interrupted.

"Exactly. When I'm finished excavating the final shape, I'll just remove the dividing berm and it will become one pond."

"Very clever," Joshua said.

"Thank you. Come over here and see this rock," Pam said, walking to the side of the building where Bertha had pushed the stone from the hole.

Joshua examined it from all sides and then tried to move it, but realized it weighed several hundred pounds. "Where did you find this?"

"Buried about three feet deep in the second hole. I think it's sacred," she said in a reverent tone.

"It looks like a block of chiseled granite."

"Sacred granite," Pam corrected him.

Joshua regarded it with a puzzled expression. "I have no idea why it would be buried in the ground, of all places."

"Did the monastery have another building behind the writing room a long time ago, perhaps during the first half of the century?" Pam asked.

"Not that I'm aware of." Joshua shook his head. "But I think you would have to ask Matthew or Aaron or another one of the brothers who knows the history of the abbey better than I do."

"Do you think they had a dungeon or something consecrated down there?"

"That's it!" Joshua said, seizing upon the idea. "Or perhaps an old cemetery and that was a tombstone." He lowered his voice, trying to add suspense to the mystery. "I bet you'll dig up a couple of corpses."

Pam's eyes opened as wide as possible. "God, don't say that!" she said, smacking Joshua on the arm. "That's disgusting—the thought of my little tractor exhuming bodies." Still, the possibility made her pause. "Isn't that illegal?"

An hour later, when Pam climbed onto the Kubota, she knew that her conversation with Joshua gave new meaning to "digging carefully." She tried not to imagine that every inch the backhoe cut into the dirt was an inch closer to unearthing bones of some unknown, long-forgotten person. Her progress slowed to a painful crawl.

About six feet from where she had found the first stone, she hit another object—too hard to be a coffin or body, she immediately concluded. Scraping away the dirt, she saw it was a second stone, identical in size and shape to the first one, and below that another, and to the side, yet one more. Sacred stones, she confirmed.

After five hours of excavating, Pam had retrieved a total of nine stones and had laid them end to end by the back side of the dining room, awaiting further identification. She was certain that, like a true archaeologist, she had found a bona fide treasure.

෴

At sunrise the following morning, Brother Marc stood at the front of Saint Cross Abbey's courtyard looking down at the small lake, and smiled. It had been nearly a month since he had ventured outside the abbey walls, about the same time the wildlife on and around the lake had scattered for quieter nesting grounds. But now a calm had returned along with his dearly loved wildlife, and Brother Marc was happy once again. Brian Beezer's plan had worked perfectly.

Several days prior, when the monks of Saint Cross Abbey had agreed to the recommendations put forth by the teenager, a letter was distributed to visitors and seekers alike. It was so widely circulated that, two days later, a small reprint appeared in *The Lumby Lines* under an obituary for Gary Pole, both of which were generally overlooked.

The changes at the monastery were both instant and widespread. Emergency Fire Department volunteers were called in to assist with the mass exodus, which brought traffic to a standstill in Franklin. The first to leave were the innocent curious, those who wanted to see the abbey firsthand but had enough sense to know when they had overstayed their welcome.

The next wave of deportees were the sidewalk vendors, who dropped their awnings, boarded up the windows, and hitched their transportable carts to powerful four-wheel drives as they mapped their course to the next stop: word had spread that a town called Lumby, not far away, would be hosting a festival within a few weeks and that there could be numerous opportunities for selling their goods, whether the town was amenable to the idea or not.

Finally, the last to leave were the freeloaders, who had no interest in the monks, their monastery, or their philanthropic efforts unless such contributions were directed toward them. Perhaps it was expected that they would be the first to leave, but several disingenuous requests were made and rejected by the monks before the deadbeats accepted the fact that this free meal ticket had been canceled. Pulling up stakes in the front fields, they easily turned their backs on the litter they left behind, which would require several days to collect. The scarred lawns left over from small campfires that had been set each night would take the summer months to regrow.

With all of the departures came welcome arrivals; the beloved animals returned to the grounds, as did the local parishioners, who had broken twenty years of Sunday-morning habit and stayed home during the invasion. The dedicated and earnest seekers who remained were invited to fill the vacated rooms at the guesthouse.

Mackenzie McGuire, accompanied by Terry and Brian, was finally able to complete the projects outlined by the monks. On one of their last days working at the monastery, Brother Matthew approached Brian.

"Do you have a minute to come inside with me?" he asked.

Brian looked worried. "Am I in trouble?"

Matthew smiled. "Not at all. I would like you to look at something."

Both Mac and Terry watched as Brian followed the monk into the abbey.

Although Brian had walked the corridors of the abbey several times before, he still felt tremendously ill at ease going into the main building. He was fully aware that, in his short life, he had bent most every rule there was. To be surrounded by men who always took the high road seemed incongruous.

"I knew your grandfather's brother quite well," Matthew said as he led Brian to his private office.

Brian stayed two steps behind Matthew. "Were you one of the monks at Montis Abbey when he lived there?"

"I was," Brother Matthew answered. "I also knew your grandfather, although we rarely saw him."

"He used to say that you guys believe in the false promises that God makes," Brian answered.

Matthew considered the teenager's comments. "Ah, and is that your opinion?"

"I haven't really thought about it," Brian answered with a slight smirk. He had deliberately stayed away from anything religious for longer than he could remember, although he wouldn't be able to say why. "My grandfather said the monks coaxed his brother into a religious life before he was old enough to think for himself." Brian paused. "He hated Montis Abbey. He said all of you killed his brother."

It was as if a hot arrow had entered Matthew's chest, and he stepped back to regain his balance.

"That's not correct," he finally said slowly, and then tried to take a step forward. But it was as if he was wading through wet cement. He looked down at the floor. "First, your granduncle began coming to the monastery alone when he was quite young. It was always his desire and his decision alone to take vows and join the community. And his death was an accident. In 1962, there was a horrific storm—winds and rain pelted the orchards and we knew the beehives were in danger," Matthew explained in a low, pained voice. "I remember grabbing branches as we walked so as not to be blown over. Once we reached the first hive, your granduncle, Brother Benjamin, continued to the north end of the apiary and began strapping down the hives closest to the woods. In a strong gust, a large overhanging limb from a pine tree broke off and smashed down on the hive. It caught Benjamin on the shoulder. The bees were so agitated that they stung him again and again." His voice trailed off and he was quiet for a moment. "He went into anaphylactic shock as Brother Lawrence and I carried him down to the abbey's infirmary. We gave him an injection of epinephrine, but it was too late, and he passed away before the ambulance arrived from Wheatley." Matthew paused again, standing in silence. "It was tragic. Your granduncle was such a good, good man."

Brian pushed his hands deeper into his pockets. "Then why did Grandfather say all of those things about you and the abbey?"

Matthew lowered his head. "He needed someone to blame. His brother was the only person in his life he was close to, and when Benjamin died, a part of William died as well. That hole became filled with anger toward a lot of people."

Brian thought back to the many years he had wanted to be close to his grandfather, the many times he had tried to joke with the surly old man, only to be brushed aside. "Is that why he felt that way about us?"

"Us?"

"Mom and Dad, me and Timmy?" Brian said. "He never really liked us," he added under his breath.

Matthew suspected this was the first time Brian had ever revealed a sliver of emotion on the subject. "How William Beezer felt really had nothing to do with you, or with any of us. He was angry with the world and saw everything through that bitterness."

Brian exhaled deeply. "But to live your whole life like that . . ."

Matthew put his hand on the young man's shoulder. "Is so very unfortunate. Yes."

Brian thought for a long moment, considering everything Brother Matthew had said. "Sorry for saying you killed him," he whispered.

"Was it the truth? Did your grandfather say that?" Matthew asked, looking directly into Brian's eyes.

"Yes, he did," he said.

"One should never have to apologize for speaking the truth," Matthew said.

Brian felt a deep relief because he now had an explanation for the gnawing ache he had felt since he was a child. "I didn't mean to bring back sad memories."

"Thank you, but there were so many good memories of Benjamin as well. Perhaps one day I will tell you some," Matthew said as they entered his office. "Now, to a different subject. I'd like you to look at something." Matthew handed Brian several pieces of paper: one was a map of the world with a dozen locations identified by small black dots; another appeared to be an organizational chart; and the third was a long list of projects or business names. "If you like solving problems, this might be fun for you."

Clearly intrigued, Brian sat down and spread the pages out on the coffee table. "What is it?"

"Information about the Saint Cross Foundation. The map identifies where our money is given, the organization chart lists who oversees our various initiatives, and the other is a partial list of our projects that are under way around the world."

Brian looked first at the project list.

"It's called micro-philanthropy," Matthew explained. "Instead of gifting large sums of money that get consumed in the running of the foundation, we try to reach the people whose lives can be greatly improved with either a gift or, more frequently, a loan."

"Loan-sharking to the poor?" Brian asked, raising his eyebrows.

Matthew coughed and Brian looked up.

"Oh, sorry. Just joking," Brian said, and returned to looking at the page.

"We believe that poverty can be fought one person at a time. By distributing a large number of very small grants, we give individuals the opportunity to build new lives for themselves. They, in turn, help others in the village."

Brian moved his index finger quickly down the list, stopping every few seconds.

"But how can a loom that costs just eighty dollars"—he scanned the page—"matter to someone?"

Matthew went to the bookcase to find a book for his visitor. "To someone who owns absolutely nothing, it means everything. Brian, millions of people live at a poverty level that we can't even imagine. Their only possessions in the world are the clothes on their bodies. That's all."

When Matthew turned around, Brian was looking intently at him.

"But if it's that bad, they can just leave."

"But how? They need shoes to walk twenty miles to the next village. And once there, how would it be any different? They are uneducated and face such dire health problems," Matthew explained. "They can't just pull themselves up by their bootstraps, as many say they should."

Aware that he didn't understand the entire picture, Brian asked again, "So the loom?"

"A real situation: we loaned Kira the money for a loom. She acquires wool and cotton thread from a villager who used to walk days to sell his fiber—"

"But," Brian interrupted, "she spent all her money on the loom and has no money to buy yarn."

"Correct, so the first transaction is barter, in anticipation of future profits. She then weaves a length of fabric and gives it to her sister, who hand stitches a satchel. The original fibers were worth a penny, but the satchel is worth fifty cents."

Brian's eyes lit up. "So, the incomes of three people rise."

"From zero to something even though some of the initial exchanges are in trade. The net worth of the village increases because now there is a small level of commerce producing money that will trickle throughout."

"Very cool."

"I'm glad we have your approval," Matthew teased.

Understanding the concept now, Brian returned to the list and reconsidered each project in light of Brother Matthew's explanation.

He then looked at the world map. After several minutes of focused concentration, he finally said, "This must be a nightmare to manage."

"It's becoming so, yes," Matthew said.

"Have the specific countries offered their assistance?"

"We never really considered asking them," Matthew admitted.

Brian frowned. "Why not?"

"I'm not sure," Matthew said, thinking back to when they had initially created the foundation. "One man is overseeing the foundation, but we fear that he's so busy with the details that some larger questions aren't being asked."

"So, what do you want me to do?" Brian asked.

"Simply think about it, when you find free time. I'll give you a chart that shows how we have structured the foundation and eventually I would like your thoughts."

Feeling the weight of responsibility descending on him, Brian immediately pushed away the papers and sat back in the chair. "I know nothing about this," he protested.

"You know nothing about running a pharmacy either, but I understand you made some good observations and suggestions to the Franklin Drug Store about product placement and customer traffic. Frequently an outsider can see things that someone close to the situation can't." Matthew could see that Brian was strongly resisting. "Think about it like one of your deals. Have fun cracking the nut."

"But this is different—it's about people's lives. It's serious," Brian argued.

"Yes, and that's what makes it so gratifying. Why don't you put the papers in your back pocket, and if you decide to look at them at some point, fine. If not, you're still always welcome here."

Tracked

After the *Endeavor* had disappeared from sight, most of the spectators had moved from the fairgrounds to downtown Main Street, not knowing the fate of the balloon or its pilot. Congregated in front of the library, some took the opportunity to get caught up with the local news.

The Lumby Lines

Wagon Tales Mobile Vet Clinic

BY CARRIE KERRY   May 16

As Doc Campbell nears retirement, a young vet with new ideas is motoring north from Wheatley to care for some of our beloved companions. Forgoing the traditional office with sterile examination rooms, Dr. Faith Glasser has redefined veterinary house calls and roadside services by putting her practice on the chassis of a six-wheel Winnebago and comes a-callin' when . . . called.

Services offered include standard physical exami-
nations of small and large animals, stool and blood
analysis (there's a centrifuge instead of a microwave
in the kitchen), dentistry, vaccinations, surgery, and
euthanasia.

What further sets Dr. Faith apart from other vets is
the treadmill that lies under her "office" and is pulled
out whenever her patients need a cardio evaluation or
aerobic exercise. (I was told that Dr. Faith was making
daily visits to our town prior to last month's Weiner
Races.) For those animals that don't survive her skilled
services, cremation is also available.

When the caravan transporting the remains of the *Endeavor*
reached the intersection of Main and Farm to Market, the crowd
on the steps of the library waved them near. For the chase crew
and those who had volunteered to follow the balloon, the return to
Lumby was demoralizing.

Jimmy D and Mark Walker were the first to confront the group.
As Jimmy began to replay the details of he *Endeavor*'s mishaps, one
of the chase vans, with the crushed basket roped to the roof, drove
directly past them on the way to the Feed Store. The trailer followed
carrying the partially charred envelope.

"So, as you can see," Jimmy said, watching the procession, "it
didn't go quite like we had hoped."

"It was a disaster waiting to happen," an old man said, waving his
walking cane.

Morty Alberts, who had gained some notoriety because of his cows,
yelled from the top step, "Who agreed to this festival anyway?"

Jimmy scanned the top row of onlookers to see who had asked
that question, and when he saw Morty, his defenses went up. "The
town council voted on it quite some time ago," he replied. "Was that
you asking, Morty?"

"Yeah, it was me," Morty yelled back. "It cost the town a lot of money to make the balloon, and now there's nothing to show for it."

Another man in the front joined in. "It's that Indonesian fellow's fault. He should have been in the balloon."

"Yeah," a woman agreed. "It's the foreigners' fault that Chuck is in the hospital."

Caroline Ross stepped out from behind the group. "That's not true!" she said fiercely. "We asked for their help."

"And look where it got us," another naysayer called out.

"Further along than we would have been without them," Caroline snapped. "And when no one else stepped forward to do the work, Kai did it without complaint."

A woman standing close to Caroline said loudly, "You should be on our side and not his. He's a foreigner we know nothing about."

Words of agreement rippled through the group.

"I didn't know this was about sides," Caroline said tartly. "But it's wrong to point fingers at someone who's done nothing but help us."

"And it's not a complete loss," Mark added, since Caroline's temper was not helping calm the waters. "We all came together and successfully built a balloon."

"And it crashed!" Morty sneered.

"Because of the mutiny at takeoff," one of his sons added.

"Yeah, it was a mutiny," a woman yelled out.

Morty couldn't resist the temptation of further riling the crowd. "So, what are we going to do now? Waste more town money?"

Jimmy stepped forward once again. "We have to build another balloon for the festival."

"But the festival begins next Thursday!" Morty argued.

"We definitely have enough time," Mark said, "if everyone works together."

∽

Gabrielle Beezer sat outside the Green Chile listening to the crowd. Although the day had been unusually slow at the restaurant, it was still open and she would need to begin dinner preparations shortly. She jumped up when the phone rang in the kitchen—probably another take-out order.

"The Green Chile," she answered.

"Gabrielle?" a woman asked.

The phone connection was extremely bad, and Gabrielle heard more static than voice. "Yes, hello?" she almost shouted into the phone.

"Gabrielle, it's Joan Stokes." The connection improved slightly.

"Joan!" she said in surprise. "Where are you?"

"I'm in Bali for another few days, but I wanted to get a message through," Joan said succinctly. "I tried calling Jimmy and Russell, but there was no answer."

"No, most everyone is involved in the balloon flight today. What's up?"

There was a long pause, and Gabrielle held the phone tighter to her ear.

"I saw the island this morning," Joan said. The sparkle in her voice could still be heard half a world away.

"And?" Gabrielle asked, preparing herself for the worst.

"It's wonderful!" Joan exclaimed. "It's just as Jamar described: beautiful sandy beaches and palm trees. A small mountain rises from the center and waterfalls cascade down to open lagoons."

"It sounds like paradise," Gabrielle replied.

"Oh, it is," Joan said. "Also, I had a chance to meet with a local attorney who came well recommended. He looked at the copy of the contract I had and said everything was well documented and legitimate."

"That's great news," Gabrielle said, beaming.

"So, please tell everyone that the deal is going forward."

"Oh, Joan, you've made my day."

"Also, you need to tell Russell immediately. I'm having the attorney in Java call him today or tomorrow to give him some details."

Gabrielle looked through the front window of the restaurant and saw the crowd starting to disperse. "I will," she said quickly. "Safe travels back," she said and hung up the phone. As she continued to stare across the street and watch the crowd thin, she wondered how she was ever going to get her friends to buy an island paradise from one of the two men they no longer trusted.

∽

The following day, within hours after signing the final deed papers for the Round House train depot, Caroline was standing on Fiddlers Elbow Road at the planned entrance to Bricks, meeting with the inspector from the Chatham County Department of Transportation. Behind her stood an entire crew of excavators, and behind them, half a dozen parked trucks that were overflowing with gravel for the new road.

"The entry is no different than what was used when the Round Station was in operation," Caroline explained. "In fact, our application shows that we will be widening Fiddlers Elbow for turnoff lanes once the center is approved by the town council. Right now we simply plan to lay a dirt access road to the building."

"You'll need a new asphalt apron," the inspector pointed out.

"That's fine," Caroline said, stifling her impatience. After facing off with the town mob the day before, she was still short of temper. "Anything else?"

The inspector took one more look at the papers. "Nope. Everything else appears in order."

"Thank you," Caroline said with some agitation. Turning to the general contractor, she just nodded and said, "Go."

The speed at which they worked was more than impressive. By the end of the day, the enormous bulldozers had cleared and graveled a twenty-foot-wide road through the dense woods all the way to the Round House.

As Brooke drove slowly up to the new turnoff for Bricks, she saw Caroline hammering in a sign: PROPOSED FUTURE HOME OF THE ROSS ARTS AND MUSIC CENTER. The head of the Ross Foundation was wearing torn jeans and an old denim work shirt with the sleeves rolled up. Dirt smudged her face and a small cut on her forearm was covered with dry blood.

Caroline stretched her back with both hands held high as she watched Brooke get out of the car.

"Isn't this amazing?" Caroline asked. "Look! We have a road now."

Brooke had heard about Caroline's outburst in town yesterday, and she was glad her friend had recovered her good spirits. "I was just out here two days ago and there was nothing. What a change," Brooke said.

"Amazing what a little money and permission from the DOT can do." Caroline smiled. "Why don't you follow me in?"

The drive through the woods seemed to take seconds compared to the hour it had originally taken them to hike through the dense brush. At the cleared field, the road gently swept to the right of the building and then ended at the entrance doors. The long grass in the adjacent fields had been mowed up to the tree line, and most of the brush was cleared along the outside train tracks as far as the eye could see leading away from the depot.

"One thing that can be truthfully said about young Caroline Ross," Brooke said, "you don't putz around when there's a project at hand."

Caroline laughed, dancing on the balls of her feet.

"Isn't it a gem? So secluded, yet it will be totally inviting for both the artists and patrons." She unlocked the front door and bowed formally to Brooke. "Please, come inside."

Brooke stepped slowly inside and, for only the second time, looked around the circular building. It was very much as she remembered it, only much larger. She visualized the end result.

Brooke had been working on the Bricks project twelve hours a day, scrutinizing the old blueprints until late in the evenings while Joshua studied. After creating and considering four radically different designs, Brooke had settled on one, the only one that offered a viable solution for each of Caroline's diverse requirements. That plan was now on paper, rolled up and tucked securely under Brooke's arm.

She continued to survey the surroundings. "Wow," she said quietly.

"It just takes your breath away, doesn't it?" Caroline said.

Brooke turned around, her gaze following the curve of the walls. "I hadn't noticed the details around the windows, or the pulley system for the enormous doors."

"I'd like to keep those," Caroline said. "I don't want the history of the Round Station to be lost or removed, so the original windows and doors should stay if at all possible."

"I think we can easily work with that," Brooke said. "Is there a place where I can spread out the proposed design?"

"There's a table and chairs in the train," Caroline answered, thinking back to when it was last used during her picnic with Kai.

For the next two hours, Brooke walked Caroline through her recommended design for Bricks, which allowed for individual studio spaces, a gallery, practice rooms, and a small concert hall. Caroline questioned several facets of the proposal but was in full agreement after Brooke explained the reasoning behind each choice. They were two independent thinkers and two good friends working together toward one vision.

"In truth, I missed some of the details the last time I was here," Brooke said, "and they are worth revisiting. For instance, to see if we want to accentuate the windows more. The artisan trim and brickwork around them should be preserved at the very least." She made a note on the prints.

"What about the cobweb of tracks?" Caroline asked.

"We can incorporate some of them into various raised floors in the exhibition hall. But for purely practical reasons, much of the track will have to be removed."

Caroline had grown fond of the switch levers and turntable roundabouts that were used to maneuver the trains into, within, and out of the depot. "That's unfortunate," she said with a sigh.

"We really don't have much choice. There are just too many rails on the ground for us to build around."

"Oh, I understand."

"I'm also sure that the county would regard the exposed rails as a code violation," Brooke explained. "And what about this great train? Do we build around it?"

Caroline laughed. "No, it will be moved out. I called several rail companies, but they weren't interested in taking it off my hands. It seems this specific model burned coal very inefficiently and it would be more costly to refurbish it than to buy new."

"So, what will you do with it?" Brooke asked.

"I don't know. I've been thinking about auctioning it," Caroline replied.

Brooke smiled when she heard that. "How funny. To whom?"

"Whoever wants it. It could be a unique addition to someone's backyard."

"Or a new town tavern?" Brooke proposed.

"Exactly. You need to think creatively when looking at an eighty-year-old locomotive. I would just like to know where it's going when I talk to the town council."

"Have they reviewed your nonprofit business application?" Brooke asked.

Caroline's smile was quickly replaced by a scowl. "Steady progress was being made until I lost my position as Lumby's favorite granddaughter."

Brooke was mystified by her change in mood. "What in the world are you talking about?"

"Several of the council members don't like the idea of Kai and me being together."

Brooke's eyes opened wide. "Is it becoming that serious between you two?"

"No, absolutely not," Caroline said. "Kai is committed to God. He'll be returning to Saint Cross and then to Coraba, where he is to become the island's pastor—presumably remaining quite single and celibate."

Brooke looked at her good friend with sympathy. "You really like him, don't you?"

"More than I should," she said, smiling weakly. "You should have seen me yelling at people yesterday. It was because I was defending Kai."

"Oh, Caroline," Brooke said, placing a hand on her friend's arm.

"I know," she said, rubbing her temples. "This is bad on so many levels."

Brooke had a flood of questions, but treaded lightly. "Does he know how you feel?"

Caroline pulled away. "Oh, God, no, and I have no intention of telling him."

Brooke leaned back in surprise. "Why not?"

"He has been preparing for this moment for the last twenty years. Coming to Saint Cross was his final step before committing himself fully to God and the Church. His life is laid out before him, and I don't want to be a . . ."

"Temptation?" Brooke asked.

Caroline passed a hand through her hair and then squeezed the back of her neck tightly. "More like a complication, I think," she said. She gazed up at the high ceiling, and her tone turned wistful. "But when we're together it's as if he has always been in my life. I have never felt so comfortable with anyone."

"A soul mate," Brooke suggested.

"I'm afraid so," Caroline said sullenly. "But it isn't meant to be."

TWENTY-EIGHT

Pressure

Federal Express made more deliveries to Lumby, specifically to the Feed Store at Ninety-two Main Street, within the next two days than they had during the prior twelve months. Once again the theater was crammed to the rafters with boxes of materials for another basket and another envelope.

Hannah had not left her makeshift sewing room since the deliveries had begun. Other than to receive occasional help to rotate or adjust the massive sections of nylon, she remained alone. Her door was always closed, and she asked that meals brought from Jimmy D's be left on a crate she had placed in the hall. Some wondered if she had broken under the stress. Only Kai knew that not only was she all right, but she had found a sanctuary.

Kai, like Hannah, was working around the clock, to build another basket in accordance to the specifications Hannah had given him. Unlike the *Endeavor*, which had barely passed the one hundred thousand cubic feet minimum for a lead balloon, Hannah said she was making the envelope "a bit larger," and advised Kai that his basket should be sixty inches wide by eighty-four inches long.

"But, Hannah, that's five feet by seven feet," Kai said in disbelief.

"That's correct," she said, smiling. "Large enough for a pilot and four two-passenger partitions." Kai continued to be puzzled, and she added firmly, "We're not letting Chuck go up alone again. That's for certain."

Kai picked up a pencil and began to scribble equations on a scrap of cardboard. "Do you know how large your envelope needs to be?"

"To the exact cubic foot, yes," she said.

Kai and Hannah shared a conspiratorial smile. "You know the town has never seen the likes of this before," he said.

"Or ever will again," she replied, winking.

Then she turned on her heels and walked down the hall. Kai heard the door to her sewing room gently close.

࿎

Brooke drove down Farm to Market Road with the intention of returning to work to apply to the blueprints the changes that she and Caroline had discussed. Approaching Montis Inn, she noticed that the parking lot was full and several cars were pulled over onto the grass along the opposite side of the road.

Not having talked with her closest friend in days and looking forward to seeing Pam's progress on the small fish pond, Brooke turned off the road and wedged herself between two large trailers that bore the logos of hot air balloon companies.

Although the number of cars suggested a lot of activity at the inn, the courtyard was deserted, and as Brooke walked over to Pam and Mark's private residence, she saw no one along the way.

"Hello?" she called, knocking on the door and then opening it slightly.

"Brooke? Is that you?" Pam called from one of the back rooms. "Come in."

"Who owns all these cars?" Brooke asked as Pam walked out of the bedroom drying her hair with a towel.

"The festival committee is meeting in the community room," Pam explained. "So, what brings you by?"

"No reason in particular, although I'd love to see your pond."

"Ah, the waters from hell, as I call it." Pam laughed.

Brooke's face filled with concern. "Are you still having trouble?"

"I just spent the last hour standing in water up to my shoulders trying to install the pump and fountain, so now's probably not a good time to ask me that question. But let me show you what I've done so far."

Pam seemed in good spirits, Brooke thought, so the project couldn't be a total disaster. And when Brooke finally saw the pond, she was flabbergasted. "Pam, this is really amazing!" she said.

The pond had graceful curves and a center spray of water fanned out above the surface from an in-water fountain.

"It's beautiful," Brooke exclaimed. "It's so much bigger than what I had envisioned."

"Same here," Pam joked. "Pull up a stone and have a seat. I haven't bought any outdoor furniture yet."

"What are these?" Brooke said, looking at the chiseled granite slabs.

"We're not exactly sure, but I feel they are religious in nature. I kept on digging them up, which explains why the pond is so much larger than I had planned."

Brooke inspected all four sides of one block. "They look like obelisk blocks—surprisingly comfortable to sit on, I must say," she said as she took a seat.

Pam did a double take. "What do you mean, obelisk?"

"You know, where squared stones are stacked on top of each other to build a monolithic shaft," Brooke explained.

"Does that mean it's sacred?" Pam asked.

Brooke was measuring the blocks with her eye. The proportions seemed right for stacking. "Sacred how?"

"Perhaps the monks used them in some ancient ritual," Pam suggested in a mysterious tone.

"Perhaps," Brooke said, skeptical.

"Or perhaps they built it as a monument to God." Pam's imagination went wild. "Maybe a thirty-foot-high stone cross that could be seen far across the valley."

"Yeah, if this was four hundred years ago." Brooke laughed. "You should ask one of the monks who lived here."

"I have a call in to Brother Matthew," Pam said, rubbing her sore knee. "So, what have you been up to?"

Brooke listened to the mesmerizing cadence of the fountain's spray. "I just came from Bricks. It will be a wonderful arts center for our town—quite a unique place."

"Charlotte would be so pleased," Pam said. "She touched so many lives before she died."

"That she did," Brooke concurred. "I feel sorry for Caroline, though. She could certainly use her grandmother's support and advice right now."

"What's wrong?" Pam asked.

"I think she's taken the brunt of the prejudice that some folks feel toward the Talin brothers."

"I'm surprised they're not more liked," Pam said, disappointed. "The whole time they've lived here, both have been considerate and pleasant. Jamar is quite a charmer and fast talker, but Kai is just the kindest person. I like him a lot."

"So does Caroline," Brooke said, cocking her head.

"Ahhh," Pam said in a long sigh. "But he's retuning to Coraba to become a priest."

"And so goes one problem that's out of Caroline's control," Brooke said.

Thinking about Caroline, she asked, "Do you like working with her?"

Brooke responded warmly, "A great deal, plus it's a wonderful project."

Pam smiled. After so much frustration, it felt good to finally relax and listen to the gently splashing water while getting caught up with Brooke.

"How are things at the firm?" she asked.

"Incredibly busy—the two owners have taken the summer off. There's even talk that they might sell out and retire."

Pam gave Brooke an assessing look. "Would you be interested in buying the firm?"

"Sure," Brooke replied, shrugging a shoulder. "But the question is: could I afford it? It's the oldest architectural firm in the area. Their revenues must be somewhere around six million a year. Joshua and I don't have that kind of money." She paused, contemplating the possibility. "But it would be a dream to own a small company like that one." She slapped her hands on her knees, dismissing the subject. "I'm sure nothing will happen for another six or twelve months, so I have time enough to think about it. So, how are you two?"

"I think we're fine, although I haven't seen Mark at all since he started helping Jimmy with the hot air balloon festival. He's been all but consumed by it."

All of a sudden the fountain in the pond stopped, and bubbles appeared on the surface in the general vicinity of the submersible pump. Frustrated, Pam jumped up and walked to the water's edge. Just as she leaned in to look, the fountain shot out a forceful squirt and saturated her all down the front. The flow of water died again for a few seconds, then resumed its normal flow.

"Ugh!" Pam yelled out, wiping water off her face. Then she saw Brooke laughing, and joined in. With a few final shakes of her wet hands, she said, "This project has taught me a lot about humility."

"Perhaps too much water pressure from air in the pump?" Brooke suggested. "So anyway, I thought Mark was only involved in making the town's balloon."

"He was," Pam said, "but during the trials he started helping with the plans for the festival. The committee members have been here all morning, working on the details." Pam leaned forward to stretch her sore back. "It's different—Mark has been so serious and preoccupied."

"Like you when you were in corporate?"

"Oh, I certainly hope not," Pam said, but then she thought back on the years she had come home from the office at midnight and left before dawn. "In some ways, I'm sure I was far worse. Don't ever tell Mark I said this, but I miss the way he was before all this balloon stuff started."

"You mean a little out of control?" Brooke asked.

Pam laughed loudly. "Yeah, except he was a lot out of control. Now he's more predictable but less fun."

Brooke was sure his latest burst of focused enthusiasm would eventually fade. "He'll return to his normal, totally capricious self as soon as the balloons have flown. So, have festival guests started to arrive yet?"

"Some, but we're holding our breath in preparation for the onslaught."

In the community room at Montis Inn, a dozen men and women studied the proposed fairground map for the festival events.

"I don't see why we need to designate a separate parking area for the chase crews," Dennis Beezer said with his finger on that portion of the diagram.

Simon answered, "They need to be assured of an immediate exit with no traffic blocking them as soon as the balloons lift."

"Ah, I see," Dennis said. "What about the actual launch sites? Will each registrant be assigned a specific location or space?"

"We plan to have—" Mark began, but was interrupted when someone knocked on the front door of the inn. "It's open," he yelled, and everyone looked that way to see who the newcomer was.

"Can I join the party?" Chuck Bryson stuck his head in.

"Chuck!" several called out simultaneously.

"Well, look who the cat brought in," Jimmy said, getting up to give him his seat. "Good to see you up and walking."

"Hopefully it's better than my driving." Chuck faked being dizzy as he walked. He saw his good friend, Simon. "Just pulling your leg, Sheriff Dixon."

"Probably a good thing if I give you a ride home tonight?" Simon suggested.

Chuck rubbed the side of his head. "Perhaps so."

"We're reviewing the fairgrounds map," Mark said, and passed Chuck a copy. "Dennis, to get back to your question. There's a grid on the fairgrounds with each space marked. During sign-up, each registrant will be given a specific launch location for the weekend."

Mark waited for everyone to study the map completely and voice any other concerns they might have. "All right, moving along. We need to sign off on the schedule before giving it to Dennis for the final printing." He passed out mock-ups of the catalogue. "Although the festival will officially begin Friday morning, there will be a barbecue open to all at the fairgrounds Thursday evening from five until nine. The food will be provided by the four restaurants in town, and the high school will be bringing over enough tables and chairs to seat a hundred and fifty at a time. Some people will bring their own chairs, and we're thinking most people will be tired from the drive in, so they won't be hanging around too long."

"Who will be cleaning up?" one of the town council members asked.

Jimmy folded his paper. "Festival volunteers will see to it Thursday night."

"So, now we're turning to the festival," Mark said, holding up the schedule. "We have three full days, Friday, Saturday, and Sunday, for all the balloon events. Before creating the schedule, we polled several balloonists and touched base with a few national balloon organizations to discuss normal timelines for this type of event."

Both Jimmy and Mark were anticipating strenuous objections from a few older council members who were not directly involved in structuring the various events, but no objections were raised.

"Each of the three mornings will begin with a 'Scout Flight at Sunrise,' where two or three balloons will launch at five thirty, shortly before dawn," Jimmy said. "It will be great for any spectators who are there that early, by the way. Lights will flood the balloons as they ascend into darkness."

"Also," Mark added, "it seems the Scouts are invaluable to the other balloonists; they watch to determine wind speed and direction across the different altitudes. On Friday morning at seven, there will be the Mass Ascension led by our town's balloon. Based on preregistration, we estimate about half of the pilots will be able to accommodate at least a few passengers, so there will be ample opportunities throughout the weekend for anyone who wants to try."

"And we'll hold a special space open just for you, Chuck," Jimmy promised with a laugh.

As Chuck nodded acknowledgment, Mark continued. "At two o'clock, the special balloons will be inflated and tethered for all spectators to see. It should be especially great for the kids."

"What's a special balloon?" another councilman asked.

"Basically anything that's not round," Jimmy answered. "Animal figures, flowers, cartoon characters, lighthouses, you name it."

"At five o'clock, there will be the Hare and Hound Race," Mark said. "The concept is that our lead balloon, the 'hare,' will launch, fly, and land. The other balloons, the 'hounds,' will ascend twenty minutes later. The objective is to drop a marker closest to the point where the lead balloon has landed." He paused. "Any questions?"

The room was far too quiet, Mark thought. He looked at Jimmy, who just shrugged.

"At eight in the evening, there will be a 'Night Burn,' where all of the balloons will be tethered and inflated in the fairground. The burns are synchronized so all the flames blast at once. We hear it's one of the most impressive parts of any festival." Mark himself was looking forward to seeing that the most. "It really should be a great sight."

Jimmy sat forward on his chair. "Saturday will be very similar, with the Scouts and the Mass Ascension in the morning. There will be a separate flight of the special balloons at two o'clock, and then the Distance Race begins at four thirty. The rules for that are on the last page of the pamphlet. Immediately following that, there'll be another town dinner at the park."

"Are all of Morty's cows gone?" Chuck asked.

"Gone, and the grass has been raked clean," Simon assured him.

"Where did he take them?" a councilman asked.

"Take who?" Jimmy asked.

"Where did the old geezer take his cows?"

"To some leased grazing fields south of town," Jimmy answered.

Mark pressed on quickly, wanting to keep the meeting on track. "On Sunday, after the Scouts, there will be a Bull's-Eye Competition, where we set a target, somewhere in a ten-mile radius, which the balloonists must hit with a marker."

"How is that different from the Hare and Hound?" Chuck asked.

"That's a good question. With the hare," Jimmy answered, "all will be leaving from the fairgrounds and they need to, in essence, find the hare. With the bull's-eye, they are told exactly where the target is, and each chooses where best to launch given how they think the winds will carry their balloon to the target."

"Clever," Chuck said, smiling.

Mark continued with the scheduled events. "Then at two o'clock there will be a speed race, but thus far we only have six balloons out of forty-four signed up." Mark paused, coming to the end of the schedule. "Finally, the Mass Ascension Sunday evening brings the festival to a close."

All were studying the brochure, flipping pages and reviewing the rules and regulations that Mark and Jimmy had so carefully laid out.

"So, let's get to your questions now," Jimmy said.

But no one had questions. None of them had any idea what a hot air balloon festival should be like. All they knew was that crowds of people would be descending on the quiet town of Lumby all too soon.

TWENTY-NINE

Atlantis

When Joan Stokes returned from Indonesia, flying into the small airport at Rocky Mount, she was pleased to be back. Although she had been gone for only two weeks, and this was just one of many trips that took her into remote corners of most foreign countries, it was always Lumby that called her home.

Not surprisingly, the drive from Rocky Mount to Lumby was the most precarious part of Joan's twenty-thousand-mile journey; she was rounding one of the hairpin turns at Priest's Pass when Howard, the town's wayward moose, stepped in front of her car. Joan slammed on the brakes, her heart racing as she looked down into the deep gorge beside her. What a place to die after traveling so far, she thought, and then concluded that Howard, beloved or not, really needed to flourish elsewhere. Right then, Alaska didn't seem far enough away for her comfort.

As Joan drove up to Main Street Realty next to Lumby Sporting Goods, Hank was waiting by the front stoop wearing a stylish Bahamas shirt and yellow shorts. A suitcase with stickers from around the world was tucked between his skinny legs, and from around his neck hung a large sign that read WELCOME HOME.

Joan removed the "On Vacation" notice and turned on the lights. She picked up the mail loosely piled on the floor inside the front door, rolled her chair up to the desk, opened *The Lumby Lines*, and sat back to review the real estate sections she had missed while island hopping around Bali.

The Lumby Lines

Real Estate

June 4

Two granite tombstones with adjacent burial lots at Catholic Cemetery in Flagstaff, Arizona, available for trade. Will consider everything and anything of equal or greater value of $5,800. Call Brian Beezer at home.

Unfurnished garage available now. $15/month. Call now 925-0746

Six beehives seeking immediate occupants for spring pollination. Rent is free if we can keep the honey. 925-5253

Quonset hut on quarter acre available month of July. Must keep lawn mowed. Call Lumby Realty for other great deals. 925-5555

Charming RV in back of house still seeking responsible tenant. One bed, one bath with hookup. Quaint. $55 per month. 925-4439.

Hay barn for rent. Two tractors on blocks stay and cow stays in pen. Call McNear. $25/mo.

House for sale. 22 Cherry Street. A real fixer-upper with great potential, just needs some attention. Well dry. Call Main Street Realty.

Certified piano teacher available to tutor your child any age 10–14. Experienced. Please telephone 925-0174

Chicken coop for rent—good for about two dozen hens. New perching rods. Long-term lease only. $2.25/mo. 925-2985

Spacious attic for loner type. No smoking. No electricity, but extension cord can be run from master bedroom downstairs. Bathroom with working toilet in basement. 925-4992

60x20 horse barn with one-acre turnout pasture. 4 stalls. Hayloft but no hay. Very negotiable. Deer Trail Lane vicinity. Must have four-wheel drive to access. 925-4638

For sale by owner. Rustic cabin unoccupied for 26 years, like new. No driveway but good hiking path to front door. Bring bear repellent.

Location Location. Impeccably maintained 4/3 on Cherry Street one block from downtown Lumby! Perfect for large family. $96,900 firm. Call Joan Stokes at Main Street Realty 925-9292 and let the best Realtor in town find your dream home!

Joan made a note to call about listing the rustic cabin and then waded through her voice-mail messages, returning those that she deemed critical. She then opened her suitcase in the middle of her office and withdrew one very important compact disc that held all of her photographs from the trip. She felt fortunate to have had her pictures processed onto a CD at the L.A. airport during her layover to Rocky Mount.

With irrefutable evidence in hand, Joan quickly walked up Main Street, waving at Simon Dixon, who was talking to Jeremiah, no doubt asking him once again to steer the blind mare away from the flower beds in the park, to which Jeremiah would once again reply that he would do the best he could given that he was as blind as poor Isabella.

How Joan loved the town and the people who formed its heart and soul.

Crossing Main at Farm to Market Road, she noticed a new bench in front of the Lumby Bookstore and an inoffensive sign in the raised flower bed: NO EATING! Joan laughed. It was probably meant for Isabella, although the letters were too small for any horse—vision-impaired or not—to read.

Gabrielle was sweeping the sidewalk in front of her restaurant, softly humming to herself.

"Lahar awaits!" Joan said in her trilling soprano voice that still carried the delight of a child.

"Joan!" Gabrielle smiled. "When did you get back?"

"A few hours ago." She waved the disc in the air. "And I have all the proof right here."

"No photographs?" Gabrielle asked, looking crushed.

"Yes, hundreds of them right here," she explained. "I used my new digital camera."

Gabrielle eagerly took Joan by the arm. "Come in and tell me all about it. Is it really paradise?"

"Yes, and it's all ours if we want. I could have stayed on *our* island forever."

"Doesn't that sound nice?" Gabrielle said dreamily. "*Our* island. I so want to see your photos. Why don't we get everyone together over at the library tonight and you can show your slides?"

"It's a compact disc," Joan said, feeling very much in the know with the new technology.

"Great. They have an integrated computer," Gabrielle said, showing a little savvy herself. "We can use their big-screen monitor. Do you think seven o'clock would be all right?"

"Lahar Island at seven o'clock—it sounds perfect. Tell everyone to bring their checkbooks. Russell will be there and will have the contract prepared for all of our signatures."

"So, we're buying the island tonight?" Gabrielle asked, barely able to contain her excitement.

Joan nodded. "Almost. We'll be making an offer, but I'm sure everything will go smoothly on their end. Now I really need to get home and shower. It was such a long flight."

∽

At ten minutes to seven, Jamar entered the library several steps behind Joan Stokes and heard voices upstairs. He assumed that all the people present that evening were potential investors. But instead of the small group he was expecting, there were easily sixty townsfolk in the crowded room, some of them investors and some interested bystanders. Jimmy D was setting up the computer in preparation for Joan's show.

Jamar took one of the three chairs that faced the audience. When Joan sat down next to him, he leaned close to her. "You look tired."

"A little," she admitted.

"I know how exhausting those long flights are. It would be my privilege to give you a back rub."

Joan looked at Jamar in surprise at what seemed to be an inappropriate suggestion. But maybe giving back rubs to strangers was a form of hospitality in Coraba. "No, but thank you anyway."

"To Joan Stokes!" someone said loudly. Another man in the back raised his glass of wine and said, "To Lahar Island!"

Everyone applauded. Just as the lights dimmed, the door briefly opened. Kai slipped in and stood against the wall.

Although Joan was exhausted from her long flight, her voice danced with delight as she began to speak.

"As Jamar promised, our island is a jewel in the turquoise ocean of Indonesia." She pressed the up arrow on the remote control Jimmy had given her. The first picture jumped up on the movie screen and everyone gasped.

Flooding the room with brilliant color was one of nature's most spectacular sights: a lushly forested island with unblemished white beaches that stretched off the ends of the screen on both sides. In the center a small cove was gently outlined by a row of mature palm trees. The water lightened from an azure blue in the foreground to a light emerald green in the bay.

Gabrielle, seated near the front next to her husband, squeezed Dennis's hand. Kai scanned the audience for Caroline.

"Lahar is one of the islands in the Malay Archipelago. By boat, this was the first I saw of our island." Joan walked over to the screen, her small body dwarfed by the large projection. "If you look carefully," she said, standing on her toes, pointing to the cove, "you can see a small dock that will accommodate a boat up to about fifty feet. The steps to the villa are behind these palm trees. I was so excited when we walked up, I almost felt the ground shake beneath me."

"Ahs" were heard throughout the room.

"This next picture," Joan said as she pressed the button, "is the east side of the island—even more beautiful than the south side. Although lined with beaches, it has virtually no boat access because of the coral reef that lies about a quarter mile offshore."

As she clicked to the next picture, Joan heard many exclamations. "The north side of the island has spectacular waterfalls. It really is more breathtaking in person than what you see here," she promised everyone. "And finally, on the west side are jagged rock cliffs, but one can see the mountain best from this direction."

Another picture showed a panoramic view of Lahar and another island.

"Which island is that, Jamar?" asked someone sitting on the far side of the room.

Jamar smiled and shrugged. "I don't exactly know. There are so many of them."

"Perhaps someone can find a map," a man said.

"I have one here," Dennis replied, holding up a recent *National Geographic* magazine.

He walked up to the front of the group and opened the insert to a large map labeled "Lesser Sunda Islands."

Several people, including Chuck Bryson, who had been standing in the back by the wine table, got up and stood around the table.

"Here's the one Adel asked about," Dennis said, pointing to an island.

"Savu," someone tried to pronounce.

Chuck leaned in. "What's that line running through the archipelago?"

Jamar got up and glanced quickly at the map. "It could be a province separation, a political jurisdiction, or even a fault line, I suppose. You never know about maps."

"Ah," Chuck said, and joined everyone else as they returned to their seats.

For several hours more, Joan shared with her friends all that she had discovered about the island. The villa was discussed for thirty minutes, with Joan showing several pictures of each room from every angle.

When the last photograph appeared, everyone broke into roaring applause.

Russell then walked to the front of the room. "Joan said that many of you are seriously interested in acquiring this island. I suggest that an offer be faxed to the brokerage firm in Java tonight. I will transfer a sizeable deposit into their attorney's escrow account tomorrow. So, those who are interested must sign the contract we have drawn up and write a check for their portion of the purchase price based upon the sheets I mailed out a few days ago."

Caroline stood at the end of the line. Although she had had no intention of investing when she arrived at the library that evening, Joan's photographs were breathtaking enough to give her second thoughts. It was impossible not to get swept up in the allure of paradise, especially one so close to Kai's home. She looked around the room to see who was pulling out their checkbook, and caught Kai's glance from across the room. He looked straight at her and subtly shook his head. From that gesture alone, it was obvious to Caroline that Kai was advising her to stay clear of any deal that his brother was putting together. She stepped discreetly out of line.

The room was so energized that after everyone signed the contract, the party moved en masse down the street to Jimmy D's.

"So, when do you pack your bags?" Jimmy asked Gabrielle and Dennis as they shared one final beer.

"We need to work up a time-share schedule for everyone," Dennis said.

"But," Gabrielle continued with a grin, "we're hoping to go the first few weeks of November. How about you?"

Jimmy looked around to see who was within hearing distance. "I'd like to give Hannah ten days on the island for her birthday next month."

"You two will have a wonderful time," Gabrielle said.

"Well," Jimmy admitted, "I may not necessarily be accompanying her. Right now, I'm only buying one plane ticket. If she would like me to join her, then perhaps."

Gabrielle and Dennis didn't know what to say, and an awkward silence fell among the friends.

"I'm sorry," Gabrielle said, reaching out and touching Jimmy's hand.

He tried to smile. "Mea culpa. But I know if I can fix it as well as I screwed it up, there's hope for us yet."

"To paradise!" someone yelled out from down the bar.

"Paradise!" the crowd shouted back.

THIRTY

Direction

"Do you need anything at Brad's Hardware?" Kai called through the door to Hannah, who remained steadfast about not letting anyone into her sewing room.

"Yes, I do," she replied. "Brad ordered two Clover's needles for me. Would you see if they've come in?"

"Anything else?" he asked.

"Nope, I'm all set," she said, her last words drowned out by the rattle of the sewing machine.

A minute later there was a knock on her door.

"Did you forget something, Kai?" Hannah asked without changing the speed of her sewing. She was stitching a French seam about twenty feet in length, carefully folding the raw edges that closed into themselves.

"It's not Kai, it's Jimmy," came a voice from the other side of the door. "Can I come in, or"—he paused—"can you come out?"

The sewing machine continued at the same speed. "I'll be out in one minute," she said.

Jimmy walked back into the main room of the theater and saw the basket Kai was close to completing. Double the size of the original, it had several partitions, whereas his first basket was one large opening. Jimmy wondered why the size and design had changed so significantly.

Hannah stepped into the theater without Jimmy noticing. "Did you need something?"

After so many years of being married to someone quieter than a mouse, Jimmy was no longer startled when Hannah appeared out of nowhere.

"I just came by to see how you are. Do you have a minute?" he asked.

"I could use a break," she said, sitting down in the front row of chairs.

Jimmy pulled up a cardboard box in front of Hannah and sat on it. But his weight crushed the empty carton and he rolled sideways to the ground.

Hannah laughed, and Jimmy, who was half perched, half lying on the collapsed box, joined in.

"I'm glad I can still make you smile," he said, getting up and pulling over a stool.

"You had quite a party last night. I was sitting on the windowsill looking down at people leaving until the early hours of the morning."

"I wish you'd joined us."

Hannah shook her head. "You know I'm not very good around rowdy crowds."

"There was certainly a lot of celebrating," Jimmy acknowledged. "I'm buying a small corner of paradise and giving it to you for your birthday."

Hannah was surprised. "You're buying the island for me?"

"A share of it, yes. That's the least I can give you." He reached out to take her hand, but then thought otherwise.

"That's very kind of you, Jimmy."

He smiled. "You said you needed time and distance."

"I still do," she said, looking down at her lap.

"I'm assuming you don't want to come back to the house after the balloon is made. Will you find a room to rent?"

"Probably," she said, blushing. "Part of me really likes living in the sewing room up here. I know you'll never understand, but it's contained and smaller than I am, and in a strange way I feel it's all mine. But at night the sound of all the animals downstairs behind the Feed Store drives me crazy."

"There are no chickens at our house," Jimmy suggested.

"But between the walls here, as little space as there is, I can be myself," she said. "I can figure out what I like and don't like without being influenced by what you need, or what you say and do."

"Look, Hannah," Jimmy said, gazing sadly at her, "I know I haven't been the best husband. I guess in truth I liked having you at home, knowing that you would always be there for me."

"But I need to be there for myself first," she said.

Jimmy spoke softly. "I see that now. And I know the only times I encouraged you to go out were when I needed you with me."

"It's not all your fault," she admitted. "It was always easier for me to hide from people or to blame you." She lifted her head. "I want to change. I want to get out and do things, but in my own way and for my own reasons."

"And I want to help you," Jimmy said. "Hannah, if you want me to resign as mayor, I will in a second."

She looked into his eyes and knew he was telling the truth. "No," she said, smiling slightly. "Lumby needs you."

"But I want us to have a chance to work things out."

She placed her hand on his. "We do have a chance."

◌

When Kai walked into the theater, he found Jimmy and Hannah talking quietly.

"Am I interrupting?" Kai asked. "If so, there are other errands I can run."

Jimmy waved him over. "Not at all," he said, getting up from the stool. "Your basket is tremendous—much larger than the other one."

Kai smiled and winked at Hannah. "I just build what the boss tells me."

Jimmy looked confused and turned to his wife. "You gave Kai the dimensions?"

"I did," Hannah said, sounding more proud in those two words than Jimmy could ever remember.

"It appears Hannah knows more about balloon construction than any of us," Kai said casually.

They all turned when they heard someone walking up the steps.

Chuck Bryson stumbled in carrying a large propane cylinder. "Well, good morning," he said when he saw the three standing by the basket. "Is this what you wanted, Kai?"

"Exactly, but you could have just given me the dimensions."

"Nothing like the real thing," he said, dropping the cylinder next to burners that had been placed in one corner of the room.

"And you actually need four of them?" Chuck asked.

Hannah stood up. "We do," she said. "I need to get back to work."

"And so do I," Jimmy said, heading for the door.

Chuck was still scratching his head. "This balloon must be huge to need that amount of propane."

Kai glanced at Hannah, who just grinned.

౷

When Jimmy walked out of the Feed Store, several changes along Main Street were noticeable. Whereas the street had been mostly empty a short time before, now a dozen four-wheel-drive vehicles towing large trailers were taking most of the parking spaces along both sides of the road. Most trailers were black or white, and all had colorfully painted signs and logos touting hot air balloons.

Jimmy saw Simon standing in front of Wools talking with one of the visitors, whose van was blocking the fire hydrant.

"And so it begins," Jimmy said to himself.

The sidewalks grew busier as Jimmy headed toward city hall. Jeremiah and Isabella were surrounded by tourists having their pictures taken. Some serious readers who had time on their hands had brought their own chairs and were comfortably camped out in front of the bookstore, while children ran in and out of the candy shop next door.

Passing the police station, Jimmy noticed Caroline Ross sitting in her car reading some papers. She had just come from city hall to submit the next round of required paperwork for her music and arts center. He knocked on her roof, startling her.

"You scared the crud out of me, Jimmy!" she said, rolling down her window.

"Sorry," he said, "just your friendly mayor."

"Yours is about the only face I've recognized all morning," she said, looking wryly up the street.

Simon Dixon was now talking with several men who had pulled their motorcycles up on the sidewalk.

"And the festival is still several days off," she said coolly.

"And next Monday our small town will be back to its normal quirky self," Jimmy assured her.

"Somehow I doubt that." She waved and drove slowly off.

Caroline had fought the urge to see Kai, but it was a losing battle, so she drove down Main Street and parked in front of Jimmy D's. After looking up at the theater for several minutes, she crossed the street and mounted the stairs. Kai stood in the corner of the room stacking empty boxes with his back toward her. The basket was near completion and his obligation to the town was coming to an end.

"It looks like you're packing to leave," Caroline said.

Kai's heart quickened at the sound of her voice but he didn't turn around. "I think my final days in Lumby are drawing near."

Caroline walked in and sat down on an old couch that had been pushed against the wall. "After seeing Joan's photos of Indonesia, I can understand why you want to return home. It's breathtaking."

"That's not why I'm leaving," Kai said, finally facing her. "The elders and a entire village of people are expecting my return. The town gave the little they had to send Jamar and me to Saint Cross to finish our religious study. By becoming their priest I will give my family a stature in our community that they would not be able to achieve otherwise. If I don't return, they will be ostracized."

Caroline cared so deeply for him. "So, you're doing this for them?"

"And for God," he said, sitting next to her.

"But what's left for you?"

Kai moved closer to Caroline and reached for her hand, but then pulled back. "It doesn't matter," he whispered.

THIRTY-ONE

Grounded

At six in the morning, Mark Walker and Simon Dixon were the only two patrons in S&T's Soda Shoppe, well engrossed in discussing a revised parking plan for the festival.

"I knew it was going too well with the town council," Mark complained. "I just didn't think they would list all their issues and send out a formal memorandum."

Simon laughed. "Don't worry. We'll take care of each complaint one at a time."

Dennis Beezer walked in, looking drawn and pale. He was carrying a piece of paper that was ripped on the top and bottom.

"You really need to get some sleep," Mark said.

"This just came across the wire," he said, handing the paper to Simon. "It hasn't even hit television news yet."

"What is it?" Mark asked.

"My God!" Simon murmured. He looked up at Mark and then back down at the Associated Press news release. "Last night, there was a volcanic eruption and earthquake near Lahar, and our island sank, creating a large tsunami that damaged three nearby islands."

"I can't believe it." Dennis groaned.

"Was anyone hurt?" Mark asked.

Simon looked down at the news bulletin. "No. No deaths have been reported." He reread the story. "This is just devastating."

Dennis looked at Simon. "How do I tell Gabrielle?"

"As gently as we tell the rest of Lumby," he answered.

∽

The news of small but beautiful Lahar sinking into the Indian Ocean spread more quickly around Lumby than it did around the world. The fact that plate tectonic activity along the Malay Archipelago was credited for Lahar's fate, and that the highest point of the island was now one hundred feet below sea level, was not a front-page news story in any publication except, of course, *The Lumby Lines*.

The residents of Lumby had to wait several hours to read the written word of exactly what happened and learn the stories behind the story. For that reason alone, there was more than usual supposition, speculation, and rumor running rampant along Main Street.

Jamar had not heard a word of Lahar's fate as he walked toward the library later that morning, having been dropped off at the post office by a commuter from Wheatley. He was oblivious of the whispers and occasional finger-pointing that went on behind his back. He was far more focused on his newly hatched idea of becoming a United States citizen. After spending five months in this country, he had tasted enough of the American way to know he wanted more.

Jamar was lost in thought as he walked up the library's stone steps.

"Shame on you," an old woman said to him, shaking her finger at him.

Jamar looked up but assumed she was speaking to someone else—or more likely, to herself.

At the information desk, Jamar asked where he would find books or documents about obtaining U.S. citizenship.

The librarian leaned over the desk. "There are none here," she whispered with a sneer.

"That makes no sense. This is a library," Jamar said.

"It's best you take your business elsewhere," she said, pointing to the front door.

Jamar realized that he had just been asked to leave and was quite taken aback. Everyone in Lumby had been so nice. As he walked out, he brushed shoulders with Russell Harris at the door.

Russell looked up at Jamar. "Tough luck, really," he said. "Call me if you need legal advice and I can recommend someone over in Rocky Mount."

"What—" Jamar started to say, but Russell continued hastily inside.

Although Jamar and Kai had been at odds since leaving Saint Cross Abbey, Jamar thought it best that he talk to his brother, and headed down Main Street toward the Feed Store.

Simon Dixon came out of the Daily Grind just as Jamar was passing by.

"I'm surprised to see you in town," Simon said.

Jamar shrugged his shoulders. "Why? No different than any other day."

"Except for what just happened to Lahar," Simon retorted.

"What are you talking about?" Jamar asked, not really interested.

It became obvious to Simon that Jamar hadn't heard the news. "There was a volcanic eruption and earthquake near the island, and the entire thing sank into the sea last night."

Jamar's eyes opened wide, his jaw dropping. "Who would have predicted the odds for that happening?" he said.

"Lumby residents were given no warning for this," Simon said.

"Well, it shouldn't have been that much of a surprise. I told several folks that Lahar is Indonesian for the word 'lava,'" Jamar said, shrugging his shoulders. "And where there's lava, there are volcanoes."

The Lumby Lines

Sheriff's Complaints

BY SHERIFF SIMON DIXON   June 7

7:52 a.m. Wheatley commuter called. Nude cyclist fell off bike at Hunts Mill and Loggers.

8:18 a.m. Sam called. Someone left another dozen live chickens on the back porch of the Feed Store.

11:44 a.m. Resident reported that large rock propelled from construction site next door owned by Steve Iron landed on gazebo. No one injured but gazebo is total loss.

12:01 p.m. Gordy Ellers requested assistance after falling into his barberry patch. Covered with thorns so he can't sit to drive himself to hospital and Martha is in Rocky Mount shopping for a new kitchen table.

12:33 p.m. Moose vs. Volvo on State Road 541 at Priest's Pass. Guardrail damaged but no injuries.

12:42 p.m. Truck vs. Moose on SR 541 at Priest's Pass. No injuries but front axle sustained some damage. Will attempt to drive to Lumby.

1:12 p.m. Truck jackknifed in front of Wayside

Tavern on SR 541. 10,000 ball bearings are now loose on road. Driver slipped on several and broke his ankle. LFD and LEMS dispatched.

6:27 p.m. Allen Miller, age 8, reported that his kite hit street wires and he can't pull it down.

11:10 p.m. Caller having just left Jimmy D's reported that the Main and Farm to Market streetlight seems to be working again.

༄

At Saint Cross Abbey, Mackenzie stood on the roof of the small chapel and surveyed the property around her. Ever since the seekers had left, Saint Cross was a different place, with a quiet, reverent atmosphere. After completing four additional projects that Matthew had identified, she was scheduled to begin a large job in Lumby the following Monday.

"I certainly will miss this tranquility on the next job," Mac said to her son, who was well above her on the chapel's roof.

"Where will that be?" Terry asked.

"At the Wayside in Lumby," Mac said.

Terry laughed. "What are they doing, extending the bar?"

"Building on to the pool room and adding a new deck out back," Mac replied.

After positioning another piece of slate, Terry set down his rubber mallet, sat back, and rested his arms on his bent knees. "Were you expecting me to join you?"

Mac looked up sharply. "Of course. You're the best carpenter in Lumby. Why do you ask?"

Her son gazed down on the courtyard, where several monks were pruning roses. "Brother Matthew mentioned a few one-man projects that need doing around here."

"Yes. He asked me a few days ago if you'd be interested, but I told him that he needed to talk to you directly."

"He said, to begin, they would like a large gazebo down by the pond. He offered one of their rooms in the guesthouse while I work here so I wouldn't have to commute."

Mackenzie hid her disappointment. She would have liked Terry to work with her on her job. "Would you prefer to work here rather than in Lumby?"

Terry had a wonderful bird's-eye view of the monastic compound. Some of the brothers sat in meditation on stone benches positioned throughout the grounds. He nodded his head and chuckled at his own preference. "For right now," he said, "I think I do." He looked at his mom, who was smiling up at him. "But don't get any wild ideas. I'm not going to church every day or anything crazy like that."

"I won't," she promised. "Did you give Brother Matthew a bid?"

"I wanted to talk to you about it first, and also get your thoughts on what the bid should include."

"Terry, I'll always help you, but you know how to do everything I do. You've been ready to be on your own for some time. Just price the job fairly and do good work you're proud of," Mac advised.

"And if I underprice the project?"

"You take the loss and learn the lesson," his mother said firmly. "But you couldn't ask for more honest clients."

"Boy, wouldn't you just burn in hell if you ripped off a bunch of monks?" he said. "Brian should think hard about that."

Mac raised her brows. "What does young Mr. Beezer have to do with it?"

"Brother Matthew asked Brian to look at some papers about their foundation. Matthew wants his opinion on some philanthropic stuff. It seems Brian gave them some really good suggestions before and Matthew wants him to do some more research."

"And Brian agreed?" Mac asked in amazement.

"Yeah. That's probably what they're talking about right now," Terry said, scratching his head. "Who would have thought? In fact,

Brian pretty much jumped at the chance to get his hands wet in 'big business,' as he called it."

"And you think he feels some responsibility?"

"Oh, he knows his toes are to the fire. But I think he may have gone overboard. When I went by to see him last Saturday afternoon, he was locked in his bedroom with a slew of books and was taking notes like mad."

"Books on what?"

"On everything from running a nonprofit to poverty reports in South Africa to agricultural forecasts in Chile."

"Good for him," Mac said. "I just hope he's not too creative in his newfound entrepreneurship."

ﾟ

Brian, who had worked with Mac and Terry all morning, was in the library at Matthew's request. They both stared at a graph that highlighted the monastery's philanthropic efforts throughout South America. Projects in six of the seven selected countries showed high activity and admirable growth. However, notes regarding the seventh country, Bolivia, were disconcerting.

"What's going on there?" Brian said, pointing to a side box.

"I don't know," Matthew said. "The person overseeing Bolivia and Chile resigned six months ago, but his stewardship was supposed to be picked up by Enrique Rodriquez in Brazil."

"Well, something has gone wrong," Brian said.

Matthew pulled out another page from the folder lying on the table. "You can read this," he said, handing it to Brian. "It's a letter from one of the women in the northern province of Bolivia. She opened a small market with a micro-grant we gave her last year and she was doing well. But now, it seems, much is lost."

Brian squinted. "I'm sorry," he said, "I can't read a lot of her writing."

Matthew smiled. "She tries to use English, but when she doesn't know the word, she continues the sentence in Spanish. She's saying that the local bankers are seizing eighty percent of each day's income."

"So bankers are thieves down there?"

Matthew's mouth tightened before answering. "Some are, but she might be referring to the loan sharks. They charge interest up to ten percent *a day*."

"Then just send her more money," Brian asserted.

Matthew replaced the letter in the file. "We could, but without solving the larger problem, wouldn't the same thing happen again in four months?"

Brian thought about his question. "Yes, I suppose so."

"Sometimes throwing more money at the problem isn't the right solution," Matthew advised. "Unfortunately, she is one against many."

"So you level the playing field. If there were one hundred on her side, the bankers would leave her alone."

"That's true. But it would take our small foundation years to make that type of change."

"And the local government?"

"Unfortunately, many are as corrupt as the bankers," Matthew said in dismay.

Brian rubbed his knees. "Are any other organizations doing philanthropic work in the area?"

Matthew raised an eyebrow. "Probably, but I don't know."

Brian stood up and began pacing the floor. "It seems to me that you need a coalition to stand up against these thugs. If Saint Cross alone can't build up the masses fast enough, perhaps other foundations who are facing the same problem would jump at the chance to work together so that progress that's made becomes permanent."

"An interesting idea," Matthew said.

Brian spoke more quickly as his ideas became clearer. "Someone needs to be on the ground, meeting with the other foundations and working hand in hand with the villagers."

"Enrique can begin the process, but—" Matthew abruptly stopped and put his finger to his lips. He studied the young man standing before him, looking so much like his granduncle, with the same passion in his heart. He just needed to be set in the right direction. "Brian," Matthew said slowly, "how would you like to go down to Bolivia for a few weeks and start to do what you are recommending? Brother Marcel is planning a trip there, but he will need assistance."

Brian looked at Brother Matthew in disbelief. Franklin was the farthest he had been from Lumby and now the world was opening up before him. But with that opportunity came a responsibility so large that thinking about it made him nauseous.

THIRTY-TWO

Releases

"I thought it would be only you, Brooke, and Joshua," Pam whispered to her husband as she scanned the backyard of Montis Inn. In addition to a dozen friends, another twenty inn guests were milling around, enjoying the ambiance. "Sending out a couple of invitations was really just a big spoof," Pam added. "You know, after I almost drowned my tractor, who would think anyone would come to the official fish release?"

Mark put his arm around his wife's shoulders. "It seems either there are a lot of folks who want to go fishing or you have tons of friends who look for just about any reason to party. And our guests just love this sort of stuff."

The pond looked splendid. Pam had moved large boulders and stones to form a cascading fall of recirculated water at the far end, and had planted lush vegetation along the banks. The surface was covered with water lilies and water hyacinths. It was a perfect garden oasis.

Hank, who had arrived early that morning, appreciated the view as he stretched out on a lawn chair at the base of the weeping willow. He wore a wide-brimmed straw hat that looked stylish with his Hawaiian print shirt and khaki shorts. Sandals were taped to his feet.

As he was not the designated driver that night, a fresh strawberry daiquiri was nestled in the grass next to him.

Pam surveyed the impromptu party. Gabrielle and Dennis Beezer were trying out the double hammock with their youngest son, Timmy. Simon Dixon was playing with some children by a ceramic frog spitting water. Brooke and Joshua tried to get comfortable on the granite blocks, which Pam had carefully arranged around the pond. They were talking with Brother Michael, who had just delivered more rum sauce to Lumby. Caroline and Kai, seated next to each other at the picnic table, were conversing quietly.

Pam tapped a fork against her glass to get her guests' attention. "Thanks, everyone, for coming," she began. "This really was more of a joke than a planned party, given how long the project has taken. But it's done."

"And the tractor still works," Mark added helpfully.

Many broke into applause.

"We're going to release the fish now," Pam said. "The first one is Einstein, who, as you'll see, is brilliant orange with one large white patch on its head." Pam knelt down and lowered the bucket into the pond, allowing the pond water to flow slowly into the container, and then she tipped it over so Einstein swam free. His long flowing tail could be seen by all.

Brooke squinted. "Is that a koi?" she asked.

"No," Pam answered. "Actually, it's a goldfish."

Chuck, standing behind Pam, chimed in, "*Carassius auratus*. *Carassius* from the Latin *karass*, which is the crucian carp, and *auratus* meaning gold. And these are a further subspecies called comets, which originated in the U.S."

Brooke acknowledged the fulsome answer. "Why not koi?" she asked.

"These are more gentle on the water plants," Pam answered as she watched Einstein swim to the far end of the pond.

For the first time that day, Hank became keenly interested in the Montis pond.

"Next is Lips," Pam said, releasing a stunning white eight-inch comet with a red patch over its lips and a spotted red-and-white tail. "A Sarasa comet, I think. Is that right, Chuck?"

He nodded. "Indeed. Instead of gold or gold and white, Sarasas have red-and-white patterns." He peered at the fish. "A very nice specimen."

Hank silently agreed.

"How long do they live?" Timmy asked.

"If all goes well and there are no predators, ten to fifteen years," Pam said.

Hank silently disagreed.

After all ten named fish were released, more margaritas were served.

"I'm so glad you stopped by," Pam said, walking up to Brother Michael.

"What you did here is amazing. I'd like to take some pictures to bring back to Brother Matthew," Michael said. "He'll get a kick out of seeing the dog rocks again."

Pam reacted as if she had been struck by lightning. "Dog rocks?"

"These stones we're sitting on," Michael clarified.

Her eyes lit up. "That sounds mysterious. Do you know what they are? Did you use them for a ritual or, perhaps, meditation?"

"Well, not exactly." He chuckled. "A long time ago, during the summer months, we frequently had a bonfire where the brothers would roast hot dogs."

"Don't tell me," Pam said, catching on. "Is that really why they're named dog rocks?"

"I'm afraid so."

"But one of you must have carved them so carefully, so . . . sacredly," Pam said in one last breath of hope.

"Not really," Brother Michael replied casually. "They were left at the side of the road by the Army Corps of Engineers who were work-ing on Woodrow Lake at the time."

Everyone heard the air go out of Pam's bubble. She had so hoped the granite stones had a deep history and rich spiritual significance.

"But that doesn't mean they weren't special to Montis Abbey," Mark chimed in.

"Monks sat on them and dripped toasted marshmallows," Pam said. "How special is that?"

Mark leaned over and whispered to his wife, "They were very religious derrieres."

She laughed, smacking him on the arm.

"Oh," Michael said, remembering one more thing, "Brother Aaron did, in fact, break his leg jumping off one once."

Pam shrugged her shoulders. "Not exactly what I had expected, but at least I know the truth."

"With that, I really need to be off," Michael said, saying good evening to everyone.

At dusk, Mark lit the torches he had placed around the back of the inn, and all watched as the fish began eating the insects that landed on the pond's surface.

"You did a wonderful job," Mark said, taking his wife's hand and leading her over to a large stone.

"You know, I really didn't," she said as they sat down close together.

"I know this was hard for you," he added, rubbing her neck gently.

She looked at him doubtfully. "Why didn't you say anything?"

He raised a wineglass. "I had total confidence you would work it out in your own way," he said. "And I was hoping that if you couldn't, you would feel comfortable talking to me about it."

Pam put her head down. "But I didn't. Not because of you—I was too embarrassed about my miserable failures."

Mark put his arm around Pam and turned her slightly to face the pond. "Look at what you created. It's stunning. And look at all our friends who have come to cheer you on. There can never be failure with a life so rich in love and friendship."

"Mark, be real," she said, snapping him out of his Hallmark reverie. "This pond cost us about twenty-six thousand dollars."

"We'll use Bertha down at the stable," he reminded her. "Do you remember our first vegetable garden? After the irrigation system and seven truckloads of premium compost and miles of fencing, I think that first tomato must have cost, oh, four thousand dollars." He chuckled. "But it was the best damn tomato we ever tasted."

"It was good, wasn't it?" She grinned.

"Delicious."

Pam leaned over and kissed him. "I love you," she said.

On the other side of the pond, Joshua saw Kai sitting alone after Caroline left and walked over to join him. "Have you ever explored the orchards?" he asked.

"Once at night. But I really haven't had time," Kai said.

"Oh, it's spectacular, especially at sunset. Come with me," Joshua offered.

They strolled in silence until they crossed Farm to Market Road and then spoke casually about the upcoming festival. When they reached the top of the first hill, Joshua stopped and turned around. The front of Montis Inn glowed from the setting sun, which was about to drop behind the mountains.

"I must admit," Joshua said, "I do miss Montis Abbey sometimes. When I was a novice, I often came here after vespers. Even in the cold of winter I was somehow warmed by the trees and the sight of the monastery."

"But still you left," Kai said.

"The hardest decision I ever made," he said, continuing to walk along the row of trees that led them deeper into the orchard.

"Did you ever have second thoughts?"

Joshua laughed. "And third. Part of me longed to take vows and make a life commitment. Occasionally I think a small part of me would still like that."

Kai looked up in surprise. "So you're not happy?"

"Oh, no, just the opposite. I couldn't be happier. But we are all so complex and multifaceted that I would never expect one decision, let alone one life, to meet every desire I might have. There are compromises: a vocation you love pays less so you willingly accept a smaller salary. A friend is in need so you sacrifice your private time to be with him."

"That's exactly what I was trying to explain to Caroline," Kai said. "Sometimes there are so many dependent upon you that you must forfeit everything."

Joshua stopped and looked at Kai. "That's not what I'm saying at all, Kai. You should never sacrifice yourself or allow others to define your life."

"I thought we let God define our lives," Kai argued.

"Unless He comes down and shakes your hand, I don't think so," Joshua replied. "Hopefully God will influence our decisions and we will follow His word wisely, but you're the only person who can decide what path to take." Joshua grabbed the end of a large limb with its hundreds of offshooting branches, twigs, and leaves, and pulled it downward. "Look at this tree. From one trunk this tree has a thousand paths taking it to the sunlight. The decisions you make are similar to selecting different branches. Each choice leads to another branch, and so on."

Kai broke off a twig in frustration. "I am so torn. I know what I want but I know I have to let Caroline go."

"Do you actually think that your parents and the island elders would want you to return to a life you didn't want to live?"

The question so startled Kai that he fell silent for a moment. "No, of course they wouldn't," he finally answered.

"And wouldn't they want you to be happy?"

Again, Kai had never asked himself that question. "Yes, I'm sure."

"Returning to the island with remorse and resentment in your heart would be as unfair to them as it would be to you. I don't think your island wants a martyr any more than God does."

Joshua's words stung so much that Kai turned away.

"If you look deep into your heart, I know you'll see which limb to choose," Joshua promised.

⌒

The following morning, Russell Harris left his office below Chatham Press and climbed the two flights of stairs to Dennis Beezer's office. The staff was scrambling to finish printing the extra flyers for the festival, which had been on hold for last-minute changes.

Dennis's head was buried in some copy when Russell tapped on his open office door.

Looking up, Dennis saw the town attorney. "No offense, but I always get nervous when you take the time to come up and see me," he said.

"I've asked Jimmy to join us. He should be here any minute."

"Come in and sit," Dennis said, returning to the copy. He had to use every second he had if deadlines were to be met.

A minute later, Jimmy rushed into the office. "Is there a problem?"

"Do I really have that bad a reputation?" Russell asked, shaking his head.

"Not at all," Jimmy answered insincerely. "So, what's wrong?"

"I know both of you are extremely busy, so I'll give you the short version. I received a call today from the provincial land registration office in Java."

"Did you tell them our island sank?" Dennis asked dryly.

"Oh, they're aware of it," Russell said. "Which is why they were calling."

"Yes?" Jimmy asked suspiciously, drawing out the question long and low.

Russell shook his head and laughed. "It seems that the province wants to accept the offer we made for Lahar."

"That's nuts!" Jimmy said. "There's nothing for them to sell or us to buy. It's a hundred feet under water."

"They agree. But they feel that it would be a boon to their economy if Americans, especially a group of Americans, bought one of their islands. So, they would like to sell us Nanas Island instead."

"What does Nanas mean, earthquake or mud slide?" Jimmy asked warily.

"Actually it means pineapples. There is a sizeable pineapple plantation on the island."

"And the government owns it?"

"They repossessed it as a foreclosure from a cartel that was using it to move drugs."

Jimmy laughed. "This story just gets better and better."

"Where is it located?" Dennis asked, pulling an atlas from his bookshelf.

"About fifty nautical miles from Lahar—still in the same province and archipelago. The island is double the size of Lahar but they would accept the original price we offered."

"It's probably a barren rock," Jimmy said.

"From the photographs the government's attorney sent me, it looks more spectacular than Lahar did on its best day. And it has far easier accessibility to the main islands. The plantation has one main house with twelve rooms and at least eight small cottages that were used by the crop workers."

"So what's the hook? There's a million dollars of back taxes that need to be paid on it?" Dennis asked.

"No." Russell shook his head. "They are so worried that we will walk away from the offer that they are waiving all taxes until next year."

"It's almost too good to believe," Jimmy said, looking from Dennis to Russell. "So we have an island after all?"

"If that's what everyone wants, it appears so. There will be a few weeks of legal procedures, and each person listed on the title of the island will have to sign the provincial release and new deed, but initially, everything looks easy to execute."

"Thanks so much," Dennis said as he stood and shook Russell's hand. "Once word gets out, our townsfolk will be lining up outside your office to sign all the documents you have."

THIRTY-THREE

Streetwalkers

When those involved with the balloon festival walked outside, they immediately took note of the deep blue sky with no clouds. The leaves on the aspens were motionless—there wasn't even the slightest breeze. Although the weatherman forecasted unfavorable weather, everyone felt confident that when the festival began the following day, Lumby would be blessed with perfect flying conditions.

Leaving the Chatham Press building, Russell shook his head at the traffic jam all the way through town. Most of the cars had out-of-state license plates.

Simon was standing on the corner of Main Street and Farm to Market Road.

"So what did you do to cause this gridlock, Sheriff Dixon?" Russell teased.

Simon shrugged his shoulders in disbelief. "I don't remember ever seeing so many people converge on Lumby in one day."

"Not such a sleepy town anymore, is it?"

"Not until Sunday night. I think most folks are just arriving now," Simon said. "So, are you going to the fairgrounds?"

"I wouldn't miss it."

At five o'clock, the fairground gates opened to the long lines of visitors and townsfolk who were eager to enjoy the barbecue dinner. Many commented that the calm air was almost ominous. The nautical flags bought on sale at Lumby Sporting Goods and stapled to tent posts drooped. Not a breeze in the sky stirred a single leaf.

A few naysayers mentioned that a weather system was supposed to push through during the coming hours, but most people stayed in good spirits, seeing old friends and meeting new. The talk from table to table under the large tents was focused on two subjects: balloons and the piloting thereof.

"It seems to be going well," Jimmy said to Mark as they walked around the fairgrounds. "How many would you guess?"

Mark scanned the area. "Around a hundred and fifty."

Jimmy exhaled in relief. "Good. If these numbers keep up, we should be in the black by the end of the weekend. The last thing we need is to lose money on the festival. Are we all set for the opening ceremonies tomorrow?"

"I think so," Mark said. "Let's plan to meet here at five in the morning. Those in the Scout Flight have been told that there will be a five thirty launch, so they'll need thirty minutes for preflight and inflation. I would think that most of the other pilots will be here to watch the wind directions."

"I talked with Kai and Hannah this afternoon. They plan to bring the lead balloon over at six fifteen. There's an expectation that we'll inflate well before anyone else flying in the Mass Ascension."

Mark and Jimmy continued to stroll up and down the passageways between the tables.

"I know how concerned you've been since the prototype flights, but don't worry," Mark said. "We won't look like a bunch of idiots. Look around—everyone's having a wonderful time."

"And they're not even drinking," Jimmy said. "Bad for business—I'll need to haul all of those full kegs back to the bar."

"Better that than someone getting out of hand," Mark said.

༄

At two a.m. Friday morning, winds preceding a cold front began to stir, and within two hours they were gusting to twenty miles an hour. At five a.m., just as pilots and crew began waking, thunder crashed and a gentle rain began to fall. One look outside, and professionals and amateurs alike rolled over and went back to sleep.

The official start of the festival came and went without pomp or ceremony. A small red flag was hung at the locked gate to the fairgrounds, if anyone ventured that far to confirm that the day's activities had been canceled.

The steady, soft rain continued to fall throughout the afternoon, stopping only a few hours in the evening. Torrential downpours began at midnight, when the buzzer rang in the Walkers' private residence.

Startled, Mark jumped out of bed.

"It's just the front desk," Pam said. "Someone probably wants to check in."

Mark heard the rain on the roof. "Or check out." He pulled on a pair of pants. "I'll take care of it."

Twenty minutes later, after welcoming the final two couples who were to arrive that day, Mark crawled back into bed, snuggled close to his wife, and immediately fell asleep.

At one o'clock, their phone rang.

Once again jarred from his dreams, Mark griped, "Who's calling at this hour?" He picked up the phone. "Montis Inn. How can we help you?"

"Have you seen the television?"

"Who is this?" Mark asked.

"It's Jimmy. Turn on the weather station."

Mark reached over and clicked on the channel. He saw a map

of the United States with a large weather mass that began well out in the Pacific and extended over the entire Northwest. Under the map scrolled the words "Stalled Front Forces Advisories in Five States."

"We've got a problem," Jimmy said. "It's supposed to rain for another four days."

Mark rubbed his eyes. "We have no control over that. Go back to sleep."

"But we need to think of an alternative. Something for the people to do," Jimmy said desperately.

"In the rain?"

"That's the problem. Everyone is getting really wet and frustrated. They know no one is going to fly tomorrow, but we want to keep them around in case it clears on Sunday."

"Why is it so important that they stay?"

"It would be such an economic letdown to all the businesses if everyone bailed now. A lot of people have worked so hard to make this happen—to make the balloon." Mark heard Jimmy's voice crack.

"Hannah being one," Mark said.

"Yes, Hannah, along with many others," he said. "So, do you have any ideas?"

Pam rolled over in bed. "Who is it?"

Mark covered the receiver with his hand. "Jimmy—he wants an alternative group event."

"Why?" she asked.

"So people will stick it out and hopefully we can fly on Sunday."

She put her head back on the pillow. "Have a street walk."

"Pam said we should hire prostitutes," Mark said.

"No!" She grabbed the phone from Mark. "A street walk, not streetwalkers," she told Jimmy.

"What's that?" he asked.

"We used to do it in Leesburg," Pam said. "Take the tents from the fairgrounds and stretch them across Main Street, canopying the entire town, then ask the merchants to move some of their inventory to the sidewalks. And the visitors do a street walk."

"Brilliant!" Jimmy said. "I'll be by first thing in the morning to coordinate it."

"I thought now was first thing," she said, and hung up the phone.

෴

Although hammering rains continued Saturday morning, by noon the townspeople had lifted the tents over Main Street. Additional tarps stretched from storefront to storefront. Jimmy had also secured the theater, after the balloon was carefully packed up, and began showing round-the-clock free movies with popcorn at a nickel a bag. The library opened its doors and replayed *National Geographic* videos of the history of flight.

Jimmy stood under the tent in front of the Feed Store and assessed the street walk. Other than an unnervingly large number of loose, apparently homeless chickens that were busy pecking at the grass, everything seemed to be relatively normal. The tarps worked for the most part to keep out the rain, and a significant number of visitors were now congregating along Main Street, strolling in and out of the town's quaint stores.

A motorcycle pulled up in front of him.

"The road's closed to traffic," Jimmy called out.

The man removed his helmet.

"Well, if it isn't young Mr. Beezer," Jimmy said. "Simon's sure to give you a ticket."

"He's the one who sent me to find you. Told me to use the bike."

Jimmy raised his eyebrows. "You're helping with the festival?"

"Yeah, some I guess," he said, shrugging his shoulders. "Terry and I put the tent up over at the park and then Simon's been needing a hand."

Jimmy looked surprised. "What does he want?"

"He needs you at the station. Seems there were a few folks who enjoyed Lumby's hospitality a little too much last night."

"Drunk?"

"Wasted," Brian said, laughing. "Get on the back and I'll give you a lift."

Jimmy took a seat behind Brian. "Nice bike. Where did you get it?"

"It was my final trade," he said, sitting taller. "Remember those cemetery lots? Some lady really went nuts for them—seems her folks are buried right next door and she was willing to pay just about anything."

"So you sold them to her?" Jimmy asked, intrigued by Brian's continuing saga.

"No, I traded them for her summer time share on Vancouver Island. Then some burned-out attorney wanted that more than his midlife-crisis motorcycle, which he said he couldn't use anyway because of all the rain in Seattle. So, that was that."

Jimmy shook his head. "Brian, you could conquer countries if you put that mind of yours to good use."

Brian and Jimmy shot off just as Jeremiah rounded the corner by Brad's Hardware. On his blind mare Isabella, Jeremiah had ventured out into the rain to buy some chocolate ice cream at Dickenson's. The most direct route, which both had taken together for the better part of twenty years, was along Main Street—except on this day, the merchants had set tables and displays up on both sidewalks, and the street had been closed to all traffic. Poor Isabella thought that they must have been transported to a different town as she stumbled along for half a block, until Gabrielle gently grabbed her halter and led the startled mare and her owner away from the commotion. Isabella showed her opposition by leaving numerous droppings along the way.

Other than a few soiled shoes, nothing else marred people's appreciation of Lumby's ingenious solution to the canceled balloon events.

ᥬᥩ

Kai was drenched and exhausted. He had searched for Caroline the day before and was now battling the crowds, going from store to store in hopes of finding her. Finally, making his way to the end of Main Street where the masses thinned out, he sat down on the wet step at Brad's Hardware and put his head in his hands.

His heart ached. When Caroline left the party at Montis the night before last, he knew she was fighting back tears. But Kai couldn't say words that would have comforted her . . . not then, not when he was feeling such torment. But after talking to Joshua and carefully considering all he had said, Kai felt as if everything had become clear. And he needed to see her.

"You're getting wet," a familiar voice said.

Kai looked up. Caroline stood under a large umbrella, wearing yellow rain gear. She looked more beautiful than anyone Kai had ever seen.

He jumped to his feet and grabbed her arm. "Where have you been?"

She was startled by his quick movement. "Here. I've been helping with the tents all day."

"I was looking for you all yesterday. I even went out to Bricks last night."

"In the dark?" She asked.

"Yes. I thought you might be there. I didn't know where else to look."

Caroline kicked a stone next to her shoe. "I needed some time to be alone." She paused. "Being with you is so hard. I want something that I know you can't give me."

"We need to talk," he said.

Hearing thunder roll, he took Caroline's hand and together they ran to the back of the Feed Store, under an open shed filled with dry bales of hay. She slid off the hood of her rain slicker.

Kai put his hands on her shoulders and drew her closer. "I've been so wrong," he began.

"About what?"

He laughed weakly and shook his head. "Almost everything," he said. "But Joshua helped me understand. I thought my obligation to my town was more important than any responsibility I had to myself." He took her hands and held them together. "I felt that I had to give my life to God and my community under any circumstance. But I would be miserable if I returned to Coraba, and now I understand that the villagers and my family wouldn't want that either. If I go home, it must be because I choose that life, because I want to be a priest for my village above all else."

"And do you?" Caroline asked.

"No," Kai said, pulling her toward him and kissing her lightly. "I want to be with you. I need you in my life."

Caroline trembled, hearing the very words she wanted to say to him.

"I love you," he said, and embraced her passionately. "I don't know what the future holds for us, but I'm sure I want us to share it together."

"So do I," she said. She placed her hands on his face and drew him near, kissing his mouth.

He took her by the hand and led her to the hay bales, urging her to sit next to him. He rubbed her hand between his. "I can't even think of the challenges I need to overcome in order to stay and work in your country, but I will take them one at a time."

"Work?" Caroline asked.

"Yes, of course. But there may be some possibilities, either with a local church or even perhaps the school."

"You had mentioned that you would like to be a teacher."

Kai smiled. "Geography and history, yes. And if that means returning to a university to complete any requirements I don't already have, I look forward to that."

"And I would like to be there with you," she said.

He kissed her fingers. "I can't ask for anything more."

THIRTY-FOUR

Winds

On Sunday morning, every pew in every church in Lumby was filled with balloon pilots and residents praying for a break in the weather just long enough to allow one flight. Reverend Poole at the Presbyterian church seized the opportunity of preaching to a full house by blowing the dust off his favorite sermon: "Knock, Knock, Who's There?" At the Episcopal church on Main Street, the homily began with a joke that deftly ended with, "There but for the crates of cod go I."

Keeping the faith for divine intervention, the parishioners continued to look to the heavens until their prayers were answered around noon, when small breaks in the clouds appeared through the lingering drizzle. An hour later, all rain had stopped and swaths of brilliant sunlight could be seen moving across the rolling hills of Mill Valley.

By midafternoon, the front had moved through and deep sapphire skies offered hope for spectacular flying. Although strong back winds followed the front, they passed quickly.

So, to the delight of those who had stayed, the green flag was finally raised at the gates to the fairground along with a hand-painted sign that read MASS ASCENSION LAUNCH 5:00 P.M. Word spread throughout Lumby and the surrounding towns that the festival was not a complete loss; there would be one extravagant ascension flight at sunset.

Having exhausted all other forms of entertainment and eager to take off, festival participants began driving into the fairgrounds as soon as the gates opened at four. The launch grid, which had been so carefully designed and explained in the festival brochure, proved totally ineffective for two reasons. Most of the brochures that were distributed on Thursday night were used as head covers at one time or another during the weekend and then were quickly discarded after becoming saturated. Also, a large number of people had departed for home the night before, leaving their assigned launch areas available for others who were positioned farther out. It quickly became a first-come, first-served policy, with the earliest arrivals grabbing the premier launch sites—bar one that was unconditionally reserved for the lead balloon. That pad was several times larger and strategically placed in the center of the field.

Mark and Kai had been assigned the responsibility of transferring Lumby's balloon from the empty stall at the back of the Feed Store, where it had been stored to accommodate the moviefest the day before, to the fairgrounds. Hannah stood with Caroline several yards from the men, watching intently.

"This thing is heavy!" Mark said, straining to lift one corner of the folded balloon.

"Probably close to three hundred pounds," Kai replied.

"We need more people. Hey, Sam," Mark called out to the owner of the Feed Store, "can your boys help us back here? And can you get rid of all these chickens? I'm going to step on one for sure."

Within seconds Sam and his three sons were standing around the balloon.

"We're going to throw it on the old flatbed that's parked in back," Mark instructed, pushing a chicken away with the toe of his boot. "All right, ready? On three." But before Mark said "one," the boys heaved it up to waist height and were headed toward the door.

Once outside, they carefully laid it next to the truck. "Okay," Mark said, "we don't want to slide it on the rough planks of the flatbed, so let me get up there. I'll swing it over and in if you can lift it high enough." He jumped up, ready to receive the balloon. "Again in three. One—"

The boys swung the folded balloon forward.

"Two—"

They swung it back.

"Th—Wait!" Mark screamed, and lunged his body to stop the balloon from landing on the flatbed.

The balloon hit Mark in the chest and sent him flying backward. The balloon fell to the ground.

"Jeez!" he screamed in pain, lying flat on his back.

"What happened?" Hannah yelled, running up to him.

Mark got up slowly and she immediately saw small marks of blood on the back of his shirt.

"Nails," Mark exhaled. "There are a ton of nails sticking out from the boards."

"Good thing you saw that," Kai said, giving him a hand to get down. "They would have torn the balloon to shreds."

Sam threw his son some keys. "Let's use the store's hay truck. I assure you it's as smooth in back as a baby's bottom."

⁖

When all of the balloon components finally arrived at the launch site, Kai turned his attention to the basket: installing the propane tanks, dropping in the burners, and connecting all the rigging. Mark and Hannah, assisted by several people, positioned the balloon and began unfolding the nylon in preparation for inflation. Dennis and Brian Beezer offered to lend helping hands.

From the corner of his eye, Mark saw Jimmy D and Sal Gentile, the marshal of the hot air balloon festival, arguing with the president and vice president of the U.S. Hot Air Balloon Association. Mark stepped closer to hear the debate.

"Look," the president said, "we overlooked the fact that your town's application and hosting capabilities were all but forged by a minor, but we're not going to be flexible on this one. You really need to follow our flying regulations"

"But he has a license," Jimmy protested.

"Not in our country, he doesn't," the gentleman said. "Several other pilots have submitted a formal protest, so you need to either find a licensed pilot or pull the balloon."

Jimmy walked up to Mark, shaking his head, Sal a few feet behind him.

"We have a problem," Jimmy told Mark.

Several people who had overheard the comment stopped working and moved closer to listen.

"A complaint has been lodged that our pilot, Kai, is not only not a local but also not a U.S. citizen," Jimmy said.

"Is that a legitimate complaint?" Mark asked, looking at Sal.

Sal held up the regulation manual. "Unfortunately, it is."

"Isn't it a little late to be complaining now?" Mark asked.

"Any procedural complaint can be lodged within thirty minutes of launch," Sal said, looking at his watch to confirm there was ample time.

"What can we do?" Kai asked.

"Without a pilot, Lumby will need to withdraw the balloon," Sal said.

"We can get another pilot," Mark suggested.

Jimmy shook his head. "Those who came without their own balloons have long since left town. And the others are already committed."

Mark looked crushed. "So we have to eliminate ourselves? Not after all this work. That's ridiculous, Sal."

Sal shrugged helplessly. "It's not my regulation, folks. You need a licensed pilot—end of discussion."

Brian stepped forward. "I can do it," he said, so softly that no one heard.

"What?" Mark asked.

Brian cleared his throat. "I've never flown a balloon this big, but I got my balloon pilot's license a few weeks ago." He cast a sheepish glance at his father. "Sorry, Dad."

"Is it a commercial license?" Jimmy asked.

"Private, but I can manage an envelope to one hundred thirty thousand cubic feet and can carry up to nine passengers," Brian explained.

Jamar walked up to join the group. "If he would like some help, I would be honored to assist."

Everyone saw Jamar's sincerity and thought that perhaps this was his way of offering restitution to the town residents for trying to sell them an island that sank.

"It might be a good idea for both you and Kai to be on board," Jimmy said.

Dennis took hold of his son's arm. "Are you sure you can do this?"

Brian looked at the basket and the massive balloon stretched out on the grass. "I'm positive," he said.

Dennis smiled. "I'm proud of you, Brian. Now, how can we help."

"Actually, Dad, if you could step back and just let me do what I was taught, that would be great. Kai, would you give me a hand?"

As the two young men began to inspect the envelope, Kai gave Brian a crash course on the specifics of the balloon, the basket, and the heating system. The questions Brian asked were focused and targeted, giving Kai a strong sense that the young man had a firm understanding of the technical operations of hot air flight.

At Brian's request, Mark and Jamar held the balloon's mouth open. The fan was turned on and cool air rushed into the pocket. Within minutes, the envelope was no longer flat.

The balloon had been lying down, and its size didn't become apparent until the air began to lift the top layer of nylon six feet off the ground. People were in awe, seeing how much bigger it was than the *Endeavor*. A buzz of comments swept through the fairgrounds, and spectators flocked to see the lead balloon.

As the balloon began to take shape but was still lying horizontally, the brilliant colors and bold pattern that Hannah had stitched so carefully were revealed. Unlike the *Endeavor* and many of the smaller envelopes, which had simple patterns, this balloon had bold horizontal bands of intense color. In the center, bright yellow began the upward and downward change of color, with a darker yellow band above and below, then oranges and reds and finally light blue and dark blue at the top and bottom of the envelope. It looked formidable and substantial.

In the middle of the envelope, along the brightest yellow band, was some dark, intricately sewn lettering, but it was impossible to read since much of the balloon still rested on the ground.

Once the balloon was half inflated with cool air, Brian turned on the burners and hot air began to blow into the envelope.

People stood in breathless wonder as they watched the envelope grow. The bold horizontal bands showing the colors of the rainbow gave it a sense of endless height. Just when the envelope began to lift off the ground, still listing, the spectators were finally able to read the black lettering: *BOUNTY*.

Everyone gasped and exclaimed.

"Hannah," one of the residents called out angrily, "why did you name it that? The mutiny was on the other balloon."

"Yeah, that's an awful reason to name this one," another man added, blasting additional criticism at her.

Hannah stood strong, facing the crowd, and for the first time she found depth and bravado in her otherwise weak voice.

"The name isn't from the mutiny," she retaliated loudly so all could hear. "I named this balloon for our bounty, for our generosity and unselfish benevolence, for our kindness of spirit, the richness of our community and everything we share. I couldn't think of a better name for who we are individually and who we want to be collectively. It is our gift to ourselves and to the festival. It *is* the bounty of Lumby."

People stood quietly, some ashamed of their mean accusations, others wholeheartedly embracing the words Hannah had spoken.

"Yes, that's exactly right," someone yelled.

Another started to clap and then cheers turned to thunderous applause all around Hannah. People regarded the stitched word and saw the true wonderment of their small town.

Once the commotion settled, a man raised his arm. "And why is there a cross at the top of the balloon, Hannah?" he asked.

She shrugged her shoulders and smiled. "The way I see it, when you're that far off the ground and that close to God, you want to stay on His good side by making sure He sees something He approves of."

Everyone laughed and began applauding again.

When she turned back around, she gasped in amazement. The envelope had righted itself and was floating beautifully above the tethered basket. The setting sun penetrating the nylon brought out the brilliance of the colors.

"Everyone is so proud of you, but no one more than me," Jimmy said, kissing her lightly on the cheek.

"Actually, I might have you beat. *I'm* proud of me," she said, alight with satisfaction. "And you've done a pretty good job yourself. A lot of people really appreciate everything you've done."

It had been a long time since he had heard such a compliment from his wife. "Don't tell Brian Beezer, but I'm actually glad he tricked us into holding the festival. And now that we all know we've broken even for the festival, even with the rainouts, everyone is breathing a sigh of relief."

Hannah looked up at the balloon again. "It's quite something, isn't it?"

But Jimmy kept his eyes on his wife. "Smiling like that, you look so different."

"I feel different," she said.

"When this is over, perhaps I can help you find another project that you would like just as much," he offered.

"I've been thinking about opening a tailor's store," Hannah said.

"What a wonderful idea. You're so talented, you would have customers lined up for miles."

"Well, maybe not miles, but I think I would enjoy that." Hannah laughed and slipped her arm through his.

∾

As the hour progressed, the other envelopes inflated, with the *Bounty* in the middle dwarfing all around it. Sal Gentile floated several test balloons for the pilots to determine wind direction and speed. Brian Beezer watched each with a hawk eye, noting almost indiscernible changes. His father stood behind him and marveled at his focus.

At 5:00 exactly, Jimmy raised the horn and, with one long bellow, officially began the festival.

At the *Bounty*, Brian was the first to step into the basket, taking his position in the pilot's compartment. Terry McGuire ran up to him and shoved a baseball cap on his head. Brian took if off and read the stitching. "*Bounty.*"

"It's from Mrs. Daniels," he shouted, and waved to his friend.

"Are you ready for others?" Kai asked.

"Ready," Brian said with a nod. "Jamar, you first, and then you can help the others get in."

Kai looked through the crowd for Caroline.

Hannah and Jimmy were next to board. Hannah was in awe when she looked up into the vastness of the envelope. She leaned against her husband. "When I was sewing it, I never realized how enormous it is. But it goes on forever."

"As we will," Jimmy said, squeezing her shoulder. He turned to Brian. "You've turned this festival into a success for the town. Thank you," he said, shaking the young man's hand.

"My pleasure." Brian then waved to his parents. "Come on, folks, you're next."

Gabrielle looked at her son and then at Dennis and ran to the basket, tugging on her husband's arm.

"Where's Mark?" Jimmy yelled out.

They scanned the crowd. "He's not here," someone called back.

"I saw him drive off a minute ago," another yelled.

Kai suddenly spotted Caroline making her way through the crowd.

"Hurry!" He waved to her.

She ran up to the basket. "Are you sure it's all right?"

Jamar offered her a hand. "There's no other place my brother would want you to be than by his side," he said, and helped her step over the rim.

Caroline was touched by Jamar's genuine kindness. "Thank you," she said, and then turned to Kai. "Did you call your family?"

"It will be all right," he said, squeezing her hand. "We spoke for nearly an hour. They were surprised and disappointed at first, but after sharing with them how I feel, they were very happy that I have found my own road in life."

"I love you," Caroline whispered.

Kai leaned over and kissed her on the check. "And they extended a personal invitation to you to come to Coraba," he added.

"We'll make that the first of many journeys together," she said, beaming.

"We have one more space," Jimmy said, looking out into the growing number of spectators. He spotted his old friend. "Chuck! Come over here!" he yelled out. "You almost died last time you went up. You deserve this more than anyone. Let's see if we can make this flight a little nicer for you than the last."

With a nod of accord, Chuck clambered aboard.

After getting his passengers' attention, Brian quickly but succinctly reviewed the rules of flight. Dennis watched as his son instructed the adults with clarity and caring. Suddenly, he saw that the young man Brian had become embodied all of the talent and potential Dennis had ever hoped possible.

"Release the tethers!" Brian called out, and the large crowd standing around the *Bounty* broke out into thunderous applause. Brian opened the valves and the burner ignited, sending a huge flame toward the mouth of the balloon. The *Bounty* lifted gently off the ground.

"Bri-an, Bri-an," the crowd started chanting. But his focus was on the burner and the envelope, and he never heard them.

Ten feet and then twenty feet, the *Bounty* rose from the ground. The quaint village of Lumby could be seen by all the passengers: the charming main street of small stores and restaurants with its colorful awnings, church steeples, and the beautiful town park with one stray cow standing by the old cannon. Short streets of tidy homes turned into rural roads that led to small farms, which dotted the landscape throughout the valley.

From both the ground and the air, it was a sight that would never be equaled.

THIRTY-FIVE

Away

Several people were relaxing on the front porch as Mark approached Montis Inn. He had made a mad dash down Farm to Market Road to get home before the balloons lifted. Brooke and Joshua were sitting on the stone steps. Pam, who had been keeping a close eye out for him, waved in relief.

"Come on, Mark," she called just as he turned off the Jeep's engine, "the party has already begun."

"Can you see it from here?" he asked, searching the skies.

"Not yet," Pam said. "Come have a margarita."

"We should see it any second," Mark said, running up the front porch steps.

"Look!" Pam said excitedly, pointing toward town.

At the tops of the trees and just barely visible, they could see a balloon begin to rise.

"That's the *Bounty*!" Mark said. "You can see the horizontal stripes. It's just amazing. It looks like a huge rainbow."

Everyone was transfixed, watching the balloon slowly rise. Even from a distance they could see the burner flames ignite and shut off every few seconds. When half of the envelope was visible, the bright yellow center band of the balloon broke above the tree line. *Bounty* was clearly visible throughout Mill Valley.

"Wow," Brooke said, "it's huge."

"Are you watching?" Pam called out to Brother Matthew, who was crossing the road.

"A spectacular sight," he called back.

"Look, there's the basket!" Mark said, moving behind Pam and wrapping his arms around her. "It looks so small under the envelope."

"Can you tell how many people are in it?" Pam asked.

"Nine, I think," Mark said, squinting. "Where are the binoculars, honey?"

"Just inside the door."

Within seconds Mark had returned with the binoculars glued to his eyes.

"Hey, there's Jimmy and Hannah!" He began to wave with his free hand. "And Dennis and Gabrielle are up there too. Look, honey!" he said, passing the binocs to Pam.

She studied the basket. "Who's the pilot? Is that Brian Beezer?"

"Yes, and I bet he's doing a great job," Mark replied.

The *Bounty* was truly a spectacular sight. Drifting a hundred feet above the town and floating southward, it seemed to deliberately follow Farm to Market Road but, in fact, was totally dependent on the kindness of the winds.

"It's going to go right over the orchard!" Mark said, sounding like an enthralled boy. "Where's the camera, honey?"

"Right by the door," she answered.

"Isn't this great?" he asked, and ran into the inn, returning a few seconds later. He jumped up on the railing to get a better view. "We need one of those, honey. I think we should hire Kai and Hannah to build a balloon for Montis. We can offer flights across the entire area. Can you imagine what Woodrow Lake must look like from that height?" He paused for a moment, further developing his plan.

"Then we can take the balloon to France for vacation. Imagine the Montis balloon flying over all those castles and vineyards."

Pam caught Brooke's eye. "The old Mark is back," Pam whispered, and the two friends laughed.

Within minutes, the *Bounty* drifted over the apple fields of Montis Inn. Those standing on the porch were not only mesmerized by the sight but could hear the blasts when the valves of the burners opened.

Shshshshsh.

Twenty seconds of silence.

Shshshshsh.

"That must be deafening when you're in the basket," Brooke said.

"Kai told me balloon flight isn't as quiet as most people think," Joshua said. "We'll all go up next week after the dust settles."

Mark was fixated on the balloon. "Hey, where's it going?"

The *Bounty* had quickly descended and was drifting about fifty feet above the ground. Mark looked through the binoculars and followed the path. "It's Howard!"

"The moose?" Pam asked.

"Yeah, he's standing in the middle of Farm to Market Road." Mark kept his eyes glued to the binoculars. "It looks like he's eating something—maybe spilled feed. And there's a whole bunch of traffic heading right for him, but he's not looking up."

The *Bounty* dropped another ten feet and finally caught the moose's attention. Startled, Howard bolted across the asphalt and into a neighboring field without ever looking back.

Mark saw the burners on the *Bounty* suddenly ignite, and within seconds the balloon was rising again, drifting above tree level. "Wow, Brian is pro!"

"Look!" Pam said. "The other balloons are up."

Within minutes, the skies between Montis and Wheatley were filled with hot air balloons of every size and color.

Brother Matthew looked up to the heavens and smiled. "It must be a miraculous view from the balcony."

The Lumby Lines

What's News Around Town
BY SCOTT STEVENS   June 16

An end to a very busy week for our town.

Our town's motor vehicle department has requested that residents stop registering their cars as either hearses or farm equipment unless they do indeed fall into either of those categories. They would like to clarify that using a personal vehicle to drive a deceased pet to the cemetery does not warrant a reclassification and is not entitled to a reduced registration fee.

The Wayside Tavern, which has suffered from dramatically reduced patronage since the accidental discharge of bear repellent in their bar, will now be opening an hour later each day, at 11:00 a.m. instead of 10:00 a.m. They apologize for any inconvenience.

The U.S. Hot Air Balloon Association has sent a letter of thanks to the residents of Lumby wherein they award our humble town their strongest praise and highest honor for "extraordinary hospitality that has been unsurpassed in all of their years of conducting annual festivals. We thank the residents of Lumby who graciously offered their warm homes, their time and effort to ensure an enjoyable and successful event."

For some unexplained reason, town residents continue to add pennies to the Jeremiah and Isabella mound, which is taking up an increasing amount of floor space in the lobby of city hall. It is estimated that two to three dollars a day are being donated.

Since no one has claimed ownership of the loose chickens that have been plaguing the Feed Store and disrupting many good movies on the second floor, they have been captured and will be blessed and immediately thereafter auctioned next Sunday at 11:00 in the Episcopal church parking lot.

Attention was recently drawn to Lumby's 1892 cannon, which several youths attempted to auction off on the Internet. Acknowledging that the cannon had been long forgotten, several councilmen thought to fire the cannon in a ceremonial event at the end of the balloon festival. After being wheeled from the corner of the town park onto Main Street, the cannon was fired just as the final balloon launched. Contrary to the councilmen's understanding that the cannon was empty and that it would be a "blank firing," an old cannonball was still in place and impressively rocketed through the air, crashing into the second-floor window of the Chatham Press. Dennis Beezer had no comment on the incident.

Godspeed to all.

Gail Fraser has written *The Lumby Lines*, *Stealing Lumby*, and *Lumby's Bounty*. She and her husband, the artist Art Poulin, live with their beloved animals on Lazy Goose Farm in rural upstate New York. Gail and Art feel fortunate to be down the road from their close friends at New Skete Monastery, who are the authors of *How to Be Your Dog's Best Friend*. When not writing, Gail tends to their garden, orchard, and beehives.

Prior to becoming a novelist, Gail Fraser had a successful corporate career, holding senior executive positions in several corporations. She has a BA from Skidmore College and an MBA from the University of Connecticut, with graduate work done at Harvard University.

Please visit www.lumbybooks.com and join Lumby's Circle of Friends.

THE LUMBY READER

Spend more time with your favorite Lumby characters.
Discover new wonders of the Lumby lifestyle.
Share your Lumby experience with friends and family.

MARGARITAS WITH THE AUTHOR

The bells at the Episcopal church have just tolled six. One block down on Main Street in the Green Chile, Gabrielle Beezer places a pitcher of frozen margaritas on the table along with several tapas. She serves Art Poulin, the author's husband, and Pam Walker, while Mark helps himself. Hank, never one to miss a social affair, is leaning against the palm tree in the corner of the room. On the floor by his feet is an umbrella-decorated drink amidst crumbled tortilla chips. Dennis Beezer walks into the restaurant, having just returned from the Lumby Bookstore. He joins the others at the back table.

Dennis: Gail's still at the book signing, and given the number of folks there, she may not be joining us for a while.

Gabrielle: Should I bring her a margarita?

hank: i will do the honors. perhaps they want my signature as well.

Dennis: Why would they want that?

hank: i'm fla-fla-flabbergasted you ask. my following is as loyal as that of any famous american icon.

Dennis: Flamingo.

hank: whatever.

Pam: Perhaps we should all go over to the bookstore.

Art: No, I think that would just make her more nervous.

Mark: That surprises me. She seems really extroverted.

Art: Actually, just the opposite. She would make a great contemplative, living a solitary life.

Pam: With her animals and you, of course.

Art: (laughs) Yes, I would hope so.

Gabrielle: So, I understand you paint the covers for the Lumby series?

Art: I do, but it came about very circumstantially. While Gail was writing her first book, *The Lumby Lines*, I was experimenting with different artistic styles. After reading her novel, I thought it would be fun to capture your town on canvas. Folk art seemed to offer the endearing qualities of Lumby. And then, a few months after I finished the painting I call *Moose Stroll*, Gail showed the painting to her first publisher, and the look of the series was launched.

hank: it was brought to my attention that i, hank, do not adorn your paintings . . . an incongruity that baffles all of us.

Art:	I assure you, it was only at my wife's request.
hank:	i'm totally speechless, but if i wasn't, i would surely assert that my role in our town is as pivotal as . . . who, you might say?
Dennis:	The renegade chickens at Sam's Feed Store?
hank:	i will be sure to reply to that comment in my next *lumby lines* editorial.
Dennis:	No doubt.
Mark:	So, Art, does Gail influence the compositions of your paintings?
Art:	Very little. Knowing Lumby better than I, she may suggest a detail or two. But so far she's only nixed Hank.
hank:	which will be discussed with the author in due time.
Pam:	And prior to painting, you sang for the U.S. Army Chorus?
Art:	Yes, under six administrations.
Gabrielle:	At the White House?
Art:	Many, many times. Certainly at all the major holidays and usually when dignitaries visited. Those were the most enjoyable since we frequently sang in the guest's native language. French was by far the easiest, but I also enjoyed Italian and German.
Pam:	Are you bilingual?

Art: Yes, my parents were French Canadian. When I was brought up in Waterville, Maine, we spoke only French in the household until I was five or six.

hank: humph.

Mark: Maine's a gorgeous state. It has a climate very similar to ours, doesn't it?

Art: We both have long, cold winters. Very much like where Gail and I now live, in northern New York.

Mark: Lazy Goose Farm.

Art: We have a good time there. Gail is constantly having some odd misadventure with the tractor, although I'm the only one who can explain how the snowblower ended up in the fish pond. Great fodder for her novels.

Pam: Is Gail as funny in person as in her writing?

Art: She's funny because she can be an innocent goof sometimes. She tries so hard to do the right thing—a little like you, Pam. As we do each week, we went to New Skete Monastery last Sunday. During a silent part of the liturgy, she was unwrapping a cough drop and squeezed one end too hard. The cherry drop turned into a small projectile that hit the Bible on the podium and then ricocheted toward Brother David. It came to rest on the white marble floor— quite noticeable. That was funny enough, but Gail was clearly horrified and at a total loss. Since we sit among the monks and nuns, breaking rank to pick it up would have been quite obvious. We all got a good laugh out of it and I'm sure some twisted variation will be in one of her future novels.

Gabrielle: Do you see yourself in her novels?

Art: I see different parts of myself, especially in *Stealing Lumby*.

Pam: Are you Dana Porter?

Art: (laughing) I wish I were. His paintings sold in the millions.

hank: i must say—

[The front door of the restaurant flies open.]

Gail: You'll never believe what just happened!

LUMBY LIVING:
TIPS FROM HOME

Welcome back to Lumby Living: Tips from Home. In this bountiful issue, we turn our sights on one of the great treasures of life: heirloom vegetables. From the Potting Shed, Brooke Turner offers her preferences and experiences with heirloom tomatoes and corn. And as with other Lumby Living contributions, we give you some ideas on how to use those fresh vegetables by, once again, offering culinary recommendations from Montis Inn, the Green Chile, and Saint Cross Abbey.

The townsfolk of Lumby are always looking for personal favorite recipes and well-kept secrets, so, if you would like to contribute your own tips from home, please visit www.lumbybooks.com and join the Lumby Circle of Friends. There, you may add your contributions, share your thoughts on a variety of subjects, and chat with others who have embraced Lumby.

THE POTTING SHED

Hidden in the nooks and lying on the shelves of Lumby's community potting shed is a wealth of information: gardening treasures passed down from previous generations, an endless number of catalogues and seed sources, old yarns about long-forgotten flower beds, and amazing insights from many of Lumby's residents. For this edition, Brooke Turner introduces us to the wonderful world of heirlooms.

Heirloom... The word immediately evokes fond thoughts of ancestry, heritage, antiquity, and keepsakes from the past. Although "heirloom" occasionally refers to, among other things, tapestries, fine crafted furniture, china, and of course roses, "heirloom" is also frequently associated with vegetables of bygone years.

All heirloom plants are open-pollinated cultivars, meaning they will grow true to the seed—the seed contains and passes on a complete imprint of the plant. Excluding nearly all hybrids, open-pollinated cultivars repeat themselves one generation to the next, one century to the next. It is that regermination that assures us that all the original qualities—the robust smells, colors, and tastes—that were appreciated by our forefathers are what we can enjoy today.

One endearing facet of all heirlooms is the history and the lore that each plant carries with it, many having been cultivated by our great-great-ancestors. Although there is debate as to the minimum age a variety must reach before being called an heirloom, some gardeners agree that the plant must have originated before 1950, at which time hybrids were aggressively introduced into our country's agriculture. A further requirement is that heirlooms are not commercially grown or used in large-scale farming.

"Loomers," or those folks dedicated to the preservation of heirloom vegetables, garden for different reasons than your average green thumb:

- They want to preserve and strengthen a specific variety of gene pool.
- They are interested in cultivating their own rare variety.
- They appreciate the history behind the variety.
- They find heirloom gardening consistent with natural, organic "unmanipulated" gardening.
- The quality of the fruit an heirloom plant produces is unsurpassed.

It is solely for this last reason that I have been an avid heirloom tomato gardener since I was a child kneeling next to my mother in the rich compost of her small backyard garden. In my mind, there is very little similarity between a deep red Brandywine bursting with intense favor, and the pale, bland-tasting tomatoes that have been altered for commercial gain: to resist disease and rot, easily ripen off the vine, and withstand a long shelf life in the grocery store. What they have bred out of today's tomatoes in order to transport and sell more produce is everything that makes the fruit so spectacular.

And so we take it upon ourselves to grow tomatoes as they were grown long ago. The effort required to study, select, and plant these cherished varieties only makes the harvest that much more rewarding. Whether you have a half-acre garden or just one small patio pot, there is an heirloom that will delight you.

Of course I try several different varieties each year, but there is always space in my garden for my old favorites:

Anna Russian: One of my personal favorites. Brought over from Russia in an immigrant's satchel and then kept in Oregon for several generations, this tomato plant can grow nine feet high and is a prolific producer of pink, heart-shaped fruit that average about sixteen ounces each. The fruit grows in clusters of two and three, and has a superb, deliciously sweet taste. It has dense oxheart-shaped foliage that protects the fruit from strong sun. It's an indeterminate vine, which means it continually produces fruit all season, on a vine, compared to a bush, and requires approximately seventy days from planting to harvest.

Mortgage Lifter: An old-time heirloom that was reportedly developed in the 1930s by M. C. Byles of Logan, West Virginia. Crossing German Johnson, beefsteak, and other European varieties, Byles cultivated a large, delicious fruit that he sold for a dollar each. The profits he made from that small business paid off his mortgage in six years, hence the name. This variety is a great producer of smooth, reddish-orange fruit that averages a pound each and has one of the best beefsteak flavors around. The fruit are naturally crack-free and disease-resistant. Indeterminate vine. Eighty days.

Abraham Lincoln: Ten years after it was originally developed by H. W. Buckbee Seed of Rockford, Illinois, in the early 1920s, this variety was described in the Shumway Seed Catalogue as "the largest tomato ever grown . . . nine tomatoes in a single cluster with a total weight of seven pounds; the average weight is about a pound and we have grown many weighing three pounds." The tasty eight-ounce fruit is bright red that darkens as it matures. A high-yielding indeterminate vine. Ninety days.

Red Brandywine: A very famous heirloom cultivated in the Amish community in Chester County, Pennsylvania, in the late 1800s, which is supposedly named after the local Brandywine Creek that used to irrigate many of the nearby farms. This disease-tolerant variety offers eight-to-fourteen-ounce full-flavored tomatoes of relatively low acidity. The large potato-leaf foliage offers a wonderful contrast with your other plants. Indeterminate vine. Eighty-two to ninety-eight days.

Big Rainbow: This tomato, whose name so perfectly depicts the variety, seems to have been a well-kept secret in the Amish farmlands for years. First introduced by SESE Heirloom in Polk County, Minnesota, it offers a spectacular-looking and -tasting tomato. When planted in rich soil, the vines can grow up to ten feet tall, often yielding fruit as large as grapefruit—twenty to twenty-two ounces. The beautiful tomatoes are multihued of every color between red, orange, and yellow. The beefsteak-shaped tomatoes have a superior taste with plenty of sweetness. Indeterminate vine. Ninety days.

German Johnson: Very popular heirloom that originated in North Carolina and is purported to be one of the parents of Mortgage Lifter. In the South, it's a tremendous yielder, but even considering the fewer fruits it produces in cooler climates, it's well worth the effort. The robust flavor, pink-red meat, and huge size, which averages fourteen to twenty ounces, make this my hands-down winner for the best slicing tomato. The plant is fairly resistant to disease. Indeterminate vine. Seventy-eight days.

Amish Paste: A family heirloom originally from Wisconsin, Amish Paste has proven one of the best for making tomato paste. It's a consistently high producer of plum-shaped, meaty tomatoes with solid flesh and very few seeds. The deep red fruit is mildly sweet and grows in clusters of two to four, each eight to twelve ounces. Outstanding for sauces and canning, as it cooks down to a thick, creamy sauce. Indeterminate vine. Eighty-three days.

And my favorite heirloom corn?

Country Gentleman (or "Shoe-Peg"): Developed in the Connecticut Valley in the late 1800s and named after a famous nineteenth-century agricultural magazine, this is an amazingly interesting corn, as the kernels are not in rows, as on most ears, but instead are randomly organized. Although the white kernels are narrow and deep, they have a wonderful milky texture (outstanding for making creamed corn and great for canning) and have a great taste. The seven-foot stalks yield three to four seven-inch ears each in ninety-two days.

Golden Bantam: William Chambers, a farmer from Greenfield, Massachusetts, cultivated this variety in the late 1800s. After his death, a friend sold the yellow sweet corn seeds to Burpee, which featured them in their 1902 catalogue. Because of its taste and popularity, Bantam is considered one of the grandfathers of yellow corn, to which most other heirlooms are compared. The stalks grow to approximately five feet and yield four to five seven-inch ears. Eighty-three days.

From Saint Cross Abbey

Braised Lamb Shanks

8 large lamb shanks, trimmed of excess fat

Salt and pepper to taste

4 tablespoons olive oil

3 carrots, peeled and thinly sliced

3 yellow onions, coarsely chopped

3 celery stalks, thinly sliced

10 garlic cloves, thiny sliced

1½ cups robust red wine

2 16-ounce cans diced tomatoes (do not drain)

4 cups chicken stock

4 cups beef stock

½ teaspoon dried sage

1 teaspoon dried rosemary

½ teaspoon dried thyme

2 bay leaves

Preheat oven to 400°F. Season lamb shanks with salt and pepper. Warm oil in large Dutch oven over medium-high heat on stove. Add lamb shanks and brown on all sides, about 10 minutes. Remove shanks and set aside. Pour off most of the fat. Add carrots, onions, and celery and cook for 6 minutes. Add garlic and continue cooking for another 2 minutes. Add wine and simmer for 5 minutes. Turn off stove. Return lamb shanks to Dutch oven and add all remaining ingredients. Cover lightly and place in oven. Bake for 2 hours or until meat falls off the bone. Place shanks in serving bowl, remove bay leaves, and combine tomatoes with remaining liquid to be used as sauce over shanks. Serves 8.

From Saint Cross Abbey

Herb-Roasted Potatoes

4 pounds baby Yukon gold potatoes, washed but not peeled, cut in half

3 teaspoons Italian or Rotisserie herbs (for this and similar recipes, we always use Whole Foods 365 Mediterranean Rotisserie Seasoning)

5 sprigs fresh rosemary

3 sprigs fresh thyme

⅓ cup olive oil

Salt and pepper to taste

Preheat oven to 350°F. In a large bowl, combine all ingredients, folding over with large wooden spoon or using your hands so that all potatoes are nicely covered with oil and seasoning. Arrange potatoes in single layer on baking sheet. Roast, stirring occasionally, for about 1½ hours, until potatoes are cooked on the inside and golden on the outside.

From the Green Chile

Beef in Black Bean Sauce

2 teaspoons cornstarch

½ cup chicken or beef stock

1 tablespoon soy sauce

½ teaspoon sugar

4 tablespoons olive oil, equally divided into two portions

1 medium onion, sliced into bite-size pieces

1 small red bell pepper, seeded and sliced into bite-size pieces

1 small yellow bell pepper, seeded and sliced into bite-size pieces

4 garlic cloves, sliced

12–14 ounces of skirt, rump, or fillet steak, sliced into bite-size pieces

Salt and pepper to taste

8 ounces black beans (half a can), lightly rinsed

In a small bowl, dissolve cornstarch in stock and add soy sauce and sugar. Stir until sugar is dissolved. In a large, high-sided skillet, heat 2 tablespoons of oil over medium-high heat. Add onion, peppers, and garlic. Sauté for 2–3 minutes, until soft. Remove from skillet and set aside. Heat remaining 2 tablespoons of oil in skillet over high heat. Add steak strips and a dash of salt and pepper. Cook steak for 2–3 minutes, until steak is done to your preference. Add cornstarch mixture, vegetables, and black beans. Stir gently to mix thoroughly. Serve with steamed rice.

From Saint Cross Abbey

Penne with Gorgonzola Cream Sauce

1 pound penne pasta	⅓ pound Gorgonzola cheese
¼ cup butter	Salt and pepper to taste
1 cup heavy cream	½ cup chopped walnuts

Cook pasta until al dente (tender but firm to the bite) according to directions on box. While pasta cooks, in a large saucepan melt butter over low heat, then add the cream and cheese. Stir continuously until the cheese has melted. Add salt and pepper to taste. When the pasta is cooked, drain, setting aside 1 cup of water that was used to cook the pasta. Toss pasta into cream sauce. If desired, add a small amount of pasta water to thin. Transfer to serving plate and sprinkle with chopped walnuts.

From Montis Inn

Montis Crab Cakes

½ cup plain bread crumbs

1 medium celery stalk, finely chopped

¼ cup red bell pepper, seeded and finely chopped

2 tablespoons red onion, minced

2 tablespoons flat parsley, finely chopped

2 tablespoons Dijon mustard

2 tablespoons mayonnaise

2 large eggs

1 teaspoon Old Bay seasoning

1–1¼ pounds lump crabmeat, picked through

⅓ cup all-purpose flour

2 teaspoons olive oil

Preheat oven to 350°F. In a large bowl, mix bread crumbs, celery, red bell pepper, onion, parsley, mustard, mayonnaise, eggs, and Old Bay seasoning. Gently fold in crabmeat. Place flour on plate or waxed paper. Divide crab mixture into six mounds. With floured hands, form each mound into flat patty (similar in shape and size to a hamburger). Dredge in flour. Add olive oil to ovenproof skillet and place over medium-high burner. Place all crab cakes in skillet and cook about 2 minutes on each side until lightly browned. Place skillet with crab cakes in oven and bake 10 minutes or until center of each crab cake is very hot. Serve with lemon wedges or tartar sauce; one crab cake per guest.

From the Green Chile

Scrod en Papillote*

6 ounces fresh spinach, well washed and trimmed

1 medium onion, chopped

4 fish fillets, about 6 ounces each (scrod, haddock, or sole can be used)

4 teaspoons butter, equally divided

1 teaspoon salt

½ teaspoon black pepper

2 plum tomatoes, coarsely chopped

½ red onion, finely chopped

½ cup dry white wine

2 teaspoons olive oil

4 sprigs fresh thyme

8 lemon slices

*en Papillote means "in paper" and refers to a method of baking foods in a folded pocket made of parchment paper. For each pocket, begin with a 15-inch square of parchment, which will allow ample paper to fold edges over many times to make a tight seal.

Preheat oven to 400°F. Cut 4 pieces of parchment paper, about 15 inches long. For each piece of paper, fold in half diagonally, forming a triangle. Open and spray with a nonstick cooking spray. Divide spinach and onion equally and place in the middle of each piece of parchment. On top of each, place one scrod fillet and one teaspoon of butter. Then sprinkle on ¼ teaspoon salt and ⅛ teaspoon pepper. Evenly divide tomatoes and red onion and place on top of each fillet. Drizzle each fillet with 2 tablespoons white wine and ½ teaspoon olive oil. Finish by placing fresh thyme sprig and lemons on top.

Fold parchment paper loosely over each fillet, folding edges tightly together, creasing as you go to make an airtight seal. Set on baking sheet and lightly spray outside of parchment paper with nonstick cooking spray. Bake for 15 minutes. Pockets will puff up. Transfer to serving plate, and make slits at top of pocket, being careful of the hot stream that will be released. Serve with rice.

From the Green Chile

Pineapple Pork

2 pounds pork loin

4 tablespoons olive oil

6 garlic cloves

½ medium red onion, finely chopped

½ medium pineapple, trimmed, cored, and cut into bite-size pieces

1 tablespoon lime juice

½ cup fresh coriander leaves, chopped

¼ cup fresh mint, chopped

Cut pork loin into ¼-inch-wide strips, then lay each on its side and cut those lengthwise so they are long, bite-size pieces. Heat 1–2 tablespoons oil in skillet over medium-high heat. Add garlic and onion and sauté for about 3 minutes, until softened. Remove from skillet and set aside. Turn heat to high and add pork in 3 or 4 batches, replenishing olive oil as necessary. Stir-fry each batch for about 4 minutes or until pork is thoroughly cooked. When all pork is cooked, return garlic and onion to skillet. Stir in pineapple and lime juice, then gently toss in coriander and add mint. Serves 6–8.

From Montis Inn

Woodrow Lake Beachcomber Dip

1 pint sour cream

2 cans whole clams, well drained

2 cans fancy crab, well drained

5 ounces sun-dried tomatoes, drained

Baguette

In a large bowl, combine all ingredients. In small batches, blend in food processor for 6 to 12 seconds, until desired consistency is reached. Place in refrigerator for at least an hour. Preheat broiler. Slice baguette on the diagonal. Place bread slices on cookie sheet and broil for 1 to 2 minutes, until bread in slightly toasted. Turn slices over and toast other side. Place in basket and serve immediately with dip.

QUESTIONS FOR DISCUSSION

1. Going on a hot air balloon ride seems to be at the top of many people's wish list. Is it on yours? If not, what other adventure would you like to try, if only just once?

2. Pam appears to face almost insurmountable challenges when she decides to build a koi pond by simply "digging a hole and filling it with water." But she becomes unnerved when she doesn't excel at excavating. Is it natural to assume we can do anything if we just put our minds to it? What projects have you undertaken that demanded more than you thought you had the time or skill for?

3. From a very early age, Kai thought he was being called to religious life and subsequently based many of his decisions on that intention. His course changes, though, when he meets Caroline. When you were young, did you have a strong sense of who you wanted to be? And did that come to pass or are you now living a very different life?

4. In *Lumby's Bounty*, several people try to live up to the expectations of others—Caroline with the residents of Lumby and Kai with family and island villagers, to name a few. Are the expectations of others a positive or negative thing? And how can we

manage those relationships and expectations while keeping true to our own goals and values?

5. Pam really sees Mark change when he assumes much of the responsibility for the hot air balloon festival, but then she's delighted when he returns to his "normal self." Is it natural to overlook some of the abilities in a person whom we see every day? And how do you respond when someone in a close relationship with you changes so dramatically?

6. Jamar thinks himself more of a ladies' man than do most of the ladies of Lumby. Do you think there is sincerity and a good heart beneath all the winks and hair combing? Is there something attractive about Jamar that Kai lacks?

7. The "seekers" bring chaos to Saint Cross Abbey until the monks who initially respond with open arms become a bit wiser. Does anything positive come to the monks out of being deluged by the seekers? Are you dealing with "seekers" in your own life?

8. Gabrielle and Dennis Beezer believe they have failed as parents because of Brian's behavior, especially when he commits the town to a balloon festival they know nothing about. Should they shoulder all of the responsibility for the way their son turned out, both good and bad? At what age do teenagers or young adults become accountable for their own actions, independent of their parents? Have you had similar experiences with your own children?

9. Now that Brian has a positive channel for his talents and energy, do you expect great things from him, or are there still a lot of life's lessons he needs to learn? Do you think his relationship with the monks will stay on a business level, or will it grow deeper and more spiritual once Brian experiences the overwhelming poverty in South America?

10. Lahar represents an escape to paradise for many people in Lumby. Do you have such a place in your life? If so, where is it and why is it special to you?

11. During her marriage, Hannah never seemed to flourish, and increasingly became very withdrawn. It takes a physical separation from Jimmy D for her to collect her thoughts and begin to understand and like who she is. Do you know anyone who has had a similar experience? Have you ever been in a relationship that limited your growth? How did you respond?